Poppies and Silk

Book Two of A Texas Bloom Series

Tanya Fischer

DOGWOOD GROVE PRESS LLC

POPPIES
and
Silk

Cover Art by *eudornaworks*

Print ISBN: 979-8-9864085-1-4

Formatted via Atticus

Edited by Britney Waldrop @brineywaldropedits

Publisher: Dogwood Grove Press LLC

Content Warning

This story contains content that might be troubling to some readers, including, but not limited to, depictions of and references to death, suicide, death of a murdered adolescent and the aftermath, sexual harassment and sexual assault, off-page child sexual assault, teen pregnancy, surprise pregnancy, mentions of off-page abortive surgery to an adolescent and its aftermath, abuse of women and adolescents, violence, graphic sex, graphic language, harm to an animal (but no death), homelessness, childhood trauma, PTSD, bondage, kidnapping, gun violence, and illegal sex trade of underage girls. Please be mindful of these and other possible triggers.

To the community of friends, family, and readers that have been so supportive. To my critique partners, Darla and Dancey—it would have been a lonely process without you.

Prologue

Winter near Austin, 1879

"Y̲ou have to stop crying." Moira O'Connel's voice was an anxious whisper in the late-night gloom of the saloon's back porch. "They'll hear you. Then how will we get work?"

Poppy didn't give a fig about the work her mother sought. "You promised. You promised—"

Moira wasn't listening. She held up a staying hand and spun, staring hard at the ramshackle door behind her. When it remained closed and silent, she turned to her only daughter. Poppy was sixteen, garbed in rags, and starving. The money from her childhood doll, the only valuable possession she had ever owned, was long gone.

"This meeting is real important, Poppy Mae. You have to start paying your way. You're old enough now."

Poppy shook her head as though to empty it of her mother's cajoling. "You told me that you'd look for normal jobs." The accusation was waterlogged. Weak. "We could be laundresses. Or housemaids. We could do something else, anything else, but this."

The cold light of the full moon illuminated Moira's face, which twisted at the naïve words. "You don't understand the trade. The men on our trail have agreed to leave us be if you help work to pay off our debts. This will give us protection. We won't have to run anymore."

Their debts?

The debts her mother had amassed by stealing from the wrong men?

"My friends in Dogwood had parents who had normal jobs. They got along just fine." Better than how they were presently doing.

Life for Poppy in Dogwood the year before had been wonderful, a dream. She had bounced between her friend Lucy's family hotel and Francesca's general store apartment. Their lives had been as dissimilar from hers as silk to burlap, but both friends had shared their homes and families without hesitation.

"Not this again." Moira drew herself up to her scant five feet. "I give you a good life, a better life than I was ever given. I work an honest living and have never left you wanting."

The lie brought forth the awful words that Poppy had suppressed for years. "I don't wish to be who you are! I've not even finished my final year of schooling." She didn't want to be a saloon worker! Why couldn't she have a normal life, a loving family that didn't demand this of her?

Moira's expression hardened, chapped lips compressing. "It shouldn't be difficult to do it so that we have a roof over our heads. You did it for free once before, or don't you remember?"

Blinking at the woman who, more often than not, felt like a resentful older sister rather than a mother, Poppy whispered, "How could you say that, Mama?"

The injustice of the lifestyle her mother defended and championed was harder to bear every year.

For the first time since Moira had signed her daughter's body over to the men upstairs, she looked repentant. "I didn't mean it."

She had meant it, or she wouldn't have said it.

People said things they didn't mean all the time. And sometimes they said the truth. Especially if it hurt.

Poppy wiped her running nose on her stolen jacket's bulky sleeve. It reeked after a month's hard travel. She recollected stealing it. The icy morning dew had crunched beneath Poppy and her mother's flying feet, and they had taken the first jackets they could find from some unsuspecting family's clothesline. That day, she'd only *thought* she knew cold. Now, temperatures dropped steadily, and Poppy and Moira's breath tangled together in steaming clouds. Never could she remember being so cold.

Sucking in a mouthful of glacial air, expecting a furious response but obstinately trying one last time, Poppy suggested, "We could find a church. Ask for help."

As she'd suspected, Moira's eyes flashed. "We're not charity cases. I never got help from churches before, and I'm not starting now."

Poppy would rather be a charity case, begging on her hands and knees, than go upstairs and lie on her back for strange men. Smelly men.

Mean men.

Her breath came faster, so fast the bitter air withered her throat and hoarsened her words. "I won't do it. I won't. You promised—"

"I know what I promised!" Moira cried quietly, peeking behind her again. Her frenzied hands seized the lapels of Poppy's stolen jacket. "You have to. You've gotta go upstairs and do whatever the boss tells you, Poppy Mae. Because if you don't—I don't know what they'll do to me." Moira must have done something very, very bad this time. The fear in her voice was real...before it turned coaxing. "It's just for a few months. Then—then we can go somewhere else and find one of those respectable jobs you keep talking about. We can start over."

If Moira hadn't pledged the same thing a thousand times before, Poppy might have believed her. But now, she was asking for more than *make yourself scarce when I'm workin'*. She was asking Poppy to take up the trade as a prostitute.

All those dreams she had made with her friends in Dogwood washed away like gold dust in a flash flood. Learning to sew and read dress patterns with Franny at Hobb's General was all for naught if she went upstairs.

She couldn't do it.

She wouldn't.

Taking the silence for acquiescence, Moira smoothed flyaway curls from Poppy's chilled temples.

"Straighten yourself up and meet me upstairs in five minutes. You need to look your best, hm?" Moira's voice was falsely light, and she delivered one last tremulous smile before she disappeared through the crooked back door. The lamplight filtered orange through her frizzing red hair before the door shut behind her, shrouding the small, petrified figure in obscurity.

A trickle of heat teased the numb tip of Poppy's nose, tempting her to follow.

Come in. It's warm in here.

She moved to bite her nails, but they were down to the quick, so she chewed the skin around them instead. The heat beckoned as it slipped below the door.

"No," she whispered.

The holes in her soles felt every nail and board of the rickety porch when she stepped back. The cramping in her stomach was alleviated.

She took another step. Then another. She eased down the two porch steps, then drifted halfway across the back alley. The door was small now, that promise of warmth and food far enough away that she could clearly recall their price.

She was a whore's daughter, but was wanting a respectable life too much to ask?

A minute had come and gone. In four, Poppy was expected to walk up the stairs of the saloon, eyes watching her, judging her worth. Nameless men would finger coins in their pockets amidst bar smoke and tinkling piano keys and wonder if they had enough. They would speculate how to explain the coins' absence to their waiting wives at home.

One man's face materialized in her mind's eye. Young, wealthy, handsome. His remarkable blue eyes sparkled; his hands offered treats.

Poppy whirled and dashed into the night, swallowed up by darkness.

POPPY'S SANCTUARY WAS a church porch, and she huddled in the deep recess of the doorway.

It was another nondescript town with poorly graded, uneven roads and weathered buildings set a mite too close together. But at this time of night, it terrified her. When she ran from the saloon, her jacket had snagged against crooked nails in the bowed boards like hands pulling her back. Wild-eyed, she had tarried long enough to untangle herself before bolting again. She had skulked from wagon to wagon, alley to alley, until she had been halfway out of town.

Poppy had stopped, gulping great lungfuls of freezing air, when she discerned the building off to itself. It glowed pure white, a beacon in the winter moonlight. The narrow little church stood straight and new with perfect right angles and a squared center door. A proud steeple hovered above her.

To Poppy's knowledge, Mama had never stepped foot in a church. Senses sharp, eyes shifting, she climbed the steps with more disinclination than she had any cathouse stairway.

Now, she hid from the wind's bite, wedged in the corner against the door, wracked with chills. Thoughts of stacks of hotcakes, crisp bacon, and the bright orange yolk of a perfectly fried egg helped to pass the crawl of time. She was exhausted, but her eyes remained wide and alert even when the first bird broke into song and lightly tiptoed along the frosty churchyard.

She hoped Mama wouldn't be too angry with her for running.

Was she looking for her, even now?

Mama would never look for her here.

With that last thought, Poppy fell into a fitful sleep.

Men's voices roused her.

Two men strode along the stiff grass, heads tucked and hands deep in woolen coat pockets. They were stomping frost from their boots, grumbling about the cold, when the grizzled old man with a porous red nose noticed her. He glanced at his slim, middle-aged companion.

The latter wavered before he removed his hands from his pockets and crouched a couple of feet away.

"Are you lost, child?" His drawl was thicker than molasses in midwinter.

"No, s-sir." She hoped she didn't sound as disconcerted as she felt. Not with men in general. Just the nice ones.

"Oh." The slim man stood, knees cracking, and murmured something in his cohort's white-tufted ear. He withdrew a key from his pocket. "Would you like to come inside while you wait for service to begin? It's mighty cold out here. Mr. Howell will have the place warmed up in no time."

Mr. Howell nodded, inspecting her from beneath flocculent eyebrows.

Warmth sounded glorious. Poppy had long since lost feeling in her feet, and her red hands were tucked in the folds of her sleeves. The men had to help Poppy—stiff and immobile with cold—scramble up. A strong odor wafted from her coat interior, and she lowered her face, embarrassed. Her nose ran.

Unlocking the door, the slim man said in judiciously informal tones, "I'm Reverend Daniels, and Mr. Howell is the caretaker. I haven't seen you in town before. What's your name?"

She considered introducing herself as Poppy Mae, but shame at her unkempt appearance and unpleasant smell encouraged formality. "Penelope O'Connel, s-sir." Her teeth wouldn't quit chattering, her lips slow and clumsy.

Ushering her inside, shrewd brown eyes took in how tightly she held her sorry coat. Reverend Daniels' voice darkened. "You in some kind of trouble, young lady?"

Not even her own mother could have compelled her to lie, so Poppy averted her eyes from the authority in his and remained silent. The silence was damning, and she surreptitiously mopped her nose with the corner of her sleeve. Fortunately, the reverend had more pressing matters to attend to. Sighing, he politely guided her to the back pew, trying very hard to pretend she was not there while he shuffled through the papers at the pulpit.

FOLK WOULD POUR into the church soon, and final additions to his sermon pressed him while concern for the lost child niggled, distracting the reverend. If God saw fit, this child's mother would claim Penelope O'Connel once the noon bell struck.

Alas, people filed in and took their seats in the pews.

He preached.

Noon came and went.

He disregarded the whispers among the curious townspeople, who pretended to ignore the urchin in the back pew. The child had sat still and quiet, the occasional rifle shot of her growling stomach causing those nearest her to flinch. Children swiveled in their pew to stare remorselessly. Their parents studiously faced the front.

She confided in no one, not even Helga Pavloski, who provided her with a slice of buttered bread from the church pantry.

Reverend Daniels took his time bidding farewell to everyone, banking the coals in the great wood-burning stove against the western wall, and still the child sat unclaimed on the last pew. Grinding his teeth, he walked to the front door and paused. A frisson of resentment passed through him.

Haven't I suffered enough?

He immediately apologized to God for the small thought. A wise man knew the answer to that question could always be no. There was nothing he could do but get her out of this worsening cold snap. The closest home to the church was his own, and he could feed and stow her there while he fetched the authorities.

Reverend Daniels opened the front door, keys jingling, and glanced back at the waif.

She had twisted in her pew as though afraid she'd be locked in.

"Best we walk fast and get out of this chill, girl," he said. An icy wind sucked all the warmth from the back of the room. He grew impatient when she didn't jump speedily enough to satisfy him. "Come on, now, time's a-wasting."

FROM BENEATH DARK russet brows, Poppy glanced at the fractious man walking alongside her.

He blew out smoke and rubbed his gloved hands together.

She should return to the saloon, find her mother, and apologize. It shouldn't be hard to find her way back.

Instead, her feet followed the preacher while burning resentment glowed in her heart. The unkind old bat she had accepted bread from had ruined the gesture, ensuring Poppy felt every bit as worthless as an abandoned girl deserved.

"Skin and bones." The woman had sniffed when Poppy took the food. "And none too clean, besides. It's a sorry sight, seeing beggars from the street at our own doorsteps. Don't your parents have any shame? Well, they shan't get a penny from me, I vow."

The greasy, buttered crust was still clenched in Poppy's left hand. She would give it to Mama. Only starvation alone could force Poppy to eat anything from that woman's hand. For now, she could breathe and walk and feel just fine without it. And what she felt was impotent fury.

At her mother.

At her lot in life.

At this preacher man who clearly wanted nothing to do with her.

He was speaking.

"Do you have a mother? A father?"

Poppy's teeth didn't chatter anymore, but she kept her blue eyes stalwartly on the busy lane. The town was awake, people were every-where, but there was no flash of bright red hair. "I have a mother."

"Do you know where she's at?"

"I lost her."

"I thought you said you weren't lost. Is that why you waited at a church?" His brows pressed together at her lack of forthcoming details. "Did you think maybe you would get help?"

"Yes, sir."

"Where was the last place you saw her?" He sounded less and less patient.

Poppy didn't answer. She thought about lying, but what was the point? Everyone would discover soon enough that she was the daugh-ter of a woman who couldn't read or write or do anything but serve men and neglect her only child. The thought felt mean, and behind it was a strong emotion that warmed her despite the low temperature, climbing her throat and making her eyes brilliant.

If she divulged that she'd last seen her mother in a saloon, his eyes would assess her again, but knowingly. The impatience would give way to apathy. He'd wrinkle his nose in disgust like that church woman and take her straight to the sheriff's office instead of letting her step foot in his home. Those were the looks she hated, worse than the pity. As though the parents' sins became the children's sins by default.

Moira never tried to change that. When Poppy came to her mother's room when the workday was concluded in tears from the taunts of the school children, Moira's response was always heated. Defensive. She would mock the children and claim that half their daddies visited her, and who were they to act high and mighty? Rather than feeling better, Poppy would feel corrupt. Dirty.

"You'll need to tell the sheriff everything when he comes by," Reverend Daniels pushed determinedly. "That way, you can rightfully be reunited with your mother. Here, come inside, and we'll find you something to eat before I leave."

Reverend Daniels' home was a modest replica of the church, though it had settled and sagged. It had white clapboard siding, small windows, and a wide covered porch that seemed to flow with the yard's slope. Though it wasn't level or square, and the grass was winter-brown, a smoke stack puffed in welcome, and a small dog yapped excitedly from inside.

Besides a stray or two that she used to feed, Poppy had never owned a dog.

The reverend's hand, not quite touching her shoulder blades, guided her up the unlevel steps. It was easy to follow along when decisions were made for her. She had followed Moira, but the wrongness of every choice her mother made intensified with every passing year. Just when they'd settle in one town, something would transpire to upset Moira—a slight from another girl, a regular moving on to someone younger, or the owner of the saloon docking her pay.

It was always something, and it was never her mother's fault.

When Poppy dithered at the door, the reverend reached past her and opened it.

"Don't worry, he won't bite you," he assured her when a wriggling silken-eared spaniel yapped and jumped around her feet. "Might lick you to death."

When he reached down to pet the little dog, chuckling, a tight wariness within her relaxed. Bad men wouldn't pay any mind to a bad-mannered puppy, would they? Especially when that puppy had made a mess by the front door.

She was ushered to the little kitchen that had settled deep in the corner of the house. It was warm and smelled of that morning's coffee. Water was in the reservoir on the stove, and bacon lay cold and limp on a chipped hand-painted plate. She hungrily inspected the water and slid her pinky into her mouth, teeth scraping the nub of her nail.

Reverend Daniels grabbed an old dishtowel and nodded toward the bacon. "Help yourself. I'll clean this up and head to the sheriff's office. We should be back shortly. Just—make yourself at home and get warm." It looked like he would say something else, but he nodded once at his instructions and departed. The silence in the house was deafening.

Once he was out of view of the small front window, Poppy dropped the buttered bread to the floor and watched dispassionately as the dog made quick work of it. Mama would never take charity from church people anyway. Her feet carried her straight to the reservoir. The enormous, soiled jacket crumpled to the floor, and in seconds, Poppy had her sleeves peeled to mid-forearm. The first splash of warm water on her face was rapturous, but she didn't allow herself to linger at the tank. She found a basin on one of the open cupboards, and she filled it with water and a piece of slippery white soap. For five minutes, she scrubbed and scoured, getting as far down her neckline as she could. Her nailbeds burned, and her face was tight, shiny, and clean. After a quick pass of her tongue over her fuzzy teeth, she returned to the basin, dipped a washrag in the soapy water, and scrubbed inside her mouth until her gums bled and her teeth squeaked.

Once she felt human again, she plucked the coat from the wooden floor and hung it on the stand by the front door to air out. No one marched up the lane, and her heartbeat slowed. The fabric at her neckline and the sleeves up to her elbows was drenched, but her face, hands, and arms were clean, and her teeth no longer felt like moss had taken up residence on them.

She turned to the plate of bacon. Liquid brown eyes watched her every move as she gnawed through three pieces simultaneously, and she was on the fourth when she heard it.

Coughing, simultaneously weak and hacking, erupted in a back room. Poppy stopped chewing and glanced at the dog, who ignored the coughing and licked his lips. His body trembled pathetically. She neglected the residual bacon when the coughing worsened, and she returned to the basin. Once she had dried her hands on the dishtowel hanging on a curved hook, she tracked the sound down the long, narrow hall to the last room on the left. Pressing her ear against the door, she listened, disregarding the clicking nails on the wooden floor near her feet.

Something clattered to the floor inside, and a feminine voice wheezed, "Walter."

Poppy chewed her lip, knocked, and opened the door without waiting for an answer.

It was a bedroom with a single window, covered from floor to ceiling in dusty bookshelves, dressers, trunks, and clutter. It smelled in the room, and Poppy's eyes found the culprit of the sweet-sour stench. Though Poppy was starved, the woman on the bed looked like a cadaver waiting for the undertaker. She was anywhere between forty and a hundred years old, sharp-nosed, and skeletal. The eyes that rolled within hollow sockets landed on her, the dark cavern of her mouth gasping for air.

A memory of Holly, a young prostitute in Alabama who had died of consumption, gave Poppy the resolve she needed. Though she didn't have the tools for bloodletting patients, she could follow the doctor's other steps. Poppy looked despondently at the filthy dress that encased her, worn and frayed at every hem and two sizes too small. One day, she would have the means to fashion her own dresses, tailored to perfection, and she would never, ever be this filthy again. But, for now, it would have to do. Besides, the poor woman wasn't much cleaner than she was.

When the wrinkled lids closed and the woman hacked into a bloody handkerchief, Poppy got to work.

THE SHERIFF TAILED the preacher up the porch steps, both careful not to appear too somber. Reverend Daniels claimed he hadn't had a good look at the girl and that this morning's discovery could simply be a coincidence. They stamped their feet of dirt and frost at the front door, inspiring the dog inside to bark energetically.

Inside was humid, the culprit a pot of gently simmering water on the stove. A soft voice murmured at the back of the house, and Reverend Daniels' severe brows rose. He spotted the soiled coat hanging on the rack beside his spares, and his tread was soundless and quick on the thin hallway rug, the sheriff hot on his heels.

"—must slow down. Your cough could come back and make you choke. I know washing up took a lot out of you, but you look so much better. There. That's it. Is the compress helping? Holly used to love a warm compress on her chest, said it reduced the tightness. Are you hungry? Oh, but you must eat something."

Reverend Daniels swung the door wide open.

The little waif had transformed into a young woman in a too-small brown wrapper. Penelope O'Connel had his wife's skull-like head propped, tilting weak tea into her dry, cracked lips. Mrs. Daniels' face was ruddy but clean and shining. Normally she was deathly pale, typical with those afflicted with consumption, dubbed the "white plague." Made it blasted hard to keep people on to help with her.

The girl had straightened the bedclothes, brushed his wife's hair, dressed her in a clean shift, cleaned the bloody handkerchiefs and debris, and unfastened the drapes. With an exhausted sigh, his wife reclined, a hot water bottle wrapped in cloth balanced on her emaciated chest.

As though sensing them, Poppy turned around, immobilized at the sight of two men loitering in the doorway. The yappy little dog had barked, but since he did so with such frequency, she hadn't paid him any mind. Now, the loom of two sets of male shoulders boded ill.

Mouth dry, she stammered, "Your wife, she needed some help. I didn't mean to go nosing around."

"Oh, no, no trouble at all," the reverend placated. His earlier aggravation was gone. "I usually have a woman to help, but she hasn't made her rounds in some time. Afraid of becoming consumptive herself, you see."

Nodding, Poppy clenched her hands together in her skirts. "I used to help when—when the women of our boarding house became ill with it. I never get sick, so..." She trailed off and glimpsed the tin star peeking from behind the bigger man's jacket. "Did my mother ask you to come get me?"

Poppy was afraid to hear how angry Mama was. Moira was probably sitting, leg jiggling, in the sheriff's office as they spoke. Lawmen always made her mother nervous, especially sheriff's offices and their promise of iron bars if you got on the wrong side of them.

The sheriff backed from the doorway and gestured down the hall. "I have some questions. Let's go sit in here so Mrs. Daniels can rest."

Licking her cracked lips, Poppy hurried to the front parlor. She prayed they didn't smell her when she passed by. After cleaning Mrs.

Daniels, she had scrubbed herself again, this time with water that scalded. It had calmed some crawling, fraught compulsion within her.

Perching on the edge of the settee, she folded her hands like one of her teachers during parent meetings, hoping it displayed a tranquility she didn't feel. She waited.

The sheriff cleared his throat. "I'm Sheriff Woolhart. Unfortunately, no one's come forward looking for you."

Poppy's impassive stare displayed no surprise. Of course, her mother hadn't come to the sheriff's office looking for her. Moira must have decided to wait at the saloon with the presumption Poppy would eventually reappear.

Or maybe she's glad to be rid of you.

Sheriff Woolhart cleared his throat and prompted, "Can you give me an idea of what your mother looked like? What her name was?"

What her name *was*? The past tenses befuddled Poppy.

Frowning, mindful of the ill woman dozing in the back, she said, "Yes. Her name is Moira O'Connel. She's wearing a big jacket, like that one." She pointed at the coat on the coat rack. "Her dress is yellow with little white flowers on it. She has red hair, blue eyes, and lots of freckles."

The preacher and sheriff shared a troubled look.

"Where did you last see her?"

Eyes downcast, Poppy picked at the frayed threads of her rucked-up sleeve. "I'm not sure. We were on someone's back porch last night, but it was dark, and I did not go inside. We arrived in town yesterday, and it got dark so fast."

"So you don't know what building it was?"

"Somewhere in the middle of town, in that direction." She pointed northeast, toward the front door. Both men noticed her raw fingertips, nails bitten to nubs, the skin ragged. A white scar shaped like a crescent moon curved beneath her smallest finger.

Sighing, Sheriff Woolhart directed another look at Reverend Daniels, who rubbed his hands briskly together.

"Miss O'Connel, would you mind rustling us up some lunch while the sheriff and I discuss something?"

Grateful to be away from two sets of probing eyes that saw through lies, she stood, circled the men, and vanished into the kitchen.

Once the door had shut behind her, Reverend Daniels asked quietly, "Well, what do you think?"

Taking his hat off so he could scratch his head, Sheriff Woolhart murmured, "I think we have a positive identification on the poor soul that Bill found this morning."

The reverend made a sound of frustration and grief.

"Yep. Hair color, eye color, and freckles match. Even if Miss—what was her name, O'Connel? —even without the description, the girl is the spittin' image of the bod—of her mother, minus the red hair."

Scrubbing his eyes, Reverend Daniels thought of earlier when he'd wondered if he'd suffered enough. *It could be worse*, he thought. *It could always be worse.* Scanning behind him to ensure blue eyes weren't peeking from the doorway, he asked, "Was the woman wearing a yellow dress?"

The sheriff's jaw clenched, and his voice was a low growl. "She wasn't wearing anything at all. She'd been assaulted, strangled, and dumped on the side of the southward road leaving town. Bill covered her up with a saddle blanket and had his boy fetch me this morning. I'd just got back to the jailhouse when you showed up about a lost little girl. What is she, twelve? Thirteen?"

"I think a little older," Reverend Daniels mused, scratching the scab of the nick he'd made shaving this morning. She was built like his Martha, small and spare. Then, thinking of his wife, he paused and shuffled his feet. "I think, if she's got no place to go, she could be a real help around here. It's getting harder to find help for Martha, especially when she gets bad like this."

With a sympathetic nod, Woolhart surreptitiously checked his pocket watch. He still had questioning to do and paperwork to file on the body, not to mention he had an idea of just which porch Penelope O'Connel had visited last night. The town was generally respectable, but the seedy cathouse in the middle of town had plenty of business, most of it bad.

So that he didn't feel rude, Woolhart asked politely, "How is Gerald? He doin' well in that sanitarium?"

For the first time that morning, Daniels smiled. "Gerald's doing wonderful, just wonderful. Sends me a letter a week to tell me all the therapies the doctors have him doing. He should come home soon." He continued in this vein for some time before Woolhart progressively inched to the front door.

"I hate to rush off, but—"

"No, of course."

"You want me to break the news about her mother? It'd be a real help if she'd identify the body."

Knowing it was wrong but feeling inexplicably protective of the girl that had been so gentle with his Martha, Reverend Daniels whispered, "Do we have to tell her anything?"

The crease between Sheriff Woolhart's brows deepened. "We can't keep somethin' like that from her."

"It can't be any good for her," Daniels argued. "It's better to think her mother's out there somewhere, not dead in a ditch."

They muttered low to one another for a spell until an agreement was reached and Sheriff Woolhart departed, but the girl eavesdropping didn't pay them any mind. Reverend Daniels' words echoed in Poppy's mind like a metronome.

It's better to think her mother's out there somewhere, not dead in a ditch.

Mama was dead.

Poppy's eyes were wide and staring, and it was almost too late before she remembered she was supposed to be cooking lunch. She found canned green beans in the larder and half a smoked ham.

Dead in a ditch.

She sliced the ham and laid the slices neatly in a cast-iron pan to warm on the stove.

Dead in a ditch.

The jar was a challenge to open, even with a dishtowel around it. Poppy's fingers trembled and sloshed liquid on the floor when the lid finally gave.

It'd be a real help if she'd identify the body.

When the sheriff eventually left and Reverend Daniels walked in, a plate of warm food waited for him on the breakfast table. Poppy busily scrubbed a week's worth of dirty dishes at the sink, her back turned to the room, and he never once suspected that she had overheard his conversation with the sheriff. He didn't know her well enough to notice the hunch of her shoulders or that the pinch of her mouth was something she did to keep from crying. Later, when she disclosed that she was sixteen and accepted the position as his wife's live-in caregiver, he was too preoccupied with his own troubles to notice that she didn't ask after her mother again.

In truth, she never wished to speak of Moira again. Poppy knew she was responsible for her mother's unspeakable end.

Mama was dead.

And it was all her fault.

POPPIES AND SILK

Chapter One

DOGWOOD, TEXAS

May 1888

Poppy stepped onto the boardwalk at Hobb's General Store, her portable hand crank Singer sewing machine in tow. It was dreadfully heavy, and after two days' travel, it would be a relief to set it securely on a table and pull its cover off. Placing such an expensive machine in the boot of a stagecoach or throwing it onto a pile of luggage in a train car had been out of the question. The sewing machine was more than just her livelihood; it had become a friend, comforting her in the darkest year of her life.

Her mouth parted at Dogwood's changes, with its fresh boardwalks, recently constructed brick buildings, and new road signs. Of the dozens of towns that Poppy had inhabited throughout her childhood, the old cow town was her favorite. She'd spent the best two years of her adolescence here, and the old friendships she'd established were easily renewed the year before. On a whim last summer while lying prone on her empty bed, Poppy had rolled over, grabbed a sheet of foolscap, and wrote a lengthy letter to Francesca Hobb. She hadn't spoken to Francesca since she was fifteen, when her mother had unceremoniously whisked her away from where she had finally sprouted roots.

Francesca had written back straightaway and began a long-distance friendship that Poppy cherished. A year later, she stood and admired how different the general store was from the one in her childhood.

The generic, tattered little store had upgraded; its woodwork was extensive, the words HOBB'S GENERAL STORE more embellished on its painted sign. A window's thick-paned glass encompassed the entire front. Even the door had a glass window. A headless mannequin stood sentinel at one end of the window wearing one of Franny's clever creations where she took a factory-made dress and added elaborate embroidery, drapes, folds, and flounces. The dress in the window was green and white striped, analogous to the navy and white day dress Poppy wore. She was beyond grateful she no longer had to wear mourning colors in the summer heat. Now, she could don her lacy gloves, jaunty hat with its summer flowers made of silk, and bright, breathable dress.

The store's front door swung open, its bell tinkling, and Mrs. Hobb sauntered out, arms outspread. Her smile was as wide as her arm span. "Poppy, look at you!"

Unlike her store, Mrs. Hobb remained fixed in time; Viking stature, booming laugh, and face spotted with skin tags and moles.

Poppy smiled and allowed the woman to enfold her in an infamous bear hug, transporting her ten years into the past. Just over five feet tall, she was almost a foot shorter than the older woman, and her face squashed between two pillowy breasts.

"Look at you," Mrs. Hobb repeated deafeningly. Nearby pedestrians glanced their way. "All grown up and pretty as a new penny. Get inside, girl. Let me look at you a spell."

Brawny arm across Poppy's shoulders, Mrs. Hobb steered her out of the noisy street and into the insulated quiet of the general store, the tiny bell tinkling merrily behind them. Through the window behind them, Poppy saw Mr. Hobb struggling to drag the largest of her bags to the Dogwood Hotel next door. He was as diminutive as his wife was immense. Imagining him lugging her bags up two sets of stairs and into the attic space brought an amused, guilty quirk to her lips.

"I should help him, Mrs. Hobb."

"Nonsense!" Mrs. Hobb cried. She didn't spare her husband a glance. "He'll get Mr. Ricci to help bring everything in for you." When Poppy curiously scrutinized the store, she added, chuckling, "You can take a tour later. Someone upstairs is chomping at the bit to see you."

They funneled through the hinged bar top that blocked customers from the family living quarters, but Mrs. Hobb paused at the staircase Poppy, Lucy, and Franny used to race up at the end of the school day.

"Franny," Mrs. Hobb began, "looks a little different now than when you remember her. Her face—"

Poppy rested her hand on the woman's sturdy forearm and said soothingly, "I know, Mrs. Hobb. She opened up to me about it, and I sent her lace veils. They're pretty and easy to see out of."

"Oh," Mrs. Hobb said, surprised and pleased. "She's wearin' a pretty one today, goes down to her collar."

Poppy smiled. "Perhaps it's one of mine."

With that out of the way, she was shepherded up the stairs, and Mrs. Hobb called a warning, "Guess who's here Franny?"

A soft voice called back, "I saw from the upstairs window, Mama."

Francesca's footsteps were light for a woman as statuesque as her mother. She was as diffident as Mrs. Hobb was bold, but she met them at the landing, and her smile was visible even through the intricate lace of the lilac veil she wore. One of Poppy's creations, it matched Franny's lilac and cream day dress.

Poppy had fibbed a little.

Although Francesca had mentioned a slight skin condition in a letter months ago, Lucy was the one who had carefully explained the extent of their friend's condition. Lucy compared the number of skin disfigurements to the quantity of stars in the sky. Saddened by the admission, Poppy had chosen to be matter-of-fact with Francesca in her following letter, which was sent with a package of half a dozen lace veils.

"Franny, it's so good to see you," Poppy beamed. She didn't attempt to hug Francesca; Lucy had cautioned that their friend was as flighty as a church mouse.

"Please, come in," Francesca urged, excitement exaggerating the tremble in her voice. "I have so much to show you that letters could never do justice. I am so glad you decided to stay the summer at Dogwood."

"I couldn't wait to come." It was true. Poppy felt breathless with excitement, winding through trails of a home crammed with too many things. "I would have arrived sooner, but Reverend Daniels and I had to take care of a few things before he released the house to the church."

Nearly all of their belongings except for their nearest and dearest were sold. Letting go of Mrs. Daniels' and Gerald's possessions was almost as painful as accepting their deaths. But the reverend, weary of mourning, had wanted to remarry. To do that, he had to leave or suffer the condemnation of the entire town. What kind of preacher married a younger woman only six months after his wife's death?

But they hadn't understood.

Poppy knew that Reverend Daniels had been faithful to the end. He hadn't been married in truth to the fragile waif on bedrest in half a decade. The most physical intimacy Mrs. Daniels had achieved with her husband in years was a pat on the hand and a peck on the cheek. And when a new woman had arrived in town, the reverend's eyes had followed, falling more in love and feeling more shame than any person ought. No, the townspeople hadn't understood.

At his insistence, he and Poppy had split the estate sale proceeds. The house, however, had belonged to the church and would go to the preacher that replaced him. Poppy gave Reverend Daniels her blessing and told him with feeling, *"Be happy."*

Following her advice came with a price. He and his new wife moved west, and Poppy took the next train northeast to Dogwood.

Francesca, Poppy noticed as she trailed behind, had bad posture. Her shoulders, rounded from hours upon hours of sewing, belonged to a woman three times her age. The Hobb residence had two spare rooms, and both were filled to the brim with the materials it took to run a successful seamstress business. The first room had racks and racks of cloth, from the thick, sturdy wool and leather that formed coats, to the sheerest tulle, muslin, and lace that would become shifts and nightclothes. Eyes widening at the abundance, Poppy had to drag herself away to follow Francesca into the next room.

A tabby cat slinked from a room at the end of the hall and froze, lantern-like green orbs on Poppy.

"Oh, that's Button. She's quite skittish," Franny explained confidently. "She's imprinted on me, and only I can pet her, you see."

Poppy hummed indulgently, which persuaded the cat to jet into Francesca's bedroom in a blur of gray and black stripes.

The second room they entered was smaller and better lit, with a long oak table pushed flush against a wall with a large window overlooking the building next door and the alley below. But what made Poppy gasp were the matching hand crank Singer sewing machines on each desk. Though they were similar to her own portable Singer, they were larger, and their golden Acanthus flower decals gleamed in the window light against the black paint.

"You have matching sewing machines?" Poppy breathed, setting her sewing case carefully on the floor by the table leg. They were newer than her machine, which was so expensive that she still paid monthly installments.

"Daddy ordered them last winter," Franny giggled, urging her to look closely at the newer, updated features. A small fortune sat on the tabletop, and Poppy's mind whirled, barely listening. "—and we can sew side by side and catch up. Isn't that exciting?"

They spent the afternoon in the sewing room with a platter of coffee, sweets, and sheaves of paper strewn across the long worktable containing orders and dress patterns. The upstairs apartment became warm and redolent of coffee and parchment, and their laughter carried down the stairs, compelling the elder Hobbs to smile behind their counter. The cheerful sounds were irresistible. Mrs. Hobb would walk upstairs, peek in the room, and grin broadly at their huddles over the patterns. After the third time, Poppy asked Mrs. Hobb to visit while they discussed their business strategy.

Pleased, Mrs. Hobb grabbed that week's newspaper and sat in an overstuffed armchair in the corner while the younger women murmured together. Then, a moment later, she made a noise that raised their heads. Her sparse eyebrows had drawn together, and her small blue eyes flew over the page.

"What is it, Mama?" Francesca asked.

"Wha—oh, just readin' that some girls have been going missing from Newton all the way to Brazos County." She peered closer, a woman in need of reading spectacles but too stubborn to wear them. "'From ages thirteen to nineteen, each goes missing in the night.' Well, I don't like the sound of that, not one bit. That's just two counties over."

"Those poor girls, not to mention their families." Poppy straightened. The tabby cat, who had tentatively peered around the doorframe, disappeared again. "Does it say anything else? Were there signs of a struggle?"

Mrs. Hobb's mustache trembled while she scanned the article. "Doesn't say. That's a shame. How do we know what to look for if they don't give us any dad-blamed details?"

Fighting between amusement at Mrs. Hobb's language and concern at this announcement, Poppy lifted the pencil she'd discarded and documented the season's fashion, flipping through pages of that year's edition of *The New York Fashion Bazar*. Stripes were most definitely in, and considering they gave an illusion of length to petite statures, she scribbled notes happily.

Poppy would model the dresses Francesca had spent the last six months creating, meet the Women's Circle, and show off the patterns and dresses to the upstanding women of the town at Mrs. Smithe's biweekly luncheons.

Scratching a mole on her chin, Mrs. Hobb mentioned offhandedly, "I was sorry to hear of your mother-in-law's passing. What did you say it was, Franny? That wasting disease?"

Stiffening imperceptibly, Poppy stopped writing but didn't look up. "Tuberculosis."

"Ah."

"The same as my husband. They were both ill from consumption for a very long time." Silence followed. "But it did not kill her as it had killed him. He passed from pneumonia." Poppy continued writing. "She died of a broken heart."

No one said a thing while Poppy's pencil scratched, then Francesca and her mother murmured awkward condolences. Poppy quirked her mouth at them as though to say *"don't be silly"*, but neither questioned further. Which was just what she wanted.

She had lied about the nature of Mrs. Daniels' demise.

Poppy's husband's death had blanketed the Daniels' home in a suffocating black pall. Despite his constant fatigue and weakness, Gerald had been the light of the family, more alive in his spirit than his body could ever compete with. She had never met anyone so determined to live. Drawn to him like a moth to the flame, Poppy had been powerless to resist his animated conversations, constant teasing, and general happiness.

Her late husband had an enduring patience for his bedridden mother's simpering during the day, and in the evening, he would take Poppy about town. Stopping to rest every other block never troubled her. And when he had died the summer before from a sudden relapse following a summer cold, it had shocked everyone. He started coughing on a Monday and stopped breathing the following Sunday.

His mother never accepted his death. She cursed Poppy, her husband, and finally, God. Her raving had exhausted her and put dark circles beneath the eyes of the other members of the household.

Poppy had responded as she always had with pain and loss. She grew numb to it. Her feet would move, and her hands would soothe Martha, but her mind was carefully blank. Sleeping was impossible in her empty bed, so she stayed up at all hours of the night sewing, sewing, sewing. Gerald had helped her acquire her first real sewing machine the month before his death, and its first creation was a half-made suit.

In two sleepless nights while Martha existed in a laudanum-induced slumber, Poppy had completed the suit and placed it lovingly on her husband's body before he was lowered into the ground.

Poppy battled Mrs. Daniels' will to die for six months before she finally lost.

Discovering Martha's body was carved into her memories. The scene had robbed Poppy's breath, and she had gasped on nothing, like a banked fish. It must have been how Gerald had felt on the eve of his death when his lungs had filled with fluid, drowning above water. Her mother-in-law's hands had stiffened into claws, tangled in bed linens, her mouth a perfect grimace reminiscent of the cat that had fallen victim to the Hanover's wagon the Sunday before. For a weak moment, Poppy had considered closing the door and fetching the preacher. But then, the reverend hadn't fully recovered from his son's death, either.

So, Poppy had set aside her dread, entered the room, and locked the door behind her.

When the preacher and sheriff arrived at the scene, Martha Daniels appeared to be sleeping peacefully on fresh bed linens. The vomit-laden sheets were soaked in a barrel outside, and the empty laudanum bottle was stashed at the bottom of the wastebasket.

No, no one needed to know the grieving Mrs. Daniels' true end.

Mr. Hobb took that moment to call from the stair landing, "Dear, that girl from outside of town is here to see you." His voice was not much louder than his daughter's and was a touch effeminate.

"All right, tell her I'm comin'," Mrs. Hobb bellowed, heaving herself from the plush armchair with an excessively loud grunt. "Girls, you have fun. I'll be downstairs tending to Alwine."

Poppy watched the woman clomp from the room, the house swaying lightly. So entertained, she was about to inquire about Alwine, but the stiffness in Francesca's bearing stopped her.

"Oh, but I hate that girl," Francesca said feelingly. She turned away in the hush of that statement to fiddle with the mannequin torso in the corner, veil fluttering. Then, she stole a look at Poppy. "Well, it's just that Mama is always taking in beggars from the streets. One year, one of them broke in and came upstairs to find the safe, and it frightened me nearly to death."

"Someone came into your room?"

"No, Daddy heard someone breaking the door lock from their bedroom—their window is above the storeroom—and caught the man stealing from the shelves. Mama was right behind Daddy with a rifle."

"How terrifying."

"Mama said he was a fellow she'd given expired cans to. He was drunk. I can't abide beggars and thieves. It's bad enough to beg on the streets but to steal from the hand that fed you?"

A cruel derisiveness to Francesca's words reminded Poppy of Mrs. Pavloski and the crust of bread.

I wonder if you've ever been so hungry, Franny, that you would break into someone's property to steal?

Years ago, during one of their escapes from a saloon owner her mother had wronged, Moira had broken into a farmer's chicken coop to scavenge eggs. Unable to find any, they took a chicken instead and camped in the woods. That week's rain had been interminable, and they couldn't light a fire. It had been one of the rare times that Poppy remembered weeping, huddled in the slow, miserable drizzle over the dead chicken they had no way of cooking.

Had the Hobb's beggar been that hungry?

Had he children to feed?

Franny had never been that hungry. That desperate.

"I'm sorry you had to experience that," she responded abstractedly, brushing off a pattern sheet she had written measurements on. Then, unable to help herself, she asked, "How old is the girl your mother looks after?"

Francesca grew vague. "I would not know. Younger than us, perhaps. I've seen her from the window when she leaves. She comes every day, and she wears the same dress."

Poppy thought of the brown wrapper she had worn when the Daniels had taken her in, how it had cut into the flesh beneath her arms. It was so odoriferous that she had burned it once Martha had loaned Poppy one of her own. Now, she envisaged a young woman wearing the same dress every day, watched by another from the window above in veils of mourning and a malevolent gaze.

Detecting censure, Francesca added, "She lives in the brothel outside of town. That's what Mama says. And she doesn't speak a lick of English."

"What does she come here to ask of Mrs. Hobb?"

Francesca shrugged. "Food. One time she asked for rags for her menses, bold as brass. Mama gave her an armful. I think I'd prefer death before I ever asked for those, don't you think?"

This show of superciliousness curdled Poppy's warm feelings for Francesca. Another emotion welled. Some dormant insecurity that she'd thought long incapacitated after years of being a respected member of society.

Franny knows I was raised in brothels. Why speak of this to me?

Desperate to change the subject, Poppy smiled and asked about the dress they would put on the mannequin in the storefront. Like a switch, Francesca dropped her small-minded attitude and returned to her normal, friendly guise.

"I CAN'T TELL you what it means to us that you're here," Mrs. Hobb repeated fondly as she walked Poppy downstairs. "I worry about Franny, you know. She's a good girl, but not real worldly. The last time she left upstairs was when Lucy got married, and that was six years ago."

Francesca's reclusive nature was reminiscent of Mrs. Daniels. In both circumstances, both shut-ins were frightened of the outside, were waited on hand and foot, and were renowned and whispered about in town.

"And I am so grateful you invited me to stay the summer."

"Stay as long as you need! Let's go out the back door, our alley connects to Tony's hotel, and we usually walk in from the back."

Amused, Poppy nudged Mrs. Hobb's biceps with her shoulder. "I remember."

Mrs. Hobb led her through the back storage room where sound was muffled by floor-to-ceiling stacks of feed and wooden crates of household staples. Dust swirled in the air when they opened the door, the scent of pine, sweet grain, and burlap was replaced by the dirt and manure scent of the alley.

"I'm grateful to Mr. Ricci for allowing me to stay in Lucy's attic room this summer. I only wish he would permit me to pay rent—"

"Balooey," Mrs. Hobb scoffed. "You're family, and no family of ours pays a durned thing. I'd have you with me if it wasn't for all of Franny's valuables. Lucy's family and their friends stay in the family section every weekend, and I know for a fact Tony likes the company. Well, half the time, he's at Trudy's, anyhow."

Poppy gasped at the familiar name. "Trudy, as in—"

"Yep! The saloon owner in low town. She and Tony have been an item for some years. Happily unmarried, being's he's still married to the sourpuss back in Georgia."

Her friend Lucy used to speak of her parent's estrangement in the privacy of her attic room during the year they shared it. The infamous Mrs. Ricci had been the Dogwood Hotel ghost, haunting the family despite being alive and well in Georgia.

Mrs. Hobb continued to whisper about the failed marriage until they reached the gas-lit back porch. The Dogwood Hotel was an immense three-story building positioned proudly on a corner lot. Fresh white paint on the clapboard siding looked pink and gold in the sunset, black shutters bracketed each window, and flower boxes cradled blooming pink and white peonies. The two women bid farewell on the back veranda, and Poppy made her way cautiously inside the hotel, lightly closing the screen door behind her.

It was warm near the kitchen to her left, and the corridor was alive with the sounds of cooking and women hollering orders to each other. Her stomach growled at the smell of stewing bacon, onions, and greens. Ahead, a familiar suited back manned the reception desk. Poppy's mouth curved. Tony Ricci, her friend Lucy's father and the owner of the Dogwood Hotel, had always been unfailingly kind to her. Sewing case in hand, she eased her way around the desk so as not to startle him while he perused his ledgers. When she stood in front of him, waiting, he looked up at once without recognizing her.

"May I help you?" he asked professionally, then, squinting, he grabbed a pair of wire-rimmed spectacles and settled them on the bridge of his nose. His smile revealed a familiar gray tooth. "Poppy, is that you, dear?"

"Yes, sir." She smiled and couldn't help feeling more comfortable at the hotel than she had with Francesca in the general store. "Thank you again for opening your home to me."

"Think nothing of it." He clasped her fingers with his right hand over the concierge desk. His left arm had been amputated at the elbow from The War, and she admired the smooth sleeve's craftsmanship, tailored to fit the missing limb. "We must tell Minnie you're finally here. She'll be overjoyed to see you." He released her hand and gestured for her to follow him to the kitchen's hallway entrance near the back door.

Minnie was the hotel's main chef in their dining section, and she also oversaw the work of the hotel and kept it running. If Tony was the business sense, she was the common sense. Poppy recalled the woman's kindness as a child and her relentless need to fatten her up. Poppy was smiling even before Tony opened the kitchen door and called for Minnie. When the slim woman turned, perspiring from the heat of the stoves, she let out a cry of welcome.

"Poppy, honey, when'd you get here?" Minnie wiped her hands and crossed the kitchen to hug Poppy with the kind of fierceness that squeezed the oxygen from the lungs, belying her slightness. "Just wait until Lucy gets a look at you, my, oh my. Still need a little fattening up, don't you?" She held Poppy by the shoulders in the hall, appraising her, a long-distance relative that liked what she saw. A tenderness softened Minnie's white smile. "You grew up jus' fine, didn't you? I knew you would. You had that same fire in you that Lucy and my own daughter have. That fire that's got heart in it."

Feeling disconcertingly touched, Poppy fought to keep her smile pasted on. "Thank you, Minnie. You haven't changed a bit."

"Whoo-wee, you need some spectacles yourself," Minnie whooped. "I've got more white up top than black these days." She patted her graying hair then, unable to keep still, put a hand between Poppy's shoulder blades and directed her to the door across the kitchen that concealed the family's section of the hotel. "Let's get you settled. Mr. Hobb brought your things to the attic."

Mr. Ricci left them to it and returned to man the front desk. Minnie led Poppy upstairs, regaling her with tales of a decade's worth of renovations, the hotel's bankruptcy, and Lucy's return that gave it life while Tony struggled with his own demons. Then, she went on to talk about Lucy's marriage to Ben Stone and their three children.

"You got any young'uns? You're about, what, twenty-four now?" Minnie puffed, climbing the slight wind of the narrow attic stairs.

"No, ma'am." She had known there would be questions and was braced for them. Countless times, she had reassured herself there was nothing wrong with being childless, that it was normal for many couples. "Gerald and I were never blessed with children, but we'd spoken of adopting before he'd passed. And I turned twenty-six last November."

The silence from Minnie was one of understanding. Even so, Poppy refused to allow her lack of children or husband to hamper what she felt was a joyous homecoming.

"Oh," she breathed. "It's so different up here."

As teenagers, she and Lucy had spent most of their summer days upstairs in the attic bedroom, the circular window open to circulate the stuffy air of the bare wood rafters and floors. Now, the vaulted ceiling was painted a cheerful white, and the hardwood floors were sanded and stained a rich walnut. A large, handwoven rug graced the center of the floor, a splash of color, and Lucy's childhood cot was replaced with a full-sized bed. A quilt and cozy knitted throw blanket beckoned. The rolltop writing desk was the same, and Poppy gratefully set her heavy Singer atop it, gliding her fingers across the artfully arranged stationary and small stack of stamps.

"Lucy had everything spick and span for you," Minnie said proudly, opening the round window wide to allow a gentle breeze in. "Mr. Ricci put a screen in the window, so you shouldn't hafta worry about creepy crawlies while you sleep."

Warm from a sudden burgeoning of feelings, Poppy turned to the older woman. "It's wonderful. All of it. I'm so glad I came."

Minnie embraced her again, incapable of helping herself. "We sure are, too. And you stay as long as you want. Lucy keeps the boys with her in the second-floor room. Isa or Sol usually sleep up here but can take a different room."

"Thank you, Minnie."

After Minnie's brisk footsteps faded down the staircase, Poppy released a pent-up sigh and sat on the soft bed, exhaling until all the stresses of the last year eked out of her. The smile she'd forced all day melted, and she sat there, simply feeling.

It was peculiar to be alone.

For years, she was companion to Mrs. Daniels. Then, when Martha's son had arrived home in remission from the sanitarium—and had fallen rapidly in love with Poppy—she'd been held by marriage. Those first two years of marriage had been unsurpassed. Meanwhile, both mother and son had remained healthy until the third year brought with it an influx of illnesses throughout the town. Martha and Gerald had caught every cough, cold, and fever. The fourth year had been the worst. Gerald suffered relapse after relapse of his illness, and he stalwartly rebuffed returning to the sanitarium despite Martha's and Poppy's pleas. And when he had finally shown improvement the summer before, it was all the more crushing when he'd so unexpectedly passed.

Now, Poppy was untethered. Floating.

Whether Dogwood was the place to tie herself down again, she didn't know. There were plenty of people that loved her here. But there was also a wealth of support in the town she had turned her back on.

To pass the time while the street outside darkened and a man on stilts lit streetlamps, Poppy unpacked. Six dresses in protective coverings were hung on an exposed wooden dowel anchored to the wall, and her unmentionables fit tidily in the standing armoire's drawers in the corner across from the bed. She smoothed the delicate lace and silk before tucking the drawer away.

Poppy lit the kerosene lamp as the shadows stretched and darkened in the attic's interior, washing everything in warm yellow light. She sat at the desk and smiled at the blue writing paper. For an hour, she wrote letters to the two dearest friends she had left behind, the scratching of Lucy's handsome fountain pen her only company. Mary and Anne had been confounded at Poppy's decision to leave, but they hadn't grasped the difficulty of living in a town where all her good memories were dead and buried. Both friends had growing families, and as much as Poppy cherished their company, their futures had just begun while hers had snuffed out. Reverend Daniels had offered to help her buy a small house, but the notion of staying had felt akin to a prison sentence, one of constantly seeing her friends live the life she couldn't have. And that small, resentful thought, more than anything, had decided her.

She refused to stay and resent her friends' happiness. They deserved a lifetime of joy and not to constantly worry about their poor, childless widowed friend.

Penning the letters that announced she had safely reached her destination granted her a soft, genuine pleasure. She was young, on an adventure. Her life was just beginning, and the future was bright.

All she had to do was be bold enough to reach for it.

Chapter Two

T he following morning, her glow of pleasure had reduced to a flicker.

Childhood insomnia clung to Poppy well into adulthood. After eating supper with Minnie and Mr. Ricci once the diner had closed, she had offered them a good night and had retired to her attic space to perform her nightly ablutions. She undressed, scoured every inch of her body with a soapy rag, scrubbed beneath her long nails with a boar bristle brush, filed them, and cleaned her teeth. A year ago, Gerald would watch her from the bed with a faint smile and dark, appreciative eyes. Now, she performed her ritual alone. There was no one to take pleasure in the sheer muslin nightgown that settled over her body but her.

Once dressed for bed, she wrote a list of every task Francesca and she had planned in the last year. Then, she removed the cover of her Singer sewing machine and finished her latest project.

Ideas often came to her at bedtime while she tossed and turned. More often than not, she would bound from the bed and begin sketching in one of her many journals, patterns burned in her mind's eye until they materialized on paper. Every dress she had, she had made herself, every silken nightgown, wrapper, and cotton combinations. She found patterns from simple country stores boring, so she enhanced them, adding the small details that made clothing beautiful in Paris and New York. She had more than one Worth magazine and would pour over them for inspiration.

She christened her attic space the first night by completing the luminous silk nightgown with complicated bobbin lace inserts and a matching dressing gown. It was risqué and would be an expensive purchase for a client, but she looked at it and wanted it. If Gerald were here to see it, his eyes would grow enormous.

Her true passion was this—the making of sensual creations that drew the eye and engendered lust. In spite of his father's admonitions of fleshly lust, Gerald had been her biggest supporter, and her friends had worn her designs for their husbands with titillating results.

At three in the morning, she finally climbed into bed, nearly vibrating with excitement to share her creation with Francesca. Perhaps they could create a more exclusive line for married women.

However, Francesca took one look at the rippling nightgown that Poppy had gingerly placed over the cloth mannequin and shook her head.

"No, Poppy, I'm sorry, but I cannot sell that to the clientele I have already accumulated. They would be scandalized."

Poppy's heart sank. "Oh. I only thought—Lucy told me of that lovely gown you'd gifted her for her wedding night, and I thought perhaps we could offer it to a select few—"

"I did sew Lucy that nightgown, but she was passionate for Mr. Stone," Francesca defended. Poppy wondered if the cheeks behind the veil were as florid as her words. "But that was a gift I knew she would appreciate, not a part of my business. I know that you grew up with painted ladies that would enjoy this nightwear, but the women of this town are decent, respectable ladies. They don't dress like scarlet women."

For a long moment, Poppy stood in the weak morning light of the alleyway window and wondered why the people closest to her always hurt her the most. The inability to see Francesca's expression made her feel oddly alone as though she were the only one exposed, all her secrets there for anyone to see. Despite the warm wash of shame, Poppy never blushed and vowed not to start. Instead, she was pale and cold, her fingers calm and steady while they pulled the nightgown back off the dress form.

She would not be ashamed. She would not.

"I did not intend to be hurtful," Francesca added, clenching her hands. "But it is much too provocative."

As though denying any hurt, Poppy nodded reassuringly. The words "they don't dress like scarlet women" and "decent, respectable ladies" clamored in her head like a bell struck with too much force.

"Perhaps I will find someone interested in it one day." She thought, *Very well, it's too offensive, let us quit this discussion.*

But Francesca carried on, and the ringing, bell-like echo of her words worsened. "I was thinking...perhaps it would be safest if you did not mention your upbringing to the Women's Circle."

Silence.

"It wouldn't be good for business. The women are—"

"Respectable and decent, not like the saloon girls I grew up with, yes. I understand." Poppy didn't nod again, and she stared unblinkingly into the tiny holes in Francesca's lace veil.

Francesca mumbled, "Yes, well." She broke off to look for something to do before suggesting Poppy go downstairs and put a new dress on the mannequin in the store window. Only too happy to leave, Poppy stowed her silken creation back in its covering and retrieved the dress hanging in the raw material room.

Downstairs, Poppy dressed the store mannequin, spirits rising steadily with the temperature. Rays of sunlight streamed through the enormous window, casting golden patterns across the sanded hardwood, and she hummed, "Swing Low, Sweet Chariot." Mr. Hobb rummaged through inventory in the back, murmuring in light tones to himself while his wife picked up the latest *Sears, Roebuck & Co. Catalogue* from the post office. She found she quite liked being downstairs when it was just Mr. Hobb and herself. He was a quiet, industrious man, and she appreciated that he didn't feel the need to fill the silence with empty chatter.

She could pretend Francesca had never said anything cutting at all that morning. Determined to forget the whole ordeal, Poppy pulled several pins from the pink cushion in her sewing apron and popped the ends between her lips.

Something crossed the window a foot away from her. A pin dropped to the floor.

One of the tallest men she had ever seen pulled a recalcitrant young woman in bib overalls toward the front door. Behind them, a glossy black and tan coonhound frolicked. The girl looked school-age, perhaps fourteen or fifteen, dug in her booted heels and tugged the hand attached to her wrist.

They looked related. Siblings?

Each was long and lean and wore floppy farmer's hats. The man's work clothes labeled him a cowboy with fringed leather chaps over patched jeans, a worn cambric shirt, and a faded kerchief at his collar. The girl's bib overalls, rent at one knee, swallowed her, a man's oversized work shirt beneath. Two thick, honey-colored braids trailed past the girl's flat chest, bouncing with the force of her wrenching.

Her brother, Poppy assumed, said something inaudible, but his face was highly animated beneath the tip-tilted hat. His mobile brows and quickly moving lips emphasized whatever he said, and it appeared to put the girl's fire out. Poppy heard a groan through the glass.

Head drooping, the girl allowed herself to be led through the front door like a broken mustang, and her brother shoved his hat further onto his head in satisfaction while the bell announced their entrance. Outside, the coonhound settled in the shade beside the door, head and drooping ears resting on his paws as he watched passersby. The two ended their odd procession at the sparse rack of ready-made clothing near the window. It was the smallest section of the store, and Poppy watched them in fascination from her hiding spot behind the mannequin, the pins in her mouth forgotten.

Pushing his sister toward the rack in the recessed wall, the man demanded in a surprisingly deep voice, "Here. Pick one."

"I can't ride in any of these dresses, Sol," the girl snapped, her voice husky and mature despite her fresh face. She looked at the riot of colorful dresses like snakes about to strike. "And don't even think about getting one of those sidesaddles. You can't ride a horse properly on one of those contraptions."

Both of their accents were thick despite the girl's impeccable grammar.

The man—Sol—looked lost. He glared at the ready-made dresses as though they had an answer. "You don't have to ride in one; just wear one to church tomorrow like you promised."

"That was a stupid bet—"

"It was only stupid 'cause you lost it."

She made a face at him.

"Ain't you tired of those sissy town girls messin' with you about your clothes? Isa, I'm supposed to be dignifying you and you're just as wild now as you were a year ago!" He sounded genuinely upset.

"'Ain't' isn't a word. And I don't care what those girls think," Isa defended, a bit too adamantly.

Poppy felt her heart prick in answer to that childish proclamation, and she removed the pins from her mouth and tucked them neatly back into their cushion. The one that had fallen out was nowhere to be seen. She knew exactly who the two were now. In her letters, Lucy often spoke of the brother and sister duo, Isa and Sol. Sol worked for Lucy's husband as a ranch foreman, and Isa was his tagalong sister.

Isa crossed her arms beneath the buttons of her bib. "I hate church."

"SH!" It exploded from Sol's mouth, and he dramatically covered the entire lower half of his sister's face with a giant hand, knocking her hat off. Isa's eyes glared up at him from above his fingers, arms still crossed and hair fuzzing around her head like a golden halo. "Hush up! You want everyone to know what a little sinner you are?"

Her eyes rolled, and Poppy smothered a smile while Isa wrangled her brother's hand from her face. "Anyone who?" she finally sputtered, wiping her mouth. "No one's even in here."

Controlling her expression, Poppy walked around the dress form and cleared her throat.

Two sets of guilty hazel eyes shot to her. They both stood straighter and, if possible, taller. Isa looked a few scant inches below six feet, and Sol was several inches past it. Standing at a meager five foot two inches herself, Poppy had to look up at both once she'd reached them.

"May I help you with anything?" she asked.

Sol found his voice first.

"Uh, yes'm. I'm trying to get this varmint—my sister here—to wear a dress to church tomorrow. Got anything that'll fit?"

His sister had caught a bout of shyness and collected her hat with averted eyes. Poppy lost the battle and smiled at the abashed face. "Let us see what we have. Do you know your measurements?"

Isa shook her head and Sol piped up, "Got any extra long and extra skinny?"

He received a jab of Isa's elbow for that input.

Tickled but more than aware of the fragility of a young lady's pride at this age, Poppy struck a thoughtful pose and viewed Isa from shoulder to instep. She tapped her lower lip. "I was thinking more along the lines of slim and elegant."

A flush stained Isa's cheeks, and Sol's mischievous grin dissolved. He studied Poppy curiously.

"Not many women have your natural height to wear certain dresses and yet still look elegant," Poppy continued. She gestured to her own pocket-sized stature. "I will never appear elegant in, say, a riding skirt, which you should wear if you wish to ride astride. You, however, could rival the ladies in Britain on their palfreys. Mrs. Hobb has some catalogs just over here. Would you like to see them while I take your measurements?"

Isa nodded and followed Poppy without argument.

Assuming Sol would stay behind and twiddle his thumbs like most men did when women shopped, she was surprised when he followed. He leaned a narrow hip against the counter while Isa rifled through thin paper pamphlets of patterns and fashion magazines that advertised illustrations and complicated patterns dotted with tiny numbered measurements. Poppy took a retractable roll of measuring tape from her maroon sewing apron, asked Isa to hold it at her hip, and measured her from hipbone to ankle. She did her arms as well, but as they were in full view of anyone who happened to pass the shop, those measurements would just have to do.

It was uncomfortably warm in the store, and Sol unselfconsciously rolled up his sleeves while his sister paused her page-flipping to point at the more practical clothing.

Dragging her eyes from the dusting of blond hair on Sol's forearms, Poppy nodded and murmured at Isa's choices. It was clear that she was a sportswoman, and she said things like, "Oh, but I don't want to wear bustles like those when I ride. It's irksome," and "I don't like high collars, they choke me when I wrestle with Junior," and "I like that one, but *not* in pink."

"What was your name again?" Sol interrupted, steadily gazing at Poppy's profile. "We're in here every weekend, and I've never seen you around before."

Isa's eyes widened, comprehending.

Caught, Poppy tried not to feel sheepish. "Penelope Daniels."

"You a Penny?" Sol grinned.

"A Poppy," she corrected, but not unkindly.

Only Gerald had ever called her Penny.

Sol took his hat off and held a square-palmed hand out to her. His smile was incredibly broad, his teeth white and strong. "I'm Solomon Williams, ma'am." They shook hands, and his hand was warm, slightly damp, encapsulating her own. "This here is Isadora, my little sister."

No longer shy, his sister bumped him away and held her own hand out. "*Isa,*" she stressed. "And I'm not sure if we're related. I think his mama was a goat."

Sol knocked her hat forward over her eyes, and her grin was a quick flash. She had the same broad arch as Sol, with gaps between big, white teeth. Her smile transformed her face from cautiously attractive to wickedly pretty.

"Just wait till I tell Ma you called her a goat." Sol yelped when Isa pinched the soft skin beneath his armpit.

These two are a mess.

"It's nice to meet you both. I recognized your names from Lucy's letters."

Hazel eyes jerked to her again. It was disconcerting when they did that, and she noticed that Sol's were greenish brown and Isa's were greenish gold. There was no denying they were formed from the same mold.

"So, *you* are Poppy." Isa's voice was full of wonder. "Lucy told us you were coming for the summer. She talks about you all the time. But I thought you would look different, more—"

Sol shut her up with one look. His hat was still crumpled in his hand.

Curious, she asked, "More what?"

Sidling away from Sol and his twitching hands, Isa admitted, "Well, I thought you'd be older. You don't look much older than me."

Accustomed to these comments, Poppy said, "I turn twenty-seven this November. And how old are you?"

"Sixteen."

"I thought you were somewhere close to that."

"Really? Junior always says I look like a ten-year-old boy."

Poppy hid her surprise that anyone would think this girl, taller than half the men in town, looked young enough to be a little boy.

"You wouldn't look like a boy if you'd quit wearin' Drew's hand-me-downs," her brother reasoned and turned to peruse the impressive line of glass canisters that contained a rainbow assortment of candies.

"Mrs. Hobb," Sol shouted.

"It's me today, Sol," was Mr. Hobb's answering shout from the back.

"I'm gonna leave a few pennies—"

"Help yourself!"

"Thank you kindly."

Poppy observed with fascination while Sol laid a few copper pennies from his pocket at the end of the counter, grabbed a brown paper sack at the end of the row, and reached for a pair of little silver tongs.

Losing interest in this ritual, Isa moseyed over to the clothes rack. "Grab a couple of peppermint sticks for me, please. I think I'll pick out a dress I like."

Still tracking Sol's movements, Poppy replied, "Let me know if you need anything."

Sol chose three flavored candies; lemon, butterscotch, and red-and-white-striped peppermint sticks. He replaced the glass lids, settled the tongs in its nook, and was in front of her in one long stride.

He smelled like clean laundry, shaving soap, and leather. She breathed in surreptitiously.

"Take one," he offered, holding the bag open. Boyish charm guarded something wicked beneath his teasing, a heady undercurrent beneath the grin.

Poppy glanced once at the green undertint of his eyes that tried to be playful but which elicited a response entirely different from their intent. More than a year had passed since a man had held her in his arms, and she grew increasingly aware of the lack of physical touch. To hide the first alarming pangs of feminine interest, Poppy pretended that her long hesitation was an inability to choose candy. Still, a question wormed into her mind.

Was Sol unattached?

She chose a golden butterscotch and considered him from beneath her brows. "Thank you, Mr. Williams."

"My pleasure." His voice was a rich bass, as deep as the lowest notes of a cello. Popping a lemon drop into his mouth, his jaw worked, shoving the candy around until it bulged in one cheek. Dark eyelashes fanned against his cheekbones while he rolled the bag's opening closed.

A memory resurfaced as she inspected Sol Williams. Advice from a skilled Louisianan prostitute had adhered to her as a child who was enamored at the thought of being a saloon girl. Lou Lou, a Creole beauty from New Orleans, had traveled to a smaller town to be a big fish in a little pond. She'd had dark hair, a lusty laugh, and hooded dark eyes. She counseled the other women on proper seduction at the breakfast table that the working girls often frequented past noon. Poppy, ten years old at the time, loved breakfast with the other women. It felt like a family, with ribald jokes, sleepy mutterings about everyday things, and a teasing tweak or hair ruffle from the kinder, older women.

Lou Lou would sip coffee in her shift and lounge with one foot in her chair, arm propped on a widely lolling knee. Her slow, husky New Orleans drawl was the best part of Poppy's mornings.

"What y'all don't understand is getting a man isn't what you say with your mouth; it's the language you speak to them across the room."

Moira was often the one to scoff while she buttered her biscuit, and she was also the last to leave the table if Lou Lou was there. "Always worked for me," Poppy's mother would argue with her mouth open.

"Shake your bosoms and show some leg, and they come runnin' up the stairs with you."

"Yes, but," Lou Lou would reply with a red-lipped smile over the rim of her mug, "that's an impermanent trick turnin'. They see tits and muff, but do they want you? No, *cher*. You gotta look them in the eye from two tables away. They're the window to the soul. If they see you through everyone else, you speak with your eyes, tell 'em how much you want them with just one look. That's how you get your regulars that pay extra just to keep you to themselves. That's how you turn a profit."

Still with that mysterious smile, she'd taken a sip of coffee, looked at Poppy, small in her chair, and winked. Never had Poppy wanted to be loved by men more than when Lou Lou was around. The business of whoring seemed darkly romantic. She had craved it.

Until Lou Lou was murdered later that year by a crazed, jealous customer.

Apparently, her tricks had worked too well; when she'd declined to marry one of her regulars and leave the business, he had stabbed her to death in a crime of passion. He hadn't even endeavored to escape, allowing himself to be led, sobbing, to the gallows to be hanged. Poppy had watched the execution with sad eyes while Moira tsked and muttered how smart she had been not to follow Lou Lou's advice. To be murdered by the very men you serviced, what an appalling notion.

You speak with your eyes. Tell them how much you want them with just one look.

Recklessly, Poppy delayed until Sol glanced at her. Holding his gaze, she slipped the butterscotch into her mouth, the buttery sweet candy twinging the muscles in her jaw. Sol's smile slid off, and she averted her gaze before she could reflect too much about what she'd done.

Isa ambled toward them, grudgingly holding a beige wool muslin dress with a navy floral print. It was one of the simpler day dresses, trimmed in bobbin lace, a simple drapery in the front and back, and the collar was high as fashion dictated.

"It's too short, but it was the least ridiculous one." Isa glared at Sol, who had stopped ogling Poppy long enough to give the dress a doubtful scan.

"I will happily hem it to fit." Poppy took the dress and looked with an expert eye. "Probably an extra four inches. Do you have the proper"— she flicked her eyes at Sol and dropped her voice —"stays and bustle?"

Unembarrassed, Isa shook her head. "None of my dresses fit, and I don't have to wear them to school or anything. I finished my schooling early last year."

"Why don't you borrow some of mine?" Poppy suggested.

Isa's eyes widened. "I couldn't do that."

Poppy raised an eyebrow. "And why not? We're practically friends already, and I have plenty to spare in my room at the hotel."

"You're stayin' at the hotel?" Sol interjected. He shifted on his big feet.

"Yes, Lucy's old attic room. It has enough space for my clothes and the material I brought from home, and the privacy will make it easy to work."

"Oh." Isa brightened, shoving her hands in her overall pockets. "Lucy said you were helping Franny out with her seamstress business, so you'll be here a while. We stay at the hotel on the weekends, too. Lucy won't come this weekend because Jack is sick, but she should make it next weekend."

No Lucy for another week?

Hiding her disappointment that her reunion with Lucy would be further postponed, Poppy draped the dress over her arm. "I should have this altered by the end of the day."

Isa's smile was there and gone again, and she snatched the brown bag from Sol, who had continued to lean against the front counter. She danced away from his long-armed reach. "Thank you! Sol, I'll be at the library."

Sol sighed and shook his head while she disappeared through the door with a tinkle. "How much will it be for the dress and the—" He dug in a pocket with one hand and waved the other around, at a loss.

"Alterations," she supplied.

"Yeah." His laugh was deep, from the gut. He pulled the necessary amount after she gave him a figure. "Will you be here at closing?"

"I leave a little before. I work upstairs with Franny, but the plan was that evenings are my own after six o'clock."

He shifted on his feet again and settled his hat further back on his head. His hair was a glossy chestnut curtain, thick and perilously close to his eyes. "That's just in time for supper. How 'bout I meet you here and walk you to the hotel? You could have dinner with Isa and me."

Unable to stop her pulse from leaping, Poppy smoothed the sleeves of Isa's dress. "I would like that."

He delivered a breathtaking smile, tipped his hat, and followed his sister's footsteps. When he held the door open for a pair of old women, he gave them a deep, "Good morning," and winked at Poppy from the doorway. She bit her lip and watched him disappear across the street, the coonhound at his heels.

Chapter Three

S ol strode through town, whistling. It had been a grand day. His accounts looked good despite the construction of his new house. The order of mass-produced decorative spindles had arrived for his front porch, and he'd bought more white paint and wood stain from the hardware store. Isa would wear a dress to church, and Sol would no longer be the biggest failure in Texas.

He tipped his hat to a group of women and gallantly stepped off the boardwalk while they passed. Hog followed, wary of townspeople's kicking feet, but the women only tittered, the boldest calling, "Good afternoon!"

This was what he loved about Dogwood. There were towns closer to Stone Ranch, but this one had friendly people, a library for Isa, and its women were prettier. Speaking of pretty...

He thought of Lucy Stone's friend, Penelope Daniels.

Poppy.

Isa had mirrored his astonishment; Poppy wasn't what they had expected. According to Lucy's stories of their hell-raising years, they had smoked, drank, and gotten into all sorts of mischief. He would never have expected it of the woman he'd encountered that morning.

At first glance, Poppy Daniels had the appearance of a melancholy little schoolmarm, all buttoned up from fashionable neck to cuff, starched and pleated in her shiny black shoes. But when he'd looked again, he'd seen the rich auburn hair, straight, slim brows, and sad blue eyes. Even in such a serious getup, she looked startlingly young.

Hobb's General emerged in the distance, and he self-consciously doffed his hat and fixed his hair. He wished he wasn't wearing his oldest pair of jeans, and he rubbed at the grease stain on his sleeve from polishing tack had left. The only thing new on him was his boots. He bought a new pair every year now that Ben Stone's horse training business had picked up. Sol told himself this sudden worry wasn't at all because he was intrigued by the prim little stranger that had so easily maneuvered Isa.

Prim? Not when she eats candy.

He thought he'd imagined the glint of interest in Poppy's eyes when Isa wasn't looking but had told himself he was reaching into an empty barrel. After being in the shadow of his friend Junior's presence most of the time, Sol was accustomed to being overlooked. Hell, Junior's face belonged on one of those nude sculptures women swooned over, not on a man walking around in a cow town. It didn't particularly upset Sol; work was so demanding he didn't have a spare moment to be interested in a particular woman anyway. Especially now that he was raising his little sister.

And yet...

He hadn't imagined Poppy scrutinizing him. When he'd caught her at it, she'd snared his gaze, unashamed, and slid that golden candy between her lips. He'd frozen, his mind zipping and galloping along while his body remained stuck, unable to move or think. Then, she'd turned away to Isa as though nothing had happened, as though she hadn't broken his ability to speak or take in air.

After that, he believed all of Lucy's stories. Poppy must be as bold and brazen as Lucy herself, but she concealed it, keeping it a secret behind all those buttoned-up clothes.

His pace increased the closer he got to the store until he was loping across the dusty street, Hog at an ear-flapping run beside him. Isa's time slot for her bath was right about now, so Sol would have to soak later. He took a stealthy sniff under his arm and grimaced. Darned Texas heat. It was May and felt like August, and he fanned his shirt to air out any evil smells before he wandered through Hobb's General, cursing whoever had invented shirts.

"Hog, stay," he commanded, but the dog was busily lapping water from a trough by the hitching post. A group of women exited the store, and he gave the youngest lady, who was about the age of fifty, a broad wink. "You ladies stay out of trouble, now."

Mrs. Hobb was at the counter checking out an elderly couple, and when she saw him stride in, she slapped the countertop, jolting her customers.

"Well, there you are!" she cried. She shoved the burlap sack of household items at the couple with a shooing motion, and they exited the store, muttering darkly. "I about spit nails when Mr. Hobb told me I'd missed you this morning."

Flicking his hat to the crown of his head, Sol sauntered to the counter and leaned across it as if he were courting. She would jaw his ear off if he didn't act fast. "I was plumb broken-hearted. Have you left that husband of yours yet so you can run away with me?"

"Ha!" She laughed, belly bouncing. "I got him good and trained. Can't go starting over with a green broke mule like yourself."

"I'm pure-blooded thoroughbred, I'll have you know. I've never been so insulted, might just have to take my business elsewhere."

"You hush your mouth." Mrs. Hobb's jowls wobbled. "What can I do for you today, Sol?"

"I'm here to pick up Isa's dress."

Her eyelids twitched for a split second, then her face slackened. "Is that what Poppy's been workin' on all day? Well, I'll be damned. A dress for Isa, who'd of thunk."

All day? Guilt straightened his cocksure slouch. If Lucy got wind that he'd made her friend work on Isa's dress all day, it might mean eating in the bunkhouse with the men.

"Do you know if it's finished yet?"

"It sure is." She lifted the lid of the glass canister full of sun-colored candy and reached for the tongs. "Poppy can sew fast as Franny. I wouldn't have believed it if I hadn't seen it."

"Er, the butterscotch candies, if you don't mind," he interrupted, pulling out a few pennies. Isa had taken his entire bag of sweets, which were probably long gone by now. Once the brown paper bag was filled with golden candy, he folded it as small as possible. Shoving it in his pocket, he said, "I guess I'll pick it up now, make sure it fits Isa."

"She's in the back packaging it up. Isa'll like it. Poppy's got a good touch."

She sucked in air as though readying to banter until sundown, so Sol quickly settled his hat into a normal angle, tipped it to Mrs. Hobb, and rounded the counter. He was itching to see the pocket-sized woman. Maybe he'd get her to laugh.

Dim light filtered in the back storage room, its window too tiny for a body to climb through, and he peeked stealthily around the doorway trim. Poppy hummed and folded tissue paper over the material in the box in the corner. Her throaty voice made for a pretty tune.

He knocked on the trim and cleared his dry throat. "Ma'am?"

Glancing up from the little table, her eyes lit up. "Mr. Williams, perfect timing. I hope it's all right that I packaged it. It might feel more special to her if it's a gift, not a chore."

Touched, he moseyed through the doorway, thumbs jammed in his belt loops. "I appreciate all the trouble you're goin' through."

"It was no trouble at all. I altered it a little around the neckline so it would not choke her, but I don't recommend wrestling Junior in a dress like this." Would you look at that? She did know how to tease. Her eyes darted playfully from beneath her straight, serious brows.

He snorted at the image. "Legs would say it wasn't a fair fight unless Junior wore a dress, too."

Poppy almost laughed. It ignited her face, squinting her eyes and lifting her cheeks with a smile, but she smothered it. She tucked her head and clasped her hands, prim once more. He was alive with the need to make her laugh, the challenge a hunter feels spotting the flash of a whitetail in the brush before he sets off in pursuit. He liked her voice. It was a buttery soft alto instead of a high falsetto, making her earlier humming rich and nuanced.

He wondered how it sounded when she laughed.

"Is that Isa's nickname?" she asked suddenly. "Legs?"

"Among others."

Wee hairs had escaped at her nape and around her ears, curly as corkscrews. Her nails were perfect, polished ovals, her fingers quick and nimble, and a gold band winked on the left hand.

Lucy had explained that Poppy was widowed, and he wondered about her husband.

"Legs," Poppy repeated, lips curling up at the corners. Her eyes drifted from his shirt front to his leather chaps and down to the hem of his work jeans resting over his boots. "Do you know I believe Isa holds the record for the longest limbs of any woman I've encountered? It appears to be a family trait. I imagine those are tailored to fit. No ready-made suits for you, hm?"

Suits?

Spreading his arms wide, he looked down at the beat-up trousers his mother had sewn for him years ago and chuckled. "You always this polite? Naw, no suits for me."

"I could make some for you."

For some absurd reason, the thought of wearing something she had sewn with her own two hands flooded his neck with warmth, and he laid a palm atop it sheepishly. "I don't know, I'm not much the suit-wearin' type."

Speculatively, she made a quarter-circle around him as though he were a stud at auction. "No? You have excellent proportions for one. It would be an achievement for me. I've never made an article of clothing for anyone so tall. You would break another record."

She was teasing him again. About his excellent proportions, of all things. "You ladies keep records of things like that?"

Though her face was smooth and polite, her blue eyes glittered when they met his. She slowly pulled out her measuring tape from the half apron she wore and unrolled it with a raised brow. He laughed aloud and backed away with his palms out in a halting gesture before him.

"No, you've done enough just helpin' my sister out. No need to use that thing on me."

The corners of her mouth curled at the ends again, like a cat. "If you're sure."

Poppy went to the table to lift the box, and he rushed forward. "Let me." She smelled good, delicate and flowery. He held the box and repeated, "I do appreciate you helping Isa."

"Any friends of Lucy's are friends of mine." She reached into her apron, fiddling with something.

"I know, but—" he sighed. It was his turn to avoid her gaze. "It's been hard. Isa's been stayin' with me for a while. My parents have my other sister's kids staying with them, and it's a lot for Isa, havin' to share her room and all of her things. And our niece and nephews, well, they don't rightly know what it means to keep their hands to themselves.

"Not to mention," he added in a rush, a boiling pot overflowing with hissing water, all these things tumbling out, "she insists on wearin' Drew's hand-me-downs, but she's getting too old for that now. It's fine at the ranch, but she won't wear nothing else, no matter how we try to bribe her. Ma thinks she's dotty and tries to pray for her at church, which embarrasses the hel—heck out of her. So now the only church she'll go to is this one because Lucy and Ben go to it, and she looks up to Lucy. Only thing is, the town kids are messin' with her about her clothes when I'm not around, but she won't do anything about it."

Something in Poppy's expression had shifted during his diatribe. The polite attentiveness was gone. She looked animated. Engaged. "Children can be cruel. Even their parents. Does she live at the ranch with you and the Stones?"

Shifting the box in his arms, he nodded. "Yeah, but only for now. Junior and a few neighbors helped me build a house about an hour outside of town, and it's about done. Just needs a little paint to finish it off. Isa has her own room and everything."

"That's wonderful."

"It's just—I know that Isa knows I love her no matter what she looks like or what she wears. But I want to do right by her. I don't want her to be a laughingstock. Overalls were fine when she was knee-high, but she just turned sixteen. She's done with school and keeps talking about that college out west. Can you see her in some university wearing overalls and pigtails? It's not proper anymore. Sometimes I forget she's a girl, and I've never seen her out of braids."

Worrying about his sister had become a constant with Sol in the last year.

As much as Isa's tagging along and constant barrage of questions exhausted him, she delighted him. Their father had no use for females who didn't cook, clean, or mend and had too many other children and grandchildren to worry about. Their mama was a godly woman, pious and worried for the mortal soul of her youngest child, especially after failing with the first daughter so spectacularly.

Both parents exasperated Isa to no end.

Even so, their family was a good one that was loud, boisterous, always teasing, and never quiet. They were a hardworking lot that was full of affection for one another. Isa might tumble through the family's cracks from time to time, but Sol was there to catch her.

Like the month before, he'd won a bet, and now Isa had to attend church every Sunday for a year. His stipulation was that she wear a dress and her stipulation was to pick the church. Of course, she chose the church that Lucy and Miss Pickney attended.

"Their picnics are more fun," Isa had rationalized. "The women at Ma's church can't cook, and they especially can't abide by a good joke."

Sol had privately agreed.

Poppy was thoughtful, brows knitted in the center. "Excuse me," she said and left the storage room. He heard her murmur something to Mrs. Hobb, who replied with a hearty good night. When Poppy returned, she clutched several small pamphlets depicting illustrated women's hairstyles, and her eyes were bright in her pale, serious face.

"Bring Isa by the attic in the morning. I'll see what we can do."

SOL TOSSED AND turned in the hotel's spare family bedroom, the night muggy and over warm.

His mind was full of Poppy Daniels.

Unable to sleep, he donned the clothes he'd folded on the bedside table and quietly made his way down the hall. He stopped at the foot of the attic stairs, poised midstep.

Poppy's lamp was on, illuminating a yellow square of light on the hallway's damask wallpaper.

What was she doing up there?

He imagined her penning letters or embroidering. Or was she reading? He couldn't imagine what kind of book a lady would read. Isa read all sorts, but she wasn't the typical lady. Sol even caught her scouring the dictionary once.

The intensifying desire to climb the stairs and see what Poppy was up to alarmed him, so he fled. The door to the family's section was locked, and he pulled a spare key from the hidden nail before he left.

"Hog," he whispered on the back porch. "Come."

The coonhound rose noisily to his feet and plodded over, bumping his head beneath Sol's hand for a pet. Together, they meandered through the dark alleyway and onto busy Main Street. He may as well play cards until a drink and a few wins soothed his busy mind.

During supper with Minnie, Poppy, and Mr. Ricci, Sol had tried to hide how cautiously protective he was of Isa. His sister always said what she thought, and though it was highly entertaining to their nuclear family and friends, Isa tended to scandalize strangers. And Poppy Daniels was a stranger. But as the night went on, Poppy and Isa had discussed their plans for their toilette the next morning, skimming through the pamphlets and grinning over the more ridiculous styles of hair and hats. Sol's guard had gradually lowered.

Everything Poppy had said to Isa was kind and genuine.

He was thinking about how Poppy's skirts had swished sensually around her ankles after she bid them good night when a noise interrupted his slack-jawed musings.

Hog growled low, ruff stiff.

Though Main Street was dimly lit by the newly installed streetlamps, the alleys remained black voids between sleeping buildings. Two shadows struggled in the narrow passage between the barber shop and the feed store.

Voices hissed at each other—an angry male and a shrill female.

"—you following me? Have I not expressed quite clearly—" The man's voice was disjointed and aggressive, the whine of the woman's voice too far away to make out. The scuffling between them turned antagonistic. Menacing.

Heart pumping, Sol stepped into the alley's entrance. "Whoa," he shouted, his deep voice cutting through the darkness. "What's goin' on down there? Ma'am, you need some help?"

Two shadow heads turned to him in unison, and the bodies pulled apart. The man scurried off at the other end while the woman dropped her head into her hands, quietly sobbing.

Concern softened his voice, and he walked deeper into the alley's shadows, squinting so his eyes could adjust to the dark. "Ma'am, are you alright? Can I walk you home?"

The woman looked up, sniffled, and fled.

Cursing, Sol didn't bother to chase after her, calling Hog back when the damned fool tried to slink away and investigate. The scene left a bad taste in his mouth, so he abandoned his plans and retraced his steps to the hotel. When he locked the family door, hung the key, and tiptoed into the hall, he checked the attic staircase.

Poppy's light was off.

Chapter Four

It was peculiar how certain people's company stifled Poppy's creeping, pervasive loneliness. Isa and Sol's presence beneath the attic floor—their big white smiles, irrepressible humor, tattered clothes, and fondness for each other's well-being—soothed an old hurt within her.

Poppy's evening although sleepless had not been restless. She'd lain in the dark in an introspective recline, listening to night sounds from the open window. It had felt good to hem the dress for Isa even though Francesca had sniffed at it; her friend thought their energies were better spent securing well-to-do women's business in town.

And Sol...

She had fallen asleep for the first time without missing Gerald. Instead, her dreams had repeated the scene of Sol turning to her and laughing, his greenish eyes crinkling in the corners.

She woke as she'd fallen asleep. Smiling.

The church dress that Francesca had chosen for Poppy to model was a navy print muslin trimmed in brown velvet. Poppy looked slim and elegant in its sufficiently flounced and draped lines, advertising the immense skill required to create such a piece. The matching hat was small and perched atop her intricately twisted updo, and she was setting its trailing brown velvet ribbons to rights when a rap on the attic stair's doorway below interrupted her musings.

"Miss, er, Poppy, are you awake? Can I come up now?" Isa's unsure voice echoed up the landing.

"Of course!" Poppy rushed to the railing which corralled the stair's opening.

The middle part of Isa's honey-blonde hair gleamed white, and the back of her new dress gaped. How unfortunate that the dress's buttons were in the back. Isa would need help donning it until she was dexterous enough to reach behind and do it herself. The hem in the back dragged across the floor, too long without a bustle to raise and shape the drooping skirt.

"Let me help you. But, first, you'll need to remove the dress so we can attach the bustle."

"You mean one of those cages that makes sitting a curse?" Isa asked warily.

"No, I did not imagine you'd want one of those. I have a spare Tampico bustle. See? It's soft, and the ruffles give it its shape instead of springs or crinoline. And it's only ten and twelve inches, enough to shape the skirt but not so uncomfortable you cannot sit a pew for an hour."

Using the paneled folding screen in the corner, Poppy helped Isa dress, and her seamstress's heart broke at the girl's yellowing, threadbare combinations. The underwear was also several sizes too large, and she speculated if it had been handed down from the girl's mother. She said nothing so as not to twinge Isa's pride, but her fingers itched to make Isa at least three pairs of combinations. A lady should own proper undergarments, especially at that tender age.

"This feels so strange," Isa admitted several minutes later, peering into the framed mirror beside the armoire. "I've never owned a dress this fancy before."

Poppy pretended she wasn't reeling from shock. As she had helped Isa undress in a sure and perfunctory manner, the young girl's secret had unraveled to the floor. Isa was not flat-chested, but a buxom girl with a full bosom despite her lean stature. Her chest had been wrapped in a sash of thick cotton material, flattening her breasts close to her body. Though Poppy had been matter-of-fact about it, Isa had colored and contended that, "They hurt too much when I ride."

Now, Isa's unbound breasts filled out the front of her dress, adding five years to her appearance. Her eyes carefully skated past them in the mirror.

"You are lovely," Poppy said truthfully. "Would you like me to teach you how to style your hair?"

While Poppy flipped through the pamphlets on the writing desk, Isa asked curiously, "Is this what men want?" She turned to view her profile in the mirror, which was long and reflected her image from head to hips. Her hair, white at the ends, streamed in waves to her elbows.

"Some men, yes," Poppy said. She grabbed a hairbrush and handed a pamphlet to Isa. "Do you like this one? Wonderful. Let's brush your hair out. You're to dampen it with your wash water. It makes it easier to style."

Isa studied the simple drawings in the little book. "And what of other men?" It was clear she wanted to have this conversation. "What do they want?"

"I really cannot say."

"I think this is what men who want wives want. If one was to catch a man who did not want a wife, she'd wear red and pull her neckline down to here."

She pointed to her navel.

Holding in a laugh, Poppy said, "Very true, but the difference in those men is they do not want to be caught. Those men are the...catch and release variety."

"Like if you tried to domesticate a raccoon?" Isa asked. "You can raise them, feed them, pet them, but they're still crazy as a sitting hen if you kept one in the house?" Her eyes widened in inspiration. "And the same can be said for women. Socrates said, 'By all means, marry. If you get a good wife, then you'll be happy; if you get a bad one, you'll be a philosopher.' And I don't know a single unhappily married man that doesn't blow smoke to anyone who will listen."

Amusement colored Poppy's words. "I see what you mean. I only know one Socrates saying."

"What is it?"

"'Be as you wish to seem.'"

Isa's eyes were uncomfortably shrewd in the mirror's reflection, and Poppy distracted her, coaching her to plait and twist her hair. They secured the braid tight against the skull above the nape with pins. Palms dampened with scented water smoothed flyways and gave Isa's hair a golden sheen.

"There is another quote I love," Isa blurted, eyes huge on her reflection. "It says that the emerging woman is strong-minded, strong-souled, and strong-bodied, and that strength and beauty must go together."

"That's wonderful." Poppy looked at Isa's profile, inspired by such a bright mind. "Who said that?"

"Louisa May Alcott. She wrote *Little Women*. Have you read it?" Isa's voice grew breathy, excited.

Feeling a little shame that she wasn't much of a reader, Poppy shook her head. "No, I'm usually up sewing, not reading. But I have heard of it. It's a book about sisters?"

"Oh, it's much more than that," Isa gushed. "I have an extra copy of it. The next time I'm in town, I'll bring it and give it to you."

"Oh, no, I couldn't—"

"Yes! You shall love it. Please."

Unable to hide a fond grin, Poppy finally acquiesced. "Very well. Thank you. I would be honored to read your favorite book."

"Oh, *Black Beauty* is my favorite book. One day I'm going to own a horse just like him." Isa blinked, and her color grew rosy, smile flashing. "I have a spare copy of that one as well. Have you read it?"

Poppy shook her head.

After they had discussed every spare book Isa owned, they looked at the changed young woman in the mirror.

"I don't even look the same," Isa commented.

"But you *are* the same, remember that." Poppy scrubbed her hands, dried them, and reorganized the desk. She wanted to file her finger-nails. No, that would be strange. She would have to wait until tonight. As an alternative, she laid the brush just so and straightened the pile of pamphlets. "It may change people's reactions to you because they are only human, but you are still the same you on the inside." Poppy sensed Isa watching her movements.

"Hm. I think Sol's reaction will be apoplexy."

"I think he will find a way to win more wagers against you."

Isa grinned at her reflection. "I may let him."

SOL'S REACTION DIDN'T disappoint.

He waited near the kitchen in faded black trousers and an outdated, dingy cream shirt that had once been white. Poppy descended first at Isa's request, and the full force of Sol's smile had stalled any of the words she'd rehearsed at the top landing. He wasn't wearing a hat, and his chestnut hair gleamed in the light from the foyer windows. He took in her dress, her hat, her fresh-washed face.

"Mornin'." His voice was, if possible, deeper in the mornings.

"Good morning." He moved to the side to let her pass, but she hovered. Her eyes anchored to his face, a mysterious smile blossoming.

Isa's booted feet descended the stairs, mostly hidden by the multitude of borrowed petticoats. Sol's eyes widened in a satisfying display of disbelief, and he pulled his thumbs from the pockets of his trousers.

Isa smiled uncomfortably when Sol circled her. He scratched his head dramatically. "What—who?" He looked at Poppy. "Where's my sister? What have you done with her?"

Isa smacked his chest with the back of her hand. "Stop being an idiot."

Sol sighed in relief, rubbing his pectoral muscle. "Oh, there she is."

Sniffing, Isa whipped her skirts away from Sol to avoid grazing his pant legs and led the way to the hotel's front door.

He watched the door swing open with a proud, effervescent smile. "Mrs. Daniels, I don't know how you did it, but I might owe you more money." He made to dig in his pocket, and Poppy placed a hand on the firm muscle and tendons of his arm.

"Don't be ridiculous. And call me Poppy."

Sol stilled, smile vanishing, while he peered down at her upturned face. She knew she was closer than was proper, and when he pulled his hand from his pocket, he snatched her fingers before she could back away.

"I do appreciate your kindness." He drew her hand up and kissed the skin over her knuckles. His lips were soft, and her entire body felt an answering pulse, every nerve connected solely to the area his lips touched.

The door swung open again.

"Are you two coming?" Isa looked suspiciously between Sol and Poppy, who wore twin expressions of innocence. Sol's thumbs were back in his pockets, and Poppy held her hands behind her back, breast upthrust.

A wagon waited for them, and Sol assisted them onto the bench. Isa scowled and wiggled in the center. Poppy's attention had focused on the hand Sol had touched during the ride to church, and she frowned at it while Isa chatted the whole way. She explained that it was the church that Lucy and Ben had married in six years before, it was better than her mama's church which was filled with nothing but mean old people, and the librarian went to this church.

After parking, Sol helped them down and walked arm in arm with Poppy while Isa fidgeted at their heels. She didn't feel as alone in the sea of strangers as she had expected. She waved to Mr. and Mrs. Hobb before taking a pew with the Williams siblings. Service was a blur. Poppy was too busy absorbing the details of the people around them.

There were many curious looks her way, and the back of her neck seemed to blister from all the eyes on her. She was sixteen all over again, an unknown entity listening to Reverend Daniels' sermon. This time, she wasn't hungry. She wore a fine dress and smelled nice.

And she wasn't alone.

They sang hymns, and Sol's deep baritone melded with her smooth alto. It was challenging to ignore his warm body brushing against hers. After singing, they sat, and the only words she heard from the sermon were *lust*, *covet*, and *fire*. She was relieved and disappointed when it ended and everyone flooded the walkways. She hadn't walked two steps before a squat matronly figure approached her.

"You must be Mrs. Daniels," the woman said with the effusive charisma of a natural leader. "I'm Imelda Barnett, the Dogwood Women's Committee chairwoman. Mrs. Hobb tells us you will show the Women's Circle some of your designs. Is this one of them?" After the flood of words, she stepped back and eyed Poppy from the opal cameo at her neckline to her velvet hemline. Poppy made to speak, but Imelda beat her to it. "That's lovely. I'd love to order one of a similar design. You will be very popular with the women indeed, and just look at you, cute as a button. How old are you, dear?"

Veiling her surprise at such a question, Poppy managed, "Twenty-six, ma'am, but I've sewed patterns with Francesca Hobb since I was fifteen."

"Yes, what skill, not a stitch to be seen," Imelda hummed, plucking at Poppy's cuff.

This must be what the general store mannequin feels when customers come in.

"Thank you, Mrs. Barnett."

"Oh, no, dear, call me Imelda. Everyone does." She patted Poppy's cheek in a grandmotherly fashion. "You are just so very darling, aren't you? Such a tiny thing, like a doll! You must meet the Women's Circle."

Smiling through growing dislike, Poppy allowed Mrs. Barnett's plump fingers to wrap around her wrist and lead her through the throng toward a group of brightly dressed women.

Halfway there, a gentleman of average height passed through Poppy's line of sight.

After a stunned pause, she strained her neck to look behind her and catch sight of him again. There were too many people. Heart racing, she almost released Mrs. Barnett's capriciously strong hold on her wrist to chase the gentleman in the expensive suit.

That looked almost like…no, it couldn't be.

Poppy hadn't seen Ace since the Louisiana brothel her mother and she had escaped from before coming to Dogwood. Just thinking the name of the man who had bought her for a weekend brought a cold sweat along her upper lip. She wondered if the old woman could feel Poppy's pulse racing in her wrist. Her heart threatened to fling itself from her chest, her head had drums in it.

It couldn't be Ace, not in Dogwood, and certainly not in a church, of all places.

She had to be mistaken.

Despite her reassurances to herself, she didn't recollect a single name when Mrs. Barnett introduced her to some of the Women's Circle. The broad smiles, large flowery hats, and pastel dresses swirled around her, and she blinked away the double vision.

The chairwoman was speaking again, and Poppy forced herself to listen. "Mrs. Smithe's luncheon is tomorrow at eleven o'clock. Be sure to bring some samples, dear."

Talk of business and sewing grounded her.

Bring some samples?

Of course, she would bring samples. She wasn't an imbecile.

"Yes, ma'am," she said placidly. "Where is Mrs. Smithe's?"

"It's the blue house on Carolina Drive." Imelda continued to give directions, but something else caught Poppy's attention.

From behind her, low tones of conversation drifted to her. She interrupted the flow of chatter with the women as quickly as was polite. "I will be there, thank you, Mrs. Barnett. It was very nice to meet you all. Excuse me, please."

Whirling on her heel, she listened for the exchange that had raised her hackles and caught Isa's bright hair floating a head above the colorful trio that had cornered her. A young woman in pink ruffles and matching ribbons stood toe to toe with Isa, flanked by two younger girls at her side. Though Isa had her arms crossed securely over her breasts, her chin was high. The ominous glitter in her eyes didn't bode well for the girls that corralled her.

The girl in pink asked scathingly, "What happened to your overalls? Did you run out of brothers to steal clothes from?"

Her friends sounded like a couple of jackals, yipping to be heard.

Jaw clenched, Poppy rounded the three girls with the speed of a cutlass, blockading Isa from them.

Their countenances altered from surprised guilt to sullen defiance.

"I don't believe we have been introduced. What is your name, young lady?" Poppy was irritated that her voice was so soft. What she needed was Mrs. Hobb's booming bark, or even Lucy's clear ringing tones, to scare these three well-dressed rats back into the hole they originated from.

The two younger girls glanced at each other, defiance dissolving into alarm. They melted into the bodies around them, leaving their older, more hostile friend behind. The young woman in the pink ruffles grew uncertain as Poppy sustained an expectant air.

"I'm Hattie Fowler. My mother is Dorothy Fowler." Hattie Fowler tilted her head insolently. "She's in the Women's Circle. She and Mrs. Smithe are best friends."

Poppy was not impressed. "How do you do. I'm Mrs. Daniels, and Mrs. Barnett has just invited me to the Women's Circle luncheon. I shall happily discuss your comportment with your mother while I am there."

"I—"

"Or," Poppy interrupted, brows lowering, "we can come to an understanding, and you can apologize to Miss Williams. She is my dearest friend, you see."

The little tormentor's cheeks pinkened, and her mouth opened and closed for several seconds while she decided whether to comply with these terms. Then, "I-I beg your pardon, Isa."

From beside Poppy, Isa crossed her arms. "I don't accept."

Stifling a sigh at her oblivious young friend, Poppy affected a smile. "Don't be silly. You must accept."

Temple flexing once, twice, Isa finally grumbled, "Fine. I accept, Hattie."

While the girls contemplated each other with well-developed hostility, Poppy dismissed Hattie Fowler and steered her tall, young friend away.

"Come, let us find Mr. Williams. I'd like to get a few more measurements today during your fitting."

"My—"

"Yes, we can probably have another new dress ready for you by next week. Shall we?"

Taking the hint at long last, Isa led the way to the front doors, and Poppy felt a sharp pride when she didn't look back.

A head taller than the other men, Sol was easy to find. The group of men stood in the shade of a cluster of pine trees. Some smoked, drawing disapproving glances from their wives nearby.

"Did you mean it?" Isa asked when they were halfway to Sol, slowing her wide strides to match Poppy's small ones. "About measuring me for more dresses."

"Would you like that? I would never presume—I just detest when girls tease others for wearing different things."

"Yeah, Hattie is a real cow turd," Isa said matter-of-factly.

Surprised laughter burst from Poppy.

Sol, hearing her laughter, looked up and raised a hand. He detached himself from the men and met them in the yard.

"Sol," Isa prompted, "can you pay Poppy to make some dresses for me?"

Poppy watched Sol's mouth part for endless seconds before he cleared his throat. "Sure, that ain't a problem."

"'Ain't' isn't a word," Isa said automatically.

Flicking her ear before Isa could dodge it, Sol asked exasperatedly, "How many do you want, squirt?"

At this, Isa appeared lost and looked askance at Poppy.

"Well," Poppy began slowly. "You'll need day dresses. Perhaps we can start with two. Would you like to try a split skirt and see if you like it?"

Isa's eyes lit up. "Yes, I'd like that very much. But I have a request. There's this dance in a couple of weeks, and if it's not too much, I'd love a dress to wear to it."

"I don't see any issue with an evening gown. Would you prefer one that's off the shoulder? It's a little more daring."

Ignoring her brother's head shake, Isa asked determinedly, "It's what ladies back east wear?"

"Yes."

"Then, I want one."

They ignored Sol's sigh and chatted about colors and designs while he went to grab the wagon. Halfway through questioning which colors would flatter her coloring the most, Isa snagged an older lady who turned out to be the librarian, Miss Pickney, and introduced them. While Poppy curtsied, she noticed a woman intensely watching Sol bound from the wagon he'd brought around. Unfailingly polite, he tipped his hat to Miss Pickney when he reached them.

"Y'all ready to head out? Miss Pickney, you need a ride?" He led the straight-laced librarian to the wagon, nodding at her banter the whole way.

Isa also talked, but Poppy barely heard.

The woman beneath the tree hadn't taken her eyes off Sol once.

"I DON'T REALLY prefer men's clothing," Isa said back in the attic room.

A slender pencil in her mouth and tape in hand, Poppy busily procured more detailed measurements. Then, figures in mind, she freed her mouth and wrote them down. "Why do you wear them, then?"

"Well," Isa began, then stopped. Took a deep breath. "I have this friend. He's a boy. He's my best friend, frankly. We spend a lot of time together, but he only treats me like a friend when I dress in overalls. Every time I wear a dress, he treats me differently. Like I'm not even there, or like I am an annoying little sister he wants nothing to do with."

"Hm." Poppy had an idea of who this "friend" was.

"So, I wear overalls everywhere. It was fine up until a couple of years ago. Ma took in my niece and nephews, and people whispered about my sister, then me, and she started to worry that I'd end up like Katherine." She muttered, "As if I'd ever be like her."

"Your sister, Katherine—" Poppy began delicately, but Isa cut her off in her usual inexpugnable way.

"—is a scarlet woman at the Hound Dog Saloon in Lufkin."

"Ah."

"Ma said Katherine was always chasing after boys. She had a baby when she was my age with a boy from school. After she dropped out and ran away with a different boy, my parents kept the baby for her. Then, the baby died." There was a hush. Poppy paused in her writing and stared unseeing at the paper on the desk. In thoughtful tones, Isa continued, "Ma hasn't been the same since. And for a long time, we couldn't find Katherine to tell her or know if she was alive *to* tell. One day, my brother Earl found her by accident in Lufkin and said she had three more kids and was raising them in a saloon. Pa and Sol went out there and brought them home. But Katherine wouldn't come. Said she liked it there. That was two years ago."

Remembering her own mother, Poppy nodded. "Sometimes you can try and convince them until you're blue in the face to work at any other place but a saloon, but they'll make every excuse to stay." *It's not as simple as you make it out to be, Poppy Mae,* her mother would defend. Feeling Isa's curious eyes on her, Poppy changed the subject. "Well, I promise you will soon have a beautiful dress to wear at the dance next month."

Isa climbed back into her overalls and grinned. "Thanks, Poppy. I can't wait to see Hattie Fowler's ugly face. You should have seen it today when she saw that I had bosoms. Oh, I forgot to wrap them." She disappeared behind the divider again. Poppy was still chuckling when she descended the stairs, unconsciously looking for Sol.

He was lounging in a rocking chair on the back porch with a wrinkled bag of candy.

When he saw her approaching, he held it out without saying a word.

All the candies were butterscotch.

Smiling her thanks, she discerned how the noon sun set the jade in his eyes to glittering and slid the candy between her lips. Sol's normally jovial expression darkened. Neither said anything. She propped a shoulder against a wooden post and rolled the candy around in her mouth, arguing with herself.

I could seduce him. He would let me.

But then, she couldn't. Not truly.

Something about Sol stood out despite his approachable personality and amiable smile. He held doors open for everyone and never met a stranger. He worried about girls bullying his sister, so he bribed her into dresses. Even the prickly librarian secured his full attention before they dropped her off at her little townhouse. Sol was far too good for Poppy, and she would do well to remember it.

"Would you like to come to my housewarming shindig the weekend after next?" he asked, a husk in his voice. "It's the weekend before the dance."

She shouldn't.

She should make an excuse.

The memory of the hungry-eyed woman from the churchyard decided her.

"I would love to."

It wasn't a wise decision. Poppy would beguile Sol purposefully if she was alone with him for any amount of time, especially in the darkness of a house party. Poppy would draw him to the side where it was darkest, touch the line of his biceps, run her hand along the width of his shoulder, then grab the length of his hair. It would be all too easy to tug his head down to hers. She hadn't admitted to herself until that moment how very attracted she was to Sol.

But is he attracted to you?

Sol leaned back in the rocking chair, holding quite still, the lines of his body tense. His eyes watched her alertly as though sensing the shift in her thoughts. The candy in his cheek was forgotten. The knuckles of the hands gripping the armrests were white and bony.

Seeing her answer, she moistened her lips.

"Are you married?" she heard herself ask.

His smile was slow. "No, ma'am."

She took a step forward. Sol was out of his chair and looming over her in the next instant, and she smelled butterscotch and a hint of shaving soap. Saw the dark intensity on his face.

The screen door opened.

He continued the momentum from his abrupt advancement and flew down the stairs before Isa could open her mouth from the doorway. His hand raked his hair, frustration evident in every line.

"What's the matter with him?" Isa huffed, tying off a braid with a strip of rawhide.

Poppy mused in a surprisingly calm voice, "I think something stung him."

"Was it a yellow jacket?"

"I'm not sure."

"Oh. I better get some tobacco from Mr. Ricci." Isa opened the screen door. "Yellow jacket stings make him swell up something fierce."

Poppy dropped her face in her hands to hide her laughter.

Chapter Five

Poppy clenched her magazines and patterns to her breast during the buggy ride to Mrs. Smithe's luncheon the following day. She was sure she would be found out. Someone would identify her as the daughter of Moira, the Social Pariah, and Francesca's business would fail.

It hadn't helped that the nightmare had revisited her, the one that always jolted her awake. Purple bruises on gray, naked skin. A shallow ditch. A man draping a saddle blanket over a too-still body with matted red hair. The man had a dark, shadowy face. He whispered sinisterly, *"Don't tell your mama."*

She had woken up in a cold sweat, thoughts reeling.

Why had that dream returned?

Not even after Gerald's death had that night terror plagued her.

And so, afraid to fall back into slumber, Poppy had lit a lamp and worked on Isa's evening dress into the wee hours of the morning. Tranquility had returned slowly, her mind determinedly blank, but beneath still waters, it roiled with words left unsaid and thoughts left unthought. Her fingers tremored and wouldn't abate no matter how she flexed or shook them.

By sunrise, she'd succeeded in suppressing the nightmare into nonexistence. It was locked away, forgotten as securely as the key to Pandora's box. Her next anxious flare-up ensued when she couldn't find the patterns inspired by Worth's designs. That snag was quickly mitigated; they were on Francesca's worktable.

Once she'd thanked Mr. Hobb for the ride and stepped into Mrs. Smithe's blue house on Carolina Drive, all her worries had proved unfounded. The Women's Circle delivered abundant warmth with their coaxing hands and crinkling smiles. Most of them were a decade older than Poppy herself, excluding two; a shy transplant from New Braunfels and a talkative brunette that spoke excitedly with fluttering hands and ready laughter. Poppy gravitated toward them.

The first woman Poppy distinguished from the rest was Hattie Fowler's mother. Dorothy was a plump, well-dressed woman with her nose in the air and a cruel smirk on her face. The second was the mystery woman beneath the tree, devouring Sol with her eyes. Poppy marked her immediately.

It was Mrs. Smithe.

Mrs. Smithe was a fortyish woman with average, blunt features and light brown hair shot through with silver. A rose cut diamond ring glittered on her finger, its setting excessive in size. Her pastel green dress boasted extravagant flounces and ribbons, and she wore a scarily wide smile when she introduced Poppy to the other women in the front parlor.

Poppy deliberated over if Mrs. Smithe knew Sol intimately, and she ignored the slow, simmering temper at the intemperate idea.

Displaying dresses and patterns seized an hour's worth of attention, and Poppy busily answered two or three women's questions at a time while the other dozen chatted amongst themselves. She happily wrote all the orders in her log. Francesca would be delighted at the amount of business they'd received in one day.

After refreshments, the conversation shifted from dresses to the interesting women who planned to make them.

Poppy firmly safeguarded the privacy of the mysterious Franny Hobb, so the hostess turned the attention to Poppy. Mrs. Smithe questioned Poppy's history, connections, where she hailed from, and if she'd be staying. Prepared for the housewives' curiosity, Poppy disclosed what they expected to hear. She was from a respectable family in a small town, was taught all she knew from the woman who raised her, married an educated preacher's son who died of tuberculosis the year before, and came to Dogwood for new prospects and a fresh start. The women were tickled that she made a living all on her own without a husband, father, or brothers to answer to, and talk promptly switched from Poppy to husbands.

Poppy settled between the two women her age, the quiet Bertha Muller, who only smiled behind her hand, and the boisterous Kitty Powers, who talked nonstop.

Mrs. Smithe chatted fondly of her husband while she sipped her tea. "Yes, my Nelson is often very busy with work out of town. He's in sales, and we do very well if it is not too uncouth to admit." She smiled around the rim of her fine china.

"What does he sell?" asked a curious, no-nonsense woman with iron-gray hair.

Poppy wondered if Nelson was weak or scholarly.

Like Gerald?

Even as that unfair thought shamed her, the voice of her baser needs added, *It might explain why she watches Sol Williams.* There was nothing weak at all about Sol. He could pick her up with one of his giant hands.

Was that why Mrs. Smithe was intrigued by him? Perhaps she was lonely with her husband constantly gone, and a single, attractive man drew her eye just like he had Poppy's.

Kitty turned and whispered to Poppy and Bertha, "All these dolls are giving me the willies. What do you think?"

Bertha giggled behind her teacup.

Poppy cast an appraising eye around the parlor. It was a large room with two windows overlooking the street they'd poured in from, and the women perched on mismatched wooden chairs and settees. It was luxuriously decorated with velvet drapes, dark-green wallpaper over wood paneling, a thick patterned rug, polished side tables, and a pianoforte.

And on every available surface were dolls.

Most were porcelain with round, pink cheeks, their tiny lips painted red, the faces shiny and glazed. They wore bonnets and matching little dresses of every color and were propped on the mantle, the top of the piano, end tables, and even tucked into the nooks of the bookshelf that housed more knick-knacks than books. Some of the dolls had real hair. Those reminded Poppy of the childhood doll Moira had sold.

It wasn't the dolls themselves so much as their quantity, cramped in what had promised to be an elegant room.

Bertha whispered, "My grandmother collected dolls when I was growing up, but most were cloth, nothing nearly as splendid as these."

"Splendid or not, I wouldn't have one in my house." Kitty mimed a grimace of fright. "Am I thankful we only have boys."

"I hope Mr. Muller and I are blessed soon," Bertha shyly admitted, cheeks as pink as the doll on the sideboard at her shoulder.

"How many children do you have, Kitty?" Poppy asked.

"Too many," Kitty chuckled quietly, glancing around slyly. The other women were still enraptured with Nelson Smithe's business prospects. "Four boys total. I told Robert not to touch me with a ten-foot pole. You can just imagine his reply."

Bertha and Poppy smothered their laughter, and as if the turn of Mrs. Smithe's conversation ran parallel to theirs, their hostess said, "—entirely lucky to have a gentleman for a husband. Even after being gone for weeks, he is very considerate of my headaches."

As though anxious to ask but curious beyond deportment, a mousy woman inquired, "Does he not visit the saloons when he's home?"'

A shadow passed over Mrs. Smithe's face, and her blunt features flashed fierce and ugly before she forced laughter. "Nelson? Oh, never. A scandal would not be good for business."

The mousy woman deflated and confessed, "I wish my Ray were as thoughtful."

Mrs. Smithe softened and leaned toward the woman sympathetically. "It is no fault of your own, dear. Those loose women tempt them and take the good men of the town."

Poppy looked down at the half-empty teacup in her hands.

Other women piped in, agreeing.

"Oh, yes, those soiled doves are always ruining marriages and tearing good, God-fearing families apart."

"It's terrible, an epidemic, not just in our little town."

One voice, louder and coarser than the others, barked, "I don't know what you all are complaining about. Have you taken a good look at my husband? Those saloon women are a godsend." The blunt, iron-haired woman sat unapologetically with her eyebrows raised.

Everyone sat in shocked silence for a moment, then a smattering of reluctant laughter spread.

"Too right, Mrs. Levitz," said a tall, plain woman. "I love my Job dearly, but I just cannot abide his halitosis."

More women agree. Though the group had a sense of womanly camaraderie, there were still hints of indignant comments about saloon women, and numerous women sneered at the marital act itself. The tea in Poppy's cup rippled along the surface as though a small, invisible current lived within the porcelain. She took a sip.

During their five-year marriage, Gerald had often been too sick and impotent to ease her needs. When he was too exhausted and incapable of performing, he'd hold and kiss her as much as she desired. Then she would smile and turn over to sleep, glimpsing the relief he tried hard to conceal. He never knew that when she rolled over she would inhale slowly, deeply, making an effort not to weep at the crawling, unsated feeling in her skin.

Did normal women not feel that way?

Like they would die if they weren't touched, deeply and passionately, blood racing and skin shivering?

Was it because it was in her blood? Her whore blood? Ace had told her when she was thirteen, *You're a natural. It's in your blood.*

She had never forgotten.

It was a silly, weak obsession to dredge and fondle that old wound. Even worse, to do so in a room filled with bored women. She knew it. Understood it. But her hand still trembled, so she gulped down the remaining tea so she wouldn't spill it.

The only comfort she felt was that, although they laughed politely along with everyone else, Bertha and Kitty did not feel the need to pipe in.

TOWARD WEEK'S END, Poppy was back in the general store window.

She undressed the mannequin, much to the wonder of a group of passing boys. They stopped, pointed, and began to joke amongst themselves. Shooting them a wry look through the glass, Poppy swiftly draped the naked bosom of the cloth mannequin with a blue taffeta dress, chuckling when its audience booed and heckled. Hiding her grin behind a show of mock sternness, she shooed them away with a hand. The oldest boy pretended an interest in her and presented his arm for a stroll. His laughing cohort bodily dragged him away.

Shaking her head and giving in to a smile, she glanced away when the bell chimed at the front door.

A strong smell of perfume and cigar smoke followed.

"Trudy, how are ya," boomed Mrs. Hobb from the counter. "Your order is ready."

"My thanks. Got any more spittoons? We got a group of no-goods who think it's funny to sneak into the saloon and steal 'em," replied a voice just as brash as Mrs. Hobb's, though higher in tone.

The conversation droned on, but Poppy stopped pinning the back of the dress to fit the mannequin. She remembered Trudy well. She was the saloon owner that employed Moira the decade before, and it was Trudy who'd had suggested Poppy spend more time with Lucy and stay out from underfoot. Before Lucy was stolen and taken to Atlanta by Mrs. Aurora Ricci at fourteen, Poppy had lived with her at the hotel for an entire year. She preferred it to her pallet on the floor behind the paneled divider in her mother's room. At first, Trudy hadn't been supremely likable, but her no-nonsense manner and fairness had warmed Poppy toward her.

Making a decision, ignoring Francesca's advice to keep her head down about her past, Poppy stepped away from the raised stage in the window and said, "Ms. Trudy? Is that you?"

Halfway to the front door with an armful of sacks, the older woman peered around then walked closer as though having trouble seeing. Did she need spectacles like Mrs. Hobb? She must be nearing fifty. Ms. Trudy had the same brassy hair, frizzy and broken from the apothecary's lightening chemical treatments. Caked makeup penetrated her large pores and cracked at the seams bracketing her mouth.

"Who's askin'?"

Familiar with the woman's insolent manner, Poppy met her down the aisle of canned goods so she could get a good look. "It's Penelope Daniels. But it used to be O'Connel. Moira was my mother. She worked for you."

A spell passed while the woman frowned, and despite once being a handsome woman, the light glaring from the window didn't do her aging skin any favors. "Pen—do you mean to say you're Poppy Mae all grown up?" She unexpectedly scrambled to hold her sacks one-armed so she could wrap the other around Poppy. "Get over here, girl. I would never have recognized you if you hadn't said nothing. Just look at you." Her eyes seemed to glimmer with genuine pride as she crushed Poppy close, bathing her in cloying perfume and smoke.

Briefly, Poppy clenched her eyes tightly closed, unable to speak. *Poppy Mae.* No one had called her that since the night her mother was murdered. The images of last night's nightmare hovered insidiously, a vapor around her falsely bright smile.

"How are you, Ms. Trudy?" Poppy eased away under the pretense of helping with the slipping burlap.

"Oh, same day, different man," Trudy chortled. "Got nothing to complain about. What about you? I haven't seen you in a dog's age."

Poppy gave the same watered-down story of becoming widowed in the past year, uprooting her life, and giving Dogwood another chance as an adult to see if her and Francesca's seamstress business boomed.

"So's the money good?" Trudy asked bluntly, a gleam of business interest in her eye.

Pausing, feeling no need to confide, she said slowly, "It's a promising start, but I'm sharing the profits with Franny. I'm doing well now, but I'm staying in Lucy's attic room for the summer. When the summer ends, I need to consider getting my own living quarters."

The expense of a house was one of many things that kept her up at night.

"You can always stay with me and my girls," Trudy laughed, then broke off. She was close enough to see the white seriousness of Poppy's face, her shuttered eyes. "No, no, I'm just funnin'. You know how I go on. I'm sure Tony wouldn't mind you staying as long as you'd like. Or you could pay him rent if he'd let you."

"No, I truly couldn't," Poppy said gravely. "I'd like to have a place to call my own. I'd like to have a new start in life, which is why"—she took a deep breath—"I must ask you to keep my past to yourself, Ms. Trudy. If people knew of my...upbringing, it could be very bad for business."

If there was one thing Ms. Trudy knew better than most, it was how to run a business. She nodded once, smartly. "You won't hear a peep from me, Poppy Mae."

"Thank you."

"How's your mother doing, hm?" Ms. Trudy asked, and the casual politeness impressed Poppy. She knew as well as the back of her hand that her mother had stolen an entire week's worth of cash from Trudy's safe. Then, she had fled six towns in a single weekend, Poppy crying and digging in her heels behind her.

"My mother passed away almost ten years ago." Poppy's face was its most serene.

"Oh," Trudy grunted, shifting feet and jerking the parcels in her arms upward. "I'm sorry to hear that. Who looked after you?"

"A preacher and his wife. They treated me well."

Trudy's mouth worked as though she was chewing on something not particularly edible, then she blurted, "Well, I hate to say it, but dying was probably the kindest thing your mother ever did for you."

The blow of such a tasteless declaration turned Poppy to stone.

Trudy barreled ahead.

"She didn't look after you the way you needed. I'd tell her again and again to save up and get you some decent clothes and shoes. The times I had to tell her to stay away from the booze and laudanum and to ask after you and your schooling instead, I couldn't even count. It was my idea Tony kept you with his Lucy, you know. I told him if any child had potential, it was you. It would do you good to see what a normal, lovin' family looked like. Of course, I never meant for his harpy of a wife to get wind of it and take Lucy away, but that's water under the bridge."

Another shock.

Lucy's mother had taken her away because of Poppy?

"It scared us all half to death when your mama skedaddled with you without a word. We had a deputy after you, mostly the law listened because of the stolen—" Here, Ms. Trudy realized she had stuffed one too many feet in her mouth and changed course. "But they couldn't find either one of you. All we could do was hope you'd make it out all right."

The store was empty around them except for the faint sounds of Mrs. Hobb muttering in the storage room.

Ms. Trudy stood before her earnestly, like she would do anything in the world for Poppy. Would she? Would she do anything?

Francesca, her dearest friend, said decent women didn't want the nightwear Poppy had to offer. But what if the women weren't *decent* at all?

Mind made up, she asked Ms. Trudy if she'd like to see the item Poppy had created that was unavailable to the public. As though grateful for this opportunity to demonstrate how much she truly cared, Trudy followed Poppy to the hotel. She took one look at the sensual creation Francesca had discarded without a second thought and ordered one for each of her girls.

"You remember where my place is?" Trudy asked at the attic stair landing.

"Of course." Poppy was still swimming in rebellious satisfaction as she wrote the orders on her sheet of blue parchment.

"I'm just checkin'. There's a new place just outside of town called The Dusty Rose. You don't want to go there, missy. The things I've heard—I won't even let Bella work there, and that one tries my patience every day."

"I appreciate the concern," Poppy said carefully. "But I won't be delivering to your establishment. Do you think Mr. Ricci..." She trailed off.

Ms. Trudy would have smacked herself on the forehead if her hands hadn't been full. "'Course, we just talked about that, didn't we? Yeah, just send Tony with 'em, dear, and I'll pay you directly."

They said their goodbyes, and Poppy merrily scribbled on her paper, developing the sensual line of nightclothes right beneath Francesca's veiled nose.

"CAN YOU GO downstairs and ask Mama for another box of sewing needles?"

"Certainly."

Poppy and Francesca had been unfailingly polite to each other since the uncomfortable morning the week before. Their combined excitement at the number of requests from the Women's Circle luncheon had healed whatever wounds Francesca's cutting remarks had flayed open. And what had not healed was soothed with the balm of Trudy's secret orders.

The flow of chatter between the two friends had returned, outmatched only by their measuring, cutting, sewing, busy hands.

Poppy reached the midway mark down the stairs and paused. A line of people at the till had both Hobbs in a tizzy, and Poppy crept as unobtrusively behind them as possible into the storage room. Maybe she could find the box of needles herself.

She was reading the labels of a cluster of crates on sturdy metal shelves, muttering, "Sewing supplies, sewing supplies," beneath her breath, when someone rapped on the door beside her. The little window was near the ceiling, far too high to see who wanted entrance, and she wondered if it was Sol. Her palms immediately began to sweat, and she wiped them on her apron and approached the solid oak door braced with iron bolts.

Curious, she slid the bolt up and unlatched the fortress of a door.

Large gray-blue eyes peered at her.

A girl a few years younger than Isa stood in the alley. Her pale hair was plaited and wrapped around her head in a coronet, but it was dark with grease and fuzzy on one side where she'd slept. Her noxious child's frock was so stained that it had rendered to a dark, indecipherable color. Dirty toenails peeked at the end of her bare feet, and she clutched a doll to her chest, an incongruently fine one with real hair the same shade as hers. Despite the general unkemptness, Poppy could see extraordinary prettiness beneath it all.

"*Wo ist Frau* Hobb?" the girl asked, her great eyes sliding past Poppy to the storeroom.

Poppy's disappointment that the visitor wasn't Sol became excitement. This must be Alwine, the girl who came to the store daily to beg who Francesca hated.

But who could hate such a pitiable child?

"Mrs. Hobb is very busy," Poppy said kindly, keeping her words slow and precise. "Are you Alwine?" She stumbled over the name.

"*Al-veen*," Alwine corrected, just as slowly and clearly. "You?" She pointed with a finger holding the doll at Poppy's chest. They were the same height.

"Mrs. Daniels. Um, *Frau* Daniels."

Alwine said nothing but investigated the storage room again.

"Are you hungry? Would you like some food?"

Understanding this perfectly, Alwine nodded and said, "Yes."

Poppy moved and let the girl in, trying not to wrinkle her nose at the dress's odor. If only she had ready-made clothing in Alwine's size—but wait! Poppy wasn't much larger than the girl herself, and she had a simple wrapper that she could gladly give away.

"Mrs. Hobb, Alwine is here to see you," Poppy called softly into the general store's main room.

Mrs. Hobb bustled to the back, leaving her husband to service the two remaining customers.

"Ally, honey, how are you? You hungry? I made you some corned beef. Let me go get it from the kitchen." She hurried off, muttering, "Don't leave her alone in here, all right, Poppy? She's got sticky fingers."

But the girl remained in the center of the storeroom, eyeing Poppy's rose day dress unselfconsciously, stroking the doll's hair. It had a remarkable likeness to Alwine, from the shade of hair and eyes to the beauty mark in the corner of its mouth.

Smiling, Poppy pointed at it. "I like your doll."

Alwine hid her doll behind her back.

The action amplified Poppy's growing pity, and she was grateful when Mrs. Hobb's heavy footsteps on the stairs interrupted the awkward moment. Once in the storage room, Mrs. Hobb shut the door and handed Alwine a white plate loaded with meat and bread.

"Here you go. What else you need, hon?"

Alwine's only answer was to set the doll aside, grab the plate, and sandwich the meat between bread. She made three thick sandwiches and began to eat them one at a time, ravenous as the skittish coyote

Poppy had once caught devouring a carcass in the woods. There was no shame in Alwine's movements as she gorged herself, eating in great bites, barely chewing, swallowing audibly. Discomfited, Poppy excused herself and slipped out the back door.

Some sentiment trembled within her, like the reverberation of a steel pole struck by something hard. Her eyes felt dry and irritated, and she didn't offer a good afternoon to the pair of men loitering on the hotel's back veranda. Her feet climbed the family stairs, but her mind was elsewhere.

A simple wrapper hung in the back of the armoire, and she folded it and wrapped it in thin brown tissue paper. Her feet flew faster now, down the stairs, through the back door, clacking across the porch. Alwine was clutching an old, bulging flour sack from Mrs. Hobb. The white plate on the little corner desk was empty.

"Wait," Poppy panted. "I have something for you." She set the wrapped dress on Alwine's full arms.

Without dropping her doll or the flour sack, Alwine shook the dress out. The brown tissue paper fluttered to the floor, revealing a dark purple wrapper that was only a little worn, a fine ball gown compared to the frock she wore. Alwine whispered something and finally presented Poppy with a smile, who returned it.

Then, Alwine balled the dress up, stuffed it in her bulging flour sack, and walked out the door without a backward glance. The tissue paper drifted across the floor from the draft as the door closed, and Poppy plucked it up, avoiding Mrs. Hobb's unfaltering gaze.

"That was right nice of you."

Poppy shrugged. "It was nothing. A used dress shan't change her living conditions."

"Nope, but it'll make her feel human."

Poppy's nose stung at that, and she held in a sniff with great effort. "She lives at that brothel outside of town, doesn't she? That Dusty Rose place?"

"Yep, and it's a damned shame. I've offered Ally a cot here, but she shakes her head and goes off yammerin' at me for minutes at a time, no matter that I can't understand her. And she's better now. She used to come in here and just help herself to the things in the crates. She was half-wild. Even now, got the manners of a pig."

"Yes. No one ever bothered to teach the poor thing basic hygiene or manners. Even I knew—" Poppy broke off, clenching her teeth together. The tissue crumpled in her hands. "I am very afraid of what will happen to her. Or what has already happened to her."

Mrs. Hobb's hand, large as a bear paw, was gentle on Poppy's shoulder. "Me too, girl. Me too."

A sudden thought made a line of concentration divot between Poppy's slim, straight brows. "You said she comes here every day?"

"Yep. Every day at dinnertime. Sometimes earlier. Some days she stays longer, sometimes it's quick, like today."

"What would you say if we took her under our wing?" Poppy asked slowly, the register of her voice heightening with enthusiasm. The idea took shape right before her eyes, and she turned to the vaguely stupefied Mrs. Hobb. "What if we were to help and teach her to care for herself?"

A landscape of wrinkles folded Mrs. Hobb's forehead. "I thought of that, but with the store, all I've got time for is to hand her some things or feed her before she flies off again."

"Oh, no, Mrs. Hobb, I did not intend to make you feel you hadn't done enough. What you're doing for her is wonderful. But I think, perhaps, I can help when she's here to help teach her a few things. Perhaps, on the weekends, Isa can help."

Both of them warming up to the thought, Mrs. Hobb and Poppy put their heads together and began planning to help Alwine.

In all the excitement, Poppy forgot the sewing needles.

Chapter Six

Sol was wound as tightly as a top. Lying awake in his bed after branding indignant, bellowing steers to think about a woman was a novelty. He thought of fanciful, foolish things.

One evening was spent recollecting how Poppy's blue eyes were dark on the outside and pale in the center. Another night, he stood over the washbasin, remembering the length of her lashes from his aerial point of view. The bed felt stiff and uncomfortable while he fretted over what she was doing. If other men had noticed her. It was like to drive him insane, this unwelcome infatuation.

Thirty years of peace—and now four straight days of hankering for someone he'd just met. It was downright inconvenient.

So why had he seized the first chance he got to escape the ranch? His constant shadow went to their Ma's, and he raced to town before six o'clock. If anyone asked, he was going to work on his house.

No one asked.

Just in case, he shouted false plans to Lucy and Ben as he rode off on his roan gelding, Copper. They watched him with some bemusement from their porch. Sol wanted to take advantage of his freedom and visit the bathhouse several blocks over, but he'd forgotten to bring clean clothes. He'd be damned if he donned the same soiled jeans he'd worn all day after scrubbing the stink off. The advantages of working shirtless most of the day meant his dark cambric work shirt was clean, so it would just have to do. Plus, it was nearly six.

Almost closing time.

Copper made good use of the water trough while Hog slinked to the hotel's back porch to beg Minnie for scraps.

The bell chimed above him, and Sol doffed his hat. His sweaty hair was matted to his head, so he shook it out and combed through it with his fingers.

His eyes skimmed the counter. There was no shining auburn head there or on the stairs. Mr. Hobb worked the counter today and nodded once at Sol while he gathered tobacco and Macassar oil for the lawyer who worked in the courthouse across the way. Sol leaned against the counter after the lawyer left.

Mr. Hobb was loading a paper bag full of lemon drops.

"Uh, put some butterscotch in there too, if you don't mind," he said, distracted, and caught himself glancing up the stairs again. Realizing how it looked, he smashed his hat back on his head. "Is, er, Mrs. Daniels around? I was gonna pay her for the dresses she's working on for Isa."

"Sure is. Let me fetch her." Mr. Hobb replaced the tongs and rolled Sol's bag of candy.

Poppy descended the stairs behind the squat little man a moment later in a daffodil yellow day dress. Forgetting how it looked, Sol ripped his hat off his head again and felt his Adam's apple bob. It wasn't right for a woman to be that pretty. She looked sweeter than the lemon drops in his bag, and he had a palpable urge to discover if she tasted as good.

Last Sunday, he thought he'd be close to finding out. Then, Isa had burst out the back door like a splash of creek water, and he'd hightailed it to the little rundown stable in the hotel's backyard. He couldn't take any chances that his precocious little sister would see the state he was in. Reduced to hiding, Sol had propped his arms on the stall wall to rest his head against them, breathing deep and willing his erection away. He wasn't a saint. He had slept with the occasional discreet woman. Single neighbor women had trailed him in the darkness of barn raisings, dances, and—God forgive him—late-night church socials.

But he never wanted to throw a woman over his shoulder and stride to the nearest vacant room like he had with Poppy on that back porch.

"Hello, Sol." Poppy lifted the wooden flip-top countertop and stepped through it, easing it back on its hinge. Sol was amused by her gentleness. Mrs. Hobb typically sailed through it, allowing it to bang down louder than a gunshot, scaring the bloomers off of every customer in the store. "The evening dress isn't quite finished, but I did manage to make Isa a split skirt if you would like to bring it to her?"

"Oh, it's no rush. I was in town, just figured I'd come by and pay you for your troubles."

"It's no trouble at all. Would you like to see what I've done so far?"

"Sure."

Poppy slid her hands into her maroon half apron's lumpy, ruffled pockets. "It's in the attic. Do you have time...?"

"'Course," he said, sliding his hat on for the second time in so many minutes.

You look like a dadblamed idiot.

He followed her through the storage room and out the back door, watching her skirts sway from side to side. The thought of being alone with her in the attic made his palms sweat and his pulse surge in the veins in his neck. She peeked back at the brown bag in his hand, and her lips tilted up.

"More candy?"

He laughed sheepishly. "I've got a sweet tooth Texas-wide ever since I was little. We didn't get candy except during Christmas. Ma would put one piece each in our stockings. Now that I'm older, I go a little hog wild."

"Have lemon drops always been your favorite?" She murmured her thanks when he opened the screen door for her, and it warmed his insides.

"I go through days where I like lemon drops, then horehound, then I'll move on to some other flavor. Isa sticks to peppermints, says it makes her breath smell good. Like anyone gets close enough to notice."

They climbed the family staircase side by side, and she nudged his arm with a shoulder. "Be nice." There was a smile in her voice. "What's your favorite flavor today?"

As though he would admit that it was butterscotch right to her face.

He grinned and shrugged instead.

The smell had altered in the attic since he'd last rested there. It held the scent of some flowery powder, fresh and feminine. It smelled like Poppy. Sunlight streamed through the circular window, and as she opened it to let the breeze in, dust motes swirled lazily in the golden haze. Despite the vaulted ceiling's adequate height, he lingered near the center so he didn't bump his head on the lower-hanging rafters. Her bed was neatly made, but the writing desk was littered with sheets and sheets of paper depicting clothing patterns. He ducked his head and ambled over, curious. The designs were complex, like a cyanotype for clothing.

He whistled low.

"You drew this?" he asked, impressed despite himself.

"Yes. See? The underskirt is sewn, and the overskirt is pinned, ready to be sewn. I should have it finished by tonight and can start the bodice tomorrow. It should look like this."

To his surprise, she pointed to a delicate, miniature painting of a dress tacked to the wall behind the desk. The dress was soft green with a sweetheart neckline, the sleeves drooped below the shoulder, and the bodice form-fitting. His eyebrows went up.

"This is even nicer than her church dress."

Poppy presented what she'd accomplished on the wooden frame mannequin in the corner. "The ruffles and pleats take the most time, especially because I have to constantly rewarm the iron in the grate."

That must make it dreadfully hot, considering summer temperatures alone transformed the attic into an oven.

She looked up at him, close enough that he could see her lashes were tipped in gold. The filtered sunlight turned her eyes multifaceted, more vivacious and intricate than a robin's eggs. Her pupils were large despite the light, rendering them catlike. When he looked at the bow in her upper lip, the bag in his hand crinkled.

She glanced at it. "Are you going to share?"

Her teasing cut the awkwardness.

"You're just about as bad as Legs. You need a nickname of your own." He dug around in the bag in a show of forced patience.

Poppy stepped closer with her hand held out superciliously. "A nickname? Very well, just so long as it's not Stumpy or Short Stack." Her nose wrinkled.

He withheld the butterscotch candy and raised a brow in affront. "My ma would wash my mouth out with soap if I called a female Stumpy. I was thinking more along the lines of Sugar." He dropped the amber candy in her waiting palm.

Poppy cocked her head, pondered the suggestion, and nodded. "I like it." She popped the candy in her mouth, eyes sparkling. He was mutually relieved and disappointed she didn't make a show of eating it. "But only you can call me that."

The declaration gave him a possessive sort of pleasure, and between the candy and the nicknames, he felt silly and self-indulgent. He tossed a lemon drop in the air and caught it with his mouth. She smiled broadly, revealing little white teeth.

"What will you call me?" he rallied, cheek bulging.

"I don't know. I like your name. Sol." She moved the word around in her mouth like her candy, tasting it, testing its flavor. "*Sol.* Yes, I like your name just as it is."

Hoping his throat wouldn't continually be this parched around her, he dug for the neatly folded bills in his pocket. "I brought the money for Isa's dresses. I figured I'd give it to you today before Ben, Lucy, and everyone arrives tomorrow evening. It's a little loud and wild when we're all together."

"I imagine." She counted the paper money, laid it carefully beneath a paperweight on the desk, then tried to return three bills to him. "You've given me far too much."

He crossed his arms. "No, I've given you exactly what your work is worth."

She didn't blush but was clearly uncomfortable and pushed the money toward him again. "No, I couldn't possibly take this. This is enough for another dress."

He backed away.

She followed, a determined glint in her eye.

"Sol," she said lowly.

"Sugar," he replied, mocking her low register, trying to stifle his delight at their game. He continued to back up until he bumped his head on a rafter, wincing.

"It's only what you deserve," Poppy chortled, then pressed the bills in her hands against his diaphragm, trying and failing for solemnity. "Now. Take this back."

His larger hands covered hers, and he bent over her. "No. And there's nothing you can do about it."

She retreated, lips parting at his cheek, taking her soft, warm hands with her. "Very well. Then, I have no choice but to make you a suit."

Make him a what?

"What?" he asked stupidly.

"Oh, yes." Poppy returned the bills beneath the paperweight and pulled her measuring tape from her apron. She pointed to the center of the room commandingly. "Stand there, if you please."

Eyebrows at his hairline, Sol dared not disobey. His reflection in the long, narrow mirror on the wall stood deferentially, hat in hand. She swiped the hat from him, set it on the writing desk, found a blank sheet of paper, and tucked a pencil behind one of her neat little ears.

"I don't need a suit. You don't have to—"

"Do you have a suit?" she interrupted.

"No."

"Then, you need one." She spoke breezily and commenced circling him, eyes roving his figure in calculating sweeps. "I think a classic black suit with a white shirt will do you well at first. Every man should own one."

Had he thought her shy? Regarding measurements and clothing, there was nothing bashful about this stranger. She used her reticulated, barrel-shaped tape measurer like a weapon, and he held still while she measured around his wrists and the length of both arms. Occasionally, she ordered him to hold the tape down. She was close, closer than any woman had been to him in a long time, and he felt his amused grin evaporate the lower her clever hands got to his waist. She would go back and forth from his person to the scrap of paper on the floor. Outside the open window, a horse squealed, followed by muffled shouting down the street. Pots banged in the kitchen far below.

He held his arms out while she measured the circumference of his chest.

"Breathe deeply," she ordered, and he complied. "Hold it. You have a deep chest for as lean as you are."

With her permission, he exhaled. "I do?" Sol's voice sounded deeper to his own ears.

"Yes. Broad shoulders, too. Do you have any Viking blood?"

"Hel—heck if I know," he chuckled. "My kin are a mix of everything. Pa swears he has Cherokee blood, but he was blonder than Isa before he went gray. What about you?"

"I'm unsure about my father, but my mother is Irish. As a child, she worked in the factories in Boston until she married and moved west." When she spoke, the sugary sweetness of her breath wafted over him. He liked that she had to stand on her tiptoes to measure his neck, and he took advantage of the proximity to study her. The freckles on her face were dense across the bridge of her nose and cheekbones. He furtively looked at her high neckline, but her neck was smooth and blemish free. No. A single, tiny brown mole resided on the left side of her neck. *A beauty mark*, his ma called it.

He wanted to kiss it.

The air around them changed. It crackled and hummed as though preceding an electrical storm. Poppy's blinks slowed, her eyelashes dark against freckled cheekbones. A part of him knew he should speak to break the tension, but he was just as caught up in the charge as she was. He could have sworn her fingers dragged against the back of his shirt before her arms encircled his waist to measure his hips. What should have been impersonal wasn't. Closing his eyes, he willed his body not to get excited.

"I'm going to measure your inseam now."

He barely heard her.

Sol willed harder. Maybe she'd stay behind him to measure it.

She skirted him again, and his eyes popped open apprehensively as she dropped to her knees before him.

Oh, hell.

His mouth went as dry as a summer creek bed.

She started inside his sole and leisurely slid the tape up his leg. Her face was directly opposite the bulge in his jeans. He hoped it wasn't too obvious that it was growing, and he gritted his teeth, thinking of drainage ditches, swarms of flies, and his toothless grandmother chewing tobacco.

Poppy's knuckles brushed against his left testicle.

How on God's green earth was a man supposed to react when something like that happened? He bit his lip viciously, and his loose fists tightened. Every vein stood out with fiercely pumping blood. The growing erection in his jeans elongated, and all the while, she took her sweet time switching legs. She didn't murmur the numbers under her breath anymore or tease about his legs' length. And when his slitted eyes glanced down at her, she was staring directly at his crotch instead of the tape. A noise must have escaped him because she cleared her throat, rocked on her heels, and stood.

"Thirty-six inches." Her voice wasn't quite steady.

His legs or his johnson?

Desperate to talk about something, anything, to keep his mind off the situation in his trousers, he asked the first thing that popped into his head. "How long ago did your husband pass?"

It was improper for him to bring it up. He tended to do that.

Now we know where Isa gets it.

Poppy gathered the paper from the floor and scribbled on it at the desk, her back to him. "A year ago, next month."

"I'm sorry to hear that."

"He was very ill. Have you heard of the sanitariums that help improve people's health?" She caught his nod. "He was in one of those for a year when I began caring for Mrs. Daniels, his mother. We became fast friends when he arrived home, and he asked for my hand in marriage not two months later."

Sol was confident that any man with a pulse couldn't be in the same house as Poppy without bending a knee for too long. He hadn't known her for a week and already wondered if her freckles reached her breasts. What would he start feeling after a month? But something intrigued him.

"Mr. Daniels, your husband—"

"Gerald."

"Gerald didn't get well after the sanitarium?" His erection had flagged considerably at this point, and he stifled the impulse to adjust himself.

Poppy leaned against the writing desk, bracing her palms against its surface. Her knuckles were so small, her profile soft and pretty as she gazed out the window. "He was well for a time. Winters were hard for him, just as they were for his mother. He would be bedridden for weeks after a common cold. But he never complained. Not even when he was too weak to hold his head up to drink broth."

So, her husband had been an invalid at least some of the time. And the man's mother as well.

"It's strange now that they're both gone."

His eyebrows rose, and he slid his thumbs into his jean pockets. "They both…"

"Yes. Mrs. Daniels passed six months after Gerald, so Reverend Daniels and I sold everything and went our separate ways."

"Are you here to stay?"

"I may." Her lips curled up, and she crossed her arms. "What about you, Sol? Why are you unmarried?"

He shifted to his left foot and cocked a lean hip. "I've been a bachelor too long. I wouldn't know how to be married to someone."

Tilting her head thoughtfully, she said, "There are most decidedly benefits to marriage. But it is a transition from being constantly alone to suddenly having this person with you every day, picking your brain about your deepest thoughts, asking about your hopes and dreams, what you want out of life."

"Doesn't sound so bad when you put it like that," he chuckled, then sobered. "I've had interested women, but I never wanted that with them enough to ask. Plus, I've helped Ma and Pa get along since I quit school. Dirt farmin' doesn't pay much with twelve other mouths to feed. Started working at the Big Stone Ranch once I was old enough to work on a trail drive. I'd give them most of my wages and stay on at the ranch. Of course, now that everyone's grown except Kat's kids and Isa, they don't need as much help. And Isa is with me most of the time anyway." He shrugged.

She observed him closely. "So, you'd consider a wife now that your parents don't need you as much?"

Warmth climbed up his neck, and he shifted to his right foot. "I don't know. I guess it just depends on who's asking."

"What if I'm asking?" she asked, features impassive.

All the warmth drained from his neck. "What?"

"What if I'm asking to be your wife?"

Mouth gaping, his thumbs slid from their pockets to dangle uselessly at his hips. *Was she—? What if—?*

Poppy threw her head back and laughed, loud and from the belly. It wasn't one of her soft laughs. This one rang through the still attic air, her hands clenched against her stomach, eyes bright with tears. When she saw he was still agape and motionless, she laughed harder, doubling over.

"I—" he began but stopped when she raised her hand.

"Oh, I can't even look at you," she giggled, wiping her eyes. "Oh, Sol, your face. If you had seen your face."

Lips quirking but nonetheless disturbed, he uttered dryly, "Well, your mouth would've swung open too if I'd asked you something like that. And here I thought you were sweet, sugar."

She flashed him a charming, mischievous grin. "More like a lemon drop than sugar."

His heart had finally slowed down enough to join in, his chuckles easier now that he was no longer frozen in terror.

The sun was setting on the way home, indigo and bright, vivid fuchsia streaking the sky through the trees. Hog trotted alongside him miserably, his belly tight as a drum from the scraps Minnie had tossed him. She spoiled the old coonhound worse than one of her grandchildren. Isa's completed split skirt was draped over his lap, but he was lost in the series of moments in the attic. The tension, her sweetness, the moment she'd accidentally brushed against him, and the moment she'd cried with laughter.

He pondered the conversation where she'd divulged life with her invalid husband and mother-in-law and thought, *Why, she's taken care of people her whole adult life.*

He wondered if she would like to be taken care of for once.

Chapter Seven

Poppy was humming and tying the last stitch to the man's white formal shirt in the hazy quiet of her attic room when she heard Lucy's boisterous family arrive at the hotel. Brisk footsteps clacked up the attic stairs, and Poppy threw the sewing onto the bed, heart alight. She'd expected them Saturday, and here they were a day early!

Lucy's bonneted head appeared through the slats of the stair railings, and she shrieked, "Poppy, are you up here? Are you decent?"

As though the years apart had never been, Poppy grinned and met her friend on the landing. "I doubt I have ever been decent, but I'm here."

They gripped each other in a hug so tight their stays creaked, laughing breathlessly. Then, still embracing, they parted enough to scrutinize each other's faces. Lucy had lost the soft baby fat that had hidden the planes of her bone structure. Her loveliness had enhanced with age, the angles of her cheekbones and jaw adding to the interesting symmetry of her face. She had wide brown eyes, full lips, and winged eyebrows. But Poppy's favorite things about her were her friend's wicked humor and constant optimism.

"You haven't changed at all," Lucy breathed, wide eyes roaming. "And yet you're completely different. You look like—like what you should have always looked like. In beautiful clothes, confident. And happy. I was afraid..."

"You were afraid I'd be in widow's weeds, crying into my veil?" Poppy asked blithely, still beaming as though she were talking to a long-lost sister and not a friend she had known for a year the decade before.

"Well, yes." Lucy didn't share Poppy's entertained air. "You've had a bit of a rough hand, wouldn't you agree?" Whatever they had missed in their ten-year absence had been reacquainted through hordes of letters.

Poppy laughed and extricated herself. "Maybe, but there have been wonderful pieces to it, and I'll tell you all about it tonight. But first, introduce me to your family."

Eyes sparkling, Lucy grabbed Poppy's wrist as though they were fourteen and was about to drag her into another escapade. She whispered, "Do you remember when we were girls, we would discuss our perfect man?"

Poppy thought about it. "I recall you wanted a gentleman that was blond and slim with a tiny mustache that curled at the ends."

Lucy's grin twisted wolfishly, and she tugged Poppy down the stairs. "Just wait until you meet my husband."

Her husband was wrangling three young boys in the family hallway, and Poppy stared. Ben Stone was nothing at all like she'd imagined Lucy Ricci—the town sweetheart and heartthrob of the hotel—would have looked twice at.

Ben stood at average height but was nonetheless a large man. His shoulders were broad, and his biceps strained in his work shirt. The blue cast of a five o'clock shadow across the bottom of his deeply tanned face nearly hid his dimples and the deep cleft in his chin. In his arms squirmed a baby with a shock of white-blond hair and stunning cerulean eyes. The baby held his arms out to Lucy, who took him habitually.

"Poppy, this is my husband, Benjamin Stone, but you must call him Ben. This little tyke is Jack, the curly-haired one running into Papa's office is Samuel, and this is our oldest, Matthew." She stroked the oldest boy's black hair, and he peeked a sapphire blue eye out from behind his father's hip.

The beauty of her friend's children melted her, and Poppy crouched next to Matthew. "I'm pleased to meet you, Matthew. I knew your mother when we were girls."

When Matthew hid further behind Ben, she smiled and stood. The youngest one, Jack, reached a little starfish hand out for the cameo brooch at her neck. She stepped closer so he could examine it, and he promptly tugged it with all his might.

"Jackie, you had better stop," Lucy warned and was forthwith ignored. When he abandoned the cameo to reach for the delicate butterfly pendant in Poppy's hair, Lucy swung him away. "Oh no, you don't. Never let him grab for the pins in your hair. You'll have a bald spot."

Ben took that moment to stretch out his hand. "Glad to meet you, Mrs. Daniels. Lucy talks about you all the time."

"Call me Poppy, please. She must have told you how we'd get into trouble once or twice."

"Heaps of it," he corrected. His chuckle revealed a gold tooth.

Lucy reappeared from chasing her second-born from the office, shutting the door smartly behind her. "We'll get reacquainted soon, Poppy. Just let me get the children settled and fed, then you and I will have a long talk, and you'll catch me up on everything I've missed while Jackie was sick. Ben and Papa will watch the children."

Ben raised a brow, and Lucy smiled sweetly at him, batting her lashes in mock innocence. His expression warned that she would owe him later, and hers replied that such a payment wouldn't be tedious to mete out.

Their conversation without words stirred the hive of loneliness in Poppy, and she hid it by catching Samuel before he toddled down the stairs. He merely squealed with laughter and tried to climb into the attic.

"This one'll be the one to give me my first gray hair," Ben said dryly. He plucked the curly-haired child up around the waist and swung him up while Samuel shrieked and giggled.

"I already claimed that one," Lucy shot at his back after he disappeared into a room, Samuel over his shoulder and Matthew clinging behind, still looking curiously behind him at Poppy. Jack nuzzled sleepily at Lucy's breasts, and she sighed. "And this one won't wean. It shouldn't be more than an hour before we're settled. I'll fetch you when I'm ready, and perhaps we can visit Franny before we eat supper together. What do you think?"

Plans made, Poppy climbed the attic stairs again, feeling an overwhelming gladness for Lucy's bounty in her beautiful family and a black pit of despondency at her lack.

IT WAS BLACK as pitch at one end of the back porch.

The light from the door lantern didn't reach their corner, and they spoke softly of everything that hadn't made it in their letters. Lucy revealed her scandal in Atlanta six years before and her subsequent absconding alone on a train to Texas where she met Ben. It sounded courageous to Poppy, though Lucy insisted that Ben had called her foolish no less than a dozen times.

"I wore him down," she said with some satisfaction. "Now, our only adventures are rounding up Samuel and Jack. Matthew, he's a perfect angel. He must get that from Ben."

They laughed.

"What about you, Poppy? I've gone on and on. Tell me what happened after you and your mother left town."

Poppy sensed Lucy's gaze in the obscure gloom and wondered how much she should tell her. There were some things she'd never even confided to her husband. For example, Gerald had never been aware that she was known as Poppy Mae; she'd been Penny throughout their marriage.

But Lucy was different. Closer than a friend. Closer than a sister. It was a relationship that had surpassed the span of time, past any miscommunications or lack thereof. Any disputes would be rectified, any disagreements settled. And she felt a curious measure of trust at that.

When Poppy's hesitation prolonged forever, Lucy teased, "Getting information out of you is a lot like getting it out of Ben."

A soft snort of laughter through her nose was all Poppy managed. Keep it short and sweet, she decided. That will be easy enough. "Mother stole money from Trudy about a year after you had moved to Atlanta. We ran a few towns over; I no longer remember the name."

Lucy made a sympathetic noise then was quiet again.

"She stole two more times, but the last time, she went too far. She stole from a saloon owner with a lot of dangerous friends. They chased us near Austin. We were tired, hungry, and it was the dead of winter. When they caught up to us, Mama made a deal with them." She lowered her voice. "She was in a lot of trouble. The night she died, she asked me to go into the trade with her to help pay our debts."

"Oh no, Poppy." A hand found hers in the velvet blackness, squeezing.

"I wouldn't do it," she whispered. Her voice sounded constricted, but her mouth smiled. Grimaced. Her eyes were dry and unblinking. "I ran away and hid on the porch of the church. The next day, they found her on the side of the road."

For once, Lucy said nothing. Did her friend see her for what she truly was?

A monster?

While Lucy Ricci had run away bravely, bringing harm to no one, Poppy had run in cowardice, and her mother had paid the price.

Before Lucy could find her words, Poppy went on, her voice forcefully brighter, "That's when Reverend Daniels and his family took me in. When their son came home, we fell in love and married. I told you that in my letters. But I didn't tell you he was scholarly, sickly, and a wonderful husband. He could dance circles around the other men in town." Smiling was easier now. "He was always laughing. He teased me mercilessly and told me I was too serious. I miss him desperately."

"He sounds like our friend, Sol." Lucy's voice throbbed with compassion.

"He was, in some ways. And very different in others." Poppy returned Lucy's squeeze and let go to chafe her thighs through her skirts. She recalled the burning look Sol had slipped to her when she was on her knees. His eyes were ablaze with a passion Gerald had never managed to ignite beyond an ember. Poppy had been kindling, aflame at Gerald's merest graze while his own fires had remained banked.

What would making love to Sol be like? Would his passion match hers? Would they reach wildfire levels?

"Isa told us you and Sol get on supremely well." Lucy's voice was thoughtful. "She said—" She hesitated.

Curious, Poppy turned in her rocking chair so fast that it scraped the wooden planks beneath them, eyes blinking in the dark. "What? What did Isa say?" She knew she sounded too interrogative, too interested.

Lucy's words became slow and sly. "She said Sol blushes around you."

Trying to keep her lips from stretching wide, Poppy forced herself to relax in her chair. "I never noticed."

"She said he buys you candy."

"No, he buys himself candy and shares it with me. I'm sure he would do that with anyone." Breezily said.

"Hmm." The sound was doubtful.

Poppy considered playing coy, then gave in and twisted in the chair again. "In your letters, you mentioned that Ben's younger brother is the looker with women chasing after him—"

"They swarm him like flies on dung."

"—but you've only mentioned Sol once or twice in passing. Why is that?"

Lucy's chair creaked. "Well, it's just that Junior is annoying and always up to something. He makes for great entertainment in letters. But Sol, I just never thought of Sol like that. He's more of a brother to me than Junior is. He's never even courted anyone before that I know of. And with Junior around, he doesn't normally garner much attention."

Poppy's snort wasn't ladylike. "I find that hard to believe. Have you *seen* him?"

Laughing, Lucy gently tapped her friend's foot with her own. "Every day, and shirtless besides. It's hard to see anyone that way when married to a man like Ben Stone."

Although she could see Lucy's meaning, Poppy's mouth formed a dubious moue. "I'm sure, but I measured Sol yesterday—"

"You what?" Lucy interrupted shrilly. "He said he was going home! What a sneaky little fibber."

Poppy didn't suppress her smile this time and confided, "Yes, he wanted to pay for Isa's dresses early."

"Did he buy you more candy?"

"He shared some but didn't buy me my own."

"He probably wants to make sure he has an excuse to offer you one. He can't do that if you have your own supply," Lucy pointed out.

"Measuring him was an... experience," Poppy whispered again, checking that no tall shadows loomed in the vicinity.

Lucy's chair creaked stridently when she leaned closer. "Do tell."

Poppy elucidated the sexual tension in hushed tones, and how she had rested eye level with a certain appendage on her knees. It was like they were teenagers again, giggling and whispering to each other.

"He invited me to his housewarming party," Poppy finished once they'd picked apart every word Sol had said to her.

"He did?" This time Lucy sounded truly surprised. "I think besides us, only his family will be there."

A frisson of anxiety scaled Poppy's spine, straightening it. "Oh. Perhaps I shouldn't go."

"Nonsense," Lucy objected. She grabbed Poppy's hand again. "He never invites women to his family functions. Never. Now I see what Isa saw; he truly does like you. You must come. In fact"— Lucy clapped and stood, pulling Poppy up with her—"I'd like for you to come visit us this week. I've missed you dreadfully, and Franny has hogged you long enough. It's my turn."

"Oh, I couldn't possibly. We have orders to fill."

"Could you sew them at my house?"

Poppy's hand crank sewing machine was portable, but if she were to visit Stone Ranch, she would, at most, complete only half the work that she usually did in one week. But temptation beckoned. In Lucy's letters, Stone Ranch was a fairytale, the way her friend had painted pictures of her life. And Poppy had worked nonstop for two weeks, weekends included, and was surely owed a bit of a break.

"I'll speak to Franny about it."

"You leave Franny to me." Lucy's approval was audible. "She never could tell me no. And she can't hoard you away up there. You're not her employee. You're her friend. But you're also *my* friend."

Encasing her excitement was a distressed layer of guilt. Telling people "no" always coated her in nervous sweat. Causing disappointment gave her stomach cramps. If she wasn't useful and well-liked, then what was she? Francesca could decide that the invitation to assist the business was a mistake, and Poppy would dissolve into tiny particles until gone. There would be nothing left. No pieces of her of any use, neither wanted nor needed. She would be wasted space again, shooed away. Easily forgotten. Or worse, despised.

Poppy shadowed Lucy back into the hotel to bid the family good night, smile in place, but the tightness around her eyes lingered.

It was another sleepless night finishing the white shirt and embroidering the white silk initials SW on the cuffs. The whole time, she worried about Francesca's reaction.

Chapter Eight

“It shouldn't be this hot in May," Junior groused, leaning against the lowered tailboard of the emptied wagon.

"It probably has more to do with the half-ton of dressed beef we just unloaded," Sol chuckled, wiping rivulets of sweat from his eyes. "And you better be careful. You're startin' to complain like Legs."

"Aw, hell, I better go grab a chaw and a cold one before it gets any worse. Where's Izzy at anyway?"

"Old Miss Persimmony's library."

The librarian's name was Miss Pickney, not Persimmony, but it riled up Isa, so they said it as often as possible. The librarian was in her forties with a perpetually sour expression. Wrinkles ringed the tight purse of her mouth, cinched up worse than a drawstring over a miner's gold-dust pouch. Her eyes protruded, particularly when a visitor used a voice raised any higher than a funeral whisper.

Or when Junior misshelved a book, which he often did.

Isa, Miss Pickney's most loyal protégé, would follow him with a thunderous expression and sweating lip, properly shelving his trail of misplaced chaos and mouthing threats to Junior like, *You're going to pay* and *You're dead meat.*

Sol didn't mind old Persimmony, though. She looked after his sister better than their own dear ma. Instead of harping about wearing dresses or taking up women's pastimes, Ms. Pickney harped on Isa's education and if she'd studied the literature she'd suggested the week before. To his knowledge, Isa was the only other person permitted behind the counter to check out, shelve, or take home books more than the allotted three at a time. For the past three years, Ms. Pickney gave excess copies of the library's donated books to his sister, each as random and beloved as the last. Isa had everything from Shakespeare to bee-keeping, from Lucy's cookbook to *A Complete History of America*.

She'd mentioned the day before that she wanted to check out a book on the art of sewing. Isa had never once expressed an interest in such a boring pastime until Poppy came around. His sister had explained that Poppy made sewing much more interesting than their ma, who only knew how to do patchwork and the same dull dress pattern that had gone out of style in the '70s.

Receiving several heartfelt compliments on her new church dress last week hadn't hurt, which Isa pretended had made no never mind to her.

Speaking of church…

Sol lifted his chin to Junior. "You comin' to church with us tomorrow?"

Junior snorted. "Naw. I want to stop by Angleman's place and look at his house. He said he wanted to add a few bedrooms and would pay decent if I helped him."

Sol wiggled his eyebrows. "You're gonna miss Isa in her new dress."

Something grim eclipsed Junior's eyes so fast that Sol must have imagined it, and he pulled a toothpick from his shirt pocket and worried his teeth with it. "I bet it's a sight." Then he grinned, squinting past the sun's glare behind Sol. "How'd you manage to wrangle Izzy into going to church anyhow?"

"I bet her she couldn't get old Granny into a bath. She tried everything except rubbing an old skunk on Granny. Spilled sour milk on her, swept a dust cloud 'round her, almost emptied a chamber pot over her head, but Ma caught her and went to hollering."

Junior roared at that.

"In the end, I owed Granny a five-dollar piece, and I bet two of it that she's been scrubbing in the creek ever since."

"So you found a dress that'll fit her?" Junior and Sol latched the tailboard up then rounded the wagon. The blond young man jumped up and gathered the reins.

"Yeah." Sol stalled tellingly, standing near the wagon wheel with his fingers in his belt loops. "Lucy's friend helped her."

"Mrs. Hobb's daughter?" An edge of disbelief colored Junior's tone. Three young ladies looked at him with interest when they passed, and he gave the oldest one a slow wink. They giggled and disappeared into a millinery.

"No, I've never even seen more than a shadow in the window of that one. Makes you wonder if Franny Hobb is even real."

"Then, you're talking about the widow." Junior's dark blue eyes lit with intrigue. At twenty-three, he'd made his way around a widow or two after swearing off whoring and booze at eighteen.

Something that felt strangely like possession erased Sol's smile from his face. "Yeah, but she's not like that." Or, if she was, he didn't want Poppy to be like that for Junior, who only had to crook a finger, and any woman Sol had mulled chasing after scurried the younger man's way. Usually, Sol took rejection with good grace, but not now.

Not with this woman.

Ignoring the signs, Junior leaned forward. "She pretty?"

Poppy Daniels, Sol decided at that moment, was a step beyond pretty. It had occurred to him before now, but considering Junior would meet her as soon as they visited the hotel to eat supper and to bed down for the night, he was inarguably convinced that Poppy was the most beautiful woman he'd ever met.

"She's nice to Legs," Sol alluded, then checked the sun's low position in the sky. He pulled an ancient pocket watch from his jeans pocket that was always ten minutes too slow no matter how often he wound it. It was past six o'clock. "Picked her out a right fine dress. She added a few inches to the hem and gave Isa a few things they're supposed to wear under all those skirts."

"You mean she's gonna wear a dress that looks like she's got a shelf nailed to her backside?" Junior asked, and humor turned his handsome face fiendish.

"Damn it, Junior, don't say—"

"I'm not gonna say anything!" Junior lied innocently. "But I think I need a little Jesus in my life, might go to church after all."

Yep, Junior would definitely tease Isa about her new dress. Sol looked up at the heavens. "What have I done to deserve this?"

Junior cackled. "I can't wait to see it. Maybe I can walk Lucy's widow friend to church so she isn't lonely."

Sol tried to hide the fact that his jaw had slammed closed with enough force to break a few teeth. "Even if she's not pretty?"

Rolling his eyes, Junior straightened the reins. The horses shifted from their bored doze. "Especially if she's not pretty. I'm not a jackass."

"That's not what I've heard." Sol dodged Junior's toothpick and laughed, loping toward the town center. Hog scrambled out from under the wagon to follow. He was grateful to escape before Junior could interrogate him further about Poppy. There wasn't a cut-and-dried answer to the attractiveness of Mrs. Daniels. He thought it over on the way to the bank and was still puzzled when he walked into the hotel.

"Afternoon, Tony." Lucy's pa was leaving the diner, probably on his way for his weekend sojourn at Trudy's place. Tony had grown an impressive mustache in the last year, and its long handlebars met at his jawline and bracketed his chin. Sol scratched at his own scruff. He needed a shave.

They discussed rising prices, the business of horse training and cowboying when two women towing three children entered the back door at the end of the long foyer corridor. Lucy's dark head, a few inches taller than Poppy's auburn, bobbed with her words.

"See, I told you she couldn't tell me no."

Poppy nodded behind her, unsmiling.

Sol tipped his hat to the other man and strode their way single-mindedly. Tony, who had just asked a question, sent him a puzzled glance. Poppy held Samuel; it was the only time he had seen that particular child so still. Sol was jealous of a toddler and grinned at the absurdity of it. He gave Matthew a playful noogie as he passed him, and Jack scowled up at him from his perch against Lucy's bosom with the defiance of one approaching naptime.

"I'd better get the boys down for a nap," Lucy said on cue. Samuel heard the word and immediately wanted down, legs running in place against Poppy's voluminous skirts. She wore her daffodil dress again, and he respected her display of strength when the little boy maneuvered his body into a limp, dead weight.

"Sam, whatcha doin'? That's not how we treat a lady," Sol admonished, whisking the boy into his arms and tossing him a foot into the air.

"Yes, that will settle him down for a nap," Lucy said dryly. "Since you have him, help me wrangle him into our room."

The unlikely group promenaded up the family stairs, Matthew close to Lucy's skirts and Jack rubbing his eyes. He encouraged Poppy to go first, and as soon as her back was turned, Samuel decided it would be hilarious to smack Sol's cheek.

"Ouch, you little varmint," he mock-growled, blowing raspberries against the toddler's neck. Samuel's screams of delight drowned out another sigh from Lucy. "That's no way to treat Uncle Sol's money-maker."

He caught Poppy peeping at him once they reached the hallway. Though she didn't smile much, he liked how her lips went catlike when she did. Downturned except at the ends, they changed course and tip-tilted as though privately satisfied with something. He deposited the boy on the bed in Lucy's room and bounded out while Samuel shrieked in dismay.

"He's all yours!" Sol laughed maniacally in the freedom of the hallway.

"Thank you," Lucy deadpanned, then stuck her tongue out at him. When Jack followed suit, Sol acted scandalized, and she laughed. "Get out of here, you miscreant, or I'll never get them to sleep."

He was still chuckling when the door shut in his face. Poppy's eyes were curious.

"What is it?" he asked, wiping his cheek. "Did Sam put something on me?" Lord knew little boys were always covered in dirt, snot, and who knew what. It would be his luck if Samuel left a little memento to dissuade any intimate moments with this woman.

Her lips went up in the corners. "No, but he did leave a mark. Right here."

He stood stock still while her soft hand drifted along the stubble of his left cheek. His ability to think wavered, and he held rigid as though in the presence of something wild and easily startled. She didn't bolt, but her hand dropped and disappeared into her ever-present apron.

"I have something for you." Her eyes dropped.

"You do?" he asked stupidly. But how else was a man supposed to answer after a woman like her touched him like he was as precious as the little ones in that room?

"Mm-hm. Would you like to come upstairs and see?"

Did he want to come upstairs with her?

If he ever said no to that, Junior had Sol's permission to use a two-dollar pistol on him.

"'Course."

Sol followed upstairs once again, but it was different without Lucy's presence. His heart beat in time to his steps. Thump, thump, thump. She smelled so good. Every rustle of her skirts sent that fragrance swirling around him. He wanted to seize the fabric and drag it to his face, see if the scent originated from the dress or the skin beneath.

The attic window was open, and the wind that whispered in was warm and humid. Isa's dress on the mannequin now owned a pinned bodice, but Poppy ignored it and went for a narrow, flat box atop the armoire.

"This is for you."

No ribbon perched atop it, but it felt an awful lot like a gift anyway, and he accepted it with a formality unlike him. Unsure, he touched it gingerly. "Is it another skirt for Isa?"

"No. It's yours." She pushed the box until it poked his stomach. "Open it." A childish expectancy flicked her eyes from his face to the box.

Self-conscious, he cursed his big hands while they fumbled against the resisting suction of the box lid. Lid discarded, a white shirt, crisply folded with the buttons out, was revealed. He wasn't sure what kind of fabric it was, but it was fine with a hint of sheen, the stitches nigh on invisible. He looked up at her.

"This is mine?" he repeated, disbelieving. When Poppy bobbed her head, lips curving higher, he felt the warm blaze of some emotion. "You made me a shirt?"

"I finished it last night."

Was that why there were always faint bruises beneath the delicate skin of her eyes? Did the woman ever sleep? Unbearably touched, he cleared his throat and strode to the bed, laying the box against the colorful pattern of the patchwork quilt. The sweat from unloading beef had dried, and he had washed up at the butcher shop, but he was still too filthy to touch anything as fine as the shirt nestled in the cardboard box.

"I'm about scared to death to touch it," he admitted, hands hovering above the box.

"Oh, for heaven's sake." Her voice was rife with amusement. She brushed past him and pulled the shirt from its nest, snapping out the creases. It was a bright, crisp white, starched and flowing in long, lean lines. Poppy said she had made it for him last night.

She had sewn it while he lay awake in his bed, wondering if she thought of him at all. "Go try it on," she urged, gesturing to the divider in the corner.

"Yes, ma'am." He liked the way her eyes flared when he said it. Then, smiling a little, he set his hat on the iron bedpost and disappeared behind the panels. He was so tall he could see over the top of it. Their eyes met. "I guess so long as you can't see the important parts." He caught a glimpse of a wicked grin before she turned her trim little back, and he allowed himself a minute to admire it, to imagine his hands running along her ribcage to the nip of her waist.

He was meticulous with the new shirt, pinching it between two fingers so he didn't make it dingy, and he buttoned it and tucked it into his old, patched jeans. After raising his arms to let some slack out, he reappeared from behind the divider and moseyed over to the wall mirror. His skin was shockingly dark against his shirt, and his teeth gleamed when he spoke.

"This," he told Poppy, turning in a half-circle, "is the nicest shirt I've ever worn."

Poppy walked over and brushed a hand along his shoulder as though clearing it of lint. "You're being flattering."

"No, I'm not. I've never had a fancier piece of duds." He made his voice serious. Sincere.

"Did you look at your cuffs?" She was almost shy.

He glanced at his wrists and rotated both back and forth. The barrel cuffs had a squared edge and two buttons, his initials neatly embroidered in silken white thread, the letters gleaming on each wrist. SW. His fingertips hovered over them, so stained that no amount of washing cleaned them. Conscientiously, he brushed the back of his knuckles over the embroidery instead. The little detail was one he'd never had before. His mother had twelve children, each with different initials. As soon as he grew out of one article of clothing, it was passed to the next child, and wearing someone else's initials wasn't a desire that any of them had. Growing up, none had ever owned a new piece of clothing that their mother hadn't sewn them. And Ma had never found the time or need for these frivolities, these little embroidered gifts.

This was special. Sol had a lunatic urge to smell his wrists. To see if her scent was on them. On him.

Didn't women embroider handkerchiefs for their beaus? They put flowers or some delicate fauna on them and an embellished pair of initials for their intended. Sol supposed it was the woman's way of branding, one of thread instead of red-hot iron. And every time that man drew the handkerchief out, she'd see it and know he belonged to her.

Sol wanted to give something to Poppy. Not candy. No, he wanted to provide her with something as precious to her as this shirt was to him. But what?

Poppy slid her hands into her apron pocket, playing with the mysterious lumps within as his silence stretched between them. "It doesn't take long to sew a shirt. And I think every man ought to have a white shirt for church. Lucy said..." She tapered off.

Worried, he dropped his arms and panicked. What could Lucy have possibly said? That he was too poor to purchase nice clothing? He didn't have good taste? Neither seemed likely, as Lucy wouldn't whisper such things about her friends. She may say what she thought but not if it was unkind.

"What did Lucy say?"

Poppy's lashes were long against her freckles. "She said you despise shirts and go without them when you can. That wearing them was unnatural to you and that she finds them all over the ranch on railings, fence posts, and the backs of chairs."

It was true. Sol's cheeks lifted with a spreading grin. "I swear on my grandpappy's grave that I'll never leave this shirt on a fence post." He raised a hand as though swearing an oath. The shirt did fit well. Usually, seams would strain and dig into his armpits, his mobility tampered by his long arms and broad shoulders. Isa called them monkey arms and had once supplied a diagram from an illustrated book where a hairy monkey with arms the length of its body swung on a tree. Junior had fallen out of his chair. Well, let's see Junior laugh at him *now*. Sol windmilled his arms and complimented her on the excellent fit, learning and noting that compliments lit her up from within.

"It's not too tight at your neck?" she asked and stepped flush against him, making his mouth dry.

He had to bend so she could see, and her fingertips were cool satin against his warm skin. *What had been the question? Was it too tight?* It felt like he was choking right now, but not because of the collar. He shook his head. This close, her eyes were fractured blue glass marbles, lines of jagged striation bleeding from pale middle to navy border. Her mouth was serious again but soft. He wanted to capture her upper lip with his teeth.

Tug it.

Up close, she smelled incredible. Her hair was glossy near her center part, but the tiny curls escaping by her ears were soft and wispy.

A maggot must have entered his brain because he murmured, "Your eyes are pretty." Then, he panicked. He was alone in a room with her. Trying to spark her would make her feel cornered. He'd better apologize. Laugh it off.

But before he could, she met his gaze seriously. "So are yours. They're nearly green, aren't they? Turn your head?" Her hand rested on his cheek and swiveled it toward the window, where a ray of light hit him square in the face. Following, hand laid flat against his cheek, she said, "Brown and gold, all sprinkled with green."

And he'd always thought they were just plain brown.

"What color were your husband's eyes?" he asked, then cursed himself under his breath. This new obsession with her husband was about as welcome as gallstones.

"Brown," she answered, unbothered. When her hand slid from his face, it felt like a caress. The vein that pressed into her high collar drew his eye; it throbbed against the lace. His own pulse was rapid.

He had once fallen from the top of a tree, careening past branches, wind rushing through his hair and taking his breath. His heart had raced just as fast, unsure if he'd make it to the ground unscathed. Hand reaching, he grabbed a branch with a strength that had stripped the skin from his palm.

Sol reached now. Reached and brushed one of those silken curls behind Poppy's ear. When her eyes fluttered closed, and she made to nuzzle into his hand, the blood in his veins thickened and heated. His fingers shook.

Footsteps on the attic stairs were a dash of cold water.

"I finally got the boys to sleep. You want some coffee?" Lucy's voice called unobtrusively, mindful of her sleeping children in the room below.

They scattered.

Sol disappeared behind the screen to change out of his shirt, and Poppy rushed to the stairs.

"That sounds wonderful." Their footsteps grew faint.

He barely got the shirt off, fumbling with the damnably tiny buttons. His hands were still shaking too hard.

Chapter Nine

S ol wished Junior would hole up somewhere else tonight instead of at the hotel. Anywhere else. Timbuktu would be perfect.

Since Junior was sixteen, the kid had pulled every attractive woman in a five-mile radius, maneuvering females to him like carriage mares toward sweet grain. Sol was used to being in the background while Junior wooed single—and some not-so-single—women from every adjoining county. At dances, Sol was the consolation prize, but he didn't mind. It wasn't long before he had his reluctant partner in stitches. But the dread that Poppy would take one look at Ben's little brother and forget Sol's existence was more than just an uncomfortable thought. He felt a hot, prickling concern about it.

Focusing on Ben's words became impossible when the subject of his concerns sauntered into view outside the diner window. His eyes narrowed.

Isa and Junior made their pushing, shoving way onto the hotel boardwalk. His sister adroitly dodged a wet willy and burst through the door, slamming it shut in hopes of cutting her pursuer off. The cowboy Casanova, whose maturity devolved ten years around Isa, wedged a dusty boot into the crack to jam the door's path.

Ben was interrupted mid-sentence by the two tornadoes.

"Where's Lucy and Poppy?" Isa asked, breathless and fanning the giant work shirt at her bibbed chest.

"They're in the kitchen finishing supper," Sol supplied, sipping plain water. Coffee kept him up all night if he drank it this late in the evening. The kitchens had closed to the public in the last half hour, and Lucy and Poppy had shooed Minnie home to her family so they could prepare one last meal and clean up. Sol and Ben had been relegated to watching the boys.

Matthew and Samuel played with wooden horses and miniature wagons at another table, and Jack was in a high chair playing with what was left of his dinner.

Junior bent over and gifted the blond baby's head with a smacking kiss. "Hey, gimme a bite." With a studious expression, Jack pinched a tiny piece of cut chicken between two fingers and raised it to his uncle's mouth. "Mmm," Junior said, then pretended to eat the dimpled hand in a flurry of pig snorts, provoking happy screams from its owner.

"Hey, Ben, isn't that the piece we fished out of Jack's nose not a minute ago?" Sol asked curiously.

"Damned if it wasn't," Ben agreed conversationally, sipping his black coffee.

Sol scratched his chin in mild interest. "No wonder it was green."

Isa and Sol watched with unholy light in their eyes while Junior gagged and stomped outside to spit in the road, startling a married couple during their evening stroll.

"I'm going to help Poppy and Lucy." Grinning, Isa turned to the kitchen, tickling the two boys who were making horse noises at the table on the way.

Junior returned, eyes watering, as Lucy set plates in front of Matthew and Samuel, who dropped their toys to eat. Glancing at Junior, she asked, "What do you want for supper? We have plenty of leftover fried chicken, and Minnie stewed liver and onions."

He made a face at the latter, and Sol smiled despite himself.

Question answered, Lucy smirked and returned to the kitchen. Sol leaned forward, hoping to glimpse inside, but only saw wood floors and a hint of the worktable. He sat back in his chair, moping, and noticed Junior watching him with a devious eye.

"She's pretty, isn't she?" Junior asked, sitting beside Jack.

"What?" Sol pretended ignorance.

"Is she?" Junior turned to Ben and crooked a thumb at Sol. "This one has been edgier than a coon around a pack of dogs. Every time I ask about Lucy's friend, he runs off."

"That's because you ask stupid questions," Sol reasoned.

"Ben, is she pretty or not?" Junior persisted.

Ben was raising his hands in a leave-me-out-of-it gesture when the kitchen door swung open again, and the three females exited, each carrying plates. Lucy set a plate in front of Ben, Isa smacked one down in front of Junior but ruined the effect by sliding hers next to his, and Poppy eased a plate toward Sol.

He stood immediately and went to take off his hat, but he wasn't wearing one. He pulled the chair out to his right, and Poppy's imparted his favorite cat that got the cream smile when she lowered into her seat. The wispy curl was back in front of her ear, and he looked at it for a second too long before he remembered to sit down. Junior watched this interaction with interest, and Sol stoically ignored the calculating smirk that played around his mouth.

Poppy sat, hands in her lap and posture erect. It reminded Sol of the way Lucy sat. He and Isa didn't sit like that; they lolled, long-limbed and loose. From the corner of his eye, Isa pulled her elbows off the table and sat a little straighter. Nonetheless, she was twitchy, always fidgeting. He had asked about her inability to sit still once. Isa had tried to explain how her mind constantly raced a mile a minute, that it was challenging to sit motionless, to not interrupt or blurt out every interesting thing that caught her fancy.

As though remembering her manners, Lucy gasped, "Oh, Poppy, I forgot. This is Ben's little brother, John Junior. Junior, this is Poppy Daniels, the friend helping Franny with her business. She's staying with us next week and coming to Sol and Isa's housewarming party." She grinned delightedly at Poppy.

Suddenly alert, Sol rested his elbows on the table. He ignored Isa's disapproving head shake. Poppy was staying at the Stone Ranch for a week? How was he supposed to get any work done? Before he could open his mouth, Junior rose to shake Poppy's hand, smile full and charming.

"Pleasure to meet you. We've all heard about you for years, wasn't even sure if you were real."

Sol scowled up at him.

Still seated, Poppy withdrew her hand. "It's very nice to meet you," she said politely, her voice butter-soft. There was a look only a notch above disinterest in her eyes, and Sol picked up his fork with renewed appetite.

Not one to be dissuaded, Junior sat, tweaked Isa's braid, and grabbed his chicken thigh. Junior observed Poppy throughout the meal, but she was lost in conversation with Lucy and appeared not to notice.

Sol knew because he guarded her with the attentiveness of Hog over a soup bone.

When Isa and Junior began their nightly ritual of good-natured debates, Lucy turned to her children, and Poppy caught Sol's eye.

"So, you'll stay with us for a week?" he asked, like it didn't matter. His plate was half-full, forgotten. "Want me to pick you up?"

"I would hate to be a nuisance," she hastened just above a whisper. "I would rent a horse, but I don't know how to ride."

"You're pullin' my leg." He felt his face stretch into a mischievous smile.

"No, truly, I never learned."

"No. No one ever *taught* you. We better remedy that, what do you think, sugar? How about I teach you to ride?"

Hooded eyes widening, she dropped her hands in her lap. "Oh, I don't know—"

"Hey." He rested three fingers against the sleeve of her left arm, but, feeling her warmth and the presence of others, he dropped them back to his knee. "You don't have to be scared. I'd never put you on a horse that would hurt you."

Poppy's hand found and gripped his under the table. "No, I know. It's just that I'm a little afraid of them. But I'd love to learn." She swallowed and looked down at the table where, just below, their fingers clenched out of sight. "Thank you."

Holding hands with her dulled his other senses. Cotton was in his ears, and he couldn't feel the chair beneath him or smell the food on his plate. His body saw only her. Felt only her supple fingers wrapped around his. Unable to help himself, he stroked the back of her petite knuckles with his thumb once before letting go.

She didn't look at him again or join the conversation as readily as before. Her eyes were unfocused, and her hand remained under the table the rest of the evening.

He wondered if it was clenched in a fist like his was.

POPPY KNEW WHAT she was doing and was determined to stop it.

She was attempting to seduce Sol.

It wasn't a conscious decision. Her body reacted before her brain decided. Gazing into his eyes, touching his face. Grabbing his hand. And this morning, she chose the seat next to him on the church pew.

She didn't hear a bit of the sermon.

His arm brushed against hers for the whole hour and a half, and it was all she could do to be still and pretend complete ignorance. It didn't matter that her heartbeat was no longer in her chest but in her extremities. Her fingers, toes, between her legs. All the edges of her hummed like a tuning fork in water, vibrating, waiting for a touch to calm them. The guilt of her feelings in such an inappropriate place stifled some of the urges, but she still couldn't look at the preacher. Taking deep, bracing breaths, she peered around surreptitiously and pretended she wasn't on fire.

Was it the wicked part of her that craved physical touch so? Her poor husband had never complained, but she knew that her needs had outmatched his, and it had weighed heavily on him when he couldn't perform. Not once had she strayed, but her thoughts hadn't been as faithful, and she had wondered if she'd been a less selfish and wanton wife, she would be content.

She hated herself for those thoughts. She was angry with herself now.

Sol was not a plaything. He was a kind and good man with a family and a community that loved him. Playing with his emotions was wrong; one day, he would make a lucky woman a fine husband. Someone better than she.

To stifle her troubling thoughts, she sought the familiar face that had initiated the return of her nightmares. She saw Ace nowhere, and her tension eased.

Her wandering eye snagged on the sheriff, who limped up to the pulpit to stand beside the preacher. People muttered at this change in routine. Sol sat straighter, and the man directly behind him craned to see the pulpit.

"Mornin', everyone. For those that don't know me, I'm Sheriff Robinson." The sheriff was salt-and-pepper old, with great bags beneath hangdog eyes. Though he endeavored to smile, the general haggardness of his expression ruined the effect. "If any of you have kept up with the news in the papers, you'll have heard that our neighboring counties have reported some of their girls are going missing." Murmurs and whispers erupted, and he raised a hand. "I'm sure you'll all have plenty of questions once I'm done here, but let me speak my piece." Everyone quietened, even Mrs. Hobb, though she trembled at the end of the pew with the need to talk. "The U.S. Marshals have decided to initiate a curfew in the following counties for the safety of our girls and young women. Every female must be home by eight o'clock in the evening unless escorted by a male relative or husband."

There were several ominous murmurs from women, even as Sheriff Robinson listed five adjacent counties and warned men to keep their womenfolk close and abide by the curfew. Sol and his sister communicated with a glance, and neither saw the quick, concerned look Junior slid Isa's way.

One young man raised a hand. "What about the dance weekend after next?"

Several young women nodded their bonneted heads.

Mouth twisting, the sheriff said, "The dance is still on, but every woman must have a male escort. No exceptions."

Isa scowled, and Sol elbowed her. "You're always with me anyway. What's the difference?"

"It makes a difference," she hissed at him. "I don't need a babysitter."

Lucy grinned from Poppy's other side. "She sounds just like Junior," she whispered, patting a sleeping Jack's bottom.

It was another half hour before the sheriff called a halt to the questions, and the preacher hastily closed service with a prayer.

Everyone wanted to loiter around and talk about the new curfew in tones ranging from worry to breathless excitement. Poppy attempted to discuss it with Lucy, but her friend was hauled off by a group of grandmotherly women salivating over the boys. Mrs. Barnett spied Poppy and whisked her into another group of women where she was forced to listen to salacious speculation about the villain who took helpless girls from their homes.

By the time she finally escaped, Lucy was gone.

Outside, Sol and a cluster of men, including Ben and Junior, were posted beneath the familiar pine. Isa strode away from the group, jaw tense and color high. Sol watched after her, eyebrows elevated in surprise, while Junior steadfastly ignored her. A group of younger men around Isa's age followed the girl with their eyes. One nodded her way and said something. The group laughed. Poppy noted that the tall one with brown hair and dark eyes didn't join in. He followed Isa's trek to the wagon, and Poppy narrowed her eyes.

"Poppy, there you are," Lucy breathed, hitching Jack and Samuel on her hip, looking frazzled. "Here, will you take Sam?"

Poppy took him abstractedly and nodded toward the young men. "Who is that? The one with the black vest and dark hair."

Lucy glanced over and raised a brow. "That's Mr. Glen's grandson, Gareth, I think. Mr. Glen is raising him since his father died in a coal mine a few states over."

"Hm."

"Why?"

"No reason. Except Gareth just noticed Isa, and I was curious."

Comprehension dawned in Lucy's dark eyes, but she was distracted by an approaching woman cooing over Jack.

At the hotel, Junior reached up and assisted Poppy from the wagon before Sol had even secured the reins. She could do nothing but accept Junior's hand and thank him. Isa scooted to the wagon's edge, but Junior disregarded her. She glared and hopped down on her own.

Poppy released his hand quick enough to make Junior blink and pet Hog's long ears to not appear suspicious. The coonhound wriggled happily at her skirts.

Not to be put off, Junior said, "There's a dance coming up. Are you going?"

"The one in two weeks?"

"Yep. You're new in town. Do you have an escort?"

Sol rounded the wagon and stood shoulder to shoulder with Isa. Both wore twin expressions of apprehension. Poppy felt the undercurrents as clearly as though each sibling held a matching sign, "No Trespassing." Neither breathed, and their ears practically twitched.

Junior stood close. His golden hair fell over his brow, and his teeth were bared. There was something disingenuous about his interest in her. She could see no passion in his eyes. He watched her, yes, but nothing like the force of will that Lou Lou had preached of. Nothing like the look Sol had given her when he'd watched her on her knees in the attic.

Junior was testing her, she decided. Trying her on like a new boot, seeing if she'd fit. But fit what? She tried to remember what he'd asked.

"I'm going with Lucy and her family," she answered, purposefully obtuse.

Laughing, Junior put his hands on his hips. "No, I mean, do you have anyone going to the dance with you? Because if not, I'd like to escort you and spin a few steps."

Behind him, a wealth of hurt suffused Isa's face, quickly suppressed into hard lines. The display troubled Poppy, and she immediately wanted to soothe those angles from Isa's face.

I don't want him.

She opened her mouth to politely decline when Sol stepped forward, thumbs in his belt loops, jaw angular. The shirt she'd sewn fit him perfectly across his broad shoulders, vividly white against his deeply tanned skin.

"I'm takin' Poppy. I already asked her." His voice was an octave below baritone. The words vibrated through her skin, making the hairs on her arms perk.

She waited for him to meet her eyes and lifted her brow imperceptibly, the barest twitch. Sol's lips, typically smiling, were compressed. *Make a choice*, they said. She wanted to kiss them. Instead, she clasped her hands and imprisoned his hazel eyes with her own.

"And I said yes."

His lips spread slowly, cold honey on warm bread. Pleasing Sol filled every crack in her heart with sunshine until she was luminous, floating in a yellow haze of happiness. Junior said something stilted, but she didn't hear, and for the remainder of the day, Poppy forgot all about her vow not to seduce Sol.

SHE FLOATED ON air in the general store.

Mrs. Hobb insisted on opening the store once church ended even though most businesses were closed on Sundays. Poppy was distractedly straightening a bonnet on the neck of the mannequin bust in the window and didn't see the man doing a double take on the street.

When the bell jingled, she glanced over to meet a pair of twinkling eyes, but her heart deflated. It wasn't Sol. She didn't recognize the man, but a deputy's badge blazed over his heart beneath his jacket. When he tipped his hat and grinned at her, she nodded and returned to the mannequin.

No, that bonnet would not do. It looked ridiculous without a head to settle on.

"Deputy Ellis," Mrs. Hobb boomed from the counter. "What can I do you for?"

Despite herself, Poppy found herself eavesdropping.

The deputy had a smooth, charismatic voice. "Well, I'm headed to Huntsville for a few days. Need some tobacco and some papers, if you don't mind."

"Don't mind a'tall."

"No one told me you hired someone else to help. Who's that?"

Poppy kept her gaze firmly on the ribbons of the bonnet.

"Pshaw, I ain't no matchmaker, Ellis. You'd best go ask her yourself."

"All right, I will."

Mrs. Hobb was still chuckling when Deputy Ellis' head poked around one side of the mannequin. Poppy blinked at him for several seconds while he looked his fill as though she were a second mannequin and he was interested in purchasing what it displayed. Her face shuttered. Wariness of the law had not abated with adulthood. Moira had cussed them, especially if one of her regulars was jailed and her cash flow stoppered, and Poppy's interaction with the sheriff who, along with the reverend withheld her mother's demise and had left a bad taste in her mouth.

This particular man flipped his hat off and offered a hand. It vaguely reminded her of something that Sol would do, but the deputy didn't quite pull off such an action. It was trite instead of amusing.

"Afternoon. I'm Deputy Harold Ellis. I just wanted to stop by and say you're just about the prettiest thing I've ever seen."

Trying to control the eyebrows that wanted to crawl into her scalp, Poppy offered her hand. "Pleased to meet you. I'm Penelope Daniels."

His eyes glanced at her left hand, where her gold band winked in the light filtering in behind her, and he hastily released her. "Oh, you're married. Beg pardon."

She almost didn't correct him, then decided against dishonesty. "Widowed."

"Oh. I'm sorry to hear that." The glitter in his eyes disproved that. "You going to the dance weekend after next?"

"Yes, Sol Williams is escorting me." She slowly avoided his gaze, worrying the ribbons with her fingers.

"You'll have to save me a few dances."

"I don't know, I have two left feet," she warned.

"Well, I've got two right feet, so we'll be a perfect match." He did a smart little jig, still half-hidden behind the mannequin, and tipped his hat to her.

Though uninterested, his boldness amused her. It had been a long time since she'd been actively courted, much less pursued by two men. She hadn't realized how lonely she'd been. Deputy Ellis left, calling a farewell to Mrs. Hobb. When he waved at Poppy through the window, she waved back.

SOL PARKED THE wagon and walked across the dirt street to the library, his hands deep in his pockets and his thoughts deep in that morning's events.

She told me yes and told Junior no. That's never happened before.

He'd be back Monday afternoon to pick her up in the wagon, and he was determined to come alone. Isa was a better deterrent to wooing than any handsomely paid chaperone, and he was dying to have another private, candid conversation with Poppy. He wanted to pick her brain, dissect every thought and feeling, to discover her likes and dislikes. And that odd, insatiable need to ask questions about her husband persisted, poking at him like a sharpened stick. He compared Gerald Daniels' academic background with his own uneducated, working-class upbringing and felt an uncomfortable stab of inferiority.

Mouth turned down, he looked up, skimming the library's stone steps for Isa. A wagonload of supplies for the housewarming party was parked behind him, and he didn't want to be here all day, endeavoring to pry his sister away from the reference shelf while someone with sticky fingers combed through his things.

Good, there she was.

His brows pushed together, creating a divot between them.

A man talked to Isa, who sat in her braids and overalls on the wooden bench beside the stone steps. A book was propped open in her lap, and she peered up at the man, her mouth moving. Her hat was off, and the May sun gleamed off her rich, honey-blonde hair.

Sol recollected the sheriff's warnings this morning.

Stride widening, thinking of those missing girls, Sol yanked his hands from his pockets. "Afternoon," he shouted from several feet away. His greeting sounded aggressive.

The man looked up. He was dressed like a city dude in an expensive suit, with a thin mustache and thickly oiled hair styled in perfect waves against his forehead. "Good afternoon," he replied warily, his voice faintly familiar.

"Anything in particular you need from my sister?" Sol asked, and his customarily friendly demeanor was decidedly cool.

You can never be too careful these days, he defended himself.

"No, I just asked what she was reading, that's all." The man backed away, nodded to Sol, and walked back the way he came without looking at Isa again. His pinstriped coat flapped behind him, and his polished shoes glinted in the sunlight.

Isa looked after him with a strange expression, like she had picked up a puppy, then quickly dropped it once discovering it had messed itself.

Sol asked forcefully, not believing the stranger for an instant, "What did he really want?"

"He did ask what I was reading," she said slowly, "but he was...oily."

"Oily?"

"Yes." She stood and closed her book, nose wrinkled. "He asked if I liked dolls. I said, 'Sir, I am sixteen. I haven't played with dolls since I was six.' And he told me that I didn't look that old. Guess I should have just stood up, huh?"

She laughed, but Sol couldn't find it in him to be amused. His eyes returned to the retreating man's back, but the stranger had vanished. Shaking his head, Sol wrapped his arm—his long monkey arm—around Isa's shoulders and steered her toward the wagon.

"Come on, let's drop this load off at the new house."

Chapter Ten

Back and fingers aching, Poppy packed. She bit her lip to control her wayward lips; she'd been smiling since Sunday.

It was Monday afternoon, and she had worked ceaselessly, scarcely eating or sleeping in order to complete Isa's evening dress. But what made her finger joints stiff, their tips sore and sensitive to the touch, was the load of blankets and drapes she had sewn for Sol as a housewarming gift. Her eyes were all over shadows, but gratification girded the profound fatigue. When she arrived at the party full of strangers, she would at least have something special for Sol and Isa's new home.

Thoughts of Sol hurried her movements, like hounds nipping at her heels. Lucy had proven that her scheming nature hadn't dissipated with age or motherhood; she had requested that Sol pick Poppy up at five o'clock sharp before she and Ben had returned to their ranch. Sol had tipped his hat in response, and the scalding message in his eyes when he glanced at Poppy coordinated with the flush of his neck.

Everything in order, bags packed neatly on the bed, Poppy snapped her fingers and muttered an oath.

"Bertha's dress."

Grabbing the altered evening gown draped over the armoire's door, Poppy glanced at her reflection in the looking glass, rushed down the stairs and across the alley, then up the Hobbs' staircase.

"Franny," she called breathlessly. "I brought Bertha's dress. She said she'd be by this weekend to pick it up, but I've already finished it."

Francesca stepped out of the fabric room. Her black veil and the tautness in her rounded shoulders said more than words.

"Just hang it on the rack with the others." Francesca's voice was chilly.

Flushed from the brisk trot to the store, Poppy acquiesced. When she returned, her friend's arms were crossed.

"I'm sorry," Poppy said for what felt like the dozenth time that day. "I know I came here to spend time with you, but I've also missed Lucy. I'll finish the other dresses at her house, and everything should be in order by the next luncheon."

Ignoring everything but the latter, Francesca queried, arms tight against her chest, "What day are you coming back? Next Monday?"

"Sunday. Unless something changes."

"Mmph." It was a very Mrs. Hobb sound.

As though the thought had conjured her, Mrs. Hobb bellowed in a sing-song rhythm up the stairs, "Poppy, someone to see you!"

The grandfather clock at the end of the hall showed ten till five.

A rush of eagerness set Poppy in motion. She looked at one of the decorative round mirrors nailed to the hall wall and brushed curling tendrils of hair behind her ears. Her eyes sparkled so brightly she hardly noticed the light bruising beneath them. "How do I look?" she asked, shoving pins in more securely and trying to remember where she had placed her bonnet.

"Who is meeting you? Is it Junior?" asked Francesca.

"Er, no, it should be Sol." Poppy stopped fidgeting with her appearance and untied her sewing apron. This weekend wasn't about work. It was about fun. But, feeling naked, she retied the apron. It felt as much a part of her as her thumbs or eyes.

"Is that the very tall cowboy?" Francesca's question held a hint of disdain, and Poppy stiffened. It was the same tone she had used to reject the nightgown.

"Yes," Poppy answered with a bite. "He's *very tall* and very kind."

"He's the one that's always sparking Mama," Francesca warned.

For some reason, the image made Poppy laugh. "Does he truly?"

Francesca didn't answer, but she didn't need to. Poppy was already crossing the stair landing. The hint of narrow-mindedness made it so much easier for Poppy to walk away without guilt.

"Have a wonderful week, Franny. See you in a few days."

POPPY COULDN'T REMEMBER the last time she'd been taken for a wagon ride along country roads and rolling hills. Sunshine broke through clouds that were great mounds of cotton in the sky, filtering the rays so that the heat was tolerable. It smelled wonderful after last night's rain. Hog must have thought so too because his nose hadn't strayed further than an inch from the ground since they'd rolled out of town. All Poppy could see of him now was the tip of his tail in the brush beside them.

The wagon seat was uncomfortable, and she braced her hands beside her body to control her jouncing. Sol talked to the single draft horse that pulled them, making kissing noises and having separate little conversations that amused her.

"Watch where you're going, Bull. You don't want to get us stuck, do you?" he chastised the dun stud.

"His name is Bull?" She turned in the seat, enjoying his profile and easy slouch against the backboard.

"Yep, he's got the biggest—" He stopped and glanced at her guiltily—"ah, well, it just suits his size."

No one was around.

Poppy bent over and peered past the horse's swishing tail.

"I see," she nodded sagely, then dropped her head back in laughter at the flabbergasted expression on his face. It was almost as good as when she'd teased him about marriage.

It was a two-hour journey to Stone Ranch, and Poppy found herself relaxing incrementally until she was as negligent as he was. The sun sank lower and lower in the west, and it smelled of thick green foliage and fresh dirt kicked up from Bull's hooves. Poppy was constantly distracted by the largeness of Sol's hands, the way the reins were looped gently through his fingers, and how they rested on his fringed leather chaps. A pair of gloves was wedged in his back pocket, and after fidgeting for ten minutes, he took them out and set them on the wagon bench.

"Where is Isa today?"

"She's helping Ma with canning. She'll be back at the ranch tomorrow."

"I like her." Happier than she could remember being in a year, Poppy plucked one of the gloves up. It was enormous and well-worn. Playfully, she removed her left glove, her wedding ring flashing gold, and slid her fingers into the glove. He watched her from the corner of his eye.

It swallowed her hand, hanging loosely past her wrist.

"Hm." Thoughtfully, she doffed her other glove, though it was awkward work with the giant fingers of Sol's ill-fitting mitt. Once both were on, she tightened the braces at the wrist and held her hands out, head cocked at the sight. "What do you think?" she asked.

"I think," he said seriously, "that you could be the prettiest scarecrow I've ever put in the field."

"Do you?" she asked conversationally, admiring her floppy hands. "What does a job like that pay?"

He shook his head, lips twitching. "I'd make a better scarecrow than you." They were nearing a narrow road with a stripe of high, green grass in its center. He sat straighter. "Would you like to see my place? It's just down this road a ways."

Poppy perked up. "Your new house is down there? Yes, I'd like to see it."

While they cantered down the lane, Sol grew animated. "Junior helped me. Isa tells us we should start a contractor business and build houses. Said we have a real affinity for it. I'm good with numbers—so's Isa—and Junior's got an eye for design."

"Does he?" Poppy didn't know why it surprised her. The young man didn't seem the creative type.

"Yep. He came up with a Folk Victorian style, looks almost like one of those houses in Isa's fairytale books. Tickled the heck out of her when she saw the cyanotype."

He discussed the jigsaw cut trim, front gables, side wings, and Victorian details. Poppy listened, watching his expression instead of the road, enjoying his passion. Then, he pointed to the left.

"There she is."

The house with fresh white paint, black trim, and a brick foundation was across the narrow road from a fenced cow pasture. No flowers decorated its barren yard, but that would come in time. The wood of the front porch was newly installed and unpainted, and the leaded windows on the top floor were as quaint as any Cotswold cottage. It was the most charming house she had ever seen.

"It's lovely," Poppy offered truthfully at his expectant silence. She smiled and pointed a limp, gloved finger at the foundation. "Look, it's level! My last house went like this." She made a shallow sloping motion from left to right, wobbling her hand at the center.

Sol's bass chuckle was rich, making her arm hairs prick. "Sounds like the house I grew up in. Probably did that because of all the kids running in and out. Ma always told us we sounded like a herd of elephants."

She was still grinning at that image when he set the brake and helped her down. Sol gallantly took her on a tour. The kitchen was medium-sized, its wood-burning stove small in its corner. Every room had a fireplace: a giant, bricked monster in the living room and smaller ones in the three smallish bedrooms down the hall. Upstairs was the attic space and Isa's bedroom, which overlooked the front yard and the green pasture across the lane. Built-in bookshelves took up half of one wall, and a wrought iron bed with a bare mattress faced them. The window at the far end allowed light in, and Poppy glided to it.

She would have loved this room as a child.

"You built Isa a young woman's dream room." She tugged the gloves off and brushed her fingers over the new paint on the sill.

Sol swiped off residual sawdust onto the hardwood. "She made a noise I've never heard from a person before. Like someone had stepped on a goose."

"You're a marvelous brother," Poppy blurted without looking at him. Her fingers pressed hard into the sill. "The way you treat her, the thoughtful things you do for her. You're a very special person."

It was so still and quiet in the room that her ears rang, the pressure of her own pulsebeat throbbing in her head. She turned with a manufactured smile, hoping he wouldn't presume her mad if she fled the room. An indecipherable expression smoothed his smile lines and cheek creases.

"Are you ready?" she asked, desperate to leave, gloves clenched in her hands.

"Sure. Yeah," Sol said as though jolted.

The remaining hour it took for the wagon to crawl to Stone Ranch was easier. They talked and learned a few things about each other.

Sol had never completed school and had worked for Ben's father since he was fifteen to help make money. His favorite sister was Isa, and his favorite brother was Drew, though he didn't blatantly admit it. When Ben returned to claim his mother's house and land from his father six years before, Sol left the elder Stone to work for him. Then, he'd been promoted to foreman after an old man named Frank had retired last year. He loved the outdoors; inside, he felt cooped up and stifled. And he hated working with a shirt on.

While Poppy told him about herself, she slid his old gloves back on. She had finished school the same year she had married. She loved sewing quilts, hated knitting, and had never been to a circus.

"And you've never ridden a horse," Sol added speculatively.

Sheepishly, she reminded him, "They are intimidating."

"Well, it's a good thing I'm teachin' you this week."

She had hoped and prayed that he'd forgotten. It was her turn to squirm on the bench. "You will be busy working—"

"I'll teach you in the afternoon," he interrupted and motioned with his reins. "There's nothing to be afraid of with the right horse. I'll teach you how to ride Sunshine. She's Lucy's horse and is old and fat enough not to get frisky."

Pretending a cold sweat hadn't popped up on her brow, a note of pleading entered her voice. "Oh, I don't know, Sol. Their teeth…"

"Yeah?" He looked wholly amused at her missish attitude, and his smug expression riled her even more.

"*Yes.* I was bitten by a horse." She refused to tell him where. Her left breast had been black and blue for days. "And I've just never been interested in learning to ride."

The smile that creased Sol's cheeks disturbed Poppy immensely. "I won't let you get bit. Just trust me. Everyone should know how to seat a horse."

She groaned and plunked her face in her scarecrow hands.

THEY PULLED UP the long, winding drive of Stone Ranch at golden hour.

Sunlight streamed through the tree line at the west and cast a sienna haze over the two-story farmhouse on the low hill, its long shadow almost caressing the outbuildings in the distance. Men loitered at the round pen beyond the red barn, chatting casually while a dark-bearded man put a handsome brown quarter horse through its paces.

They all wore wide-brimmed hats, leather chaps, boots, and long-sleeved work shirts of various colors. Some wore gloves, and those without had them pocketed or tucked into belt loops. Some had gun belts with holstered pistols, and all had knives in leather sheaths. One man, who Poppy recognized as Junior, wore his kerchief around his neck a little higher and tighter than the other men, and the straw hue of his hair appeared red in the burnished light of the sunset.

Junior noticed them first and raised a hand.

In unison, all heads turned their way. The only one that paid no mind was the man training the horse, and Poppy identified him as Lucy's husband when they sidled closer.

A woman in the garden behind the house stood from her crouch as they rounded the bend in the driveway, and she jumped up, grabbed the baby crawling in the dirt, and hurried to meet them.

"Poppy!" Lucy cried, jogging. Jack giggled, his six front teeth gleaming white. Poppy laughed at the sight.

Flowers bloomed in the farmhouse's flower beds, bright pink against the stone fireplace.

"What are those flowers?" Poppy asked Sol, slipping off his gloves to don her own.

"Azalea bushes. Ma's got lots of those around her house." Sol tugged his gloves back on. They fit him snuggly.

"You should plant some in front of your house," Poppy mused.

They sat so close that her shoulder bounced off his biceps when they hit a rut. He was warm and vibrant beside her, and she mourned the end of their journey when he set the brake near the front porch. Her disappointment intensified when Junior insisted he help her from the wagon. Sol, who couldn't quite conceal his grimace, climbed down and reached into the bed for her bags.

Squeezing her hand before freeing it, Junior asked, "Did you have a nice ride?"

"Yes, it was—"

"Oh, Poppy, I am so glad you're here. It felt like time had slowed all day!" Lucy was puffing from her trot to the wagon, and she passed Jack to Junior and steered Poppy up the front porch steps before the bewildered young man could do more than gape. "We have so much to catch up on. Come in, let me take you to your room."

A devilish glint in Lucy's eyes pulled an answering smile from Poppy. Glancing behind her at Sol, her smile widened to a grin at the smirk he shot at Junior, whose reply was a rude hand gesture. Sol followed behind with her bags, being careful with her sewing case. Junior retreated to the round pen with his towheaded nephew, head shaking in disgust.

Whispering so the tall shadow behind them didn't hear, Poppy said, "Nicely done."

Eyes alive with mirth, Lucy whispered back, "We can't have the pup disrupt my plan, can we?"

"Plan?"

"Oh, yes, the plan where I matchmake you with Sol."

"Lucy! He probably doesn't even think of me that way," Poppy lied.

Lucy glanced behind them furtively, her voice barely audible. "He is unquestionably thinking of you that way."

Hope softened some inflexible place in her abdomen, and she sucked her bottom lip between her teeth, thinking about how slow Sol had set Bull's pace on the journey there. Several times, Bull had come to a complete stop. Neither had been in any big hurry to get to the ranch.

Again, Poppy ignored all the reasons why seducing Sol was a bad idea.

LIFE ON STONE Ranch was an amalgamation of extreme busyness and pockets of comfortable silence. Loud spurts of laughter and children's giggles were interspersed with moments of crackling embers in the fireplace while Ben's aunt, Tia, visited and read to the children. Poppy liked the quiet Tia and her equally taciturn husband when she met them at supper the first night.

Lucy showed her the guest room, originally Matthew's, and though it was much smaller than the attic space at the hotel, she liked the coziness of the rocking horse in the corner and the little bed against a wall covered in childish drawings of horses, cows, and cowboys. By nightfall, Isa had returned, and Poppy was wide-eyed with awe that the younger girl had ridden her horse several miles, alone and unafraid, from her family's dirt farm to the Stone's.

The first night was good fun at supper, where everyone was loud and boisterous. Sol, Isa, and Junior ate with the family, and Poppy was relieved that Junior had ceased all flirtations with her. He returned to his favorite pastime of pestering Isa, pretending to strangle her with her braids, and once he pulled his knife out as though to saw one off. Isa retaliated with casual threats to murder him while brandishing her butter knife and by making fun of the way he used to chew on cow patties.

"Tobacco, Izzy, not cow shit," Junior had calmly replied, cutting his porkchop. "And I quit that a long time ago."

"When it's stuck in your teeth, you can't tell the difference," Isa had argued. "Like you'd reached down, grabbed the nearest turd, and ate a mouthful."

He'd glowered at her in response.

Between those two, Sol, and the children, Poppy couldn't remember a time when she had laughed so much.

After helping Lucy clean up after supper, Isa took her bedding to a cowhide couch in the parlor, and Poppy bid everyone good night. Sol caught her eye before tipping his hat her way, and it was a struggle not to let her gaze lower to the brown sliver of chest his half-unbuttoned shirt revealed. He was all cheek creases and laughing, jade-flecked eyes as he backed out of the door. Her eyes followed him through the screen, noting that he didn't bed down in the bunkhouse with the other men but in the barn.

She thought about his eyes as she sewed late into the night, unable to sleep.

SOL AND JUNIOR shouted a warning, their horses crashing into the brush near the gilly hole.

It was midday, and Lucy had explained that Isa had taken Poppy on a ranch tour while the children were down for a nap. When Sol and Junior had found neither in the yard, Junior suggested looking in the creek just beyond the tree line. Isa's favorite thing to do was swim in the perfectly round pool of water in the creek's bend. They were almost over the rise, and he held up a hand for Junior to stop. The last thing Sol wanted to see was his sister in her undergarments, and he especially didn't want Junior to see Poppy in hers.

"Isa!" he hollered. "Y'all decent?"

"We're in the water!" she shouted.

Junior nudged his horse ahead, and, cursing, Sol pursued.

A pair of heads bobbed in the reflective brown water, one dirty-blonde and one russet. It was probably cold as hell, but the sun glared from the hole in the canopy above, warming the water enough to keep their lips from turning blue. Sol cut Junior's horse off with his own before the idiot could release a single flirtatious remark.

"Isa, Pa came by. Ma needs you at the farm to help load stuff for the new house this weekend. I made plans today and can't do it." And those plans included teaching Poppy how to ride.

"Oh." The dejection in her voice gave Sol a brotherly twinge of satisfaction. He hadn't forgotten what an interrupting busybody she was. He could just imagine her shouting at him and Poppy from the corral fence, offering pointers and otherwise butting into any intimate moments between them.

"You ever swam in a creek?" Junior asked Poppy, his teeth bared in his most charming smile.

Poppy's lips were barely above the water, whereas the water level was at Isa's shoulders; she and Isa must be on their knees. "No, I haven't."

"She can't swim at all," Isa stated. "In fact, I was teaching her to swim before the two of you rudely interrupted."

"How were we rude, pipsqueak?" Junior shot back incredulously.

"By cutting our lesson short."

While the two squabbled back and forth, Sol's eyes crept to Poppy. She looked different in the water. Her hair was down and floated in a cloud around her, framing her face in damp, straggling tendrils. Her freckles stood out against her pale face, and her blue eyes mirrored the shimmering water beneath her. They moved from his shoulders to his leather-clad legs splayed on either side of his bored horse.

A wave of pungent creek water splashed their way, startling their mounts.

"Well then, get out of here, you peeping Toms!" Isa shrieked. "What are you waiting for, us to walk out in our underthings? You should be ashamed of yourselves, just wait till I tell Ma."

Both men held up their hands and laughed.

"We're gone, we're gone," Junior appealed.

"For the love of all that's holy, don't say anything to Ma," Sol placated. His mother was famously pious as though compensating for the fact that her active sex life had landed her a dozen children back-to-back.

They rode off, still chuckling until Junior opened his yap. Lord, but he had a mouth about as big as Isa's.

"Did you see the way Poppy was looking at you?" Junior hooted. "I thought steam was gonna come out of your ears."

"Don't be a jackass. It wasn't like that." Sol could feel his brows settle down over his eyes and tugged his hat lower.

"The hell it wasn't. She's been hot for you since she got here."

He wanted to tell him to go to hell but curiosity prevailed. Sol cleared his throat and asked gruffly, "Oh yeah? Why do you say that?"

It looked like Junior would rib him some more, but he surprised Sol by being candid. "Well, she never stops looking at you, does she?"

WHEN POPPY HIKED up the hill from the tree line with Isa, Sol had Lucy's old palomino mare, Sunshine, saddled and ready. He beamed at her foreboding expression.

Isa's face fell at the prospect of leaving during this interesting bit of events. Then, she brightened.

"Junior, I'll race you to Ma's farm!"

Junior, who was digging a stone out of his horse's hoof, glanced up. "On that useless excuse of a thing you call a horse?"

"Pavo is twice the horse yours will ever be, John Junior Stone," Isa snapped. She smashed her hat over her wet braids and disappeared into the barn. Five minutes later, she came out, mounted on her gelding cow pony. "You ready?"

Sighing long-sufferingly, Junior mounted his horse and nudged it next to Isa's smaller one. "I reckon I could beat you one more time before I go back to work."

With a ferocious kind of glee, Isa held up three fingers and bent low, ticking them off as she shouted, "One, two, three, race!" They thundered east, grass and dirt flying.

Meanwhile, Poppy edged around the corral with a hunted air. "I should help Lucy get dinner ready," she said, shooting wary looks at the horse in the corral. The mare only stood at fourteen hands but loomed over Poppy's diminutive height.

"Oh, no, you don't." Sol's laugh was evil. "You're not going to weasel your way out of this one. Lucy said the boys are still down for their nap and thinks helping you learn to ride is a grand idea."

Poppy's eyes narrowed on him. Her lashes were still spiky from the creek. "I'll just bet she did."

"Come on. The first thing you need to learn is how to mount." Though he sounded sure of himself, professional, every word came out like some sly innuendo. The corral gate groaned open, and he ushered her beside Sunshine. He could feel her trembling from a foot away. "Fit your foot in the stirrup, grab the pommel, and lift yourself up."

Face pale, she followed directions beautifully in a flurry of muslin and lace. "Like this?" she asked from the saddle, skirts up around her knees.

Sol got an eyeful of stocking-clad ankles and calves. Her underskirt had tucked around the back of the saddle when she'd mounted, and he rushed to tug it to a proper length at her ankles, frowning around her in order to guarantee no cowhands looked on. Then, eyeing her hem critically, he made minor adjustments here and there until Poppy laughed.

Reaching up—only a little as her lap was chest-high to him—Sol positioned her fingers around the reins. "Now, you'll want to hold them evenly together in one hand, keep 'em nice and loose. You won't saw back too hard on one side this way. Sunshine is trained well, all she really needs is you to touch the side of her neck with the reins, put a little pressure toward the direction you want to go, and she'll turn. Same with the pressure of your legs. Here. It'll be easier if I get up and show you."

Nudging her foot out of the stirrup, he mounted behind her.

"All right, put your foot back in. There. Oh, don't give me that, Sunshine," he scolded when the mare curved her head around to nip at Sol, ears back at the extra weight. Poppy's back was ramrod straight. He patted the mare's rump, dust rising in a poof and floating off. "Now, I want you to turn your heels in and nudge her belly. Don't kick her. We don't want to run, just walk. There, that's it. Now," he continued as Sunshine traversed the curve of the round pen in a resigned walk, "when you want to go left, move your fist left. Don't saw back, the reins will yank her head around by her mouth—she's used to a gentle hand and won't like that. The first way, they touch her neck, telling her where you want her to go."

Poppy gently moved the reins left, and Sunshine obediently turned. A noise of delight escaped her. Plastered as he was to her, he felt it when she laughed and willed himself not to get aroused at the proximity. Her damp back was pressed against his front, and he wrapped his left arm around her. He felt...close to her. Her joy was his. And when he urged her to nudge the mare's sides into a trot, Poppy giggled, and he was helpless not to laugh with her.

He felt lighthearted, like he would float away if he let go of her. She was a quick learner, and her seat in the saddle developed confidence, her movements sure.

"Yep, horses will like you. You've got a gentle touch. See how Sunshine's ears are pricked forward? She's enjoying this as much as we are."

"Do you truly think so?" Poppy asked breathlessly, doing as she'd been taught and gently slowing the horse with a husky "Whoa."

"I know so. In fact—" Sol broke off and slid backward from Sunshine's rump. Poppy turned around in the saddle, eyes as big as silver dollars. "I think you can walk her around the corral by yourself."

"Sol wait—are you sure? What if she gets mad at me?" Her voice tremored.

"I'll catch you if you fall. Besides,"—he swatted Sunshine's rump again—"she's too fat and lazy these days to do much of anything. You'd get one good run out of her, but she probably couldn't buck more than an inch off the ground."

Poppy didn't look heartened, but she pivoted forward and stiffened her back. He saw her narrow heels nudge the mare's golden sides, and she mimicked his kissing noises. Sunshine walked forward. Sol smiled so much it hurt and he didn't care if anyone saw. Poppy was a natural. She walked the horse around for a while before growing bored. After a questioning glance, she tapped her heels harder and urged Sunshine into a trot. Her cheeks lifted with a grin, and she turned pink all over, uncaring that her damp hair fell from its precarious pins.

Several times he called from the fence. "That's it, Poppy-girl! Look at you go!" and "You look like you've been riding all your life!" The more he praised her, the more she transformed into a completely different woman. Younger. Often, she turned to him in the saddle for support, and laughed every time he whooped and clapped. After half an hour of this, Sunshine's nostrils flared wide, and her mouth opened around her bit, winded.

Poppy eased her to a halt then draped fluidly over in the saddle, embracing the mare's perspiring neck. Her small hands were gentle in the horse's mane, untangling the strands, stroking the golden neck. Intrigued and worried, Sol hopped from his perch on the corral, walked around the horse's drooping head, and halted mid stride.

The reserved woman who hoarded her happiness like treasure was smiling broadly, her eyes glittering with tears. Seeing him, they closed, but her beatific expression remained. Over and over, she stroked Sunshine's neck. From the corner of his eye, he glimpsed Lucy watching from the porch. When she started down the stairs, he raised a hand and shook his head. Lucy halted, vibrating with curiosity, then disappeared inside without a sound.

Not wanting to break the moment but incapable of helping himself, he said with soft approval, "Sugar, you did so good. So good."

Light blue eyes opened, no longer filled with unshed tears. They crinkled at the corners. Poppy dismounted on the wrong side, and Sol caught the reins a split second before she barreled into him. Her arms wrapped tightly around him, and he reciprocated the embrace.

"Thank you, Sol." It was muffled against his shirt.

Something in his chest unfurled, spread, and made breathing hard. "You're welcome, shug." He stroked her hair from root to tip. It curled wildly, clinging to his fingers.

Leaning back, she looked up and up at his face. "No one ever taught me how to ride."

And to his surprise, she grabbed his head above his ears, stood on tiptoe, and kissed him chastely on his stubbled cheek. The thing unfurling in his chest quivered and grew. He'd never been speechless before. Poppy returned to Sunshine and crooned to the palomino, stroking behind her ears and beneath her whiskered muzzle without an ounce of fear.

Chapter Eleven

Lucy and Poppy reclined in rocking chairs on the front porch the next evening, shoes off and stockinged feet propped on the railing. They spoke of things married women often spoke of: men, children, and intimacy.

"How was your tour of the farm today?" Lucy fanned herself with a dishtowel, watching beneath drowsing lids as Tia supervised the three children at the foot of the hill. Little hands pet a young goat and lamb, and Samuel's high-pitched squeals reached the porch.

During the boys' naptime, Sol, Junior, and Isa had abandoned their chores to tour the ranch with Poppy. A grinning Sol had handed her the reins of a saddled Sunshine, and Poppy had spent two delightful hours riding at his side. Junior and Isa had raced ahead, Isa shouting, "One, two, three, race!" repeatedly, her fingers stabbing into the air. Poppy had never seen a more competitive pair.

"It was wonderful," Poppy sighed, arching her feet and spreading her toes. Golden hour was her favorite on the ranch, when everything was drowsy and hazy, the workday almost complete. "I want a place just like it. Well, perhaps a bit smaller."

Lucy's eyelids popped open. "Would you like to live somewhere close to here?" Her voice was awash with hope.

Smiling, Poppy waved a fruit fly away from her nose. "If I can make a living. It would be a dream to live near you, your family, and Dogwood."

Nodding once emphatically, Lucy said, "*Our* family. In my mind, you're a part of it. Of course, you should live nearby. I'll ask Ben if there are any places for sale. The closer, the better."

"You may well eat your words," Poppy chuckled. But the thought of living within riding distance of Stone Ranch made her abdomen clench with longing. Her toes curled. It was a desire beyond want; it was a *need*. She *needed* this life, the children underfoot, the waving grass and budding flowers in their neatly maintained beds. Needed to see men on horses in the distance and chickens clucking to announce a freshly laid egg.

She watched chickens pecking happily in the dust by the barn, remembering the one she and Moira had stolen before despairing later at the waste. Mouth firming, she vowed, *I will never feel that way again.*

"Tell me, what did you and Sol discuss during your ride? Isa said he stuck closer to your side than a burr."

At the change of subject, Poppy's mood lifted. "Oh, we spoke of everything. He has so many amusing stories about his childhood. I'll never know how he's still alive to tell half of them."

Lucy laughed, pushing her rocker back and forth with her toes. "I've thought the same thing."

"And he asked about me." Poppy's smile slipped. "I tried not to speak of my childhood, but he was curious about it. And my marriage."

"He asked about your marriage?"

"Yes. I've talked at some length about Gerald. I've wondered if it didn't bore him, but he listened to every word."

"Hm." The noise was sly and knowing.

Poppy swatted ineffectually in Lucy's direction. "Hush. But we spoke of so many things, and it was curious how he listened as though he didn't find me at all boring."

Lucy's laughter ceased. "Poppy, you *aren't* boring."

Poppy didn't believe her, but she was at peace with it. She had, in fact, come to an understanding about herself years before. "I may not be boring to you, but I'm nothing like Isa or Sol. I've never met two people more spirited. They are funny and confident, and if anyone were to say something horrible to them, they would just laugh and never think of it again."

"Hah! You've just never seen one of them riled up." A hint of a frown cut through her laughter. "Once, a neighbor boy came by to swim, and he started some pretty terrible rumors about Isa after she beat him at some game they played. Sol heard about it, and I have never seen him so angry. The next time the boy visited the property, Sol cornered him, yelling and threatening. We feared he'd kill that boy and have all the neighbors swarming the property with pitchforks. Luckily, Ben was there to call him off. The only good thing was that Junior was at his father's house at the time. He would have reacted even worse."

They were both quiet at the incomprehensible notion of Sol being anything but temperate and teasing when a speck appeared in the distance.

Lucy dropped her feet and sat up, squinting. Her face cleared. "Is that Deputy Ellis?"

Sure enough, the man Poppy remembered from the general store rode up on a chestnut gelding. He was in his mid-thirties with receding dark hair, friendly eyes, and an approachable smile. Lucy stood and waved as he reined in beside the porch.

"Hello, Deputy. Is everything well?"

"Howdy," Deputy Ellis returned, glancing around. All the men were in the northern pasture culling horses to be trained and sold. As he looked back at them, his eyes landed instinctively on Poppy's raised, stockinged feet, eyeing the darkness within her drooping skirts.

Coolly, Poppy lowered her feet, and her skirts fell around her ankles. The deputy cleared his throat.

"I was hoping to speak to the men about some news. I just got back from Huntsville over those missing girls."

Lucy's eyes widened.

Poppy stood. "The missing girls from the paper?"

Deputy Ellis nodded, mouth straightened into a grim line. He went from charming admirer to lawman in two seconds. "'Fraid so. Huntsville sheriffs have more pull, so we hope to get more manpower. We're working with what we've got, but I'm afraid we don't have many leads. And the ones we do have don't rightly fit."

"How dreadful," Lucy said softly. When he wiped his sweating brow, she started. "Let me get you something to drink. Are you hungry?"

"Well..."

Smiling, Lucy beckoned him upstairs. "Come sit a while until the men get back. They should be here shortly. It's about suppertime."

"Thank you kindly."

He dismounted, hitched his horse over the watering trough at the well house, and made his way up the porch stairs. He wasn't wearing a hat, and his face was pink with a fresh sunburn.

"Did you lose your hat?" Poppy asked when he took Lucy's rocking chair with a groan.

"Nah, it flew off right in front of someone's wagon. I meant to buy a new one, but—" He broke off and swept a hand over the pink scalp his thinning hair revealed. The tension left Poppy's shoulders while he closed and scrubbed his eyes. "I don't like giving news like this, but I reckoned I'd spread the word to a few places before I made it to Dogwood."

Lucy walked out with a Mason jar of cool water and a plate of cold roast beef and bread. He muttered his thanks, made short work of the food, and drank the water in four long pulls. Then, sighing in contentment, he handed the dishes to Lucy. "I appreciate it."

When Lucy returned from the kitchen, she looked serious. "What's been happening, Harold?"

Sitting forward, he clasped his hands together, grave once more. "Another girl went missing not too far from here. There wasn't a trace to go on, but the circumstances around the girl's living conditions put her in with the pattern of the other missing girls."

"What pattern?"

Ellis clenched his jaw. "All the girls lived in bawdy houses. Saloons, bordellos, brothels, all of 'em. That's why it's gotten so bad, we think. When it started happening last year, they were brushed off as runaways. The law figured they'd run off with some sweet talker. But enough of the saloon workers put up a ruckus and threatened to hire Pinkerton agents, so Huntsville stepped in and got a group of men familiar with this kind of crime together. They saw the pattern right away and have been working to stop it before it happens again. But their methods ain't working."

"What have they been doing?" Poppy asked. Her eyes hadn't left his face once. She worried one of her nails with her teeth.

Frustration roughened his words. "Can't rightly say. Huntsville told us to keep mum until our next meeting. But I figured I'd tell people out here what I can. And who's to say that the next girl won't be from a nice family next time?" At Poppy's expression, he held up two hands. "Not that it matters. It's wrong no matter where the girls are from, but you need to be cautious in case the men behind this try to switch it up."

"There is more than one of them stealing girls?" Poppy asked. She chewed her thumbnail, thinking of the group of men that had chased Moira clear across the county until they'd been flushed out and cornered.

There was a silence while he determined how much information to share. "Possibly. And they're organized, whoever they are. But"— he grunted, bracing his hands on his knees to stand—"I can't say more than that. I just want y'all to be watchful. Keep your women close, especially your young ones." His eyes lingered on Poppy for another tick before darting to the crowd of men riding up with a small herd of horses.

Two men and a coonhound veered from the group while the remaining cowboys herded the horses into a small paddock.

Spying the saddled horse in the shade of the well house, Ben and Sol trotted up. Hog slumped on a shady piece of grass next to the trough, panting. The badge on Deputy Ellis' shirt caused their brows to darken.

"Everything alright?" Ben asked, dismounting, and looping his horse's reins around the railing.

Sol remained mounted. His shirt only had three buttons done up, and Poppy's eyes followed the slice of sweating skin before guiltily skittering away.

"Well, there are some things I thought I'd tell you before I reached Dogwood. Figured you could spread the word and warn your neighbors." Deputy Ellis relayed everything he'd told the women, throwing a few important Huntsville names that bounced unsuccessfully off the men. While they talked, Poppy and Lucy fetched two more jars of water.

Poppy passed hers to Sol, who smiled boyishly and offered his thanks. He drank in long pulls, and she watched, fascinated, as a bead of water escaped and slid over his bobbing jugular. When she reached for the glass, their eyes met. He wiped the moisture from his mouth with the back of his hand and winked, slow and rakish.

She hid her smile and mouthed, *Behave.*

Was she supposed to resist him? It felt pointless, like defying the urge to eat when hungry or to sleep when tired. The more time she existed in his presence, the more she longed to let her body do the thinking for her.

Deputy Ellis said his goodbyes but stopped Poppy's trek across the yard. A crooked smile played about his lips. She didn't have to bend her neck to look at him, his clothes were expensive, and his teeth were small in his mouth. Everything about him was all wrong.

"Don't think I've forgotten your promise to save me a dance," he teased.

Had she promised that? She couldn't remember.

Feeling penned in, trapped between Sol on his horse and the deputy, she inched toward the porch. "I haven't forgotten."

"Well"—his eyes swept her, pausing in amusement at her stockinged feet in the grass—"make sure not to forget your shoes."

Her toes flexed guiltily, half-hidden by her skirts. When the deputy turned and strolled to his horse, she glanced up.

Sol assessed the other man with narrowed eyes, hand in a hard fist around the horn of his saddle.

SOL STOOD IN the doorway of his room in the barn, toweling off his torso after his perfunctory washing at the basin. He stopped wiping long enough to sniff the threadbare towel, grimace, and throw the cloth in the corner.

"Well, do you know any more about her?" he persisted while Ben led the milk cow, Matilda, off the stanchion. "What has Lucy said?"

It was clear from the stubborn set of Ben's mouth that he didn't want to get into it.

Well, that's just too damn bad.

Sol trailed him, shirtless, to the cow's stable. Seeing that his friend had pasted himself to his shadow, Ben groaned and shut the door in Sol's face. "I've told you all I know."

Wedging his slim body in the crack of the door before it shut, Sol called the bluff. "Balooey. I know when you're lyin', look me in the eye and say it."

Ben rolled them instead, unlatched the rope from Matilda's harness and patted her bony hindquarters.

"Come on. Why all the secrets?" Sol blocked the door and folded his arms over his chest.

"It's not my business to tell," Ben pointed out, folding his own arms stubbornly.

"Is her family a pack of wolves or murderers or something? Circus performers?" Sol paused, raising his eyebrows at a shocking, more believable idea. "Mormons?"

Dropping his arms, Ben demanded, "Damn it, Sol, why the twenty questions? You sparkin' her?"

"I'm trying to, but everyone's as tightlipped as a river clam about her. Does she have an extra toe hidden away?" He grinned suddenly. "Or something else extra?" He'd read somewhere years ago about a circus woman with three breasts. He didn't think Poppy had three breasts, but what if she did? It would take more than that to dull his interest.

"I promised Luce I wouldn't say anything. You gotta ask her yourself."

"I *have*, and every time I bring up her past, she turns flighty as a barn cat." Sol's smile vanished, and he turned and opened the stall door. He checked left and right, but the men were eating dinner in the bunkhouse, and his and Ben's dinner probably waited for them in the house. Poppy would be in there helping with the children while Isa set the table and Lucy finished plating supper.

Ben's sigh was long and beleaguered. "If I tell you, you can't let on you found out from me. Lucy will kill me. Or worse. Make me sleep in the bunkhouse with the men."

Sensing defeat, Sol crossed his heart and ushered Ben into his room, staying in the doorway as a lookout. Ben lowered his voice to a whisper.

"Years ago, Lucy talked about a friend she'd made when she was about thirteen," he began.

Poppy had been new to the school and was teased mercilessly by the other girls for being the daughter of a saloon worker in low town. Having been just as hotheaded then as she was now, Lucy had run to a pinned Poppy's rescue, shoving the other girls away. They'd become fast friends after that. Lucy had convinced her Papa to allow her new friend to stay at the hotel, unwitting that Trudy had seconded the motion. Poppy had flourished, helping in the diner during afternoons and Saturdays, wearing Lucy's old dresses, focusing on her studies, and getting three square ones a day. They frequented Franny's upstairs apartment, where the three became best friends.

"Lucy mentioned—" Ben broke off, and both men checked the barn's breezeway for shadows with skirts. "She mentioned that Poppy knew stuff that little girls shouldn't know from livin' in the saloons with her ma."

Mouth pinched, Sol shook his head and rubbed the back of his neck. He'd been afraid of that. When his niece and nephews had come to live with his ma and pa, the family had felt that same fear. Thinking of his sister Katherine always brought a scowl to his face, and he didn't attempt to smooth it away. Children didn't belong in saloons. He didn't suppose he'd ever forgive his sister for the hell she put her children and her whole family through for the life she led.

"Lucy said those people she was stayin' at, the preacher and his wife that finished raising her? They took her in because her ma was killed. And that's all I'm sayin'."

BEN HAD LONG retreated to the house, and Sol donned his shirt and sat in the still, muffled quiet of the barn, thinking. Ultimately, he left the barn and rounded the house to the side porch where the sounds of children playing were the loudest.

Poppy cuddled a slumbering Jack in the rocking chair and watched Lucy's two oldest boys kick a leather ball in the yard. She crooned softly to the baby, smoothing the flaxen hair from his forehead, her face suffused with bliss.

Sol froze as though he had walked up on something private.

Sacred.

Her face was joy intertwined with such an aching longing that his throat constricted. Isa wore that look when she spoke of books and her future. And once, Ben's mask had slipped into it six years ago when Lucy had wheeled out of the hotel kitchen with a tray of food and a blue hair ribbon. Sol could have stayed there all day, just watching her. Jack's rosebud mouth made sucking motions, and Poppy brushed the back of her knuckles over the apple of his cheek. Then, she squeezed him close, settled deeper in the rocking chair, and turned her blue gaze on the two boys chasing the ball in the grass.

"Well done, Matthew," she called in her soft, throaty voice when the ebony-haired boy kicked the ball neatly into the overturned barrel near the well house.

Matthew offered a shy grin while a half-naked Samuel crawled into the barrel to retrieve the ball. Then, both boys decided that the dark shelter of the wobbly barrel was preferable to running around in the setting sunlight. Deciding it was as good a time as any, Sol forwent the stairs and hopped onto the porch in one easy leap. Poppy's head spun and she answered his smile with one of her own. She did it more since being on the ranch.

Her movements were slower, her smiles easier.

And she was never far from the children.

"That's the only time he's still." He nodded at Jack and bent to ruffle the feathery white hair.

It brought his face close, and that familiar current sizzled through him while she contemplated his profile. What would happen if Jack wasn't there and it was just the two of them?

Since the discussion in the barn with Ben, a sad protectiveness lingered. It added a layer to his attraction, one he hadn't felt before. She had no mother. No siblings or menfolk. She was all alone in the world. He couldn't imagine a life without a swarm of family members to pester him.

"You look—" he began, then straightened and leaned against the porch post. Giggles echoed within the barrel in the grass.

"I look what?" Poppy used one foot to rock back and forth, and his lips quirked. Her shoes were still missing, and her stockinged toe stretched, barely reaching the boards. Inside the house was the sound of Lucy and Ben descending the stairs amidst deep murmurs and giggles. Must have managed a quick romp before supper.

"I was thinking you look good with a baby in your arms. Natural."

Instead of smiling bashfully or changing the subject, Poppy gazed down at Jack's cherubic face, raw emotion slackening her features, her eyes limpid. "I've wanted to be a mother for as long as I could remember. I used to have a doll that I cared for like it was my child. I would make her clothes and pretend we had a different life. A grand life."

A thousand questions pressed, but he clamped his lips shut and held them in. It was a good thing he did because, in the silence, Poppy came to a decision.

"It did not happen for Gerald and me, but I taught Sunday school, which helped a little. Leaving the children was hard, but I hadn't been myself. It was better for someone to replace me."

"Grief will do that to a person," he said, soft as feather down. "Take all the happiness out of things you used to like."

"Yes." Her eyes were brilliant, and she blinked the sheen away. Matthew and Samuel crawled back out of the barrel.

He considered her, unsure. "You lonely?"

Another silence, then Poppy looked back down at the twitching baby in her arms and smiled, honest and genuine. "Not right now."

MEMORIES HAUNTED POPPY, making sleep elusive.

She needed to sew on nights like tonight when her mind raced and images appeared unbidden from the past. But she had run out of fabric earlier that day, every project completed, and she couldn't even sew if she wanted to. A stack of books on the bedside table, gifted by Isa, summoned her, but Poppy couldn't read them. She had forgotten the kerosene lamp downstairs.

In the dark, plying thoughts swirled. What if she had said this? What if she had done that? How would life be if only she had only been a little braver?

At the forefront, the varieties of these black thoughts were almost exclusively of her mother. The specter of Moira's flaming curls and sad blue eyes drove Poppy to cover her face with her pillow, moaning low like an animal. Her mother's ghost never said anything but would watch Poppy, desperately tragic and accusatory.

If I had only gone upstairs, Poppy's mind raced. *If I had only done it for Mama, she would be alive, and I would no longer be haunted by this guilt.*

Following the memories of her mother came darker, more sinister ones.

You did it for free once before, don't you remember?

Said so many years ago, the words still flayed deep.

And she remembered.

She remembered like it had been yesterday.

Missing girls with unfortunate upbringings, news of men organizing and abducting them, the panicked fear that she had spotted Ace in Dogwood; each event brought forth the vivid weekend when Poppy had been seduced at thirteen. Ace had courted her mother, offering marriage, promising to take them away from the brothel they had resided in. More often than not, she refused to think of him. He didn't deserve her thoughts. That space in her mind should never be tainted by his ilk. And yet, the man with the boyish good looks and money overflowing his pockets, his kindness to a forgotten child, the coaxing words he would whisper in her ear...

It all wormed into her thoughts no matter how hard she pressed the pillow against her face.

You liked him, her conscience whispered. *You had loved him. And he had loved you.*

"No," she hissed in the pitch dark, throwing the pillow to the floor and exploding to her feet.

No. Ace hadn't loved her. That wasn't what love was.

Love was Gerald's kind and respectful treatment of her. Love was holding a sleeping child, the purest form of trust a person could ever experience.

Her face was damp. Was she crying? No, not tears. She was soaked in a clammy sweat. Feeling around in the dark, she washed her face, rinsed her mouth, and then completed her ritual for the second time that night, scrubbing her arms with a washcloth and her nails with her boar bristle brush. Cursing herself for forgetting the kerosene lamp downstairs, dreading to rouse anyone from sleep, she ventured into the darkened house to retrieve it.

Quiet as a wraith, she cracked the door and slipped into the hall, her nightgown a blur in the dark hallway. Hands waving, toes feeling, eyes straining, she carefully shuffled to the stairs. Once she'd reached the first floor without breaking a leg, she rifled around for the lamp she'd forgotten on the kitchen worktable.

It was gone.

Gritting an oath, she decided she might as well use the outhouse.

The darkness outside was all-encompassing, and she blinked rapidly on the porch, trying to remember the quickest route to the smelly little building with its half-moon cutout. She tiptoed barefoot around the well house along the worn dirt path, wishing the moon was out or even some stars. But the sky was overcast, the black void of night heavy, like an oppressive blanket thrown over the ranch. Once she located the outhouse and made quick, furtive use of it, Poppy threaded her way along the path around the well house, then stopped.

A horse nickered in the barn.

The bunkhouse was a dark, sleeping hulk in the distance, but the barn showed signs of life. Its door was open, the crack illuminated with a soft amber light. Sol slept in there. Was he up? Or had he forgotten to douse the lamp?

Curious and not altogether thrilled to return to her lonely room, she trekked toward the barn, straining to make out the shapes in the yard around her. She couldn't. During the day, the yard was smooth and unencumbered with objects. Now that there was no light, obstacles popped up and left long shadows in the grass, confusing her with humped shapes that hadn't existed hours earlier.

Something loomed ahead, but she saw it too late.

Gasping audibly, she struck her right knee hard against the hip-high object, but when she tried to catch herself on it, it rolled and she tumbled along with it. The noise she made when she hit the dirt wasn't loud, but someone heard her.

The barn door creaked, and footsteps padded her way, nose snuffling in the grass nearby.

It was Hog. She could smell his hot doggy breath, and his long tail whipped the barrel repeatedly as it wagged. *Thwack, thwack, thwack.*

"Someone out here?" called a quiet voice. The barn's crack yawned, and muffled footsteps neared.

Her knee burned and ached. Annoyed with herself, she answered in peeved undertones, "Yes, me."

"That you, Poppy?" Surprise colored the man's deep timbre. It was Sol. "Are you all right?"

"Yes, I fell over this—this *blasted* barrel." She smacked the wooden barrel next to her as though it had purposefully leaped up and tripped her. "I thought it was closer to the porch."

His tall, lean silhouette strode closer, and she could tell from his svelte shadow that he was shirtless. The whisper of his feet along the grass suggested he was also barefoot. Unexpectedly aware of her own heartbeat, she forced herself to listen.

"Ben brought it over by the barn so no one would trip over it if they needed the outhouse." His ironic amusement sobered. "Did you hurt yourself?"

"I bumped my knee." With delicate fingers, she touched her kneecap. The nightgown over the injury was wet. *Oh, disgusting.* "I think it's bleeding."

Crouching, a black figure blocking the light from the barn, Sol ordered, "Hold onto my shoulder. I'll take you inside, and we'll have a look-see in the light."

She should demur. She should tell him good night and return to her room.

It was entirely within her capability to walk.

But when he bent even closer, the scent of sandalwood washed over her and addled her thoughts. His breath smelled of mint tooth powder. Every scent of him was fresh and masculine, her every sense heightened by night blindness. Her heart was a wild thing. The veins throughout her body sang, nerves alive, waiting for the touch that his proximity promised.

"Are you certain?" she asked.

As though her double-edged meaning had no purchase on him, Sol said, "Sure. Come on."

You promised, she chastised herself. *You promised not to turn your attention to him.*

Ignoring the voice of reason was easy. As usual, Sol's nearness vanquished the aching void of loneliness, whisked away by his vibrant presence. The memory of him behind her on Sunshine, his patience and praise, made happiness burn within her.

Poppy held out her hand, and he wrapped it securely around his shoulders, lifting her as effortlessly as a feather pillow. She squeezed her eyes shut at the heat of his bare skin against her palm, stunned at the sudden weightlessness of being carried. No one had ever held her like this. Gerald attempted it on their wedding day, but she hadn't wanted to overtax him. Now, Sol's strength awed her, and his heat seeped through her thin muslin nightgown, warming her. She opened her eyes at the barn door, where the light expunged all shadows and secrets.

"Thank you," she managed, gripping the surprisingly silky skin of his shoulder. "I didn't wake you, did I?"

Hog didn't follow them into the barn; his tail disappeared around the corner toward the chicken coop.

"Nah, I hadn't settled into bed yet," he assured her. He was always so kind. It made her grit her teeth for wanting him. Her wariness of kind men was a distant memory.

Gerald had been good.

Sol was also good.

Not so much Poppy.

The scenarios that raced through her mind as he carried her past the barn doors and into the spacious breezeway between stalls would have shocked him. It had been so long since she'd touched a man's bare skin. And this man...he smelled so good her mouth watered, and she couldn't find her tongue.

"I'm sorry for putting you out." Her mouth was a desert. She swallowed.

"Don't be sorry," he mock-ordered. "I'm a man holding a beautiful woman in his arms. I reckon I should be thanking you."

Her lips quivered at Sol's studious concentration on his feet so they didn't trip. "Don't thank me yet. Carrying me like this might throw your back out."

Amusement lit his green-tinted eyes, crinkling the corners. "If that happens, you can throw me in the wheelbarrow over there and push me to the house."

"Push you? With my bad leg?"

"You're right. We can both sit in it and wait for Ben to milk the cows. He can wheel us to the doctor down the road."

"Could you imagine? Both of us half-dressed, me bleeding, you with lumbago—" She broke off, and they gave in to the quiet hilarity of it.

Matilda, the milk cow, peered at them from her stall, her eyes enormous and surrounded by long black lashes. Directly across from her was a door which opened to a small room lit by a hanging lantern. She could see a small table through the open doorway, a bed with a thin blanket and a single pillow, and a pair of freshly polished boots near the footboard. Sol paused just outside, something unspoken hovering in the air. A stillness. Something intangible waiting for a decision.

"I've got some, uh—" He cleared his throat. Again, minty breath wafted across her cheek. "Some liniment in there if you want to doctor your knee."

She couldn't meet his eyes. "Yes, that would be nice."

Nodding once, Sol gripped her more firmly and stepped over the threshold. He left the door open, but instead of depositing her on the chair at his desk, he settled her on the soft bed. When he stood to his full height, Poppy's neck had to arc dramatically to see him. Breathing was impossible. All her air caught and held in the vicinity of her diaphragm.

Sol's shirtless body stunned her.

A graceful leanness to him sharpened his hipbones, cradling honed muscles that pointed in a V into the faded jeans he wore. Sparse, sandy hair trailed from his pectorals to his stomach, to his jeans. The line arrowed south and made her pulse throb, deep and low. In the lamplight, his skin glowed a rich walnut from years of sun exposure.

He looked around at his meager belongings and scratched his neck. The movement defined the biceps of his arm, and *that* muscle was not lean but large, round, and corded. The bared chests of the men she could remember from the saloons rarely had such well-developed musculature, and she marveled at how the human body changed when forced to rope cattle, work fences, and lift bales of hay as though they were less substantial than air. His raw virility held her arrested, and it worsened the more sheepish he grew.

Did he think she cared about his room? Look at her. She was gape-faced and drooling into her lap.

Averting her gaze, ashamed and embarrassed at her ogling, Poppy focused on the task at hand. She looked at her knee.

A small patch of red stained her night-rail, vivid against the white. Pursing her lips, she prodded the area. It was sore, and the gown stuck to her knee from congealed blood.

"Do you have any water to wash with?" she asked, striving for lightness. Her words sounded exactly as she felt. Tense.

"Yeah. But—" He broke off and strode to the basin at his rough little washstand. "Well, no, this water's probably dirty. I just washed up with it. I can draw some more from the well."

"I'm sure that's all right." It was primly said, even while her body was warm, heavy, and hyper-aware of the man across the room. Why was the thought of his wash water so intriguing? Something was very wrong with her.

"Not afraid you'll catch something from me?" he teased, wringing out a cloth and grabbing a dusty round tin of liniment from a crooked shelf on the wall. He walked over and squatted in front of her.

Poppy's eyes immediately shot to the apex of his spread thighs, and she clamped her own shut. It was so hot in the room, she could hardly catch enough air. Licking her lips and gritting her teeth, she forgot to answer him and slowly pulled the fabric of her nightgown up, hissing as it peeled away from her knee. The fabric's slide against her skin made goosebumps erupt all over her body, and her nipples pebbled into hard, insistent points. Sucking her lip, she raised her foot to look at the wound on her knee.

A noise escaped Sol, but she ignored it. She couldn't look at him right now because he would see. He would see what he did to her.

The skin had been scraped from her knee instead of the deep gash she had feared.

"Oh," she breathed. "I thought it would be much worse."

She peered up and caught him staring at her exposed legs. It was his turn to be motionless.

Not for the first time, she had made a stupendous faux pas. Growing up, it was nothing to see a woman's bare legs or fully exposed breasts, and the language had been even worse. So, this, the baring of her knees to mid-thigh, would have been nothing in the art of seduction. The other women would have laughed at her missishness and told her to "Bare her bum" instead. In that world, displaying her legs wouldn't engender a blink. But, in this world, the *real* world, baring her legs for a bachelor in a secluded room had just proven how much of a wanton she truly was.

They remained frozen for long seconds, so long Poppy wanted to laugh or scream, anything to stop the gradual needles of embarrassment. Sol's face was flushed from forehead to neck.

Then, he surprised her.

With a gentle hand, he clasped the back of her right ankle and held it, twisting her leg from side to side for his inspection. A trickle of blood had dried halfway down her shin. He set the tin of liniment on the bed, and she absently picked it up to have something to do. With his free hand, he drew the cool, damp rag from her shin to the bottom of her knee. His hands were roped with prominent veins, his fingertips squared off and calloused. He repeated the action slowly, soothingly, and her eyes fluttered closed. There was a lump in her throat that she tried to swallow.

It felt so good to be touched. The pulse in her neck throbbed, stretching down, down into her belly. Lower. When her eyes opened, he was watching her, attempting stoicism. He was failing. His eyes were lit with fire. They jumped from her exposed skin to the pronounced points of her breasts, then along the stretch of her throat above the gown's lace neckline.

"Does it hurt?" His voice was gravel.

She managed to shake her head, her eyes closing and opening sluggishly.

As lightly as he could, he ran the damp cloth over her knee, and she winced. Her knee jumped, and the hand at her ankle instinctively slid up the curve of her calf to hold her still. His knees hit the floor, bracing himself. Poppy's breath came fast. Sol's nostrils flared, his angular jaw honing. Laying the rag on the footboard of the bed, he nodded to the liniment.

"Open that for me?"

The tin smelled of petroleum jelly and astringent herbs that weren't entirely unpleasant. Sol coated some on two fingertips and rubbed the salve over the raw flesh of her scraped knee, concentrating hard. It stung even though he was beyond gentle; she made a low noise. The hand around her calm muscle tightened and slid higher to grasp the back of her knee, which had grown damp.

"Sorry," he gritted.

He brought the two fingers back to the tin and repeated the process, spreading the glossy sheen around the edges of the scrape. Everywhere he touched was like being licked by flames. Poppy was damp everywhere, her face, between her breasts, between her legs. She spread her knees infinitesimally, and he stiffened. Even his eyeballs were rigid. Without consciously thinking, her hips inched closer to the edge of the bed. The nightgown hiked up, revealing more of the whiteness of her thighs. Her breasts were eye level with him, her nose close enough to his hair, where the scent of sandalwood was the strongest.

If only he would look at her, she'd get even closer. She'd get so close that she would melt into him and climb through his pores. There would be no distinction between where he began and she ended.

Sol didn't look up at her.

Instead, his hand released her calf...and moved to the other one. Then, both of his hands stroked from ankle to knee, the broad palms rough and warm. Her breath came in tiny pants, lips parted.

Closer. She needed to be closer.

Poppy spread her legs more, an inch, then two, until a sliver of dark shadow grew between them, hidden only by the rucked-up hem of her night rail. His hands were enormous and dark against her legs as they slipped past her knees to the curve of her thighs.

It was too much.

Poppy's mind blanked, and instinct replaced any rational thought.

His lips were close, and it was nothing at all to cant her head and trap them between her own. The feel of Sol's wide mouth—always smiling, always laughing—made her moan. Her hands fisted the blankets of his bed, the tin of liniment tumbling to the floor.

Sol broke away. He looked simultaneously aflame and unsure. Heart racing, she ignored the question in his eyes and focused on his lips. They were supple. He had tasted good. Minty. She leaned forward again, arching her back and putting more force behind her kiss.

This time, he responded. His hands gripped her thighs hard, and his lips opened beneath hers.

Besides sewing, kissing was her favorite pastime. When she'd found an affinity for it with her late husband, who was too fatigued to do much else, she would kiss him for hours. Sliding her lips over Sol's, she discovered something. He was a skilled kisser. Sol's rhythm matched hers. His lips were lush, his tongue confident.

Blood whooshed in her ears, drowning out the little moans she made in the back of her throat. The wet glide of their lips, the warm massage of his tongue against hers, it overcame her. It took little effort to push herself further across the bed until she straddled his lap. She twisted her arms around his neck, feeling his hardness beneath her bottom, and deepened the kiss. The textures of his mouth excited her, and she made love to it with hers, wishing his hand would disappear beneath her nightgown, wishing he was inside of her.

But he broke away from her mouth when she rocked her hips into his, needing that deeper connection.

Forcing her heavy eyes open, Poppy blinked up at his face, lips swollen. They both gasped as though they'd been racing, and she could feel her urgent heartbeat in every part of her body. His pupils were blown, glazed, and his reddened mouth frowned. A tendril of fear curled in her belly, cooling her ardor.

"Wait," he panted, unmoving on the floor of his room. "What are we doing?"

Wasn't it obvious?

She blinked stupidly at him, and her sluggish mind took an eternity to understand.

But of course.

Sol was decent, and men like him didn't have affairs. Did they? Or maybe, honorable men like him didn't have affairs with women like her. His rejection grew, souring in her stomach, and a hurt she hadn't experienced since Gerald's death returned.

Poppy scrambled away from him. The skirt of her gown dropped, and she was decent once more. She walked hastily to the door and into the breezeway, skin shrinking from the lowering temperature.

"Poppy, wait!" he called behind her.

She broke into a run.

She had never felt so embarrassed of her high passions, of the temperament she was cursed with. Circling the barrel, she disappeared into the house, up the stairs, and dove into the lonely little bed in the guest bedroom. Sleep was as impossible as before, but now it was the stabbing pain of current rejection instead of past guilt.

Somehow, it hurt worse.

Chapter Twelve

A year ago, Sol helped Ben introduce a stallion to the mares that were culled for breeding, and the men had shaken their heads ruefully at the stud pacing the paddock fence. The dark bay had snorted, screamed, and charged with his tail high in the hopes of the mare's favor. When he'd scented the air, neck and lip outstretched, his prick jumping against his belly, the men had laughed and made ribald comments.

Sol had never experienced kinship with a horse more than now, and he'd never felt less like laughing.

After Poppy had kissed the hell out of him and abandoned him literally on his knees, he'd spent a sleepless night full of regret and a raging erection that hadn't abated even when he'd woken up the following day. He'd paced the barn like that stallion, flushed, his clothes too tight on his body, suffused with a restless energy that only had one thing on its mind.

Now, at the breakfast table, Poppy was pale and subdued. Sol stared at her, food cold on his plate until Isa's elbow stabbed him out of his gawking. He ignored his sister's suspicious glances. He ignored Junior's stupid, knowing grin. He ignored anything that didn't have curling auburn hair and hurt blue eyes.

He didn't think he'd frightened Poppy last night. After all, she'd initiated everything from pulling up her nightgown to kissing him.

That kiss had made him forget his name, where he was, and why he should stop. It wasn't until he'd been a hairsbreadth away from ripping her gown off that he'd forced himself to halt. He prided himself on never taking advantage of women, but with Poppy, he'd never wanted to take advantage of one more. Which opposed his increasing need to protect her from harm. She was down for a single summer. If he took her, would it make him a bastard? Would Ben and Lucy find out and skin him alive? Or would she discard him and move on to someone with more to offer?

The questions had made for a sleepless night.

Two invisible hands pressed both Poppy and Sol in their chairs while everyone else gravitated to the kitchen. They studied each other, alone for the first time since the night before. Sol wanted to tell her how sorry he was, how he wished he'd never opened his big mouth. That stopping had been physically painful, and all he'd wanted was to take her on the floor because she was sensual and perfect.

But he didn't so much as emit a squeak.

You're such a coward. Say something to her, damn it.

"How's your knee?"

"It feels much better." Her eyes rose from his buttons to his face, looking tense and miserable.

Say something else.

"I could take another look at it if it bothers you," he blurted.

Not that!

The half-circles under her eyes were dusky, thin skin tinged in purple, her eyes striking against them. She drank in his tense posture. Her face softened. "If you'd like."

It was like he'd been nailed to his seat, anticipating an unforgiving blow and receiving a caress instead. His lips stretched across his face, and Poppy did that thing where she sucked her lips between her teeth to hide a smile.

"I have the afternoon free. I'd like to take you to the creek, maybe teach you to swim?"

"Swim?" Her lips reappeared, wet and glossy. She glanced at the closed kitchen door, stood, and made a show of clearing the table. Her movements were languid, her eyes interested.

He mirrored her, clearing his side with much less finesse. A fork clattered to the floor, and he swooped to pick it up. "Yeah. I reckon you learned how to ride a horse so fast it wouldn't take but a couple tries to teach you how to swim. You could probably swim laps around me before you had to go back to Dogwood."

"You think so?" She finally gave in and smiled. His face answered with one of his own.

"'Course. We could walk to the gilly hole together after lunch."

"All right." Her smile shrunk, and her eyes snagged on his lips. They had made it to one end of the table together.

Sol set the stack of platters and cutlery on the table and moved close enough to smell her. Flowers. Being near her made his blood go south, and he lifted a hand to run his thumb from her shoulder to her elbow. Her ribs flexed with her inhale.

The kitchen door cracked open, and they sprang apart.

Isa's head poked through the crack. "I want to come with you to the creek."

Sol glared at the nosey little meddler, hand twitching with the need to switch her behind.

"Of course," Poppy rushed since Sol was too furious to speak. "After we help Lucy clean up, we can walk together."

"Excellent." Isa stuck her tongue out at Sol, and his scowl darkened.

With one last amused glance in his direction, Poppy followed Isa into the kitchen.

Sol had no choice but to take the dishes to the kitchen and get his own workday started.

ISA HAD UNDERESTIMATED the measures Sol would take to garner a little privacy with Poppy. So, with some assistance from a conspiring Lucy, Isa was now stuck gathering and washing vegetables from the garden while he escorted Poppy to the creek.

"How much can you swim?" he asked when they reached the steep, sandy bank of the gilly hole. Frogs grew silent, and the noon sun beamed at the sluggish brown current that acted as an undulating mirror for the cypress canopy above.

They planted their bottoms in the sand to discard their shoes. Sol pitied her for all the untying she had to do to get those shiny black ankle boots off.

"I can doggy paddle enough not to drown, but I find it terrifying." She rucked her skirts up to undo her garters and rolled her stockings down, and Sol averted his eyes.

Look at the state of him. There was no way he could walk into the water without her noticing her effect on him. Disgusted, he unbuttoned his shirt, revealing the long red johns beneath. He hated wearing them. They were stifling and itchy in the summer, but he figured

142

they were the safest to use when swimming around women. Before Poppy could finish undressing, he stood, shucked his jeans, and strode into the creek with his back to her. The water's freezing temperatures wrung a hiss out of him and instantly amended the situation between his legs.

"Whoo!" he hooted, scaring off a couple of mourning doves in the trees above them. "It's a little chilly!"

A startled gasp made him whirl around, and his eyes widened. Poppy waded in behind him in a pair of fitted woolen combinations that tried, and failed, to veil the contours of her body. Her nipples poked against the fabric, and he could see gooseflesh pebble her skin from her arms to the exposed legs up to midthigh. He turned back around, gritted his teeth, and trekked until the creek was level with his stomach.

In his mind's eye, he saw her in his room the night before, her nightgown rucked up to her wide, lush hips. He splashed his face.

How the hell was he supposed to help her swim when he'd be constantly poking her underwater?

"Don't go any d-deeper, or I *will* have to swim to get to you," Poppy teased behind him. When he didn't respond, she added, "You can turn around. I'm decent."

"Yeah, but I'm not," he said unthinkingly on a cautious pivot. "Sorry. I didn't mean that."

Poppy's shoulders were almost submerged, and her eyes reflected the iridescent water. She didn't look disgusted or appalled, and his jaw relaxed. He hadn't realized he'd been clenching it since he saw her garters. Softly, she confessed, "I suppose I have no right to claim any decency either after last night. I'm truly sorry for throwing myself at you."

They circled each other in the water, and when her shoulders dipped below the water level, he caught her arm and dragged her closer. Her lips parted. "Well, I'm not sorry. And you *are* decent, Poppy. And you're welcome to throw yourself at me any time. I'll always catch you."

Mouth twisting wryly, her attention bounced between his eyes and lips. "You're too kind."

He grinned. "Come on. Let's teach you how to float before Legs gets here and ruins all the fun."

Poppy proved that, like horseback riding, she also took direction well with swimming. Her eyes flared in fear when he cupped her body in his arms, her feet parting from the sandy creek bottom, but when he soothed and praised her, she relaxed.

"What you want to do is take a deep breath—it's that air that will help you float—and relax your body from your head to your toes. No, don't tense up, that's what makes you sink. Pretend you're the water. Flow with it, be slow. There you go. Close your eyes. It'll help." Eyes closed, Poppy held her breath and relaxed her body. He kept his arms in a loose cup beneath her, barely touching her. "All right, spread your arms out, cup your hands, and push the water to keep yourself up."

When she did as she was told, her body floated up, and he risked a glance down to see if her feet were up as well. Her body was wholly revealed through the translucent combinations, every hollow, every hill. Breasts, navel, and the triangle at the apex of her thighs. The cold wasn't doing enough, and he throbbed beneath the water.

Stop lookin' at her, then. You came here to help her swim, not get an eyeful.

But when he glanced back at her head, she was watching him, and her eyes hid nothing.

It was nothing to pull her closer, lower his head, and cover her lips with his. This kiss was different from their first one. It was gentle. Testing. He took control of the pace, keeping it slow and languid.

He had never kissed anyone like her. She was a master; every glide of her lips was a promise, her tongue incredibly soft, her taste sweet. He wanted to taste her everywhere but couldn't pull himself away from her mouth. It was the best kiss he'd ever had.

Out of sight, Isa stopped midstep in the bushes. She watched the two undiscovered, so caught up in their own world and sharing the longest, most searing kiss Isa had ever seen. Covering her open mouth so she didn't reveal herself, Isa turned and ran back up the trail, her smile huge behind her hand.

Sol pulled away and glanced at the movement in the brush behind them. He saw no one.

"We'd better finish this lesson before someone walks up on us," he said. His voice had deepened so much he had to clear his throat. "Think you can float on your own?"

Through glazed eyes, Poppy nodded.

But throughout the lesson, their hands touched, their legs slid, and their skin grazed each other in promise.

Chapter Thirteen

Quiet as a mouse, Poppy eased her bedroom door shut and disappeared down the dark hallway.

It was close to midnight, and the house slept. She tiptoed down the stairs, pulse thrumming in her temples. Every move she made sounded inordinately loud. By the time she inched the front door closed behind her, her back was damp with sweat.

If anyone caught her, she'd merely explain she had to use the outhouse.

No one was outside. Sawing snores drifted from the bunkhouse a hundred feet away, along with night noises, but nothing else broke the stillness. The half-moon gleamed proudly above, absent of cloud coverage, and her nightgown, a sheer, lacy confection, gleamed in the black surroundings. When her eyes found the barn, her heart sank. The light was off.

Sol must be asleep. He'd worked hard the first half of the day so he could take time off for her post-dinner swim lesson. She'd felt his eyes on her through the whole supper, but Lucy had been in the mood for conversation, and he'd ultimately left with Junior. Poppy hadn't had an opportunity to speak with him since the gilly hole.

Had he thought she'd rebuffed him?

She should check near the barn. If she heard Sol snore, she'd go back to the house.

Poppy snuck down the porch steps with careful feet, hem in hand. Her breath was drowned out by chirping insects and insistent frog croaks from the creek. She was so intent on the ground, praying she didn't trip on anything, that she didn't notice the figure in the shadow of the barn until an arm reached for her.

Her swallowed scream was no more than a squeak, and Sol chuckled, reeling her into his arms.

"Sh, it's just me," he whispered.

Reflexively, she whacked his bare chest with the back of her hand, making him laugh louder. "You scared the blazes out of me," she accused, albeit quietly.

"I'm sorry." He didn't sound sorry, but she allowed him to drag her against his warm skin.

Eyes closing, she wrapped her arms around him. He smelled like he had the night before, all sandalwood, leather, and tooth powder, and she could hear the thunder of his heart. It was loud in her ear, steady but gaining speed. As his hands stroked the curve of her back and the blades of her shoulders, she sighed, "I forgive you."

"Were you coming to let me check your scrape?" His question was hesitant. Loaded.

"Yes," she lied. "Your light was off. I was afraid—I thought you were sleeping."

"No, I figured I'd leave one on in my room, let the animals in the barn sleep."

One of his hands left her back, and feather-light fingers skimmed her jaw. She looked up, trying to see Sol's handsome, lean face, but couldn't. It heightened her other senses. His thumb brushed her upper lip. Then, her lower, parting them.

"I've been wantin' to do this all day," he said, lowering his head.

Their mouths touched, and she was rooted to the grass. His lips brushed hers, implausibly soft. Rough cowboys shouldn't have such soft lips or such smooth backs. Eyes drifting shut, she allowed herself to feel every movement of his mouth on hers as it increased in intensity. At first, he teased her lips with tiny plucks until she grew impatient and stood on tiptoes, deepening the contact. She felt him smile, and wickedly, she curled her tongue between his lips luxuriously.

The rough wooden slats of the barn wall instantly pressed against her back.

Poppy twined her arms around his neck, pulling. Sol's hands cupped her bottom and raised her in one smooth motion, and her legs wrapped around him, nightgown hiking up to her hips. Their kiss grew harder, lusher, and she drank him like she was dying of thirst. Well and truly pinned, he positioned her lower, lower until they both broke away and gasped. He was hard and hot as sin against her, the front clasp of his jeans rough against the sensitive skin of her mons.

"Sol," she breathed. "I want you."

His hands kneaded the globes of her bottom almost roughly, and she couldn't prevent a moan. It felt too good.

"I want you, too, sugar. God, I've never wanted anything this much." His rueful laugh was dark and strained.

Leaning forward, she kissed the line of his neck, licking a trail with the flat of her tongue, intoxicated by his salty-sweet taste, ending it with a kiss when he stiffened against her. "Take me to your room," she suggested.

"Are you sure?" His words were a growl, his grip hard on her. "I don't think I can stop as easy this time."

"I didn't want you to the first time." She slid down, feeling the length of him. Powerless to resist, she kissed the center of his chest, her hands everywhere. He was lean and hard with interesting angles, muscles contracting against her fingertips.

"Fair enough." His voice had a tremor.

His warm, rough hand encased hers, and he led her to the barn doors, bypassing the dark barrel. It opened and closed silently as a ghost, hinges well-oiled. The light beneath the crack of his door lent the barn's breezeway an eerie cast, but Poppy had never felt safer with this man leading the way. She had been aroused before, but it felt different this time. Her heart was aroused, too, and just as stimulated. She wanted his body with the same urgency that she wanted his smile. His words of praise from the past few days consumed her thoughts.

That's it, Poppy-girl! Look at you go!

You did so good, sugar. So good.

As he opened his door, the room barely illuminated by a lamp turned down low, she acknowledged she would do anything for him when he talked to her like that. Was it because she knew he meant it? He hadn't wanted anything out of it. He didn't want a response from her; the words had just burst out, genuine and proud. There was goodness behind everything he said, everything he did. His feelings were on his sleeve, unafraid.

Once he led her in, he released her and locked the door with a simple hook latch. Poppy backed away, facing him, her back to the simple bed against the wall. She was untying the ribbons that held the neckline of her nightgown together when he turned around, and she loved the way his Adam's apple bobbed in response. Sol's eyes looked black in the ill-lit room, and they flashed when her gown slid leisurely down her shoulders to her elbows, breasts gradually revealed.

"You're beautiful." His voice was low, almost inaudible. "You look like—" He broke off, and a wry smile twisted his lips.

"What?" She cocked her head to the side, her night braid swinging near one breast.

It was too dim in the room to tell, but she could have sworn his cheeks had darkened. "You look like one of those paintings. You know, where their skin looks like an oyster pearl, and their"—he motioned across his chest, unsmiling—"here looks like peaches ready to be picked."

It was her turn to flush, but not from embarrassment. If Sol didn't touch her soon, she would die. Her skin was hot and oversensitive as though she was morphing into a living flame, burning from within. The nightgown whispered to the floorboards, and Poppy stepped out of its white circle, untying the cord in her hair, and finger combing the braid into a curling mass. Naked, watching his eyes devour her, she circled him, dragging her fingers from his abdomen to his lower back. She pressed close, embracing him from behind, resting her forehead between the muscular furrow of his spine. Her small breasts flattened against his back, and he groaned. The noise excited her, and she kissed his left shoulder blade, her hair sliding forward against his skin.

When her hands sunk to his fly, he whirled and clamped her wrists in a firm grip.

A dangerous glitter in his eyes hollowed her belly.

Slowly, he turned them until her back was to the bed again, pushing until her knees hit the mattress and she fell upon it. The hold on her wrists tightened with a small flare of pain, and before she could gasp, he pulled her up the bed. As though it had been no great effort, Sol followed on his knees until he was suspended above her, surveying every bared inch of her skin. Releasing her wrists, he trailed the backs of his hands down her arms. When he skimmed over her breasts, she arched into his touch.

Yes, there, she thought.

"You're so soft here," he said wonderingly. His knuckles brushed over her nipples, making them pucker.

Poppy moaned. His knees straddled her thighs, so she slid her legs out, stomach contracting until they were free, and spread them. The bottoms of her feet ran sensually down his calves.

"Sol," she whispered, begging.

His breath came with difficulty while he looked at the scintillating view she had exposed before turning burning eyes on her. "You're not playin' fair," he complained.

"When it comes to you," she murmured grasping his hands and firmly placing them over her breasts, "to this, I will never play fair."

He closed his eyes as though to locate what was left of his control before it left the room completely, but when he opened them again, the shape of Poppy's breasts changed beneath his fingers' manipulations and rendered him witless. Sitting back on his heels, his hands followed the bow of her waist, flowing wider over her hips. "How was all this under those skirts?" he accused. "Look at you, just perfect. You were made for me."

Throbbing at his words and tired of his playing, his savoring, she grabbed his head and pulled it to hers. Their kiss was searing, but he released her mouth to trail his down her neck and finally, *finally*, to her breasts. Having always had sensitive breasts, the first wet pull of his lips around her nipple made her groan. She clamped her hand over her mouth, afraid to wake the men in the bunkhouse. He abandoned her right breast for her left, swirling his tongue around the nipple, sucking it to the roof of his mouth, then letting it pop out. He kneaded them, brought them together, and buried his head between them with a masculine groan.

It was too much.

Poppy thrust her hips up and tried to get a connection of his hips between hers, but he was too blasted tall. Desperately, she gripped his hair and tried to kiss him again, but he was stubbornly kissing her lower, down her belly. Lower. Only one other man had kissed her there.

She stopped breathing, her pulse erratic, changing.

Pausing just below her navel, he glanced up at her. He was lying fully on his stomach like a hunter. "You trust me?"

Did she trust him? That was the difference between him and that other man. Trust. With one man, the trust had been broken. It had felt wrong.

With Sol's warm breath tickling the sensitive skin of her stomach, his eyes lighter now that they faced the lamp near the bed, glittering greenish, she felt no crawling sensations. No wanting to peel her skin off, no wanting to dissolve into the bed.

With Sol, she felt only the smallest amount of trepidation.

And curiosity.

Poppy swallowed and nodded her head. Yes. She trusted him.

Satisfied, he refocused his attention on her, skimming her inner thigh with his lips. Dark hands gripped the white flesh of her thighs, huge upon her, and she liked the contrast of dark and light, large and small. Then, thought was impossible. His warm, wet mouth kissed closer to the center of her, and her panting was deafening in the quiet room.

When he kissed her where she was swollen and damp, she almost bowed away from him with astonishment. His hands and arms hooked and pinned her to the bed. She was going nowhere. Then, his tongue slid between her outer lips and licked from her entrance to the pulsing bud at the top.

They groaned as one.

Softening his tongue, he made love to her body, and her cries were small and kittenish. She would have felt embarrassed, but the noises appeared to inflame him; he picked her bottom up from the bed and ate her alive. Poppy couldn't remember this intimacy feeling like this, the hot, wet, satiny caresses that brought pleasure into a finely honed focus. Sweat broke out on her chest and became a damp sheen on her face. Her hands delved into his thick, fine-textured hair, and she rocked her hips against him.

"That's it," he said, taking a deep breath, his voice low and rough. "Ride my face sugar."

"Sol!" His lips had formed a gentle suction over her clitoris, and her vision went blurry, sparks of white warning of the impending eruption. His mouth retreated, and she wanted to scream. "Noo, don't stop." Her forearm had a small bite mark from trying to stifle her cries, her body wracked with shivers, so close was she to that pinnacle, teetering, red-faced and tense.

He was up, shucking his pants and crawling up her body. Sol ripped her forearm from her face and kissed her. It was rough, mouth opened wide over hers, frantic. He tasted salty, and she kissed him back, bumping her pelvis against his stomach, running her feet along the crisp hair of his legs. Leaning back on one arm, he reached between them, and she peeled her eyes open enough to glance down. His erection strained from his lean body, impossibly large, long, and heavy. Lou Lou had once said some men carried double-barrel rifles, some carried Colts, and some carried derringers. As a child, Poppy hadn't understood.

Eyes watching her, face flushed and damp with perspiration, Sol asked, "Think you can take it?"

Poppy licked her lips. Her husband had been a derringer. She glanced up from the flushed, dark head with its long shaft and the coarse sandy hair at its base to Sol's concerned eyes. "I can take it," she whispered. Instinctively, she spread her legs, reaching up with her hips, body begging for contact.

At her words, his lids hooded, his jaw bulged, and his temple throbbed. He eyed her between her thighs, and she felt vulnerable and aroused all over again. There was something base and animal about him when he looked at her, like he didn't give a damn about his nakedness and that everything about hers was beautiful and sensual. The filthier they got, the less inhibited, the more excited he would be. He released his cock and lowered his hand to cup her, and she moaned, throbbing into his palm. When he tested her readiness with a careful finger, then a second, her head dropped. It was tight with two fingers, and she squeezed them with her small inner muscles, moving with him as he thrust them slowly in and out.

He bit his lip and shook his head. "I can't wait anymore."

Spreading the moisture with his fingers, he notched the broad head of his cock against her soft furrow, easing forward with steady, inexorable pressure. Slowly, her body gave, her muscles spreading wide to receive him.

Teeth gritted, a hank of hair over his eyes, Sol groaned approval. "Look at you. I knew you could take it. You're doin' so good."

His words made her pulse and keen, and she tilted her hips up, trying to wedge him inside her. He hissed at the movement, flexing in so deeply she gasped. He was halfway in, working carefully forward and backward. Sweat soaked the hair at his temples until he was fully seated within her, lowering over her to kiss her with soft lips. She could feel the tremble of his arms on either side of her head.

Poppy felt a similar strain. There was a fine tremor in her legs as they spread wide beneath him, and he was immense and hard inside her. She felt full. Tight. Their kisses changed as she shifted her hips beneath his, but he remained motionless inside her. Breathing faster now, Poppy teased his lips with hers, stroking his mouth with her tongue, trying to break the tight rein of focused concentration. Dragging her nails down his back, she reached until she had his rear in her hands, grabbed it, and rocked upwards.

The movement felt so deep she squeaked, but it wasn't exactly pain.

"This what you want?" he growled in her ear, pulling out almost entirely before sliding back in.

Poppy's moan was loud. She nodded, incapable of speech. His pubis brushed against that exposed, vulnerable part of her. How he could talk, she'd never know, but she wanted to see him moving in her so she pushed his chest up enough to peek between them. The sight of their most intimate parts together made that sensation rise again, where she was shivery and too large for her skin, and she clamped down on him.

Sol groaned, braced himself on an elbow, folded enough to suck a breast into his mouth, and drummed into her. His other hand sank low, tangling between them, and in that instant of contact against her wet, swollen heat, Poppy lost herself.

"Sol, God, yes, please," she moaned incoherently.

He took her mouth, movements rough and erratic, sweaty bodies slipping together. She bit his lip when she climaxed, moaning breathily against his mouth while his hand buried itself in her hair, pushing hard against her inner contractions. The sting of her scalp forced her to release his lip and arch backward while he grew impossibly harder and larger within her.

The look on his face…

When Sol reached his end, his eyebrows lifted in the center. His face softened.

Feeling unbearably close to him, Poppy wrapped her boneless limbs around him and pulled him against her damp, sweaty skin. Her heart raced, and her sex throbbed, soaking wet.

She wanted to remain here, just like this, forever.

Peppering kisses all over his face, she wondered if someone could expire from too much bliss. Sol allowed her pampering, letting her run her hands through his hair, along his neck and back. The grip of his hand on her hair eased, massaging instead of clenching.

Backing away enough to peer at her face, he asked, "You all right?" His voice was a husk.

"Yes." Poppy's heart had expanded to twice its normal size. "Are you?"

His head dropped back to the pillow and muffled his words. "No. I think you lamed me."

Laughing like she was ten years younger, Poppy released him, and he rolled onto his back. Gasping at the feeling of him disengaging from her body, she glanced down at the trail of wetness he'd left across her thigh.

"I should wash up."

"Don't." Head propped on his hand, biceps flexing, he rubbed the moisture into her skin. "I like it there. Especially here."

Her mouth dropped open when he dipped two fingers back inside her, stoppering his seed from escaping. Her face burned. "That will make quite a mess of your bedspread."

"Why would I care about that?"

"You'll have to burn it."

"Hold your tongue." He leaned over and nibbled her lower lip. "I want to die wrapped up in this blanket."

Rolling her eyes, she sighed and stretched, toes and fingers pointing, and said conversationally, "You are a barbarian, Cowboy."

His mouth had lowered to her nipple, and his erection, which hadn't deflated to less than semi-hard, twitched against her. "And don't you forget it."

THE ROOSTER WOKE Poppy the next morning.

She blinked and rubbed the sleep from her eyes with a fist. A glance at the little window over the bed showed it was still black as pitch outside. Idiotic rooster.

A warm, broad hand slid from her breast to her stomach, massaging.

Pleasure moved along her nerve endings slowly, sleepily, and she snuggled deeper into Sol's embrace. They hadn't been asleep long; the entirety of the night had been spent making love, kissing like adolescents for hours, talking, and learning each other's bodies. She'd lost count of how many times he'd made her laugh. She was sore deep inside, and outside, she was raw. Her lips were chapped, and she licked them. Still, her senses sang when he kissed the back of her neck, and his hand drifted lower, something long and hard poking her insistently between her thighs.

Deciding she needed to control the pace this time, she rolled and hooked a leg over him.

It was different now that it was dark. Intimacy in the light had been exceptional, but there was something singularly intriguing about touching while totally blind in the dark. Poppy's fingertips relearned his chest, stomach, and lower, where he stood stiff and proud between his long legs. Gently, she touched the delicately thin skin, drifting her fingers from shaft to head. At the crown's underside, he flinched and said something muffled.

"Are you sore?" she whispered in the dark, leaning to kiss his chest before sliding down. "I am, as well."

His words were indecipherable, and she smiled.

Not so talkative first thing in the morning, was he?

When she had crawled low enough to kiss his stomach, he held rigid. She could hear his breathing quicken.

"I'm sorry I made you sore," she cooed to him and placed a gentle kiss on the warm head of his cock. He groaned and delved his hands into her hair. "Let me kiss it and make it better."

She was very gentle with him.

Opening her mouth, she relaxed her tongue so it was soft, swirling it over and around the crown. He tasted faintly of the soap she'd washed him with last night before they'd fallen into an exhausted sleep, but mostly he tasted of clean, earthy male. Releasing him with a *pop*, she sat up and blew cool air over the tip then repeated the process all over again. After the third time, he finally found his voice.

"Poppy," he gasped from the headboard. "You're killin' me."

"No, Sol, I'm making you better." Her words were patient.

Sol's chuckle was dark, and his hands firmly gripped her under the arms and dragged her astride him. Grabbing her hips, he eased her over him, positioned her, and pushed in. The sensation was pleasure and pain, so interwoven that it made her head fall back. Poppy adjusted her knees and the angle, sliding to the hilt. Then, at the twinge of pain, she made a noise and wriggled back up.

Concern edged his voice. "Hurt?"

"Just if we go deep," she consoled, dropping her head to trail her cool hair over his torso. "Some stallion is out there bemoaning the fact that he was born with a human manhood while here, a mere man, was born with his."

Laughter exploded out of Sol, and he almost popped out.

She giggled with him but was forced to stop. It was difficult to laugh when something the size and hardness of a railroad spike was inside her. She began to rock.

Humor morphing into pleasure, Sol said simply, "I like you, Poppy."

That familiar warmth bloomed in her chest, spreading, twinging down to where their bodies met. Her hips moved faster. "I like you, too, Sol."

It occurred to her that falling in love with him would be too easy. That she should guard her heart. But that thought drifted away, along with everything else bleak and oppressive.

In his presence, all she felt was joy.

SHADOWS RINGED THEIR eyes, and their lips fought grins during breakfast. Lucy threw them suspicious glances, but Isa was surprisingly unconcerned with her brother's unreliably somber attitude.

"Hey, Ben, I figured I'd take Poppy on a ride to the property west of here. Still needs to get saddle broke." Sol buttered a biscuit as though it made no never mind to him.

Ben denied requiring extra help that day. If bodies could smile, Sol's did.

Avoiding his gaze, Poppy hesitated in stabbing eggs with her fork. "Unless you need help around here, Lucy?"

Eyes pledging to get answers—and soon—Lucy replied, "Of course not. You should enjoy yourself. I shouldn't keep you all to myself, anyway." It was so reluctantly said that Poppy nudged her with an elbow.

"That's right decent of you." Sol nodded. He was so serious over his mug that Lucy's eyes narrowed further. "Legs, you still goin' to Ma's again today?"

"Well, I thought I would accompany you and Poppy, actually," Isa began, a devilish glint in her eye. Sol side-eyed her, scowl half-hidden by his coffee cup. There were two red marks on his neck—scratches—and Poppy squirmed in her chair. Isa relished being the bearer of Sol's crotchety expression for another moment before she shrugged. "But then I remembered I'd promised to help Pa bring all the games to the new house. I'll be busy all day. I think I'll also stay the night at Ma's."

Poppy exhaled in relief and tried to ignore how Sol dissected her every move, gaze hot enough to melt her into a puddle.

Breakfast was cleared, and Poppy scrubbed and cleaned dishes with enough vigor to sling suds and slosh water on her midriff. Lucy was too busy with the children to corner her, and Sol rode up with Sunshine saddled and ready right as Poppy dried her soapy hands and forearms on a dishtowel.

"I'll be back to help at dinnertime, Lucy," Poppy called from the screen door, but she didn't hear the reply. Her feet were already flying across the porch.

Sol and Poppy rode all morning, legs brushing as their horse's hooves whispered through the tall grass glistening with dew. Hog ran happily along, chasing every squirrel and rabbit, disturbing a flock of birds roosting in the underbrush by the tree line, barking at cattle in the distance. They spoke of everything and nothing. Where they thought they would be in twenty years, their favorite sport, if they liked trains or carriages better. But whenever he asked questions about her mother, father, or childhood, she would grow vague and speak of the Daniels family instead.

He was pensive when she confided what Martha Daniels had done at her end.

"When Katherine's first baby died under Ma's care, I thought it would break her like that," Sol said. He looked west, and the noon sun streaked the longish hair peeking beneath his hat with gold and amber highlights. Poppy had forgotten a bonnet and constantly pinned her curly flyaways back into place. "Ma said she had raised twelve children and had almost lost a few, but by the grace of God, we had all lived. So...she hadn't understood why God would take her first grandchild."

"How awful," Poppy said softly. His profile was masculine, all angles and edges, firm chin, angular jawline, and deep-set eyes. But speaking of his sister's first baby, his face had eased into a quiet kind of sadness as though confused. Hurt. She reached over and touched his leg; he gripped her fingers and kissed them.

"She was a sickly little thing. Had lots of things wrong, always coughing and wheezing. One day, she caught a fever and just never got better. Doc said it was influenza. There wasn't much Ma could do; she was too little. Isa caught it, too, but she was older and healthy as a horse. Ma wouldn't go to church for months. I reckoned she blamed God."

Poppy nodded in understanding. Reverend Daniels had done the same thing after Gerald's death. He couldn't preach for weeks. He said nothing came to him that he could put in a sermon; he was simply too angry. A circuit preacher relieved him after Gerald's and Martha's deaths. "How did you feel about it?" she asked. "Did you blame God?"

Sol shook his head and shrugged. "Hell, I don't know. I always thought of God as just watching us, that what goes on down here isn't up to him. But Ma was determined that if He answered any prayers of hers, He would answer the prayer for a miracle for that baby. And when He didn't, it shook her up. So, no, I didn't blame God. For years, I blamed Katherine." He glanced over at Poppy, his mouth a crooked, bitter twist. "It was easier to blame her. She didn't even know about it for years. Could you imagine, shug? Not knowing or caring to know if your child is well?"

Shaking her head, Poppy whispered, "No."

He watched her, gazing so deeply into her eyes for so long that her heart performed leaping, twirling somersaults behind her ribcage. She was neatly snared, unable to look away even if she wanted to. Then, his eyes crinkled in a smile, and she was released. "I'm sorry, this wasn't supposed to be sad. I was supposed to charm and entertain you."

"No," Poppy said. "No. These conversations are just as important. Sometimes voicing the hardships when you're happy is better than facing them when you're not. It's less terrible."

"Maybe one day you'll tell me your hardships."

She frowned and played with Sunshine's reins, and her somersaulting heart began to wring and twist.

"But not today," he said in a falsely hearty voice. "Right now, I want to show you one of my favorite spots."

He led Copper through a tangle of underbrush in the woods, and Sunshine dutifully followed. The woods were darker and cooler, but mosquitoes whined and attempted to follow them. After nearly ten minutes of winding through trees, vines, and brush, they broke through a sunlit glade.

Yellow rays streamed on the patch of open ground where an enormous weeping willow squatted in its center. Beneath the trailing branches was the perfect place for the picnic blanket Sol had rolled and tucked behind his saddle. They dismounted and tied their horses to a fallen limb, and he whipped out the red gingham blanket, bowing and gesturing toward it like it was a throne.

They lounged on the blanket, talking, stealing kisses, and laughing.

Later, he rolled Poppy's stockings down one by one and rubbed her feet.

"Those are the sounds you made this morning," he teased, thoroughly enjoying himself. When his strong thumbs moved to the muscles of her calves, her moans increased. His eyebrows rose. "Now I'm starting to get a little jealous, you making more of a fuss over a little foot rub than lovin'."

Eyes closed in bliss, Poppy retorted, "There were far more people that could have heard me last night. Out here, we're alone. Plus, foot rubs are a specific kind of pleasure."

"Is it better than lovemaking?"

"Is the person making love to me you?"

He choked on a laugh. "I hope so!"

"Then no, this is only a fraction of what you make me feel."

Smile fading, Sol switched to the other leg. "Your husband…"

Poppy's eyes opened, and she peered at the sky through the tresses of the willow's reed-like branches. They shifted and swayed with the breeze, the bright, cheerful blue sky peeking through them. "Gerald was quite ill much of the time. It affected him. How he *performed*. And he was very distraught when we would try, and he couldn't quite—but he was a wonderful husband. He helped me so much, and if it hadn't been for him, I don't believe I would be half the person I am today." After another hesitation, she slid her thumbnail between her teeth. Her brows knitted, lifted, and frowned again. "I don't wish to speak ill of him, but what I felt with him is far removed from what I feel when we are together."

Hands warm and gentle, Sol murmured, "Well, I'm glad I make you feel good. You make me feel pretty good, too." His hands went higher, and Poppy closed her eyes again, feeling. His lips skimmed her knees, her thighs, the tops of her arched feet. When he climbed higher, she began to sigh.

They made love slowly, leisurely, their hands stroking each other's hair. Fingertips brushed cheekbones, lips, the tickle of eyelashes. And when they both collapsed, their hearts beating furiously, flesh connected, they repeated that morning's words.

"I like you, Poppy."

"I like you, too, Sol."

Chapter Fourteen

"**S**omething is different between you and Sol," Lucy remarked in an undertone while they installed the white sprigged curtains Poppy had brought. They were alone in Sol's new parlor, which smelled of sawdust, varnish, and fresh paint.

"Is there?" Poppy kept her face carefully blank, pretending ignorance. She was strangely reluctant to admit the affair between Sol and her as though speaking it would dissolve it. Her fingers tied the curtains in a loose knot, and she cocked her head at it. Hopefully, they weren't too feminine for a bachelor's home. Besides, if Isa lived here, she might appreciate the occasional feminine touch.

Lucy hopped from the chair and tugged Poppy's collar down. "Don't play coy. Look at all this stubble burn!"

Swatting the prying hands away, Poppy grinned and scooped the basket off the ground. "I don't kiss and tell, Lucille Stone."

Groaning, Lucy followed her from the parlor to Isa's upstairs room. From the leaded window, the front yard was the focal point. Wagons were already parked by the lane and in the grass, the horses loose in the hastily built paddock off to the side. Sol's family had arrived in droves to help. Men assembled a bonfire in the backyard, and a cookfire burned, a cast-iron rack braced on blocks for that evening's supper. Sol's mother and grandmother had arrived early and taken over the kitchen, so Poppy and Lucy did last-minute decorative touches while Tia and Frank occupied the boys with a wagon ride.

"Poppy, please tell me *something*. We used to share everything together! It doesn't have to be...detailed." If Lucy hadn't sounded so disappointed, Poppy could have hidden her smile. And, sensing weakness, the taller woman hastily shut the door and forgot all about the quilt and blankets in the basket. "What have you two been up to? Have you and Sol kissed?" She grabbed Poppy's hands and led her to the bed.

If Poppy was truthful, she *did* want to tell Lucy certain things. But another part of her, a secret part, wanted to keep Sol all to herself. It was too new, too precious. She half wished she was back in the attic room in Dogwood just so she could think about it.

And, it almost felt wrong to air out Sol's private matters to anyone. Even to her best friend.

"Yes," Poppy admitted, a half-truth. "We kissed."

Covering her mouth, Lucy gasped. "You did? Who kissed who first? You or Sol?"

"The first time, me. The second time, Sol."

"There has been a second time?"

"Sh, yes, keep your voice down." Poppy laughed.

"Oh, I shall swoon," Lucy said dramatically and fell backward on Isa's bare mattress. Three seconds later, she bounced up again like a Jack-in-the-box. "What was it like?"

Poppy's eyes grew distant, thinking of Sol's touches, his deep thrusts inside her when he neared his release, and the rough approval in his voice that made her body grow tight and warm. "It was—different. Very different."

The wicked smile on Lucy's face fell a little, and her deep brown eyes turned shrewd.

Warily, Poppy rose from the bed and rummaged in the basket for the sheets. "Help me put these on?"

Sighing, Lucy complied but had to have her last word. "If you two end up marrying, I had better be the first to find out."

Shaking her head at her friend's whimsy, Poppy interjected dryly, "He has to ask first, and I don't think a few—kisses—are enough to interest a confirmed bachelor into matrimony."

SOL WAS GOING to marry Poppy Daniels.

He didn't know if it would be this month or this year, but he intended to have her standing before a preacher with his whole family watching from the pews.

It was all Sol could think about.

How long did a person have to know someone before deciding that marriage was the next step?

Truth was, he'd known women—good, decent, pretty women—for years without ever having thought of popping the question. And he'd slept with enough to know that sex hadn't ever made him feel this way.

He'd kissed Poppy that second time and had thought, *If I get to kiss this woman every day for the rest of my life, then that's the life for me.* He'd known her for two weeks, and all he could think about was spending the next two decades with her. It must be what happened in most men's heads when they got a piece of a woman they couldn't get enough of. They became too tangled up in the woman's skirts, and what was in them, to realize all the other ways they didn't suit.

Best not to rush into it. Don't wanna scare her away.

Sol always rushed. He made plans one second, and the next, he was executing them. He never brooded on what could have been. No point in living in the past. He always looked ever forward. The fact that he'd spent most of his life swearing off marriage, fearing he'd drown in children and debt like his pa, no longer concerned him. His job was steady, his house sturdy, and there was currently a woman inside it that had thought about him enough to make curtains, pillows, and blankets to pretty it up.

When he'd caught her loading the bundles in the wagon that morning, striving to be secretive, he'd popped out from behind the well house and asked if she needed help. Her chagrin had amused him until he'd realized she was hiding homemade gifts.

Gifts she'd fashioned before they'd even kissed.

At that moment, all the loco thoughts of marriage became clear and tangible. Real. Poppy was the sweetest thing he'd ever met, inside and out. But when he'd approached her for a long, hard kiss, emotion swelling, Ben had sauntered out of the barn.

Thwarted yet again.

Tonight, he'd be busy entertaining his many family members, some from over three counties away, and wouldn't get another opportunity to kiss her.

Sol's thoughts changed direction, and a grin widened his mouth. He may not get the chance to kiss her, but he'd damned well make sure everyone knew he was courting her. Poppy Daniels was his, and by the time the night was through, everyone would know it.

IF POPPY HAD worried that Sol would be formally polite and treat her as an acquaintance as she'd suspected most men would, she was wrong. Again.

Every fear and worry she'd had about Sol since their first kiss remained completely unfounded. She and Lucy had just put finishing touches on Isa's room when the girl burst in on them mid-sentence, wearing her customary overalls, braids, and floppy hat.

"Are you two in here? Sol and Mr. Stone are asking—" Isa's words broke off, and her mouth gaped, big eyes roving the room.

The walls were decorated with a few watercolors Lucy had donated from her own home, and the expanse of white was no longer bare. The built-in shelves were stained to a rich, dark gloss, and Isa's library copies stood sentinel. The blanket was one Poppy had owned, a Crazy Quilt with white, navy, and azure geometric patterns. The curtains were a matching navy with a cheerful white lace border. They fluttered in the open window's breeze.

"How do you like it?" Lucy asked, playfully smacking a pillow. "Poppy brought the blanket, sheets, and curtains, and I brought the paintings."

Isa didn't answer.

Instead, she hugged each woman tight in turn. Poppy squeezed her eyes shut and held the girl close. What she wouldn't do to be a part of this girl's family....

They went outside to mingle with the many other people, and Ben's eyes lit up at the sight of Lucy. He drew her into his arms, baby Jack in his other. Before crushing loneliness could consider harrying her, Poppy's arm was hooked by another, reeling her into someone's warmth.

Sol.

The smile on his face crinkled his eyes, and simply said, "There you are."

All at once, Poppy fell in love with him.

It hadn't taken much. She would panic later.

The crush of people overwhelmed her, and she clung to Sol like a buoy in a squall.

It was nearing suppertime, and the aroma of sizzling, marinated meats drifted over them in a mouthwatering haze. Whole cobs of corn in their husks lined the iron rack over the fire. An enormous bald man in baggy bib overalls sipped out of an earthenware jug and turned everything occasionally. Two railroad spikes were nailed into the dirt alongside the house, and a pair of middle-aged men threw horseshoes at them, iron peals ringing in the air. In the backyard, several young people played a game of baseball.

Sol steered her around a section of grass off to the side. More than a dozen people were circled around a pair of straining, grunting men wrestling on the ground. The wrestlers were shirtless and lean, and a tall, wiry man with graying blonde hair announced their movements.

"That's my pa," Sol explained over the noise, his thumb brushing over the back of her knuckles. They almost held hands. "He used to be the county's wrestling champion back in the heydays before his back went out. Taught us everything he knew. Look." He chuckled and nodded at Isa, who had shoved her way between two shouting teenage boys. "Legs just noticed they were wrestling. She'll want a piece of the winner. Looks to me like it'll be Al. He's slick. See how he never stays still for long?"

The smaller man twisted out of a complicated hold, wrapped his leg and arm around the arm and head of the other man, and pulled back until the man tapped out in the grass. Sol's father boomed out the winner while half the crowd cheered, and the other half groaned. Poppy saw a swapping of silver coins and bills, and several men glanced at a cluster of wives with nervous eyes.

"Pa." Sol shouldered his way through the crowd, arm still looped possessively through Poppy's. Sol's father turned, and though his face was deeply tanned and weathered as a leather boot, he still retained a lively handsomeness that Sol himself carried. Mr. Williams had shoulder-length hair, a beard, vivid green eyes, and a broad smile the same shape as Isa and his son's. "Pa, this is Poppy Daniels. She's Lucy's friend. Poppy, this is my pa, Lonnie Williams."

Lonnie shook her hand, and his distracted air disappeared when Sol refused to let go of her arm. "Pleased to meet ya. You met my wife yet?"

"No, sir." Although Poppy saw Sol's mother that morning in the kitchens, she was never formally introduced. Mrs. Williams was as serious and no-nonsense as Sol and Lonnie were lighthearted.

"She'll be wantin' to meet you. Son, make sure you bring Miss Poppy around. Don't be a stranger." He turned back to the crowd where Isa and Al were arguing. "Isadora! You can't wrestle Al; he'll break your arm." He said wrestle like "wra-sle," and Poppy stifled a smile.

"Not if I don't break it first!" was Isa's rejoinder. The crowd laughed.

"Nope. Not happenin'." Lonnie was firm.

"I'll wrestle you, Izzy, after I win against Al," Junior called out in the middle of pulling off his shirt, sidestepping through the crush.

More women suddenly wedged their way into the crowd, giggling behind their hands. Isa glared at them, arms folded. With Matthew on his shoulders, Ben sidled next to Sol while Lucy nudged her way beside Poppy.

Junior and Al circled each other until Lonnie's cry of "GO!" set them after each other like a pair of Tasmanian devils. Al was quick, but Junior had longer arms and more brawn, easily displacing the smaller man's weight and flipping him onto his back. It took nearly five minutes before the red-faced Al would tap out. Junior made to shake hands, covered in dust and grinning, but the other man spat on the ground and stalked off.

"Aw, don't mind Al," Lonnie shouted over the jeers. "He's always been a sore loser!"

"All right, Izzy, me and you." Junior rubbed his dusty hands together.

There was an unholy light in Isa's eyes as she threw her hat down, unlaced her boots, and stuffed her stockings into them.

Sol whispered in Poppy's ear, making her shiver. "She's known for tweakin' your privates with her toes. Junior better watch out."

Sure enough, Lonnie warned, "Isa, you better fight fair or you won't fight at all!"

Isa wrinkled her nose and Junior's grin widened. Both crouched low, circling each other. Isa fingers ticked off with her pa's, "One, two, three, go!"

She went after Junior like a cat after a dog, winding around him, climbing on his back in a choke-hold that he effortlessly broke out of. It was clear he was going easy on her, but with no little exertion, and both wore twin expressions of competitive glee. As usual, tense undercurrents from Isa made Poppy chew a thumbnail. Did anyone else notice?

"This won't end well," Lucy said in a low voice near Poppy's ear, answering her question. Lucy didn't speak of the fight. She saw it, too. Concern tightened her eyes. "Junior's a heartbreaker, and he's never seen her as more than a sister. This cannot end well at all."

Poppy silently agreed but whispered, "We all had one growing up, that first puppy love. Once she matures, and spreads her wings, maybe she'll forget it and move on."

They nodded and erased their mutual frowns.

Finally, Junior wrapped it up, planting himself behind Isa to hook both arms above her head while her long legs thrashed about, struggling for purchase. After an admirable amount of time, she admitted defeat. Isa tapped out and rolled away, breathing hard. Lonnie announced the winner, but Junior shook his head, yanked Isa up hard by her arm, and dusted her shoulders off.

"C'mon, let's go out back so you can out-shoot me."

"Race you!" Isa counted, and they were off.

"What time are we leaving tonight?" Poppy forced nonchalance as the crowd dispersed.

"Probably around eight. It gets a little rowdy at night, and the boys will be tired." Lucy glanced over at Tia, who held the two youngest in both arms while they pet a docile old mule. She took in Poppy's arm in Sol's and smiled. "I'll find you later."

The shindig was raucous. Sol introduced Poppy to countless people, many of whom were hilarious and interesting. Most of them were related. However, when several young men's eyes gleamed with interest, Sol possessively wheeled her away. He steered her around, murmuring anecdotes and introducing her as "Lucy's friend," but smiles were knowing, and elbows jabbed each other. After an hour of this, amused and exasperated, she was ready to find some privacy.

"Are you done showing me off like a prize pony?" she teased after meeting Sol's brother Drew and his wife.

Sol scratched his neck, sheepish. "I reckon so. I wasn't trying to make you—"

"No." She squeezed the arm that was glued to hers. "No, I was only teasing."

They glanced at each other, smiling. "Did I tell you how pretty you look today?"

Warmth rushed all over her. "You have not. Have I told you how handsome you are in this shirt?" She pinched the starched fabric of the shirt she'd sewn for him, trying to hide her pride.

"You made it. It would make Bill over there look nice." He nodded at a slovenly man drunkenly leaning against a fence post. The jug in the grass next to him had overturned.

"Would you like to see what Lucy and I have done to your house?"

His eyebrows rose in interest. "What have you two been up to?"

She shrugged mysteriously.

"Let's go look, but we need to go in the back door, or Ma will put us to work."

Twilight encroached, and lamps sparked to life, dangling on slender tree limbs, wall hooks, and inside the house. They snuck through the back door, along the narrow hall. He released her arm, a strangely empty sensation.

Four men hunched around a dining room near the staircase, a game of Faro on the rough hewn table.

"Hey, Sol, you want in?" one of the men asked. He had immense sideburns and a heavy jaw.

"Maybe next time," Sol evaded easily, rounding the staircase banister. "We're going to take a look at Isa's room."

"Your lady friend can play, too," another offered. He had turned fully in his chair to sweep Poppy up and down with keen eyes. He was the youngest in the group, and his rugged handsomeness probably appealed to most women.

"Nah, I don't think she knows how to play the game," a third countered, dismissing the notion.

"Faro?" Poppy asked without thinking. "I know how to play."

Faro was one of the most popular card games in these parts. Anyone with a grandfather knew how to play.

Or anyone raised in saloons.

The men smirked at each other, and Poppy felt an uncustomary stab of irritation. She'd been taught by a drunken, well-meaning dealer who had too many slow nights and fits of boredom. He would invite a young Poppy to the dealer's table and teach her the games. She liked Faro because she was a hand at card counting and, accustomed to the dealer's cheating, cleverly saw when she was being finagled. She knew when to bow out with her money intact. Not that he would ever let her keep any money, but it was grand to win nonetheless.

Her eyes narrowed on the horseshoe-shaped card formation in the center of the table. It would be immensely gratifying to beat these men at their own game.

But fingers threaded through hers and she glanced up the stairs where Sol was attempting to drag her. Interest in the game evaporating, she followed, paying no mind to the low whispers behind her. His hand demanded all her attention, and she looked at the ropes of veins, corded knuckles, and powerful fingers that turned gentle when they touched her.

Would they finally get a moment alone in Isa's room?

The answer was, laughably, no. Sol's grandmother and several matrons had surrounded the quilt, chattering about the pattern. When they saw Poppy, they swooped down and interrogated her on its detail.

She heard Sol sigh next to her as he slowly released her hand and gave himself over to his many female relatives.

Later, after escaping the fluffy white heads of the older generation, Sol mingled with his family while Poppy lounged in front of the bonfire and sipped homemade wine. Sol's mother rested nearby. He had introduced them in the kitchen earlier, and Poppy had insisted on helping serve food. Now, everyone had eaten, and two fiddles keened on the other side of the bonfire. She had just gathered her courage to start a conversation with Mrs. Williams when Sol strode around the fire and held a hand out for Poppy.

"Dance with me!"

The wine was potent, and Poppy's head buzzed enjoyably, but she was still too sober to make a fool out of herself in front of Sol's entire family. "Oh, but—"

Not taking no for an answer, Sol pulled her from the stump and guided her around the fire where several couples, including Ben and Lucy, danced. She hadn't danced since Gerald had taken her out the summer before. Sol danced with wild abandon but was conscientious enough of their size difference to shorten his steps to fit hers. Her bittersweet memories faded until she laughed with the rest of them.

Sol dragged her off when the fiddles stopped and everyone bent over, faces sheened with sweat.

"Are you having fun?" His breath was sweet from wine, and he found privacy in the shadows beside the house.

"I'm having a wonderful time." It had been a long time since she'd felt no need to don a mask and pretend she wasn't beneath someone. Here, no one cared where you came from, what your upbringing had been like, or if you were acquainted with the mayor. Here, everyone was equal, and no one was a stranger.

"Good." The relief in his voice endeared her to him. He raised an arm as though to wipe the sweat off with his sleeve then stopped and dug for a handkerchief. She took it and dabbed at his face. "Good. I was worried you would feel left out, or uncomfortable, or, hell, I don't know."

Poppy raised herself on her tiptoes and kissed him, twining her arms around his neck.

Though she'd meant to keep the kiss sweet, Sol and the wine had other ideas in mind. He deepened it, cradled her face with his palms, and backed her deeper into the shadows. Someone was going to find them, she just knew it. He must have had the same idea because he stopped their kiss and rested his forehead on hers.

"Someone's going to catch us here." He craned his neck away, looking around. "Let's sneak into my room. No one will be in there."

"There's no bed," she whispered, kissing a line down his neck, arching her breasts against his chest. He cupped one in his hand and massaged it.

"Sugar, we won't need one." His voice was rough, and he turned her, hot on her trail while she eased the back door open. The men at the dining table were louder now. They didn't appear to notice them creep into the bedroom down the hall.

Sol's room was dark and shadowy, and light from the bonfire cast dim flickers against the bare walls from the two curtained windows.

"It's dark in here. No one will see," he assured, backing her beside the tall dresser, the only piece of furniture in the room.

Wedged between the corner and the dresser, Poppy's breath accelerated, and she raised her head, elongating her neck so Sol could kiss her from jawline to neckline. His hands reached beneath her skirts, and, unexpectedly, she was lifted, his arms hooking under her knees and spreading her wide. The wine made her dizzy, and she giggled until he kissed her deep and rough while she fumbled, fingers shaking, to unclasp the buttons of her combinations. She opened the slit in her drawers and reached for his trouser buttons. He was out in less than five seconds, hot, turgid, and velvet-soft against her fingertips. Their next kiss was messy while Poppy guided him to her damp heat.

Throbbing against the flared head, she made little gasping noises at how widespread she was for him. She'd never been picked up in such a way or been in this position, and she pressed down on him impatiently.

"Ah, slower, slower," he groaned into her neck. "We've gotta be quiet."

"Okay," she gasped, drunk on wine, drunk on him. She kissed his cheek, the bridge of his nose, his soft lips. "We can be quiet."

But when he worked himself in, breaching her entrance and sinking deep, she couldn't stop a keen of pleasure. He stifled it with his mouth, their tongues warring, teeth biting. Poppy's shoulder blades pressed up against the wall, and she braced her left hand on the dresser top, her right arm thrown across Sol's shoulders. He picked her up with only the strength of his arms, fingers biting into her buttocks, and sank her onto him to the hilt. They groaned as one as he slid in and out, and their pace quickened. Using the dresser as leverage, she rolled her hips into him, and the changed angle and motion that pounded his pelvis against hers had her ripping her mouth away.

"I'm—I'm about to..." she warned, shocked at how fast it was happening. It was hard to keep her moans soft, and she squeezed her eyes shut, teeth bared while her release splintered through her. Feeling it, he sped his pace, slamming her down so that the slap of her sensitive flesh against his intensified her climax.

"Never had anything feel this good," he choked out, his voice husky and rough at once, his thrusts punishing. "If you even knew what you felt like—"

Sensing his release, she kissed him to stifle his groan. His hands bit harder into her, flooding her with warmth, working his climax out with her body slower and slower until he stopped, panting with exertion. Drained. Her heartbeat was a loud thrum in her ears, her brain sloshed in her head, and when he disengaged and let her slide down, feet touching the floor, her thighs trembled ferociously. Steadying herself on the dresser, something warm and viscous trailed down her leg, and she squeezed them together.

Sol helped her straighten out, kissed her forehead, her lips, rubbed his nose into her neck, then wrapped her in a hug that stretched forever.

By the time he returned her to the bonfire, she was smiling from within, and their eyes shared feelings that Poppy was determined to ignore. She watched him approach his father, loose-limbed and grinning, clapping the older man on the back.

"I think it's safe to say you've got our Sol wrapped 'round your little finger," said a voice to her left.

Poppy whipped her head guiltily away.

It was Sol's mother, Mrs. Williams. She sat on a log that acted as a bench, and next to her was Granny, who held Katherine's youngest child in her arms.

Thankfully, his mother was smiling, though her expression wasn't as natural as her husband's or son's. Returning the smile a little cautiously, Poppy demurred, "I wouldn't say that, Mrs. Williams."

The woman laughed. Two bottom teeth were missing. "Well, I'll just say that in all my years, I ain't never seen Sol show a woman off in front of the whole family. Not once."

Pleased was a tame word for what Poppy experienced at that, but she also didn't trust it. People said things all the time. It didn't always mean anything.

Scrambling for a reply, she glanced at the child in Granny's lap. "Is that one of your grandchildren?" she asked politely.

Mrs. Williams sighed. She had a hooked nose and thin lips. It was clear that Lonnie Williams had made carbon copies of his children; not a single Williams she'd met looked like their mother. "Yep, that's Katherine's. 'Spect you've heard all about her, haven't you?" There was a hint of rancor in the latter. Next to her worn boot, a wine jar sat empty.

"Just that she's one of your daughters," Poppy lied, nervous now like she'd inadvertently walked into a courtroom during a verdict.

"She's my wildest girl. And that's sayin' something when I've got one shootin' guns and racin' horses in boy's clothes." She extended a thumb in Isa's direction, who was up to bat in a baseball game with her male cousins. "Always sneakin' out, getting into mischief, Katherine was. Now she's a whore, and I'm raising her young'uns."

Spanish moss seemed to grow in Poppy's mouth, constricting any flow of words, dry and uncomfortable. How could Mrs. Williams say such things about her own daughter to a perfect stranger? She struggled to input something, finally managed, "I'm sure your taking the children in is a blessing to them. That was very good of you."

The woman waved that away. "And do what else? Can't let them grow up in a saloon and end up just like their mama. That's what would happen. I guarantee it. You can't take them out once they get a taste of that life." She gave Poppy's fashionable party dress an appraising look, and the self-righteous fury softened. "I'm sure it's hard to understand, you bein' a pure lady and all. It'll be a gift to have one in the family. Heaven knows the other women Sol has walked out with were no saints."

Wouldn't it scandalize the woman to know that Sol's seed was still sticky on her legs?

Granny took this moment to speak up, her words lisping a little from her toothless mouth. "Remember Winona? Heavens above, she'd have given Sol a dozen children, and none of 'em would have been his."

Mrs. William's face flushed dark red in the orange light of the dying bonfire. "Sure enough, Mama. But any woman who gives it up before marriage isn't good enough for our Sol, and I told her so."

"Did you?" Granny cackled, bouncing the rousing toddler back to sleep.

"I sure did. And I'd do it again. Now, Poppy, do you have any family in these parts?" asked Sol's mother, picking her empty jar up and peering into it.

"No, ma'am. My family has passed." Poppy's lips felt as numb as her insides.

"I'm sure sorry to hear that. Is that why you've stayed in town with Lucy's folks?"

"Yes. I'm working as a seamstress."

"Well, that's fine, just fine, isn't it Mama?" Mrs. Williams was slurring and heaved herself up, eyeing the direction of the kitchen that housed the cask of homemade wine. Granny didn't answer. She snored where she sat, weaving precariously on her backless seat. Mrs. Williams waddled off, murmuring about needing the outhouse, and left Poppy to her thoughts.

Fingers clenched tightly in her lap, Poppy looked into the fire, her exemplary mood withering.

Were his mother's words true? Was that way of life ingrained into a person for the rest of their life, no matter how much they chose differently? Maybe it was. Look at what she was doing with Sol, sneaking away with him at a family function. Was she any different from the woman Mrs. Williams had chased away or Sol's sister? Or even her own mother?

I am different, she told herself forcefully, needing to believe it. *I am.*

Eventually, Lucy came over and chatted with her, though Poppy had grown quieter and less ready to smile. From the corner of her eye, Sol unsubtly observed her, a worried line between his brows.

He escorted them to the wagon when it was time to leave, and Poppy managed a smile for him, his mother's words replaying over and over in her mind. As an excuse not to hug Sol or clasp his hand—she felt far too unworthy of such familiarity now—she held a sleeping Samuel and offered a virtuous nod as her goodbye.

Poppy looked back only once, unable to resist.

His silhouette was tall and forlorn in the shadowy lane behind them.

His shifting feet and cocked head, a kicked puppy in the road, solidified her conviction that she wasn't good enough to scrape at his boots.

Chapter Fifteen

Only Tia and his mother harbored enough energy for church that morning.

Sol shifted Poppy's bags in the wagon while she and Lucy clung together, murmuring their goodbyes, and every child received a kiss in turn. She'd been reserved since the night before after their tryst in his empty bedroom. He should have divulged a desire for more than just her body.

He should have wooed her like she deserved. Instead, he'd acted worse than Hog, the way he'd panted after her. His jaw clenched at the piercing self-disgust. She deserved better, and her unceremoniously polite distance proved she knew it.

But something niggled. Despite Sol's reservations, it had been a perfect night. After he'd taken her against the wall in his room, he'd left her at the bonfire smiling.

What had happened from the time he'd deposited her beside the bonfire to when she'd left on Lucy's wagon?

Comprehension slackened his tense face.

Of course. Poppy had stood next to his mother. Usually, he and his ma got on fine, but the last time he'd shown interest in a woman, she and Granny had frightened the poor creature off. Had she said something to Poppy? He glanced over at the porch, and his jaw set again.

Of course, Ma said something.

Ten minutes in his mother's company had Poppy just as closed off to him as the first day he'd met her. What had happened?

Well, they had two hours together to find out. That dogged, unbudging part of him narrowed its eyes.

He walked around and met Poppy at the wagon step. He held his hand out. She took it graciously but refused to look at him. Touching her brought images of her under him, splayed open and glistening with sweat. She sat and gave him her profile, eyes on the driveway ahead, and the area around his chest ached like the time a cantankerous donkey had kicked him.

"I'll be back around dinnertime," he called to Ben and Lucy, then hopped on the squeaky buckboard seat and grabbed the reins. Clicking his tongue and slapping the reins, Sol eased the wagon forward and they were off.

He'd get to the bottom of Poppy's strange mood before they made it to his road.

They hadn't even reached the end of the drive when he asked, still looking forward, "What happened last night, Poppy? What went wrong?"

Poppy didn't flinch. She'd expected the question. Her voice was calm. "Nothing happened."

"That's hogwash if I've ever heard it."

There was no reply.

He forged ahead. "One minute, you're dancing, laughing, and smiling. Next minute you're staring into the fire like someone kicked your dog." When she was still unresponsive, he twisted in his seat. It hurt to look at her. Her skin was gray beneath her freckles, her mouth tight, hooded eyes expressionless. He would just have to out-stubborn her. "My ma say something to you?"

"Your mother said nothing untoward."

Like hell. "No? She tends to say exactly what's on her mind, whether it's fair or not. Drives Isa up the wall." A frisson of fear had his hands fisting the reins. "She talk about any other women I've walked out with?"

"What?"

"Come on, she or Granny had to have said something about Winona. That's Granny's favorite story, Ma running that woman off."

Poppy finally turned to him, eyes awake and absorbing his features with the same urgency his did hers. "They said some things. Winona may have been mentioned. But your mother also said you had never officially introduced any women to the family."

"The exception bein' you?"

Poppy nodded slowly, watchful.

"Did that scare you off?" he asked a little desperately. "By now, you've gotta know how I feel about you."

Her face shot around to face the front again, and he wiped his forehead roughly with the back of his gloved hand. This wasn't going well at all. For a mile, he was at a loss, struggling for something to say.

It was a good thing he'd held his tongue.

"How do you feel about me?" she asked. It wasn't a hopeful question but a foreboding one. Like she was about to dash all his hopes out the window with yesterday's wash water.

A nervous sweat popped up over Sol's back and upper lip. She wanted to know how he felt about her? He'd tell her exactly how he felt.

"I feel"—he stopped, looked at her white-knuckled grip over the sewing case in her lap, and powered through it—"I feel like I want you. I've wanted you since you told my sister she looked elegant instead of skinny. Since you ate that hard candy and all I could think about was kissing you. I think about you all day when I should be workin', wishin' I'd known you before I'd built my house so I could've asked you how many rooms you wanted."

Poppy's mouth gaped at that, and her whole body turned toward his indignantly, knees pointing accusingly. "Sol, you do not even *know* me. You may want me, but you don't know the true me. I am not who you think I am."

Not for lack of trying, he wanted to shout.

Temple flickering, he gestured at her. "I may not know everything about you, and you haven't offered much when I *have* asked, but I know enough. I know you're kind. Generous. You love babies and want some of your own, and God willing, if you do, you'll be a great mama. You can dance and play cards, you're always willing to help, and kissing you makes me forget my own name. When it comes to makin' love, I could do it with you every day until the day I die and never get tired of it. And lovin' you"—he laid a gentle grip of his gloved hand over her chin and turned her face up to his—"lovin' you is the easiest thing I've ever done."

There was a bite in the air; her lips were cold. She didn't kiss him back, but he hadn't expected her to. Sol hadn't even known he'd loved her until he'd said it, and his breath stuttered in and out at the exhilaration, the truth of it.

Poppy's blue eyes were wide on his, their expression heartbroken. "You have known me for weeks. You only think you love me. But you won't when I tell you where I come from. What I've done."

Releasing her chin, he mulishly faced forward again. He wouldn't let on that Ben had already divulged the nature of her childhood. If she wanted to tell him about her past, he'd force himself to listen. If she could suffer through it, he could suffer to hear it. "It won't change how I feel about you," he warned.

"Last night, your mother told me she took her grandchildren out of the saloons. That if they had been raised to that life, they would have ended up just like your sister Katherine. Do you think that's true?"

So that's what had happened. Ma had opened her big mouth without even knowing anything about Poppy. Anger made his words tense. "Hell, no, I don't believe that."

"Hm. Some people do, though," Poppy said conversationally. "What if I told you that I was raised in a saloon? Would you still want to put me on your arm and prance around with me to your family?"

"It wouldn't matter if you were raised with a pack of wolves, I would still want you."

Her eyes hardened. "Someone told you I grew up in saloons. How long have you known?"

"Why does it matter to you? It doesn't matter to me. It never did."

A tremor shook her words now. "It will matter very much if word gets out and everyone learns of my past. You won't want me. And your mother certainly won't."

"You can't tell someone how they feel," he gritted, "just because you're scared. You can't tell me how I feel about you. Your past is the least important thing about you, Poppy. You can't control how you were raised, and it shouldn't touch your future."

She laughed. It wasn't a pleasant sound. "What a thing to say! Something like that touches *every* part of a person. What do you think it's like in saloons for children?"

"I 'spect it's pretty awful, seeing how Pa and I were the ones to get my niece and nephews from one. They didn't act like other kids their age for months."

Poppy acknowledged this with a nod then tried again. "Did you know that I knew how to play Faro because the dealer used to teach me? Sometimes I would sit on men's laps so they'd let me play with them."

Sol tried to catch her eye, but she stared determinedly ahead.

"Mama would make me go outside when that happened or make me clean the mugs behind the counter. But most of the time, she was upstairs and wasn't around to watch out for me. One weekend..." Her words trailed away, and she covered her eyes with her fingertips.

"You don't have to tell me. It doesn't matter—" He tried to soothe her, but she brushed his words away.

"No, you need to know all the rotten parts of me. If you truly think you love me, then you need to know the worst. Because I do care about you…so much. I couldn't bear it if you found out later. If you despised me." Her eyes were pink-rimmed, and Sol clamped his mouth shut so she could speak her piece. "One weekend, my mother went to a house party. She was to stay there with a few others and asked the saloon owner to watch over me. But what Mama didn't know was that one of her regulars had planned the house party with the owner so he could get me alone. He kept me in a private room and spent the whole weekend with me."

"Poppy—" Sol's voice was as broken up as he felt inside. He gripped her shoulder, speechless, while Bull ambled slower and slower, eventually drifting to a stop on the side of the empty road.

"No, let me say it. When Mama came back early and found us in bed together, she screamed at him and chased him off, threatening to bring the law into it and have him arrested. I was only thirteen and had not started my menses, a punishable offense even for a whore's daughter."

He made an outraged noise as if to interrupt, but she clenched his gloved hand with her own and dragged it down into her lap. Focusing on a point between Bull's ears, she kept going.

"We ran. That's what we did for a long time. We ran and ran. We made it to Dogwood and settled down, and that was the best two years, being with Lucy and Franny, making friends for the first time. Ms. Trudy was a fair woman but didn't want me underfoot, so she had Mr. Ricci keep me at the hotel with Lucy. But Mama stole from Trudy, so we had to leave again.

"It happened like that for a long time until just after I turned sixteen. Mama had stolen from a man in Austin. He had a lot of friends in the trade, and, to make a point, they caught us outside the city. They told my mother"—she took a deep breath and closed her eyes—"they told her that I could work off her debt."

Sol's hand clenched hard around hers, a noise escaping him like an angry bear. "The hell they did. Please tell me she didn't agree."

Her eyes finally turned to him. They were open wide, haunted. "They told Mama they would kill her if I didn't."

No…

"But I couldn't do it, Sol," she whispered, and the tears were in her voice even if they weren't in her eyes. "I couldn't. I had asked her—begged her—to get a job as a washerwoman or something reputable. I'd told her I would stop going to school and help her so that we could pay for a room somewhere. But she wouldn't do it. She went to a saloon in the first little town we'd come across that wasn't a city, and that's how they'd found her. And the night I was supposed to go upstairs and start working Mama's debt off—I couldn't. I ran away."

Sharp relief surged through him. "That's good—"

"It wasn't good," she cried, halting his words. "It wasn't! I ran to the church down the road and hid, and the next day, they found her body in a ditch outside of town." She bit her knuckles hard, and Sol gently extricated her hand from her teeth so he could kiss where she'd hurt herself. "She was naked. Someone had beaten her when I hadn't gone upstairs. It was my fault. I killed my mother."

THEY PULLED TO a stop in front of the white clapboard Dogwood Hotel near noon in a stupor.

Sol had wanted to keep talking, but Poppy had shut down after her admission.

Which was complete balderdash.

A sixteen-year-old child was not responsible for the consequences of an adult's actions. But the more he'd tried to explain it to her, how wrong she was to believe her mother's death was her responsibility, the more unresponsive she became. Finally, he'd turned Bull back onto the road, where they bounced and jostled the remaining miles in charged silence.

He parked the wagon beside the hitching post and went to assist her, but she climbed down alone, face carefully blank. Clenching his jaw, he grabbed her bags without accepting help and shouldered his way into the hotel. He nodded curtly at Mr. Ricci's pleasant greeting, Poppy following so closely she hissed breaths down his neck. His feet stomped up the stairs to the attic, and hers did the same. Was she finally angry? Good. He preferred her anger to her playacting as a store mannequin. But mad at who? He was furious with her mother and even a smidge upset with Poppy for being obtuse enough to claim responsibility for her mother's death. No wonder she preached her unworthiness if she constantly dragged her own conscience through the mud.

When he set the bags at the foot of the bed, she shouldered past him, opened them, and neatly put things away.

"Sugar." His voice was loud in the quiet room, and she stopped. She stood in the middle of the room, fingers pressed against her stomach. Her mouth was bowed. Sad. "I want to marry you."

Poppy was shaking her head before the words left his mouth. "No. You don't." The words were toneless. "You don't have to marry me just because of what we did. People do that all the time."

Brow darkening, he strove for patience. "I don't give a damn if people do it all the time without marrying. That's not even why I'm asking."

"Do you feel sorry for me? That's a poor excuse for a marriage."

"No, it's not because I feel sorry for you," he growled. "It's because I care about you and want to spend my life with you."

"Even after everything I just told you?" Her disbelief soured her expression. Sol wanted to paddle her rear end.

"None of that matters!" he yelled, flinging his arms out.

"Of course it matters," she spat, and it was her turn to gesture wildly. "It matters! I can't give you children, Sol. Seven years of marriage with nothing to show for it proves that. And my past would be dredged up somehow, I just know it, and then there would be a scandal. I would dishonor your whole family, and your mother would have another whore in the family to lament about to complete strangers."

He took another step toward her, and fury such as he'd never felt bared his teeth. "Don't you talk about yourself like that. You think I care about any of that?" Her eyes had widened, her mouth trembled. Without thinking, he clasped the sides of her face and kissed her with bruising force. When he pulled away, her eyes were squeezed tight, her chin wobbling worse than before. He kissed her again, softer. "I don't care about any of that."

Another soft kiss.

"No person is going to say anything that will change the truth. It only took two weeks for me to love you because you are worth loving. You're the first and the last thing I think about every day. And I'll keep askin' you until you say yes."

Kiss.

"I want to make you smile and laugh and scream my name for the rest of our lives. And I'll fight for it. For you."

This last kiss was the longest, the softest. Poppy's nails bit into his wrists as she held on, unable to speak or do anything but kiss him back.

"Because you're worth fighting for." His own breath was shaky, and something knobbed and bulky had caught in his throat because he couldn't speak anymore. Her eyes were still pinched shut, her cheeks damp, the lashes wet.

Sol kissed each eye, turned on his heel, and left.

Chapter Sixeen

S ol didn't return the next day, or the next, and Poppy felt broken
by Wednesday.

Didn't she have what she wanted? Hadn't she pushed everyone
away, convinced them of her unworthiness?

You're the first and the last thing I think about every day.

She hadn't told him that he was too.

*I want to make you smile and laugh and scream my name for the rest
of our lives.*

Even after everything she had told him?

Because you're worth fighting for.

She wasn't. Was she?

Perhaps distance would prove to be the balm for his temporary leave
of senses. Lesser men than him were moved to propose marriage after
only a few weeks of acquaintance. He probably regretted every word
and would distance himself from Dogwood until summer's end. And
yet...despite the lies she told herself, she knew Sol had meant what he
said. He was honest, if anything. And if he was giving her space now,
then she only had herself to blame for her misery.

She was sewing upstairs with Franny, the crank of their machines
nearly lulling her to sleep, when they heard the ruckus downstairs.

"What is that noise?" Francesca asked when the shouting had
stopped.

It had sounded like a girl's screams, over before it had begun.

"I'll go downstairs and find out," Poppy offered mechanically, oddly disinterested.

Mr. Hobb paced behind the counter just outside the closed storage room. Poppy frowned at the sign on the door.

CLOSED.

"What is it, Mr. Hobb?" She tried to keep her voice low and unobtrusive. She heard Mrs. Hobb's deep voice through the storage door.

"It's that foreign girl," Mr. Hobb explained. "She showed up five minutes ago, screaming and carrying on. I had to close the store so that no one walked in on a scene."

"I'd better see if I can help." Poppy eased around a reluctant Mr. Hobb and cracked open the storeroom door. "Mrs. Hobb? Can I come in?"

"Oh, thank God," the burly woman expelled, opening the door wider. "Come in, see if you can help me with this child."

Alwine wore the purple wrapper Poppy had given her, but she was dirtier and more unkempt than ever. Her hair was no longer in its braid atop her head but hung in a tattered rat down her back. The ever-present doll was mussed and dangled by its arm in Alwine's hold. When the girl saw Poppy, she stepped forward and spoke in urgent German. Poppy, unable to understand a word, studied the girl's facial expressions intently. When Alwine's tear-filled gray-blue eyes snapped down to her hand on her belly, Poppy's blood went cold.

"What is it? What's she sayin'?" Mrs. Hobb asked, seeing the change in her friend's face.

Finally, Alwine shoved the doll beneath her dress, revealing bruised bare legs and feet. Even Mrs. Hobb understood that.

"I think Ally is trying to tell us"—Poppy whispered in slow, aching dismay—"that she is with child."

THEY HAD LEARNED through Alwine's broken English and the German/English dictionary borrowed from the library that the girl was afraid to go home, afraid "they" would "take" her baby. Staying at the Hobb's was her only option.

Poppy and Mrs. Hobb set up a little cot in the material room, and Francesca stormed to her bedroom in a snit and didn't come back out. Both women ignored this and took steps to soothe Alwine's confused frown. They bathed the girl, and Mrs. Hobb fought tears over their young friend's bruised body.

"What have they been doin' to ya, sweetheart?" Mrs. Hobb asked in a falsely light voice.

But Poppy's eyes were dry. She studied Alwine's doll, chewing furiously at her nails in one hand and holding the dictionary open at the Fs in the other. Two fingernails broke off at the nail bed, and she spat them out discreetly. Something wriggled in her mind, something slimy, worming beneath layers and layers of carefully guarded memories.

"Ally, do you know a man called 'Ace'?" Poppy's inquiry felt vague, far away.

Alwine wiped her streaming eyes and dodged the pot of warm water Mrs. Hob poured over her sudsy hair. "*Was?*"

Was meant *what*, Poppy remembered.

"A man named Ace?"

"*Ja*. Yes. *Er ist der Vater meines Kindes.*" Alwine's eyes filled with tears.

Poppy pointed at the doll. "And the doll?" At Alwine's blank, watery stare, she flipped through to the Ds in the dictionary and asked, "*Puppe*? Who gave you the *Puppe*?"

"Ace. *Mein* Ace."

"I thought so," Poppy whispered.

"What are y'all talkin' about, Poppy?" asked a bewildered Mrs. Hobb.

"I'll tell you when I return." Poppy was already out the door, trotting to the sheriff's office.

"I'VE NEVER WORN anything as fine as this." Isa swirled her skirts in front of the mirror, solemn with worry. "And it's off the shoulder. I hope Ma doesn't show up."

Isa's soft green dress altered her hazel eyes to peridot gems, and the corset beneath gave her lithe body dramatic curves. There wasn't supposed to be any hint of bosom at the sweetheart neckline. Still, Poppy hadn't accounted for how naturally blessed Isa was, who appeared ten years older between the dress, the gleaming honey curls tumbling from a half up-do and the rounded bosom that would be at home on a ship's masthead.

Hopefully, Sol wouldn't have a conniption.

"If your mother attends, you can explain that off-the-shoulder evening dresses are perfectly respectable. Even Queen Victoria wears them," Poppy assured. Her face in the mirror was pale and drawn, and she turned away from her reflection.

Isa had shown up that morning, tentatively asking if her dress was ready. Then, eyes wide when Poppy flourished the evening gown from the standing wardrobe, blurted that Sol would chain her to his side.

"It's good that he's escorting you, even with all the extra security." Poppy thought of all the lawmen and volunteers posted at every street for the dance.

"You're coming as well, aren't you?" Isa asked, suddenly nervous. "Lucy can't make this dance because Sam is sick. So, I was looking forward..."

Poppy had worried that Sol would renege on his offer to escort her to the dance. "If Sol still wishes to escort me, then, of course, I'm coming."

"Why wouldn't he wish to escort you?" Isa's gaze was far too astute for her age.

"Perhaps he forgot."

Isa laughed like Poppy had made a ridiculous quip. "Forgot? He's downstairs right now, waiting for us. The other day, he rode all the way to Houston to buy a suit that fit him. He spent half the day today getting ready and finding cut flowers for you, then got angry when they wilted before we arrived. I don't think he 'forgot.'" She stopped laughing at Poppy's face at that and asked, "Did something happen between the two of you?"

It took several minutes of distracting Isa and ignoring the guilt that he wasn't wearing a suit that she had made—because she hadn't finished it—and fussing with Isa's dress before Poppy was able to avoid that perplexing question.

But Isa had the memory of an elephant. She repeated, "Is everything well between you and my brother?"

"Yes, everything is very well," Poppy soothed. The relief on Isa's face was acute. Guiltily, Poppy studied her and leaned in a little. "Are you nervous?"

At first, Isa snorted. Crossed her arms over her trim, corseted stomach. "I suppose. Isn't that idiotic?" She forced a little laugh. "It's just a dance, for goodness' sake. It's nothing at all to get hett up over."

"I disagree," Poppy said. "My first dance as a young woman your age was terrible."

Instead of being mollified, Isa spun so fast her skirts windmilled, horror-struck. "What happened?"

"Absolutely nothing." Poppy ignored the stupefied expression and fixed Isa's off-center bow.

"How was that terrible?"

"Well, nothing happened because I was too afraid to talk to anyone or dance. I sat in the corner all night, and the only person I spoke to the whole time was the preacher I lived with. When I got home, Mrs. Daniels asked how the dance went, and I told her how boring it was. She was more disappointed than I was; she'd been waiting all night for juicy gossip and stories of me dancing with all the boys in town."

"Oh." For a moment, Isa plucked at the necklace she'd borrowed from Poppy—green paste gems in black settings that matched her dress—and looked uncertain. "I don't want to dance with all the boys. Just one person would be enough. Someone besides Sol, I mean."

Knowing where this was going, Poppy brightened her voice. "Do you mean Junior?"

Isa's head jerked her way in the mirror's reflection. For a long, uncomfortable moment, Isa scowled at Poppy with the grudge of someone unwilling to give up a coveted secret.

Unoffended, Poppy gentled her gaze. "I'm sorry. I should not have said anything. I should have let you come to me first."

"Who said I even—" Isa began but broke off when Poppy's brows shot high, insulted. The younger woman's scowl deepened. "*Well.*"

"Yes. Well."

Finally, the cantankerous frown dissipated. "I suppose—just don't tell anyone."

Poppy was reasonably confident several people already knew, omitting Junior himself and Sol, who would never consider anything untoward between his sister and one of his best friends. Feeling the nervous knot in her stomach settle the busier she was, Poppy picked up a black silk choker with an opal cameo. "I would never say anything, Isa. I promise. Can you help me put this on?"

While she fumbled at Poppy's nape, Isa asked slowly, testing, "Do you think he'll ask me to dance?"

After a moment's thought, Poppy shook her head. "I'm not certain. How does he treat you when you wear dresses?"

Isa's brows lowered. "Like a horse apple in the street. Smelly and not worth his attention."

Suppressing a smile, Poppy turned and looked up at Isa's youthful, pretty face. "Junior may see you a little differently one day. But for now, he doesn't see you that way, does he? He's not comfortable treating you as a respectable young woman. He's used to treating you like a little brother, wrestling, racing, and having spitting contests—yes, Sol and I saw you doing that at the party."

The young woman's cheeks reddened. "I didn't think you had."

"The point is," Poppy continued, smoothing a stray flyaway hair behind Isa's ear, "that you should have fun even if Junior doesn't look at you twice. Don't do what I did and sit like a shadow in the corner of the room. You deserve to have fun. Dance with other boys your age. I see them looking at you at church all the time."

"Yeah, to laugh."

"No." Poppy shook her head solemnly. "Several weren't even around their friends and looked as though they were mustering up the courage to talk to you."

The dark-haired miner's son was particularly stark in Poppy's mind.

As though deciding to believe her, Isa turned her face from side to side in the mirror. Her lips twisted in contemplation. "I suppose I could start spending time with more kids my age. Dance with other boys. It could be a good social exercise, like one of Ben Franklin's experiments."

"That's the ticket." Poppy beamed. "Now, are you ready to go downstairs so the men can take us to the dance?"

"Lead the way." Isa was more grim than enthused.

Sol and Junior leaned against the back porch posts, deep in conversation, but they straightened when the screen door creaked open. Poppy stepped out first.

"We're ready." Poppy's eyes widened and her breath eked out. Sol wore a new black suit and the crisp white shirt she'd made him with a matching bowler hat and tie strings. He looked like a completely different person. With the perfectly tailored suit that hugged his long legs, arms, and torso, he would have been at home in one of the big cities. Paired with his sharp, angular jawline and twinkling eyes, he was devastatingly handsome.

Sol perused her with equal intensity, and when Junior whistled teasingly from the sidelines, they both jerked their eyes away. It was getting harder to pretend they didn't feel anything beyond friendship for each other. Before Junior got the idea, Sol stepped forward and offered his arm.

"May I escort you to the dance?" He was so formal and serious that she ached. All the words from their last encounter echoed between them.

"I would be honored." She took his hand, sliding her fingers around the hard muscle of Sol's forearm. Smoothing her face of any emotion, she moved from the doorway.

Behind her, Isa stepped onto the porch.

Sol tore his eyes away from Poppy to glance at his sister, and his mouth dropped open. "Isadora, is that you?"

Raising her nose, Isa said haughtily, "You know I don't answer to that name."

"How 'bout Squirt?"

Isa straightened the hem of her skirt. "Definitely not."

Sol took a step toward Isa and chucked her under the chin. "You'll be the prettiest girl at the dance. Junior and I will have to fight the boys off with a stick. I wish Ma and Pa could see you. They'd be eating every word they said about you lookin' like a boy."

Isa revealed her white, gapped teeth in her customary quick grin, but Poppy couldn't help but notice how she avoided Junior. Or that he hadn't stopped looking at Isa since she'd stepped foot on the porch.

Clearing his throat, Junior offered, "You both look real pretty. Y'all ready to go?"

Awkwardly, he offered his arm to Isa, who hesitated before accepting it, walking through the hotel and onto the boardwalk with him in total silence.

Once the other couple was a little ahead, Sol leaned down and whispered in Poppy's ear, "You are the most beautiful thing I've ever seen. You're not leavin' my side, and I want every dance."

"Sol," she admonished softly.

They walked a block without speaking, their arms interlinked and rigid as iron. "I see you haven't changed your mind since we last talked."

"No," she whispered. *It's for your own good.* "We should dance with other people, too. Not just each other." When he didn't comment, the air grew brittle between them. She nodded at Isa's stiff back. "Besides, you need to dance with Isa. She's scared to death."

"Isa? Scared?" His obstinate skepticism turned thoughtful. "She's still not real used to dresses."

"And she's a little uncertain if she'll get asked to dance. Try not to hover or look threatening so some young man will get the gumption to ask her."

He snorted. "Junior and I talked. He'll be watching over her for me while I spark you."

"I will reject all sparking," she warned. She had never met a more stubborn man! "And what makes you so sure I'll be around to let you? Some gentleman could whisk me away for half the night."

He lowered his face to hers, brow thunderous despite his cocky grin. "I wouldn't let anyone within throwing distance of you." The green undertint made his eyes vivid against his tan skin, and they dropped to her mouth. "Your lips look so good I could just eat them up. I never wanted to kiss anyone so bad until I met you."

Poppy's head wrenched forward; Isa and Junior didn't seem to have heard. She shot him a curdling look and hissed, "Sh!" from the corner of her mouth.

He lowered his voice. "I just want to bite 'em. Did you make this dress?"

Pointedly ignoring the former statement, she said, "Mrs. Daniels and I did it last year." Her dress wasn't as off the shoulder as Isa's, but it had a deep, square neckline revealing her collarbones and shoulder blades. Her underskirt and sleeves were of matching striped material with a shimmering black taffeta overskirt and bodice. Black lace inserts gave an elegance to the sleeves and hems, matching the lacy choker at her neck, and the bow beneath her bustle was an expensive gold silk. It was the most dramatic and costly dress she owned.

And it currently felt as though it would burst into flames with the way Sol looked at her.

"I like it. I want to pull it off. Slow." His other hand came around, knuckles brushing against the smooth skin of her collarbone until it met the lace insert of her sleeve.

Breathing choppy, Poppy glanced at the other people around them. None spared them a glance. "You have to stop this."

"Why?"

"I have already told you why," she gritted.

His own teeth ground. "You can push me away, Poppy, but I'll just keep coming back."

"Like a weed?"

"Careful, shug, keep teasing me, and I'll think you love me."

Warmth spread up her chest like a breeze on an ember, lighting up from within. How could she convince him that courting her was folly?

THE DANCE HALL was a grand, long building with exposed rafters and several sections of broad double doors. As it was the end of May, all the doors were propped open, and people teemed within the hall's recesses. Lamps hung from hooks in the rafters, and fiddlers played on a raised stage in a corner. On one end of the building were tables groaning beneath the weight of refreshments, punch bowls, and endless sweets.

Sol and Junior's moods seemed to have fouled by the time they arrived, and Isa abandoned Junior's arm to cling to Poppy. They left the men behind and found a vacant bench near one of the open doorways. Warm air filtered in, and trees swayed against the twilit sky. The fiddlers started a slow, sweet song, tempting couples to file onto the dance floor.

"I'll get you two some punch," Sol muttered after Poppy and Isa had sat. He disappeared into the crowd.

Junior was quickly surrounded by a group of people, several of whom were women without partners, and Poppy watched the sparkle dim from Isa's eyes. Holding back a sigh, she caught the girl's eye and leaned closer to her on the bench.

"Remember our conversation?" Poppy's voice was firm.

Closing her eyes briefly, Isa nodded.

"Good. Now, don't look, but a young man is coming this way."

The dark-haired young man from church walked sideways between people, his face turned toward them. What had been his name? Gareth.

"Do you remember him?" Poppy whispered quickly.

"Not well. He's Mr. Glen's grandson. Garrett?"

"Gareth," Poppy hastened and tried not to laugh while Isa mouthed it. "Smile!"

Isa complied and smiled wide right as Gareth reached them. He was one of the only boys that didn't wear a stylish bowler hat, and the lamplight gleamed off his deep brown hair. Shifty eyes bespoke nerves, but his lips matched Isa's smile.

"Evenin'," he said, his voice surprisingly rich for such a young man.

"Evening," Isa parroted.

Then, they were quiet, glancing at each other, looking away, coming back for another peek. The bench trembled beneath Isa's jiggling leg, and before Gareth could open his mouth a second time, she blurted, "Would you like to dance?"

Poppy shoved her fist against her mouth to keep from laughing, hoping the boy didn't turn rude.

Gareth's grin widened. "Ain't I supposed to ask?" He held out a hand.

Smile developing into something genuine, Isa accepted it and quipped, "You were taking too long."

Together they strode off to the dance floor, still chatting. Poppy watched them, pride welling, until Junior's serge vest blocked the view of the young couple.

"Who the hell was that?" Junior's voice was unnecessarily angry, and his vivid blue eyes burned holes in the young man leading Isa in circles across the dance floor.

"That's Gareth. He's a nice young man, isn't he?" Poppy responded mildly.

"Young? He looks older than her."

She wrinkled her nose. "Not by much. I doubt he's even twenty."

A woman walked in front of Junior, purposefully slow, and was affronted when he craned his neck to see over her garish hat. He was talking under his breath, and Poppy had to strain to hear him.

"—he see she's wet behind the ears? Just because she's wearing a pretty dress doesn't mean he can..." He trailed off.

Raising her brows, Poppy suggested dryly, "Dance with her at a dance?"

The look he hurled at her was peevish. "I just meant she's young. We can't let her dance with just anyone."

Poppy stretched her back and rolled her shoulders. Her bustle belt dug into the small of her back, and she wondered if Sol got waylaid by some chatty rancher on the way to the punch table. "He's not just anyone. Lucy knows Gareth. He's Mr. Glen's grandson, and the young man moved here after losing his father. And from what I've seen," she finished defensively, "he's a polite young man and not afraid to talk to a pretty girl in a dress."

Junior finally tore his eyes from the dance floor to narrow them on her. "What's that supposed to mean?"

Fed up with his boyish immaturity, she took a page from Isa's book and spoke her mind. "It means that since her best friend will not speak to her any time she wears a dress, she decided to talk to someone who does."

Mouth opening and closing, Junior frowned but didn't come up with a defense. Instead, he gave her an accusing stare before deciding he'd rather stand off to the side, away from other people.

And her.

Equally amused and frustrated, Poppy shook her head and forgot him completely when she spied Deputy Ellis' head bobbing in her direction over a sea of people.

Feeling her stomach twist anxiously, she met him beside the dance floor.

He smiled gently at the look on her face. "I know you have questions about the German girl—"

"Her name is Alwine."

"Er, yes. And I have some answers. Why don't we take a spin around the dance floor while I tell you everything I know?"

Whatever he wished.

She took his hand and let Deputy Ellis guide her to the dance floor, the stomping of everyone's feet and the whine of the fiddle loud in her ears. The deputy nodded to several people but maintained a gravity that Poppy appreciated. It had been the same when she'd visited the sheriff on Wednesday evening to report Alwine's pregnancy. Deputy Ellis had at first been delighted to see her, but once he'd discovered she was there for business, not pleasure, he'd pulled out a notepad and remained professional during her entire statement.

As soon as they began their first spin with the fiddles, Deputy Ellis said, "After you told me that the girl came from The Dusty Rose, I asked around." She had to stand closer while they danced in order to hear him. "She's not enrolled in any schools in town, even though you said she's too young to have completed it. I stopped by The Dusty Rose and asked for the proprietor, whose name on the deed is Cash Yarbrough, but he wasn't in residence. A woman named Maude oversees the building and claims not to know of an Alwine, but I didn't believe her."

"Why didn't you believe her?"

"Well, she spoke with a strong accent, and it sounded German to me."

"And what was her name? Maude?" Poppy filed the name away to mention to Alwine later.

"Yes." Deputy Ellis nodded to another couple. "And as for the man you said...*fathered* the child," he said with utmost repugnance. "I've dug a little, and no one has come forward with any information about an 'Ace.' But," he added at her immediate slump of hopelessness, "that doesn't mean he's not out there. It's probably an alias."

"He will be a man of good standing," Poppy reminded him warily. She hadn't disclosed that she knew Ace. He believed it was information retrieved from Alwine.

"Yes, ma'am." Deputy Ellis nodded respectfully, and his smile materialized as the dance ended on a sweet note. "You're looking very well tonight, if you don't mind me saying."

Poppy had opened her mouth when a hard chest brushed against the back of her head.

"Why, thanks, Harold. I put a real effort in to look nice for you." Sol's voice was hearty and amused, but the chest behind Poppy radiated a scorching heat.

An irrational urge to laugh warred with the impulse to clout Sol for interrupting a discussion she had waited days to have. Deputy Ellis laughed and clapped Sol on the back, mistaking the crocodile smile for an honest one. They talked while Poppy stewed, and then Sol covertly slid his arm across her shoulders.

"Mind if I take the lady for a spin on the dance floor?" he asked, every tooth bared.

"Sure, sure," Deputy Ellis said. "Mrs. Daniels, it was a pleasure to—"

Sol spun Poppy away, and the rest of the deputy's words floated away, cut off by a woman in a frothy blue gown and her rotund partner.

"Sol, that was incredibly rude!" Poppy glared up at him, her hand tugging against his fruitlessly.

"Was it?" His concern was fabricated, and his toothy grin had retreated. In its place was a firm, set grimace. "I didn't think it was."

"Well, you wouldn't! You have the manners of a goat."

"You're startin' to sound like Isa." His lips curled.

"Deputy Ellis was being very helpful—"

"I'll just bet he was."

Poppy tugged harder on her hand. "I don't wish to dance with you any longer, *Mr. Williams.*"

"That's just too damned bad, *Mrs. Daniels,*" Sol ground out.

She had never felt so angry. With one last attempt to pull her hand away, she finally succeeded, but Sol grabbed her arm and whisked her to the edge of the dance floor towards the nearest open doorway. It was completely dark outside, stars and streetlights illuminating the space in an icy cold glow despite the evening's warmth. He walked her across the street, past a group of guffawing men, and into the shadows beneath a nearby store awning.

"What's got you all in a huff?" Sol demanded after he'd released her arms.

"I was speaking to Deputy Ellis about something important, and you interrupted," she said slowly as though to an imbecile.

Sol's hands gestured wildly. "What could have been so important you talked about it during a dance?"

"Ally!" Poppy hissed, glancing at the group of men nearby. They paid no mind and laughed uproariously again. "I was discussing Ally with him, if you must know."

Sol's features were clear enough for Poppy to catch his frown. He dropped his hands to his sides. "Ally? The girl that comes to the Hobbs' every day?"

"Yes, but now she's staying at the Hobbs'."

"Did something happen?"

It was the honest concern in his voice that evaporated Poppy's rancor. He weakened her knees the way he cared about people. And it was that genuine worry that persuaded her to tell Sol everything. While she spoke, he moved incrementally closer until he held her. She hadn't even realized he'd taken her in his arms until she was pressed against his front, breathing in his deliciously familiar scent.

"So, you think this man from your past, this Ace, might have something to do with Ally?" His voice was so deep it vibrated her inner ear, tickling, and she rubbed her ear against his chest to clear the feeling.

"I'm not sure," Poppy admitted softly. "There are things that remind me of him in Ally's situation. The way she has free rein, her neglected appearance, the doll. He gave me a doll, did I tell you? It was made to look like me, and it was my most treasured possession. And Ally's doll is the same, identical to her in every way except the dress."

"And you told all of this to Deputy Ellis?"

"No." Poppy lifted her head, suddenly worried. "Should I have done?"

Sol frowned and shook his head. "I don't know, shug."

"I'm not sure if I'm ready to tell anyone yet." She looked down, shame eating at her. Her nose burned, and she blinked away the irritated sensation in her eyes.

A warm, gentle finger lifted her chin up, up, up. Sol's face was bent toward hers, his eyes serious. "Hey. You don't have to tell anyone anything if you're not ready."

"What if I say something, and it turns out Ace was never here? That all these signs were just one horrible coincidence?"

"You're doing the right thing. Having too many pieces of the puzzle is better than not enough."

Tired of fighting it, Poppy rested her fingers against the proud line of his brow. "How do you always know just what to say?"

Sol's lips descended on hers, heartbreakingly soft—just as plush and tender as the kisses in the attic. Poppy's eyes burned, and she closed them, clutching him closer to her by his lapels.

A throat cleared a few feet away, and they separated guiltily.

"Yeah?" Sol asked gruffly.

"Have you seen Isa?" The tall shadow was Junior, and he sounded annoyed.

Sol reeled Poppy back into his arms, and she allowed it. He said, "She was dancing with that boy from church, last I saw."

Junior spun on his heel, dirt crunching under his boots as he strode purposefully to the dance hall.

Chapter Seventeen

Isa was having the grandest time. She had danced with Gareth three times and each of his friends at least once. At first, a derisive boy in the group had teased a short, flame-haired youth covered in freckles because Isa towered over him when they danced.

"I might be taller than him in these boots," Isa had defended the blushing young man, flashing the heels of her shoes, "but he has the lightest feet out of all of you. Do you want to dance again, Travis?"

When they returned from a do-si-do, flushed and laughing, the group had scattered except for a rigid, angry Gareth. Travis released her arm like a hot poker and melted into the crowd.

"What is it?" Isa asked Gareth right before a rough hand wrenched her around. Junior stood almost nose to nose with her, glowering like a bull about to charge.

Gareth was suddenly at her other elbow. "You want to dance again, Isa?"

Junior stood straighter, chest inflating. "What the hell did I just tell you, boy?"

Yanking Junior's tight grip from her elbow, Isa backed away until she was side by side with Gareth. "What's going on? What did he say to you?" When neither male spoke, she glanced at Gareth. The more time she had spent with him tonight, the more good-looking he had become. She liked how his lashes framed his pretty dark eyes and how he was tall enough to look her right in her eye when they danced. It was because he had danced with her that she was having such a wonderful time. Once they'd taken a few spins around the pine floor, his friends had warmed up to her, and she'd spent the whole evening doubled over in laughter.

Now, Junior had chased everyone away.

Everyone except Gareth.

Her respect for him heightened, and she tucked her hand in his arm. His brown eyes widened, and his attention skittered from the tall, threatening cowboy to her profile.

"He's not bothering you, is he?" Isa asked, ignoring Junior.

There was no time given for an answer. Isa was yanked away again, but Gareth didn't let go. For one absurd moment, she was held like a rag toy between a pair of snarling dogs.

"I don't think she wants to go with you," Gareth said, pulling on Isa's hand.

Several people turned to look, whispering low to each other. Seeing this, Isa pulled away from both of them, crossing her arms beneath her breasts. She was ignored.

"She's like a sister to me, and if I tell you to stay the hell away from her, then you'd best listen." Junior's voice was deep and menacing and totally unlike him.

Once again, she was tugged unceremoniously away, this time onto the dance floor.

"If you don't quit yanking me around like a rag doll, I am going to sock you right in the nose," Isa gritted through her teeth, mindful of the curious stares of the townspeople around them. "And I don't want to dance with you!"

"Want in one hand and spit in the other," Junior gritted back, slinging her in circles with more force than necessary. "What the hell were you thinkin', flashing your ankles, stuffing your dress? Why are you acting like some hussy?"

"Flashing my—stuffing my dress? Hussy?" So many things had spewed from his mouth that she objected to that her outraged brain couldn't think of which to address first. "How dare you!"

When she released his shoulders and made to abandon him on the dance floor, he whipped her right back around. "At least finish the dance, Izzy. People are watchin'."

"It's your own fault that you caused a scene," she hissed at him. "I don't know what you mean by it, scaring my friends off and accusing me—"

"They weren't your damned friends. They're just trying to get into your skirts!"

"Oh, just because that's all *you* care about doesn't mean that it's the only thing on other people's minds, John Junior." Her lips felt stiff and hard against her teeth, and Junior's expression was equally displeased. "And I wasn't flashing my ankles, you jackass! And what do you mean, stuffing my dress?"

He somehow managed to nod at her chest without looking directly at the cleavage displayed. "There! You can't expect no one to notice you're flat one minute and then...not the next. Why did Poppy let you do such a thing? You tryin' to look like Katherine?"

Her vision shifted to a hazy, burnt red. "I do not stuff my bodice. I wrap my bosom up when I'm wearing overalls. How could you even say such a thing? And if I look like Katherine"—she pretended to think, forcing sarcasm to drip like venom from her tongue—"maybe it's because she's my sister. Of course, we look alike!"

His dark blue eyes caught hers for the first time that day. He was taller by several inches, but Isa's boot heels made her eye level with his chin. The ever-present kerchief around his throat was black. She wanted to strangle him with it, no matter that he was finicky about people touching his neck. Whether he'd had an accident or not, he never revealed the scar or how it'd happened, but she had a darker, more ominous suspicion of the truth. Despite her rage at him, she cared about him almost more than her own self. It was a perplexing, uncomfortable sensation, particularly when he didn't feel the same way.

Except for tonight when all he displayed was anger while trying to prove he cared for her.

It felt like the opposite.

Voice hard and with an edge of finality, she said, "You better tell me you're sorry for calling me a hussy, Junior. I mean it."

His eyes, typically so pretty but now so maddening, flicked away. "You shouldn't be actin' like one."

The urge to strangle him intensified but so did the urge to cry. Nose stinging, she growled, "I'm not acting like one. You're acting like a horse's ass. Why? Because boys noticed me and wanted to dance with me—no, I don't care if you think they wanted more, they just danced and played around, and there's nothing wrong with that!"

His mouth, having opened midway through her tirade, clamped back shut.

Feeling her anger mount, she taunted lowly, "And even if I did want 'more,' it wouldn't be any of your business. I can do what I want, with who I want, when I want, where I want—" She broke off with a gasp when Junior's hand squeezed hard around hers.

He immediately loosened his grip and lowered his face inches away from hers.

"That's where you're wrong, little girl. I'm your family. Sol is a brother to me. And he and I will do whatever it takes to make sure you never end up like Katherine. No matter how mad you get at us, no matter how pretty you are when you wear dresses, we'll run off any little shit like that one over there that's got a look in their eye that says they'd like to see you flat on your back with your skirts raised."

The intensity of his words and his unblinking eyes on hers made her throat seize. Her face went red and hot, and her eyes burned. Through her tight throat, in a voice she didn't recognize as her own, she forced out, "It was just dancing."

As soon as the fiddlers drew the song to a close and began another slow waltz, she was off, breaking away from Junior's punishing hold and twining her way around colorful skirts and men's broad shoulders. She looked around for Poppy, but her friend wasn't on the bench by the side doors. Thankfully, she saw Sol outside. He was deep in conversation with Poppy, and if she wasn't so upset, Isa would have warned them that if they were trying to hide their feelings from each other, they were doing a sorry job of it.

"I'm ready to leave," she announced, breathing hard.

They took one look at her face and approached her, worried.

"What's wrong?"

Not even caring to lie, she blurted, "Junior is what's wrong. He's scared away the only friends I've made tonight. Now I want to go home."

Poppy and Sol shared a look, and her brother sighed. "All right, let me get my coat. I left it somewhere inside."

Once he was gone, Poppy gripped Isa's hands. "What did he say?"

Annoyingly, Isa's voice was still strained. She tried to clear her throat. "He said all sorts of awful, untrue things because he's an idiot. I hate him right now."

"Of course, you don't—"

"Yes, I do!" Isa cried, then lowered her voice. "He wants to ignore me all night, then when I finally find someone who wants to talk to me, he has to come up and threaten them."

"He threatened Gareth?"

"And his whole group of friends. Then, he takes me to the dance floor and tells me what a hussy I am—"

"He what!" Poppy was angry now.

"I just want to leave before he finds us." She turned as though to look for him and was surprised that he was right in their line of sight. He wasn't running after her. No, he was on the dance floor with the girl Isa hated the most.

Hattie Fowler.

Hattie wore pink ruffles again, but her dress was also off the shoulder, and even more of her skin showed than Isa's. Junior smiled down at the young woman, his charm turned all the way up. Clenching her teeth, Isa waited for Sol in breathless suspense to return with his jacket in while Junior danced with the meanest bully in Dogwood.

He knows it, too. He knows that girl is awful to me. That's why he's dancing with her.

Junior had even given her advice on how to get Hattie to leave her alone. However, his idea of a resolution was to hit Hattie right in the eye. And now, he was smiling down at the brat. When their dance was over, he looked right at Isa, caught her eye, and bent low to kiss Hattie's hand.

"Oh, that bastard," Poppy whispered at Isa's side while Isa tried to find air, which seemed to have been sucked from the room. "Isa, are you well?"

Pretending she wasn't fighting tears, Isa said as though from very far away, "I'm fine."

"Are you sure? You look...angry."

Isa finally looked away from Junior, who had just said something so hilarious that Hattie had just about broken her jaw to laugh at it. "I don't get angry," she told Poppy, her lips numb and her ears ringing. "I get even."

Without another word, Isa hurried along the side of the building of the town hall, edging through dark shadows. Behind her, Poppy nervously rushed inside to find Sol.

Mindfully blank, Isa went from doorway to doorway, searching for a tall young man with dark hair. She could find him nowhere and was too afraid to go inside at the risk of bumping into Sol or Junior. Finally, chest aching, Isa gave up and leaned against the outside wall of the building, ensconced in the darkest shadow near the back alley.

"What are you doing out here?"

The disembodied voice in the alley made her jump, and Isa stood from her slouch against the wall. The voice was familiar. Unhappy.

"Gareth?"

A figure emerged from the alley, a pale blur of a face floating in the darkness. Gareth's eyes looked like great, black pits in the shadows. Almost skull-like. Shivering, she crossed her arms in front of her.

"Oh, you remember my name." The sarcasm was another shock.

It perked something inside her, fighting away the despair she preferred to ignore anyway. "Well, I knew you weren't Travis," she answered, stepping onto the rutted dirt of the alley, sinking deeper into the black void so that her eyes could adjust. "You're too tall. Almost as tall as me."

"I *am* taller than you," he defended without heat. "Where's that Viking cowboy? He going to come outside with fists swinging because you're with me?"

That was precisely what would happen, and guilt ate at her. She liked Gareth. "Probably. I guess I'd better go inside." But when she went to turn away, his warm hand gently clasped her forearm, halting her.

"Who were you looking for a minute ago?" His voice was very close now, and Isa felt something squirm low in her belly.

"Um, you. I wanted to apologize." It was a half-truth, but now that it was out, she found that she did mourn the end of what had been a lovely night. "Junior had no right to be such a lout to you. And I told him so when he forced me to dance with him. I was having a grand time with you and your friends, and he ruined everything." She couldn't stop the outpouring of words and sealed her lips before she could further make a fool of herself.

"Oh." He still held her arm, and her breath caught when his hand trailed down to hold her hand.

She had never held hands with anyone before.

It made her heart beat all funny inside her chest, the feel of his fingers against hers. Isa was afraid her sweaty palm would disgust him. He spoke, and she blinked at him in the darkness. "I've been wanting to talk to you for a while. Since I moved here, I reckon."

He laughed wryly at himself.

"When did you move here? I live an hour away, so I've only seen you around once or twice." She stepped closer.

"About a month ago. You wore overalls and sat in the library, reading a book about this thick." He spread his fingers about four inches within her hand, and she laughed. Then, she stopped laughing because he said, "I like the way you look in them."

Swallowing hard, she repeated idiotically, "In my overalls?"

"Yeah. You looked fun. And real pretty."

"Oh." Somehow, all the thoughts and intellect she knew she possessed flew away at his words, fluttering around in the wind. She couldn't form a single interesting sentence and settled for, "Thank you."

"Isa." This time, he stepped so close she could feel the movements of his chest against her bosom. Everything was pure sensation. Unable to see more than shadows, she could only feel his warmth, smell the wool of his black vest, the faint scent of punch on his breath. "Would it be all right if I kissed you?"

She should say no. The only person she had wanted to kiss for years had just put his lips all over Hattie Fowler's foul hand. She didn't want his spoiled lips anywhere near hers, not anymore. Bolstered by this, some of her brain function woke up enough for her to close the distance between them. "Are you going to ask, or are you going to do it?"

When he leaned in to kiss her, her *first kiss*, she could feel his lips smiling.

Most surprising of all was that she liked it.

"WHERE THE HELL is Isa?"

Sol looked up from Poppy's worried blue eyes to Junior's furious ones. They stood outside, but Isa had disappeared. Poppy was moments away from explaining why Isa wanted to go home when Junior stormed through the open doorway.

"We were just about to find her." Sol's tone revealed a bit of surprise at Junior's anger, and he observed his friend carefully shield some of the burning emotion in his eyes.

"You told me to look out for her, now she's gone." Junior said it as though it were Sol's fault.

"She's sixteen years old," Sol laughed. "Not six. She'll be all right. She knows well enough not to walk to the hotel alone."

With a growl of frustration, Junior turned on his heel and strode along the building, watching people in one doorway, frustration tautening his posture, before moving to the next.

Junior was more of a scold than his own pa. A small hand on his arm broke Sol's amused stare.

"Sol," Poppy began, urging Sol to follow Junior. "I think we ought to find Isa before he does."

"Why do you say that?"

What the hell had happened while he was grabbing his suit jacket?

"Because I think Isa is going to do something to purposefully anger Junior—"

"You son of a bitch!" Junior shouted, followed by a shriek and the smack of flesh hitting flesh.

"Shit," Sol muttered, bursting into motion toward the black gloom of the alley. Junior was a dark gray smear straddling someone on the ground while Isa shoved at him.

"Get off him, Junior!" Isa's voice was shrill and outraged.

"Damn it, Isa, watch out." Sol grunted, pulling her away in order to hook Junior's biceps with his arms, dragging him off the thrashing figure from the ground.

Damn, he's strong!

"Are you hurt?" Isa asked, helping what turned out to be Mr. Glen's grandson from the dirt in the alley. "I'm so sorry, Gareth!"

"It's okay," the boy replied, panting. He spat in the dirt, a shaft of light across his and Isa's youthful faces. Gareth grinned at Isa. "It was worth it."

Junior strained against his friend's hold. Sol grunted and said, not unkindly to the boy, "You'd better clear out before he breaks loose."

After a challenging glance at Junior, who muttered threats at Gareth, Poppy managed to gently send the young man on his way toward the other end of the building. Isa waited until he was out of earshot before she rushed forward, shoving Junior hard on his chest, nearly knocking Sol over.

"How could you?"

"That little bastard had his hands all over you," Junior spat, shrugging Sol's arms off.

"He did not! We were just kissing."

"And why the hell were you kissing some boy in the dark, huh?" Junior's voice throbbed with anger, and Sol steadied him.

"Let's just calm down—"

Isa blew up. "Oh, you can kiss all over Hattie Fowler's hand, but I can't kiss a boy who has only ever been nice to me? You're such a hypocrite."

"Watch what you're callin' me," Junior warned, pointing a finger at her.

She slapped it out of her face. "And a fool." She sobbed it. "You ruined everything."

With that, she turned and fled down the opposite end of the alley.

"I'll get her," Poppy said and took off after her, calling her name.

Taking a deep, bracing breath, Sol folded his arms and looked at Junior's stiff back. "What a goddamned mess."

SOL DIDN'T SEE either Junior or Isa until they rode home together the following morning.

No one bothered to go to church for the second time that month, and Isa and Junior rode on either side of Sol, two wooden fence posts on horses. Sol's mood was low. Poppy had stayed up half the night with Isa, and he hadn't had the chance to sneak up to her attic room to make amends like he'd planned. That morning, when he'd checked on her, she was fast asleep. Poppy hadn't stirred when he'd kissed her cheek, so he'd reluctantly left a note on her bedside table before leaving.

Now, he would give anything to be at the hotel, slipping into bed with her.

Not that she would welcome him. She had been adamant that they go their separate ways even after she'd allowed his kiss under the awning.

I'll never understand women.

Uncharacteristically moody, Sol stared between his horse's ears.

"Isa, you comin' to the ranch with us or staying at Sol's?" Junior finally asked after several miles of stilted silence.

"None of your business," Isa said coldly.

Sol closed his eyes.

Here we go.

"Why are you being so bratty? Got a bee in your bonnet?"

Isa's words were a sneer. "I don't wish to talk to you, which I thought was perfectly clear after your actions last night."

It wasn't unusual for these two to argue or fight with each other. Since Isa was old enough to tag along with Sol, his friend and his little sister went after each other like cats and dogs. And if they weren't fighting, they were playing. But as they grew older, and the tongue in Isa's mouth sharper, her wits more honed, Sol knew he needed to nip it in the bud before it became a real problem.

Sol sighed long-sufferingly and reasoned, "Let's cool down some before we get riled up again."

"Nah, let her say what she has to say." Junior's voice rose. "Go ahead, *Isadora*, tell me how my actions were wrong."

"Jesus, there it is," muttered Sol, scrubbing his eyes.

As though waiting for the opportunity, Isa turned in her saddle so Junior couldn't help but hear every word. "What *didn't* you do that was wrong is the better question, *John*."

"All I did was watch out for you while Sol sparked Lucy's friend, how's that so bad?"

"You scared my new friends away, for one." Isa's color was rising, twin spots in her cheeks that made her golden skin ruddy.

Junior snorted and shifted in his saddle. "A bunch of horny toads aren't friends."

"They were funny and they danced with me, and I'm pretty sure I could have taken any of them in wrestling. There was no need for you to butt your big nose in my affairs."

"You sound just like Lucy when you talk like that," he jeered at her across Sol's horse.

Her lip curled back from her teeth. "Good. I'm glad I do. And I hope it makes you want to rip your ears off so I don't have to do it for you."

The ears she spoke of turned steadily redder. "None of that stuff would have happened last night if you had found some female friends to bandy with, not some group of boys lookin' down your bodice and watchin' you flash your ankles."

"What—" Sol started, increasingly worried at this talk.

He was ignored.

"For the hundredth time, I was not showing off my ankles or bosom, you idiot!" she shouted at him.

"Well, if I'm an idiot, then you're a hussy!" he shouted back.

Sol sat up straight, eyes wide. "Whoa, whoa—"

He was ignored again.

"And wouldn't it take one to know one?" Isa's eyes were flashing sparks, her face set in an ugly grimace that warned of impending danger. All their horses had stopped, and Sol glanced back and forth between the two.

"What's that supposed to mean?" Junior's eyes narrowed. Both leaned precariously away from their saddles to shout at each other.

"It means *you* are the whore! Not me! I've kissed one boy in my whole life, and you've kissed hundreds of girls, don't think I haven't heard all those vile stories you tell the other ranch hands. And Gareth likes me. He told me so right before he kissed me, before you ruined it. And the only woman that's ever really liked you is your mother, and considering you're a no-good son of a *bitch*, that's not saying much!"

And, digging her heels into her horse's sides, she rode off hell-bent for leather.

White-faced, Junior watched her ride away, jaw working, then wheeled his horse and galloped off in the direction of his house.

It was beyond obvious now that Sol had missed some critical information about last night's dance. More tired than curious, and worried about Isa, he galloped toward home.

He found her holed up in her room.

Knocking, he said through the door, "Isa, come out and tell me what in the world that was about."

"Go away." Isa's words sounded clogged.

Sighing, he tried again. "What happened? I'm the one that asked Junior to watch out for you, so really, it's my fault your dance was ruined."

"You can't blame yourself and make excuses for everyone, Sol," Isa said, her voice clearer. "You never would have acted like that. He was being horrible, and it was his choice to act that way. Not yours."

"Legs—"

"And I decided I don't want to go to Ma's while you're gone on your trip with Mr. Stone. I want to stay with Poppy at the hotel."

"Oh. I can ask Poppy if she's up for—"

"I already spoke to her last night. She told me I was welcome to share the attic room with her if Mr. Ricci didn't mind. And he doesn't. I asked him this morning."

The discussion left him feeling impotent.

He tried one more time. "Isa—"

"Just...go away. I want to be alone."

Strangely hurt, he backed away from the door and left her.

ISA IMMERSED HERSELF in helping out at the hotel, whether lending a hand in the kitchens, waitressing at the diner, or washing the linens. Gareth showed up almost every day on the back porch, asking if he could help her when she churned butter or washed sheets. Sol was watchful but didn't see anything wrong with his sister having a beau and wondered why Junior was so hostile about the idea. He would have asked Poppy, but she stayed hidden in Mrs. Hobb's upstairs apartment with Francesca.

Junior was absent for days, working on houses across the county with a local contractor.

Meanwhile, Isa buried her nose in books when she wasn't working and sent letters to universities with Ms. Pickney's help. She was determined to be the first woman in the county to go to a real college.

For Sol, it was a period of mourning. Isa's childhood trickled away, taking with it dips in the creek, fishing, and spontaneous wrestling matches. She'd stopped wearing overalls since the dance, choosing instead to wear the dresses Poppy had sewn for her. She even sewed her own dresses, a patient student under Poppy's willing tutelage. He hadn't seen her in braids for so long that he forgot what she'd looked like without her hair in an elegant updo.

The last thing he wanted to do was leave for several weeks while the woman he wanted to marry and the sister he loved acted too busy for him. When he rode off with Ben and a herd of horses, he didn't even get a chance to tell Isa or Poppy goodbye.

Chapter Eighteen

Mrs. Hobb clomped down the stairs, weeping. Poppy was a little startled to see the brash, gargantuan woman cry. "Mrs. Hobb? What's wrong?"

"It's Ally. She's gone!"

Fear leaped froglike from Poppy's stomach to her throat, and she croaked, "Has someone taken her?"

"No, she ran off." Mrs. Hobb's sobs increased in volume. "I think she was scared off. Franny said Ally was trying to pet the cat, and so Franny hollered at her. It must o' scared her something fierce because she grabbed her doll and ran downstairs. By the time I went to check on her, she was gone. Left the storage door wide open. Me and Franny rowed somethin' awful."

"Did this happen this morning?"

"First thing."

"And she hasn't come back?"

"No," Mrs. Hobb sniffed. "Ally could tell that her bein' here with us upset Franny, but I tried to keep her in the storage room with me as much as I could. But Franny...you know how she gets. I'd be careful goin' upstairs," she warned, dabbing beneath her eyes with her ham-sized hands. "She ain't fit for company."

Nodding, Poppy took the stairs two at a time and ground to a halt at the sewing room doorway.

Francesca stood with her back to the door, writing on fabric with chalk. A bulky robe encased her wrapper, and her veil was long and dark. How the woman could even see out of it was a mystery. An occasional sniff erupted from behind it.

"What happened?"

"Mama told you," Francesca said hoarsely. Defensively. "I heard the two of you downstairs talking about me."

"But there's no sense to it, Franny. Why frighten a child who was just petting a cat?"

"Because she followed Button into my *room* to pet her, that's why!"

Ah.

Not even Poppy was allowed into the recesses of Francesca's room. It was as shadowy and mysterious a place as the face beneath the veil.

And yet...

"That was still no reason to scare her half to death," Poppy reasoned.

Francesca suddenly whirled, shearing scissors in hand. Poppy uncrossed her arms and smoothed her face to hide her alarm. "You think I frightened her on purpose, Poppy? I didn't! I wasn't wearing my veil, and she saw me, *the real me*. She screamed, and I told her to get out, get out, *get out!*"

Pity and understanding clashed with Poppy's fear for Alwine. "I'm truly sorry that happened, Franny." She braced herself. "But Ally is in danger, and this is the safest place for her. It's important she comes back—"

"Well, I hope she never comes back!" Francesca shouldered past Poppy to disappear into the fabric room. Everything looked the same except for a sad, empty cot in the corner.

"How can you say that?" Poppy followed, brows low. "She's just a little girl, and she's in dire straits. For someone to get a girl her age in the family way...she needs a loving family to care for her, to help her learn how to operate in the real world."

"That may be, but why must it always be my family? We have enough to do as it is. Let her take charity from someone else."

"What a selfish thing to say," Poppy blurted and tried to circle the rack to see the other woman. "That poor child cannot help how she was raised. She needs help. And who better to help than us?"

"We have helped someone in need already. You. Why should we have to undergo the challenge twice? We can't just pick up every beggar from the street and open our home to them. This material room...this is my room. I need it for my business." Francesca's voice rose incrementally from behind the material rack. "And Mother put her in it knowing how much my business means to me."

It was as though a very large fist had smacked into Poppy's solar plexus. They had already helped someone like Alwine.

Her.

How could she have forgotten?

A hot, burning feeling took over her senses. She was sixteen, holding a crust of bread, rejected. Unwanted. Angry words flared through her guts and up into her mouth, bursting out.

"Is that what you truly think? That Mrs. Hobb betrayed you by helping a child?"

Fabric continued to rustle, but Francesca said nothing.

"Is that how you felt about me when I was young? That I was a beggar and no good?"

Silence. Then, "You were different."

"No." Poppy's voice rose. All the anger she'd felt since hearing Mrs. Williams' thoughtless words, reliving her past with Sol, and denying that they suited despite wanting to marry him more and more with each passing day—it all came spilling out. "I was not different. I was just as poor and unloved and wretched as that little girl who left this morning. The best thing that ever happened to me was the care given to me by Lucy's family and your family. And now you would deny another child that same care and affection!"

"My mother has someone to love. Me!" Francesca's voice was shrill. Girlish.

"That's not how you measure love!" Poppy cried, still speaking to the rows and rows of fabrics behind which the other woman hid. "They can love you, clothe you, feed you, and do everything for you and still help another person. Why you despise this girl so much is beyond me. You know nothing of what it's like out there. Nothing! It's horrible. There are places children should never be, and Ally has to go home to one every day. You'd never know because you won't leave this house. You won't even go outside! You have no idea what it's like to be hungry, to be taken advantage of by other people."

Francesca's only answer was a deep, muffled sob.

Poppy didn't feel like crying, and she ignored the rising pity. Instead, she felt furious, reckless, and more alive than she'd ever felt before. Her lungs bellowed, starving for air she couldn't seem to get enough of, hands clenched into fists. "You may allow others to take care of all your needs, but Alwine has a dignity that you lack—even when she's begging. I'm going to find her, and when I do, I will pay for her room in the hotel myself. May you be happy with your rooms all to yourself again. Goodbye, Franny."

She turned and raced downstairs, ignoring Mr. and Mrs. Hobb's wide, questioning eyes behind the counter. Muttering that she was going for a walk, she hung up her sewing apron in the storage room and strode out the door.

Deputy Ellis had said that Alwine lived in The Dusty Rose with a woman named Maude. She asked three separate strangers in stores where she could find such a residence before someone pointed the way, looking subtly scandalized.

The brothel wasn't difficult to find. It used to be one of the finest houses in Dogwood until the Civil War when Union soldiers ransacked it and drove the family out. There it had sat for two decades, abandoned with empty windows, until a stranger came along with a lawyer and full pockets, claiming the home with squatter laws.

Poppy stopped in front of the broken, rotten picket fence that encircled the ramshackle old two-story's front yard. Two bedraggled women on a porch bench mirrored the state of the listing house with its peeling paint and missing shutters. When Poppy gathered her courage and stepped onto the property, the two women hastily stood and disappeared inside. Not to be deterred, she stiffened her spine and climbed the steps. Her fist was raised to knock when a dark, hulking shadow appeared behind the screen door. Dancing backward, she barely missed getting hit in the face as a heavyset woman surged out of it like a tempestuous ocean swell.

"What you want?" the woman demanded in broken English, her face hard and timeworn as a cabin plank.

Raising her chin despite the hostile swells emanating from the woman, Poppy said in a clear, loud voice, "I am looking for a girl named Alwine. Is she here?"

The woman's beady eyes were sunk deep within the fat folds of her face, and she gave Poppy a once-over. The sneer became an ugly smile, revealing broken and missing teeth. "You work?"

Eyes narrowing at the odd question, Poppy couldn't hide her dislike for this woman. "I am a seamstress, yes, I work. Where is Alwine?"

"You work here," the woman continued as though she hadn't spoken, eyes calculating. "Men pay big money. *Ja*, you make big money here, work for me. Pretty. Young."

Her cackling laugh sent needles of revulsion through Poppy. She was getting nowhere with this woman. Taking a risk, she leaned to the side, peered into the darkness of the door's torn screen and cried, "Alwine! Alwine, come out, come back to *Frau* Hobb!"

A meaty hand shoved her hard. Stumbling backward, windmilling her arms, Poppy managed to find her footing and hopped from the first step to the ground rump-first. Thankfully, her bustle cushioned her fall and saved her bottom from most of the impact. She glared up impotently until the woman began to waddle after her, steps creaking and threatening to snap. Poppy clambered up gracelessly, flitting backward into the yard toward the road. The two women from the bench watched, open-mouthed, from an open upstairs window.

Seeing them, Poppy shouted up, "Tell Alwine to go to *Frau* Hobb's. *Frau* Hobb!"

A rock sailed past her, just missing her left ear.

"Get gone!" shouted the woman. "Leave! *Neugierige Hündin*!"

An answering cry from the back of the house made Poppy's heart leap with joy.

"Ally!" she screamed, dodging past the lunging woman toward the backyard.

Alwine and another woman were struggling near a cellar entrance, and though the older woman was larger and stronger, Alwine fought like a wildcat.

Poppy had never seen anyone use a porcelain doll as a weapon, but it was proving to be a good deterrent.

Poppy didn't think. She sprinted in hard, furious steps, thrusting out her palm in one hard motion into the center of the surprised, angry woman's face. Blood gushed. The woman screamed and released Alwine to clutch her nose.

Poppy grabbed Alwine's hand and pulled.

"Run!" she shrieked, and Alwine must have understood because it was as though wings had taken flight on the girl's bare feet.

They rounded the woman woman coming around from the front who sweated and panted after them with fistfuls of rocks, yelling insults. Poppy and Alwine ran as though their lives depended on it, skirts in hand and bare legs pumping. A stone struck the base of Poppy's spine, but it bounced harmlessly off her rigid stays. For once, her imprisoning corsets and bustles were an armor she was grateful for.

They didn't stop running for a mile, constantly checking behind them. They didn't even stop when they reached Dogwood.

Poppy's lungs were afire, and the stitch in her side had doubled her over by the time they reached the general store. They rushed into the storage room. She released Alwine's hand, rubbing the feeling back into her fingers, and engaged all the locks on the door. Their harsh breathing was loud in the room, and Mrs. Hobb's shadow darkened the doorway which connected to the front room.

"Ally!" Mrs. Hobb hustled forward and embraced Alwine. Tears streamed down both faces.

It took Poppy, Mrs. Hobb, Isa, and the help of the German/English dictionary to convince Alwine to stay at the general store. Mrs. Hobb wouldn't hear of Poppy paying for a room and set up a private screen in a corner of the storage room. She nestled the cot behind it along with a washstand and water in a pitcher, and finally, Alwine was content.

The girl refused to go upstairs. She peered up at the floor above her with frightened eyes, murmuring the same word repeatedly.

"She's saying 'ghoul,'" Isa whispered to Poppy later after poring through the open dictionary. "She says a ghoul lives upstairs and it frightened her."

Poppy's lips tightened. She said nothing despite Isa's curious stare.

Francesca's secrets were not hers to tell.

HER FEET ACHED.

The heeled, mid-calf lace-up black boots were not made to be run in.

Poppy wondered if her toes would be bloody when she got around to unlacing them. Limping through the hotel's back door after dark, she half-hoped not to run into anyone when Minnie strode out of the kitchen door.

Astute brown eyes, so dark they appeared black, took one look at Poppy and narrowed. "Lord, you look like something the cat dragged in. Get in here, let me make you a cup of coffee. You hungry?"

Forgoing the bliss of doffing her pinching shoes, Poppy allowed Minnie to cosset her and told the woman everything.

Whistling at the clean-scrubbed worktable, Minnie said, "You best not go back there. That's trouble with a capital 'T.'"

"I will if Alwine runs off again."

"No ma'am, you sho won't." Minnie wagged a finger at Poppy. "You'll get that deputy or the sheriff and let them do their job."

Poppy's mouth twisted, the roast she was chewing suddenly too soft, like mush in her mouth. She forced herself to swallow and chased it with hot coffee, burning her tongue. Minnie tutted under her breath.

"Look at you. You as stubborn as my Lucy-girl, you just hide it better'n a poker player."

"I'm nothing like Lucy," Poppy denied gently. "She's brave and strong. I'm not."

Minnie sighed and pulled a hidden wooden stool from beneath the worktable. Poppy wasn't sure if she'd ever caught Minnie sitting before. "You don't have to be a spitfire like Lucy to be brave and strong. Don't they say somethin' about still waters runnin' deep? That's you. You're just as strong, just as brave. A fighter."

"I fought today, but it unsettled me." Poppy looked down at her mug and rotated it, watching the wavering lines of the dark brew within. "I was frightened." So frightened that she felt disgusted about it now.

"What makes you think bein' scared is the same as bein' a coward?" Poppy's eyes whipped up.

Minnie leaned forward and braced herself on her slender forearms. "You're sittin' here, sad about everything you think you're not instead of celebrating everything you *are*." She laid a long-fingered hand on Poppy's. Squeezed it. "You're special, Poppy. Just look at you, startin' over all on your lonesome. Got a business, got a talent, got lots of people that love everything about you. And you've never treated a one wrongly."

Mouth pinching, Poppy averted her eyes from Minnie's kind old face. "Oh, but I have, Minnie. I was awful to Franny today. And I don't know how I can bear to look at myself."

She told Minnie about her ugly words to Francesca that morning and chewed her nails, breaking a third one off at the nail bed. It would need filing before bed.

But Minnie didn't seem to agree with her. "Now, I've done talked to Mizz Hobb enough to know that Franny's still just a little girl in a lot o' ways that count. She stopped comin' downstairs at seventeen and stayed that age ever since. What you told her was somethin' she needed to hear, and bad. But it ain't easy to be the messenger, yes, ma'am, I know that's right." She patted Poppy's hand and sipped her coffee, her dark eyes shrewd. "Now...why don't you tell me about you and Sol?"

"What about me and Sol?"

"Just that I've never seen that boy so wild about a person, but the both of you circle around each other like you're dyin' and he's the undertaker."

Poppy put her face in her hands and laughed humorlessly. "What did you put in this coffee, Minnie? A truth potion?"

Minnie cackled. "I ain't no witch, but I've got eyes, don't I?"

When Poppy finally lowered her hands, her eyes were fever-bright, her mouth unsmiling. "He wants to marry me, but I've said no."

"Whoo-wee, he works fast, don't he?" Minnie sobered. "You don't like him that way, is that what it is?"

"No, I do, and I think you know that." Poppy grimaced, mouth pinched and small while she thought. "I care for him very much. He makes me feel...happy. Happy and alive and good about myself. It's wonderful."

"But..."

"But I don't deserve him, Minnie," Poppy whispered. She hid her trembling mouth behind the rim of her mug. "He's kind and good, and everyone loves him. If I marry him and the town finds out about my past—"

"Codswallop," cried Minnie. She sat straight and braced her hands on the table. "That's balooey if I've ever heard it. Why, everyone's got a past, chile. Everyone's got secrets, stuff they ain't so proud of. But you, you don't have nothing to be ashamed of."

"People are cruel, they'll talk—"

"Oh, I reckon I know some about people's cruelty."

Poppy's mouth clicked shut. Shame swelled. A dry, cool hand rested atop hers again.

"Now, I told you before that you weren't no coward. Not for other people. But I don't want you to be a coward to yourself. If you don't reach out and take what you want, what you deserve—like happiness—then you're doin' something real shameful. You're denyin' yourself a little piece of good in the world. All because of somethin' you had no power over, hm?"

Throat working, Poppy nodded and squeezed Minnie's hand.

"Now, I know that cowboy will be back on this doorstep as soon as he and Mistah Stone get back, but before he does, I want you to think about something."

"What?" Poppy croaked.

"I want you to picture that you're sittin' next to a little girl. She has pretty blue eyes and freckles and is sweet as a peach. Now, this girl's had a rough life. Lived in saloons and been in the dirtiest, roughest places in the state." Poppy wiped her eyes. "If she were to tell you that she wanted a family one day, a husband that made her happy and would never hurt her, what would you tell her?"

"I would—I would tell her that she would have one." Her throat hurt. It made it difficult to speak. "Gerald."

"No, no, you've got to tell her the truth, Poppy. You tell her that her first husband dies, and she moves to her old town. But there's another man, a good man that makes her laugh, who asks for her hand and wants to give her a second chance at a happy marriage. Would you tell that little girl that she wasn't worthy of him? That she could have that first husband because no one in town knew her, but this one wasn't allowed?"

Poppy shook her head rapidly.

"Then why are you punishin' her, sweetheart?"

Eyes flaring, Poppy choked out, "I'm not. I'm different now than I was then."

"That's where you're wrong." Minnie looked sad and kind all at once. "You and that little girl are one and the same."

Chapter Nineteen

Sol sat on his horse in front of Hound Dog Saloon and wondered what he was doing.

He hadn't been home in two weeks, but he'd wasted half a day's travel to ride to Lufkin. The memory of the last time he'd made this trip had left him with a bitter aftertaste. All too aware that he had dismounted in front of a saloon in the middle of the day, Sol sighed and tied up his roan gelding. He hadn't day drunk since he was a dumb kid, and the thought of sitting in a dark, seedy bar with a lot of other drunk men didn't appeal to him.

He'd rather be in Dogwood bothering Poppy.

It wasn't crowded in the saloon, and Sol planted his behind on a stool facing the narrow staircase. The two women he saw were neither tall nor blonde enough to be his sister. Out of all the Williams children, Katherine was the best-looking. Except maybe Isa. The two looked more alike every day.

And both couldn't be more different.

"What'll it be?" asked a man with a thick black mustache and a stained apron from behind the bar.

Knowing better than to ask for water, Sol dug in his pocket for his worn leather wallet. "Beer, this early."

Mustache twitching in easy humor, the bartender reached for a mug.

"You know where Katherine is?" He hoped to God that she still worked here.

"Kat? Upstairs. Want me to call one of them over?" The man nodded to the women sitting near a group of men playing cards. One of them cannily glanced up as though sensing his attention.

Holding up a staying hand, Sol shook his head and muttered, "No thanks, I'll just wait here for her."

Sol was halfway through his second beer when Katherine finally flounced downstairs, head thrown back in laughter. It made his guts twinge, knowing what she'd been doing, especially when he saw that her customer was as old as their pa. He remembered when they were kids and how she was always laughing, running through the corn fields, playing and hiding instead of working. But no one could stay mad at Katherine for long. She had received the least amount of whoopings of the Williams children and had her daddy and brothers wrapped around her fingers. She could have been anything with all that charisma, could have done anything she'd wanted, but had instead turned that charm on all the young, available men in the neighborhood. He remembered the fights that broke out because of her, how her eyes had lit up when one man beat another to a pulp in the churchyard one Sunday. His mother had cried into her handkerchief while Katherine's smile had spread wide across her face, cheeks tinged with pink.

Familiar feelings of suppressed anger at his sister's choice of lifestyle soured his expression, and he pushed his warm beer away. Arms crossed on the bartop, he watched his sister pocket a wad of bills in the area between her half-exposed breasts. Like their mother, she was well-endowed, and he grimaced at all the skin that she was showing. At least she had a dress on instead of her undergarments.

Something about the shape of her dress caused his frown to deepen, and an awful, helpless anger rose in him.

She was pregnant.

Again.

Katherine glanced up as though detecting his censure from where she stood. Her smile only flickered for an instant before it widened, and she sashayed his way. When she tapped the bartop with one finger, the bartender wordlessly supplied a shot glass of whiskey. She threw back the shot, licked her lips, and winked at the bartender before rounding the corner of the bar to sit beside Sol.

"Sol! To what do I owe this pleasure?" The liquor fumes on her breath made him sick to his stomach. Up close, she looked haggard and drunk, despite her energetic tone.

He didn't think about his words, just snarled them out like he had no sense. "How can you keep doing this?"

Expression souring, she asked, "Do what—oh, this?" She waved a hand over the rounded stomach he was glaring at. "Yes, a product of the trade. But it's surprisingly good for business." She leaned closer and waggled her eyebrows. "Men like knowing you're already knocked up, makes 'em feel better about being unfaithful to their wives 'cause at least they're not planting their bastard in you. And some"—her eyes slid to the bartender at the other end of the bar—"some of 'em like thinking the baby in you is theirs."

Sol shoved two fingers deep into his ears. "God above, I don't wanna hear this."

Katherine's laugh was husky, malicious, much different from the delighted bray she used to have as a child. Several heads turned their way, and Sol took his fingers out of his ears, hating them all. In the shadows of a darkened corner, a child of about ten bussed a table. He imagined that child as Poppy, with her carefully blank face and heartbreakingly sad blue eyes. That accustomed knot formed again in his throat, and he cruelly swallowed it down.

"This is no place to raise a child. Haven't you learned how to...stop that from happening?"

Shrugging a bare shoulder, Katherine tapped the bar again. "I've tried, but what works for others doesn't seem to work for us fertile Williams offspring." She downed the whiskey that seemed to magically appear, not sparing another glance at the hopeful, mustachioed man. "Look at Ma. Popped 'em out every two years like clockwork."

"Yeah, but she was married."

"And that's the difference, isn't it?"

Voice growing colder, Sol leaned in, "The difference is she took care of us, and we were loved. We weren't holed up in a dark saloon full of drunkards and hussies."

Katherine's laugh sprouted harsh edges, and her brown eyes snapped. "As I remember it, big brother, our childhood was nothing special. I had one dress every three years, and I wore boy's shoes. We didn't have two pennies to rub together; half the year, we lived off vegetables and no meat. That boy over there"—she pointed at the boy holding an armful of glass mugs—"he makes more money in tips sometimes than our own pa did breaking his back. He eats like a king, and those clothes he's wearin' aren't secondhand. Now you tell me, which sounds better to you?"

Sol's nose was so pinched his nostrils went white. "They did the best they could, Kat."

"And I'm doing the best *I* can," she hissed at him, and for the first time, her eyes revealed some of the emotion she felt. Leaning back in the high-backed stool, she regarded him unhappily. "How's Isadora? Still walkin' around in Drew's old overalls? Ain't she full-grown now?"

"She's livin' with me at my house and already finished school a whole year ahead of everyone else her age. And she's wearin' dresses now and is the prettiest thing you've ever seen."

For some reason, the latter curled Katherine's lip, and her attractiveness disappeared; she was almost ugly. Was she jealous of her own sister? It wouldn't surprise him.

"Is this why you came, Sol?" she drawled. "To preach to me, try to make me feel bad?"

Taking a calming breath, trying to remember that she was his sister and that he loved her, he declared, "I came to check on you. We've been hearing a lot of talk about girls goin' missing. I wanted to tell you to be careful. Or warn you. Heck, I don't know. You're my sister, Katherine, not my enemy. I don't want anything bad to happen to you. Not ever."

For a moment, his words crumbled the wall encasing her features. Glancing around, she leaned forward and whispered, "I've been hearin' stuff, too. The deputy came by a while back, told us girls to be careful. 'Specially the young ones."

"Has anyone gone missing here?" he asked, curious.

Eyebrows raising, causing a deep wrinkle to crease her forehead, she huffed an incredulous laugh. "No, but hasn't anyone told you? All the girls missing are from saloons and bawdy houses. Every one of 'em."

"They told us. We've got a curfew to keep the women and girls safe. I hope you've been careful. There's no tellin' what types of men come in here." He made to take one of her hands, but she shifted imperceptibly away. Hurt made it hard to swallow, so he grabbed his beer tankard instead.

"Yeah, well, I'm a little older than the girls that go missin'. Plus, no one would steal any girls from here, or the boss would—" Her brown eyes flicked up, her face shuttered.

Glancing over, Sol noticed a well-dressed man leaning back in his chair, watching their every move. He wasn't young or particularly handsome, but everything about him screamed money and danger. A Colt winked at his belt. His eyes glued to Katherine and remained there, his look hard.

"Who's that?" he asked lightly, taking a sip of tepid beer.

"My boss-man," Katherine muttered, a frown that was more of a pout than anything on her lips. "I can't keep talkin' to you. I need to get back to work."

Laying a staying hand on her arm, Sol pleaded, "Wait. Just come back home with me. You can stay at my house until you get back on your feet. If you want, get yourself a decent job, and have your baby at home with a good doctor. You can start over. Let us help you. Please."

Katherine was already clamming up, her attention darting back to the man across the room with the hard eyes. "There's nothin' wrong with the life I have now," she sneered, sliding from the stool. Her words were defensive. "I make a good living and want for nothing. The clothes I wear are nicer than any the people back home could ever hope to have. Why, I'm practically rich compared to them. Just go home, Sol. Don't worry about me. I always fend for myself."

Watching her trounce off hollowed Sol's stomach, and when she sat in her boss's lap to give him a long, passionate kiss, he couldn't bear to watch. Leaving a dollar bill on the counter, he shoved his hat back on and strode out.

Beneath the defensiveness, she had seemed scared. For herself or for him? He told himself he didn't give a damn, but he was lying.

And beneath all that worry for her was a deep, unsettling disappointment at her obvious loyalty to people who were as worthless as a shit stain on a pair of trousers. Her selfishness. She claimed she was thriving because she had pretty clothes and good food.

She displayed no sympathy at being pregnant again.

And not even once had she asked about her children.

HE DIDN'T REMEMBER the trip back to Dogwood.

All he knew was Copper was put up in the darkening stables behind the Dogwood Hotel, and his boots were climbing the family stairs up to the attic. Poppy sat at her desk blowing on a fresh painting, her fingers colored with reds, golds, and blacks. She looked vibrant and lovely in a burgundy and pink dress, curls haloing the intricate twists of her hair. At his footsteps, she turned, took one look at his face, and rose to her feet.

"What is it?" she asked, meeting him in the center of the room. "What's wrong?"

He walked into her arms, and she didn't hesitate. She enfolded him in an embrace and stroked his back. "I can't do it. I can't keep away." He pulled back and cradled her face with his big, awkward hands. "I wish I could fix this."

"Sol—" Her voice was soft. Beloved.

"I went to Lufkin and visited my sister," he interrupted. "Katherine."

"You did?" Sol didn't say more, and her teeth worried her lip. "Here, sit down. Tell me everything."

He allowed her maneuvering and sat on her bed while she brought the chair around and sat, watching him expectantly. With a long, weary sigh, he told her everything. "After talking to you about the places you grew up in and everything the sheriff and deputy said, I got worried about Kat. I needed to check on her, make sure she was okay. Let her know that girls were goin' missing. But when I got there…"

He left nothing out. The dirty old man that his sister had been upstairs with, the round pregnant belly, the drinking. It felt good to tell someone else. Katherine was someone his pa avoided talking about and that his ma enjoyed talking about *too* much. Having someone just listen for once was restful. When he got to the end when he'd offered to bring his sister home, to help her, Poppy released a deep sigh.

"She wouldn't come home," he said, still not fathoming it. "I even offered to support her."

"She sounds a lot like my mother," Poppy admitted after a few seconds' reflection. "No matter how I tried to convince her to make a living doing something else or get help from a church until we both found employment, she wouldn't have it."

"I don't understand it." He frowned.

"You cannot make people's choices for them," Poppy whispered. "They have to want it for themselves."

Sick at heart, he nodded, wanting to forget the failure of his day. He watched abstractedly as she picked the dried paint from her fingertips. Sleepless nights put bruises beneath her eyes and red, irritated sclera housed the navy ring of her irises.

"I missed you," he said, knowing it was hopeless. "I missed you so much. Every day I wished I was here, holding you. Makes it real hard to focus on work." He tried to laugh. "But I promise I'll leave you be. I'll stop pushing you. I just wanted to see you one more time. So you know that I still care about you. Still want you. That I miss you." He stopped talking, hating how much he sounded like a bumbling fool.

She surprised him by standing. Poppy walked between his wide, lolling legs and took his mouth in a soft, deep kiss. He responded immediately, wrapping his arms around her hips, and pulled her as closely as she could come.

When she finally broke away, she gasped, "I missed you, too."

"You did?" Hope blossomed, a seed in suddenly fertile soil.

"Yes." She smiled back.

He wanted to shout his joy, but something bright red and lacy caught the corner of his eye. He peered around her. "What's that?"

On the wooden frame mannequin was a nightgown like he'd never seen. Why, he could see straight through it!

"It's a shift," she answered calmly, but her muscles went tense beneath his fingers. "I make them for Trudy and her...employees. She said the clientele love them."

He whistled. "And I can see why. Do you have more than that one?"

Her mouth softened into a smile. "Just the one for now. Mr. Ricci brought her the others last week, but I've been working on this one for some time. I think the red will be quite striking with black stockings. What do you think?"

"You can say that again." All the strain of the trip, the less-than-satisfying interaction with Katherine, not knowing if Poppy would be receptive to his visit—it all fell away. His face cracked a smile.

Shyly, she peeked over, tugging his long hair where it brushed against his shoulder. "Do you really like it?"

"Are you kiddin' me?" he scoffed, peering closer. "I'd wear it."

Her laugh was from the belly, and he looked up to better enjoy the view. Recklessly, he slid his palm behind her neck and brought her down for another kiss. It soothed a raw spot in his chest. She stopped laughing immediately, and when her tongue reached out and touched his, he groaned into her mouth. Her taste drove him senseless, and he rose to his feet and reached beneath her bustle and overskirt. He found the two globes of her bottom and grabbed firm handfuls, pulling her up against his rapidly swelling cock. Surprising him, she reached low and palmed him, her mouth wide over his and kissing so deep that every breath he took was hers. Rocking against her hand, he released her mouth and dragged his lips down her sweet-smelling throat.

"Let me take you to my house, Poppy." He smiled against her rapid pulse. "I bought a bed."

"Yes," she said, eyes glazed. "Take me home."

The unintentional words filled him with burning happiness.
Take me home.
If it was up to him, it would be her home for the rest of her life.

THEY BARELY MADE it to the house.

He'd rented a buggy and picked her up in secret behind the hotel. He couldn't keep his hands off her. As soon as they'd left the bustle of town and the road became narrower and barren of people, Sol had swooped down and claimed her mouth, letting the horse do the work while his lips had been busy. Her hands had roved over him, sliding up his shirt and touching the hot skin of his waist, slipping lower beneath the waistband of his jeans.

They reached his house just before dark, and he helped her down in a rush, kissing her hard. Her moan lit him up like a blaze, and his hands were everywhere, teeth nipping at her plump lower lip, tugging it until she clawed his shoulders, trying to climb him.

"Let me put the horse up. Go make yourself at home, sugar."

They separated, and Poppy grabbed her bag, stepping onto the little front porch. Sol led Copper to the lean-to he'd constructed since the party, parking the buggy out of sight of the road. The gelding and Hog drank out of the trough. He pumped water in a bucket by the well and carried it into the kitchen, where Poppy was bent over, lighting a fire in the stove to warm a pot of water.

He refilled the stove reservoir then set the bucket down and pressed against her posterior, running his hands up and down her hips. When she pushed back into him, arching her back, he couldn't even muster a smile. He was so aroused he couldn't see straight and rubbed his thick length against her skirts, trying to find that sweet spot that made her just as wild as him.

Their disagreements were a distant memory.

All he knew was how much he needed her and how much she needed him in return. She turned until she was directly in front of him, eyes intent, face dewy with the flush of excitement. This time it was her that dragged him down for a kiss, her tongue insistent, lips moist and soft.

Poppy's hand grasped his belt buckle and pulled, walking backward out of the kitchen, into the hall, to his room. During the work week, he came straight home, washed up, and fell into bed. His house still didn't feel like home, but with his woman dragging him into his dark room, it was the closest to home it had ever felt.

Wanting—no, *needing*—to see her, he lit the lamp on the dresser and turned it all the way up. She didn't complain, didn't even look twice at it. Her eyes were fixed, and she released his belt to unbutton the front of her bodice. Not taking his gaze from her, he tugged his shirt off, flinging it to the bare floor. Her bodice followed suit, revealing the lacy straps of her combinations. Her nipples were visible through the fine muslin, and he got up close, massaging her breasts, rubbing his thumbs over the tips until they were hard points. Impatient with her fumbling fingers, Sol took over, tugged her skirt off, untied the belt of her bustle, ripped off her petticoats, and tossed her on the bed.

When she was just in her combinations, garters, and stockings, he slid the straps from her shoulders and kissed a trail from her collarbone to the tips of her sensitive breasts.

"Oh," she breathed, her eyebrows nearly meeting in the center, face rapturous. "That feels better every time you do it."

He sucked hard on her nipple, feeling the beaded point of it against the roof of his mouth. The noises and whimpers she made had him grinding against the bed between her legs. In one rough movement, he pulled her undergarment completely off so she was bare except for her garters and stockings.

Sol loved Poppy's body.

She was wider at the hips than the shoulders with a petite ribcage and teacup breasts. He tried to span her ribs, feeling delicate curved bones and thin skin. The flare of her hips from her waist was dramatic, and he squeezed the firm flesh between her hipbones and round buttocks.

"This is heaven," he said, voice like gravel. Unrecognizable. "So is this." He cupped her mons, lowering his fingers to dip them shallowly in the crease below. His cock flexed in his jeans at how wet she was. "And ready for me. You don't know what you do to me. Feel." He put one of her hands on the bulge in his trousers, eyes closing at the pressure.

"Let me see it," she demanded, giving him a loving stroke from head to root.

"Yes, ma'am," he acquiesced, managing a grin. She was cute as a button when she bossed him around.

When his boots and clothes were off and he stood bare, erection straining toward her like a flagstaff, she sat up. Her mouth was level with the broad head. Poppy looked up at him...and kissed the tip. When her lips spread over it, he groaned, and when she began to suck, he cursed. Torturing him, she released him to look at it, leaving him glistening in the lamplight. Then, as though she liked what she saw, she fed his long length back into her mouth until he bumped against the soft palate of her throat.

He choked on a groan, cupping her head and thrusting in and out of her mouth. When her cheeks hollowed around him, applying firm suction and faster movements, he grunted and grabbed her head with both hands. "You gotta stop, you do that too good. I'm about to bust."

Eyes glittering up at him, she rereleased him and scooted backward on the bed. He crawled after her until they were near the headboard. Slowly, he unclasped her garters and slid them and her stockings down her shapely little legs, kissing the satiny softness of her inner thigh, the high arch of her foot. Though he tried to be slow, to make it good for her, his hands shook. The tip of his cock leaked in readiness. He wanted to drive into her hard enough that the headboard put a hole in the new plaster.

"I don't think I can be slow. Or easy." His words were gritted out of him, his vision tunneling to the pink area between her legs. Gripping behind her knees, he spread her wide. She let him do so without compunction or shyness, and he'd never appreciated it more than that moment. He dipped his head, biting the tender area of her inner thigh, sucking it hard between his teeth, leaving a love bruise.

She moaned long and low, thrusting her hips up, moving that silky part of her close to his face.

"Careful, shug, I bite," he teased, but instead of biting, he plucked the little bud with his lips. She gasped and murmured something, but he was beyond hearing. "God, you're sweet, you know that? Better than candy. I could just eat you up."

Making good on his word, he dipped his head low and gave her a long, slow lick. He paid lots of attention to that little stiffening part of her, loving how the rest of her got all soft. Miming what she'd done to him the week before, he blew air on her, and her choked moan made him chuckle. Playing with her was better than any shindig game. He dipped the tip of his tongue inside her, and the flavor of her was even sweeter now than it had been the last time. It made him reach his tongue in deeper, and he pressed his face flush against her, maddened by her scent, her taste.

The noises she made were almost too much, breathy little whines that she didn't have to hold back now that they were in a place secluded from others.

If he didn't get inside of her that second, he would blow against the bedsheets. He climbed to his knees and worked two fingers inside her, stretching the inner lips which had flushed dark red with arousal, and managed, "It's not gonna last long. You're too much."

Poppy nodded, her hair coming loose from its pins, eyes blue slits in her flushed face. Her nipples were the same red as her lower lips, and he promised himself he'd pay lots of attention to them soon. Lining up the head of his cock with her drenched entrance, he braced his knees and pushed in as deep as he could.

He swore. "You're so damned tight. Think you can take it all again?" He was halfway in, working past tight muscles, and sweat dripped down his temples.

"I can take it." She pulled her legs back, opening herself up as far as possible. "Give it to me, Sol. Give me all of it."

Growling at her words, he thrust in to the root, his body flush with hers. Her mouth was a little 'o.' Eyes wild, he warned, "Get ready, sugar."

He didn't make love to her this time.

He pumped her in long, hard thrusts, forcing noises out of Poppy that would wake the neighbors if he had any. Remembering how she liked to watch, he grabbed a pillow from the headboard and shoved it under her hips, giving her an unimpeded view of him sliding in and out. Their skin slapped, and he almost stuttered to a stop when she reached between them, splayed the middle and ring finger of her hand, and stroked over the girth that split her wide around him.

"You feel so good," he groaned. "That's it, make yourself feel good. Hell, hurry, sweetheart, I'm about there."

She gasped, grabbing his face for a messy, wet kiss, pulling back to whisper encouragement. To beg.

That was all it took before he swallowed her moans, pounding into her so hard the headboard repeatedly slammed against the wall. He felt her contractions squeeze him, and he gripped her hips to work through them. He was almost embarrassingly loud when he came, but it felt so good he didn't give a damn. Poppy's legs were stiff and tight, still caught up in her climax, her little fingers working herself until her gasps slowed.

Bracing his weight on his elbows, he collapsed. He could feel their mutual heartbeats in their squashed chests and below, where he was still hard as iron. Poppy's inner walls pulsed around him, lush and plump, and the blanket and pillow below her were soaking wet. He kissed her soft and slow, but she pulled back.

"I *do* care for you, Sol," she croaked, eyes wide and earnest. "I'm sorry for pushing you away."

"Sh," he said, kissing her quiet. "I'm glad you did. I've never been one to beat around the bush, and I just asked you to marry me without even giving you time to get to know me. Shooting first and asking questions later didn't work so well this time."

She put a finger over his lips. "I still shouldn't have pushed you away, though, just because I was afraid."

After several more lingering kisses and whispered admissions, they finally parted and cleaned up with the hot water from the stove and the sandalwood soap on his new washstand. Naked, they had a picnic on the bed. Pickles from the pantry and smoked ham from the larder filled their starving bellies.

Sated in every way, Sol put the plates in the kitchen and clambered back into bed with Poppy, laying the back of his head between her breasts while she stroked his drying hair with her fingernails.

"How's Isa?" He kissed her silky nipple. It hardened instantly, and he played with it absentmindedly while they lounged, and Poppy told him that all was well. She spoke more of her business with Trudy and how she felt guilty for going behind Francesca's back.

"It's none of Franny's business," he reasoned, bending her leg to massage the ball of her foot. "You're still gettin' your work done. Plus, if you ask me, your friend is a mite small-minded."

Poppy exhaled contentedly as his fingers moved to her arch. "She's just trying to protect her business. If word got out that I made intimate articles and sold them to women who *steal their men*, they would never do business with us again. Besides, Franny is already cross with me."

Sol moved to the other foot, smiling when she stretched the toes of the one he'd just finished. "Why would Franny be mad at you?"

Poppy told him about her argument with Francesca and guilt at her angry words was evident in her tone. "But she had no reason to be so horrible to Ally."

"Sounds jealous." His eyes drifted closed as Poppy ran her fingernails through his hair.

"I believe so. Franny's not used to sharing her space; just working with me every day must be a strain for her. But it was no reason to frighten Ally so badly that she ran away."

"Ally ran away?"

Poppy hesitated, and her fingers slid away. He huffed, grabbed her hand impatiently, and returned her hand to his hair. Her cat-like smile tugged up the corners of her lips, and she resumed playing. "Yes, but she came back. Mrs. Hobb gave her a place to sleep in the storage room."

"That's good." He turned his head to the side and nuzzled a breast, drawing a nipple into his mouth. She stretched sinuously beneath him, then rolled, leaving him on his back in the bed.

"I have something for you." She sounded shy. "Do not move."

He tried to ask what she was in an all-fired hurry about, but she bounded off the bed, naked as the day she was born and not a bit modest about it. She left the room and returned with her bag, pulling out a brown paper sack.

"You got me candy?" he asked, delighted.

She nodded, set the bag down, and crawled to her knees beside him. "Here." She slid a lemon drop in his mouth, a burst of bright flavor, and put butterscotch in hers. She pulled pins from her hair, released her long, curling tresses, and lowered her head.

"Whatcha doin'?" he asked, folding his arms behind his head to prop it up.

"Making you feel good," she grinned, kissing her way down his stomach. Watching her do that, completely buck naked and mischievous, made his semi-hardness swell to a full erection. She paused to glance at his arms. "Keep your hands just like that."

Intrigued, he immediately wanted to pull his hands from behind his head and take charge but resisted the urge. "For how long?"

"Until I say."

Liking this playful side of her, he tried to relax, but his body had a mind of its own. Already his cock was twitching, fully aroused and flushed. His thigh muscles were tense, abdominal muscles standing out in relief as she kissed down them, and then, to his astonishment, she turned and straddled him while facing the opposite direction.

His hands immediately went to her bottom, spreading her cheeks roughly, his face warming with a flush of male possessiveness and arousal at the astonishing visual. He almost choked on his candy and impatiently crunched it between his teeth.

"Uh-uh," she admonished from near his privates. He could feel her warm breath on his shaft. "Hands back where they were, please."

Gritting his teeth, unable to resist, he spread her once more, took a good, long look, then slowly put his hands back behind his head. "This isn't fair," he complained around his candy. It wasn't the first time he'd told her this, and he was deeply afraid it wouldn't be the last.

Poppy scoffed cheekily from beyond his view. "You'll live."

And then, a warm, wet mouth engulfed his cock. He could feel her candy shifting against the crown.

"Ah God, Poppy," he groaned, breaking the rules to scrub his face with his hands before firmly shoving them back behind his head. She was trying to break him. He was sure of it. The sight of her most intimate areas, inches away from his face and spread wide for him to see, had a sweat breaking out over his entire body.

And then, the hot suction of her mouth began to tug at him rhythmically.

He grunted in time to the tugs, his hips straining, needing her to take more of him. Half his lemon drop pressed painfully against his gums. Words were coming out of his mouth, hot, filthy words that would make the devil himself blush.

"Deeper, baby, take me deeper. Ah, you're so good at that. You gotta let me touch you, sugar, please."

Finally, he hit his limit. He growled and grabbed her hips, yanking her backward up his chest until her silky soft cleft was against his mouth.

His cock slipped from her mouth, and Poppy cried, "Sol!" then moaned loudly when he worked two fingers inside of her, licking her swollen clitoris with the flat of his tongue from side to side. Then, breathing hard but not to be outdone, she stretched as far as she could and took Sol into her mouth again, driving him crazy.

A gentle but firm hand grasped her hair and pulled her off. Poppy groaned at the loss until she realized he was shoving her body impatiently lower, lower, until her entrance hovered just above his saliva-coated head.

Poppy eagerly rose on her shaking knees until he was lined up and sank onto him as far as she could. The depths he reached at that angle made her yelp, and Sol groaned for her to be careful, to be easy, but she didn't want easy. She leaned forward, changing the angle to something manageable, and worked herself on him.

Between the view and incredible tightness, Sol didn't even bother trying to last long. He let go, letting himself be selfish, taking her hips in his hands and stroking up into her, watching her swallow him to the root. His testicles tightening, his legs stiffening, and an all over body flush were his only warnings before his vision went white and he exploded inside her. He groaned long and loud, not caring anymore that it probably wasn't manly to carry on the way he did with this woman. He emptied himself in long surges, pulling her down far enough that she was yelping again but unable to help himself. Then, breath still choppy, he sat up and pulled her back on his chest, spreading his legs so that hers were spread almost impossibly wide to accommodate them.

Looking over Poppy's shoulder, he grabbed a breast, playing with the turgid red nipple while she bounced on him, trying to find her release. He was still hard inside her and bit his lip through the sensitivity. He murmured low in her ear and slid his other hand down to where their bodies met.

"Look at the mess we made," he said in her ear, strumming that red, swollen nub that was distended and peeked from her outer lips. "Look how hard you made me finish, how much I want you." He kissed her neck, sucking the salty-sweet skin, feeling her use him. "You ride me better than any horse, sugar." He spread his legs wider and bumped his hips against hers. Her cries got louder, and he moved his fingers faster over her, biting her neck and shoulder.

She clamped down on him, shouting his name, her nipples tight and hips working him so desperately he groaned.

Poppy whispered his name over and over until he gently eased out of her with a gush. Ignoring the mess in his lap, he tucked his body behind hers.

"I've got you, love, I've got you." Her heart beat at a frantic pace, and he kissed her shoulder blades, her reddened, bruised neck. "You've just got to now. There's no more fighting it."

"Got to what?" she asked, voice hoarse. Confused.

He reached his hand down and cupped her tender flesh, smiling when she jumped. "You've got to marry me. I'll pine away and die if you don't. Is that what you want?"

Poppy sighed and laughed, and he heard her answer in it before she even spoke, his heart doubling in size inside his chest. "Yes, Sol. I'll marry you."

He wrapped his arms and legs around her, naked and sticky, and squeezed her until she squeaked.

"Thank God!" Sol laid wet, smacking kisses all over her neck and cheek.

"Just don't tell anyone yet. Let it be something special for a while, just for us." She turned enough for a kiss then burrowed deeper into his embrace.

"Anything you want," he agreed, then teased, "just so long as you know that I'm no good at keepin' secrets."

It didn't bother him that she hadn't professed her love for him.
He would love her enough for the both of them.

Chapter Twenty

During the last luncheon of June, Poppy had difficulty concentrating.

The distance between Franny and her had been a slow, painful process to mend and bridge. They steered away from any conversation other than the business of sewing or to *please pass the shears.* Work was steady, but gone was the easy camaraderie. It helped that Poppy and Mrs. Hobb kept from repeating Alwine's name in Francesca's presence, but Poppy couldn't help feeling a smidge of resentment from having to constantly censor herself.

A person that was a growing delight to Poppy was Sol's sister Isa.

She was a constant source of amusement, was beyond accommodating, and helped with the hotel and dress deadlines. Her sewing abilities had improved from competent to talented. Everything Isa touched was a challenge that she was determined to master. She even helped Mrs. Hobb with Alwine. Isa had brought a book of German fairytales for Alwine to read. However, it became smudged and dirty, and Isa had to sheepishly pay the disappointed librarian out of her own pocket. Despite her struggles with cleanliness, Alwine learned etiquette, and her English steadily improved. Mrs. Hobb happily made plans for Alwine to work in the shop and trained her to stock shelves. She would stack cans, her doll tucked marsupial-like in an apron pocket. Isa taught her the got your nose trick, and Alwine was fond of using it on Poppy, who acted satisfyingly shocked each time. The girl would dissolve into giggles, still wholly childlike despite her thickening waistline.

Although Isa still teased and charmed, Poppy noticed that her usual spark was dampened, and not once did she speak of Junior.

Now, seated between Bertha and Kitty on Mrs. Smithe's divan, surrounded by dozens of unblinking painted eyes, Poppy worried about her new family.

"Yes, Mr. Smithe arrived home just this weekend. I have missed him dreadfully," Mrs. Smithe said, her usual audience cloistered around her. "I asked him just last night if he'd remain home for the duration of the summer, and he has high hopes of the possibility."

"I don't understand why she always has to talk in circles," Kitty said, between lips that barely moved to Poppy and Bertha. Both women leaned closer. "She speaks like my husband when he's questioning people at the stand. Just say what you mean. 'My husband is married to his work and would go completely mad here with all these dolls to follow his every movement'."

Poppy stifled a smile. Bertha forced one. The latter avoided gossip almost to the point of fear.

"I am tempted to take some of them with me so I can see the look on Mr. Williams' face," Poppy said thoughtfully. It was clear to everyone in town that Sol was courting her. As he was friends with nearly everyone he met, the response of the townsfolk had been dramatically positive. Never had she been told so many "good mornings," "evenings," and "how do's" in her life. An announcement of engagement would be unnecessary. His intentions were as plain as the grin on his face.

Meaning they had to be more circumspect than usual when he visited the hotel. Luckily, Isa was there to buffer the speculative whispers.

"Where is your Mr. Smithe?" asked one of the bold older women. "We haven't seen him since you first moved here."

"Oh, he needed something from the general store." Mrs. Smithe's voice was breezy, and the lines of her face appeared starkly when she smiled. Was she wearing powder? It made her face stark white, as though she'd rested her face on a loaf of floured dough. "You know how men cannot seem to stay in one place. Like their own home!" Her laugh was a mite harsh, and silence hovered tellingly.

Grasping this, Mrs. Smithe changed tactics. "Listen to me go on. Mrs. Daniels!" Her words were the shrill bark of a lapdog, and Poppy jumped at being addressed. A dozen pairs of eyes turned to her, and she felt her stomach go topsy-turvy at the attention. "Do tell us about the juiciest gossip I heard. Is it true that Mr. Williams is courting you?"

Relaxing somewhat, Poppy settled her full teacup in its saucer. She was afraid to drink any. Her bladder had been overactive of late.

"Mr. Williams is indeed courting me." She returned everyone's smiles. She hadn't wanted anyone to know of their engagement, but was an admission of being courted any different?

"Is he that very tall cowboy?" Mrs. Smithe asked, taking a sip of her tea, pinky extended and wedding ring winking ostentatiously. The way the woman pretended not to be familiar with Sol was nails on a chalkboard as though Poppy didn't catch her staring at Sol every Sunday at church. "I must admit, I expected you to have different tastes."

Feeling the climate of the room shift imperceptibly, Poppy straightened. "How so?" There was the smallest chill to her voice. Bertha's hand moved and settled gently on Poppy's arm out of sight of the others.

Kitty was narrow-eyed and unmoving on Poppy's other side.

"Well, he is working class, is he not?" Mrs. Smithe's tone displayed no inkling of the change in the room's atmosphere. More than half the women there had husbands that worked less gentlemanly trades.

Chin rising, Poppy managed a brittle smile. "He's the foreman of a successful ranch a few towns over. He is perfectly to my tastes."

"And you're a successful seamstress," Kitty piped in. "You two are a match made in heaven."

Everyone laughed and concurred, and the tension eased.

As though needing to have the last word, Mrs. Smithe asked pointedly, "When will my dress be completed since we are on the subject?"

Hoping her face didn't break, Poppy's smile widened. "Will next Monday at noon be an appropriate time to deliver it?"

"Of course!" Mrs. Smithe clapped, and through the thick layer of powder on her face, twin spots of color ignited her cheeks.

One of the older women cleared her throat. "I say, Mabel, have you heard any more of the missing girls?"

Mabel, who was bespectacled and sharp of wit, was married to the local newspaper editor. "No, it's the same as before."

Mrs. Smithe fidgeted nervously as this talk continued, and she spoke over a pair of women that were in a discussion over it. "Well, I hope they solve this quickly. I, for one, do not like to be escorted about after curfew like a—"

A door slammed, interrupting her.

Then, garbled words and screams rent the air. Every woman turned as one to the closed parlor door. Poppy felt a frozen moment of strange recognition and made to stand right as Mrs. Smithe snapped, "Everyone remain here, please!" Face set, her skirts swished as she trotted to the door. "I know exactly what this is about. I shall return momentarily."

Mrs. Smithe slipped through the door, her body blocking the foyer, and the door was shut crisply to muffle the arguing voices.

The shouts were in girlish German.

Alwine?

A masculine voice added low tones to the shrieks, and then there was a deafening crash.

Poppy and Kitty rushed to their feet simultaneously, but Poppy reached the door first. It wouldn't budge.

"Ally?" Poppy called through the door, jiggling the brass doorknob. Had Alwine followed her here? Was she in trouble? "Let me out, if you please!"

Kitty bent low and looked through the keyhole. "Someone's blocking the door," she said frustratedly.

"Get her out of here." Mrs. Smithe's yell was clear through the oak paneling. "One of you, clean up this mess!"

The shouts became crying before the sound dissipated down the hall toward the back of the house. Then, silence. Poppy shared looks with Kitty. Bertha looked shocked.

Poppy quit the door and urged Bertha to stand and led her to the window, skirting the women seated in chairs around them. No one occupied the street but a couple of men carrying lumber. "What was the girl saying?" she asked under her breath.

Bertha was second-generation German and had admitted to being competent in the language.

"I—" Bertha began, then clamped her mouth shut when Mrs. Smithe opened the door.

"I must apologize," Mrs. Smithe tittered, but it was forced. "A servant girl was very unhappy at being let go last week and thought throwing a tantrum at the door now that Mr. Smithe was home would regain her position. Young fool."

"Mrs. Smithe," Poppy said, pulse fast. "That sounded an awful lot like a girl I know. Are you sure it wasn't her? Her name is Alwine, she is fair of hair and may have followed me—"

"No," Mrs. Smithe snapped. "As I said, it was a young woman we let go last week. Not this...*girl you know.*" It was so scathingly said that Kitty inflated indignantly, but Poppy pressed a hand to her arm. Mrs. Smithe was lying. And she realized Poppy knew it.

Recognizing she had lost control of the situation, Mrs. Smithe smoothed her coiffure while her closest friends circled her, purring comfort. "No, I am well. But unfortunately, I must cut our luncheon short. Forgive me."

As the women murmured their support, Poppy broke away first and strode into the foyer.

It looked normal. Nothing was out of place. The painted vase stood intact on the table. But what had crashed? Quickly, Poppy scoured the floor and saw something behind the chair leg beside the table. She swooped down and clenched it in her hand just as Bertha and Kitty stepped through the door. Fingers tight around the shard of porcelain, she marched outside with her friends.

Once they were far enough away from Mrs. Smithe's home, Poppy repeated, "Bertha, what was Ally shouting? Do you know?"

Looking away, Bertha tightened her hands over her little reticule. "I-I am not sure. She was making demands, just as Mrs. Smithe said. My German is very rusty, you see."

She was fibbing. Poppy could see it in the pink cheeks and down-turned eyes.

Poppy shared another meaningful look with Kitty, but neither pressed their quiet, reticent friend.

It was only after saying farewell that Poppy opened her clenched fist. Her heart stuttered, brows pressed close in confusion. She knew what Alwine's shouts sounded like, her high, girlish voice lashing out in a fury. It had most assuredly been Alwine at Mrs. Smithe's front door. Surely it had nothing to do with Poppy being in residence. Alwine knew her name and spoke it with frequency now. She also knew enough English to get her point across.

Why scream in German?

In Poppy's hand was a fractured piece of a porcelain doll's face, its single painted blue-gray eye underscored with a black beauty mark.

It was from Alwine's doll.

But why had she gone to Mrs. Smithe's home?

ALWINE WASN'T AT the general store.

"Mrs. Hobb, where is Ally?" Poppy's urgency caused Mrs. Hobb's grip to loosen on her inventory list.

"She left, ran out the door a little after you'd left for your luncheon. She does odd things like that sometimes. Is somethin' wrong?"

"I don't know. She must have followed me. Look." Poppy pulled out the broken piece of Alwine's porcelain doll. While the woman bent closer to have a look, Poppy recounted the scene at Mrs. Smithe's. "Once Mrs. Smithe finally let us leave, I found this beside a chair. It had to have been Ally."

"That's hers, all right." Mrs. Hobb went to hold it, but Poppy's fingers closed fast around it.

"I'm going to show it to Deputy Ellis."

"I want to come with you," said a voice.

Both women glanced up. Isa entered the storage room, brows straight and serious. She looked very grown up in her severe gray serge dress.

Poppy nodded. "Very well."

The sheriff's office was only a few blocks from Main Street, but when they arrived, only the deputy was there to take their statement.

"I'm sorry, Mrs. Daniels," sighed Deputy Ellis as he wrote down everything Poppy had explained. "Your friend isn't considered missing just yet. Give her some time to show up. And since you didn't see her, and neither did your friends, you don't have much of a case to go on."

Elbowing Isa before the hothead opened her mouth, Poppy said, "Oh, but I have proof. Look." She pulled out the fragment of porcelain and handed it to the deputy. "She takes this everywhere. It's an exact replica of Alwine, see the beauty mark and the gray eyes?"

Deputy Ellis frowned down at the jagged porcelain. "Where did she get this?"

"I've told you," Poppy said, softer, very aware of Isa at her side. "She got it from a man she calls Ace, the same man I've mentioned was no good. The one that got her in the family way."

"You never did tell me who that man was to you." Deputy Ellis' eyes were calculating, glancing between his notes and her face.

At first, Poppy said nothing, Isa's stare burning holes in her profile. Then, "He's someone from my childhood who was known to be an evil man. Especially to young girls."

"Were any arrests made? Any paperwork?"

She hesitated. "No. My mother took me from that town and came here."

"I see."

It galled Poppy that the customarily transparent deputy could pick and choose when to be impassive.

"Is there not anything that I could do?" Poppy wrung her hands. Isa's arms were folded beneath her breasts, brow dark.

"Just be patient, I reckon."

Poppy nodded, and they departed. Isa disparaged everything from the deputy to the pokey little sheriff's office to the way Deputy Ellis looked at Poppy like she was a steak dinner. But Poppy ignored this.

And when Isa went her separate way at the general store, Poppy slipped back out and rented a horse from the livery. She was still frightened of riding alone, but the livery horse was docile and uninterested in getting frisky. Poppy rode at a nervous trot out of town and found herself staring at The Dusty Rose for the second time that month.

Heart in her throat, breath harsh, memories assaulted her of fleeing with Alwine back to town.

She hadn't made it a foot from the picket fence when a man of average height and above-average looks stepped out of the front door.

"Well, hi there," he called across the front yard. "Can I help you?"

There was something...wrong about the man.

His face was almost handsome, but his eyes were ugly. Mean. His polite words felt like a ruse, the Big Bad Wolf beckoning Little Red Riding Hood closer.

Poppy's hands were vises around the reins. "I'm looking for a girl named Alwine. Is she here?"

The smile on the man's face widened. He sauntered across the porch and down the steps.

"I know who you are. You came here not too long ago, didn'tcha?" He wore spiked, ridiculously large spurs, heralding each step. "Big Maude said you broke Mina's nose."

"I—"

"She snores now. Wakes me up, so I gotta make her sleep in someone else's bed." He laughed like it made no never mind to him. Halfway across the yard now, his voice softened. "But you, you could snore in my ear all night, and I wouldn't mind it. How about it? You ever think about takin' up the trade? You could make a lot of money." His eyes glittered like something from beneath a childhood bed, some demon light flaring from within.

Adrenaline tensed every muscle, ready for flight, and her eyes flicked to where his fingers had splayed wide, prepared to grab. "I'm not here to work," she said, struggling to sound professional. "I'm here to see if Alwine came back."

"Ran off again, didn't she?" he asked, and his smile fell. "If I ever get my hands on her, she'll feel the strap of my belt when she's eighty."

Poppy glanced at the windows of the house.

No faces looked back at her.

No Alwine screamed from behind the house.

She isn't here.

The man lunged at her, startling the livery horse. He'd reached the rotting fence, splayed hands grabbing for her horse's bridle.

"Hyah!" she screamed, kicking the horse's sides, uncaring that she had knocked the man down to the red clay dirt.

The horse was fast despite its age, and Poppy watched her back more than her front, trees a blurry green around her.

No one followed.

ALWINE DIDN'T RETURN to Hobb's General that week.

Mrs. Hobb was beside herself, convinced that the girl had finally made a nuisance of herself to the wrong person and something horrible had happened.

Poppy and Isa visited the jailhouse daily, but there was never anyone besides a snoring tramp in the cells. Finally, Poppy gathered up the gumption and admitted to Deputy Ellis that she had visited The Dusty Rose, including with some hesitation the altercation with the strange man. Isa's eyes grew wide, and the deputy's went stern.

"Don't do that again," he commanded, and Poppy's mouth puckered. "I'll go have a look. Just... don't do that again."

On Friday morning, he stopped by the store, but his news was grave.

"The brothel's abandoned," he stated, leaning against the countertop. "Looks recent, too. Some things are still there, like they cleared out in a hurry. I bet that's where your girl went."

"Oh, no," Poppy mourned, covering her mouth with her hand. She shared a worried look with Mrs. Hobb. Isa popped out of the aisle she stocked, the can in her hand forgotten.

"Where could they have gone?" Isa asked.

"No tellin'." He reached in his shirt pocket for a pinch of chewing tobacco and tucked it deep within his lip. "But good riddance. The number of complaints we got from that place defied reason. It was months away from shutting down as it was."

"What kind of complaints?" Isa pressed.

Brows raising, and smiling at her temerity, he wedged the tin back in his pocket and shook his head. "Isn't fit for your ears, missy."

Isa's eyes contracted, and Poppy hastened to the deputy, "If you hear something, anything at all, please let us know? We're dreadfully worried. We care about Ally very much."

Eyes warming at the pretty woman on his arm, Deputy Ellis allowed her to usher him out the door. "I sure will, ma'am. You know, I did see a set of wagon tracks leaving the front of the house headed west. Maybe they're hopin' to get better business in Austin?"

Poppy filed the information in her memory and forced a nod.

If Alwine was in trouble, they would never know.

Not now.

AFTER A BUSY, backbreaking week, Sol had never been so grateful that it was a Friday.

It crossed his mind to skip home and ride straight to the hotel to see Poppy, but he smelled so bad he couldn't even stand himself.

Home, bath, clean clothes, then his sugar.

Hopefully, he didn't fall asleep the second he toed off his boots. He missed Poppy more than sleep.

But to his consternation, the windows of his house were illuminated and visible from the end of the lane. He clicked his tongue to Copper, and they trotted the rest of the way.

Is Isa home?

Pavo, Isa's horse, was bedded in the lean-to. He hitched his gelding next to him and stomped his boots at the back door before wearily walking in.

"Isa?" he called.

A lamp was on in the front room and the kitchen, and he edged toward the kitchen doorway.

"No, it's me," called a feminine voice from the kitchen.

Sol jumped at how close Poppy's voice was, and set his hat on the hall table. "You scared the bejesus out of me, sugar." He laughed and shouldered his way through the cracked kitchen door. "What are you doin' here?"

He stopped short at the sight of his aluminum tub filled three-quarters of the way with steaming water. Poppy had draped a dishcloth along the tapered back so his back wouldn't be cold. He felt a sudden lump in his chest and wiped his palms on his shirt.

"I thought you would like to come home to a bath ready for you," Poppy said, turning to him.

Sol snatched her up for a hug then released her like a hot potato. "I probably smell like the inside of a miner's boot about now. It was a hot one."

Ignoring him, she moved right back into his arms.

"I don't care what you smell like." Her voice was muffled in his shirt front. "I had a terrible week and needed to see you without watching what we said or did in front of the hotel staff. Isa said she would tell everyone I went to bed."

"Isa knows about us, then?" he asked, stroking his hands up and down her slim back.

"It's Isa, *of course*, she knows. But I think everyone knows." Poppy's laughter sounded strained. The muscles of her back were tense, her shoulders high and stiff.

Frowning, Sol stepped back and lifted her chin with a crooked finger. "What's the matter, sweetheart? You feelin' blue?"

For a moment, Poppy just looked at him, eyes huge on her face, open and vulnerable. "Yes. You could say that."

Chin trembling, she turned out of Sol's arms.

"Hey, what is it?" He followed her, but the hand she held up stopped him in his tracks.

"Bath first. Then I'll tell you everything. I swear it."

Feeling his heart sink slowly like an anchor in Mud Lake, Sol nodded, mind racing, trying to think what could be wrong.

Does she have to leave town? And me? Had Reverend Daniels written a letter, needing her back?

"Alright," he said carefully. "Let me put my horse up for the night, then I'll come in and take a bath with this nice hot water you heated for me. Thank you." He gave her a parting kiss on her forehead then walked outside in a trance.

His horse and tack were stowed in the little lean-to without him having any knowledge of doing it. All he could think about was the regret on her face, her delicate hands pushing him away.

Is she breaking it off with me? Had she changed her mind about us marrying?

The prospect made him feel physically ill. Before walking in, he had to stop near the back door to quell the nausea. Poppy wouldn't do that, would she? At least, not without a damned good reason. Had Isa said something about him that disgusted her? No, it couldn't be that. Sol had said and done some pretty disgusting things to, and in front of, Poppy, and not once had she turned him away. Seemed to enjoy them, if he recalled.

Still.

That little seed of worry poked at him as he struggled to ease his dirty, concerned face into a semblance of calm. No matter what she said, he could get through it. Maybe he could persuade her to stay if she didn't want him anymore. To give him a chance.

Walking into the kitchen, feigning that his thoughts weren't tearing him apart, Sol bestowed his most charming smile and prayed she didn't leave him while he was buck naked in the bath.

"I'm glad you're here," he told her, unbuttoning his grimy work shirt and tugging it off his head. She looked composed once more, but her eyes moved over him, waking his body up. He toed his boots off and threw his balled-up stockings in a pile, dipping his fingertips into the bathwater. "Whew, this is gonna melt me like butter. How'd you know I needed this?"

Chuckling, Poppy gathered a square of pale sandalwood soap and a thick white washcloth he was sure wasn't his and gestured to the bath. "All cowboys need a bath after working all day, and sometimes washing in the creek does not do the job. Get in, Sol."

"Yes, ma'am." He dropped his trousers without even a hint of contrition, revealing the growing erection between his legs.

She looked at it.

He looked at it.

Then, he said with mild concern, "I should see a sawbones about this. Happens every time I'm around you. It's downright inconvenient."

Poppy tried to fight her smile and lost miserably. "Goodness, how I like you."

His sinking heart lifted a few inches. "That's good, sugar, because I like you, too." When he stepped into the bath, he released a dramatic yelp for effect at the water's temperature. He cupped his gonads in his hands before dipping his rear gingerly into the water, trying and failing to ignore the growing amusement from the woman at the foot of the tub. Laughing, he gritted, "You better hush up before you find yourself in here with me, dress and all."

"Don't you dare," Poppy warned, voice quivering.

When he had settled in completely, he leaned against the damp towel and let his muscles go lax. Sighing all the way from his toes, he closed his eyes. "I needed this. You're a saint."

When she didn't answer right away, he peeked at her. That knot of worry returned. Crouching at the foot of the tub, Poppy dipped the rag in the water and lathered it with the soap. She did everything with slow purpose. Like it was an art.

Like it was the last time.

"Foot, please," she said.

He raised one of his big feet out of the water. "You don't have to do that."

"Hush."

"Yes, ma'am."

Biting her grinning lips, Poppy shot him a stern look over his five wiggling toes and washed his feet with the soft, lathered rag. The feeling was almost incomprehensible. He supposed that no one had ever washed his feet before, not since he was a child. But what loosed a deep, low groan was when her strong, capable fingers dug deeply into the arch of his foot.

It felt so good he was pretty sure he had lost consciousness.

"Hm," she said from far away, "I've only heard sounds like these when we're in bed."

He couldn't even form a reply. His mind had turned to swill, and he floated along while Poppy's fingers worked their magic over his aching heel. Finally, he heard himself say, "Sugar, if you don't marry me soon—"

Her silence returned, but her fingers climbed past his bony ankle and into the lean muscles of his calf. He started groaning again.

After she had repeated the process with the other foot and leg, Sol was incapable of thought. He floated in the water while she maneuvered him, lifting an arm to wash his torso. When she reached his back, his vision darkened, and he felt seconds away from sleep. Just as he drifted off, he heard it.

A sniff behind him.

His eyes popped open, suddenly wide awake. Not wanting to spook her, he let her take her time washing his back, hoping, praying, needing her to be the first to talk.

Finally, Poppy said shakily, "Sol, I have to tell you something."

"You can tell me anything." His words were barely a sound.

"I know, I'm just so afraid to." Her voice was a throb behind him, and he restrained the urge to turn and look at her.

Instead, he grabbed her hand and kissed it. "Whatever it is, we can get through it together."

She gasped behind him and said, "I feel so utterly stupid. You'll be so ashamed."

Tugging her hand, he urged, "Hey, come around here so I can look at you." Once she was crouched at his side, sleeves wet and nose pink, he said, "There's nothing stupid about you, and I won't have you talkin' about yourself like that. Just tell me what's wrong."

For several moments her eyes swam ominously, darting between his, searching for something, before she admitted in a small voice, "I'm fairly certain I'm carrying your child, Sol."

She promptly burst into tears.

Instinctively, he pulled her into his damp, bare chest, all the while air wheezed silently out of him. She was carrying his child? He couldn't have been more shocked if she'd climbed on the rooftop and started yodeling.

"You're sure?" he asked when his voice started working.

"Pretty sure." She sniffed, pulling away and dabbing her eyes. "I've not seen a doctor. As I'm unmarried, I didn't want to start rumors. And I wanted to tell you first." Poppy avoided his eyes. "I've been feeling so poorly ever since you left for Lufkin."

"That was weeks ago!" He couldn't hide his shock. Had she really been pregnant all the way back then?

"I know," she moaned, covering her eyes. "I am so, so sorry. You cannot believe how sorry I am. I haven't had a...you know, since I arrived in Dogwood in May."

Raised around too many women to pretend ignorance, he asked, "How late are your menses?"

After thinking for a minute, she finally looked him in the eyes, miserable. "Three weeks."

His mouth kept swinging open as though on a hinge with no latch, and he closed it before she started crying again. "It probably happened the week you visited Lucy and Ben's ranch."

"I suppose. I've never been with child before. I thought that perhaps the strain of being here, all the changes—oh, I am such a fool." Poppy's face crumbled again.

"Uh-uh, no, don't get all sad again, it's all right, darlin'." He shushed her and kissed the damp trails down her cheeks, fighting a surge of pure euphoria. "Here I thought you were telling me you were leaving town and never comin' back."

She blinked at him. "No, of course not. But this, isn't it worse? I was so afraid of your scorn, how trapped you must feel now."

Sol's laugh was loud and wildly inappropriate for the moment. "Hell, I've been tryin' to get you to marry me since my party a month ago. If anyone is trapped, it's you." His delighted grin drooped. "You're not upset about marrying me and having my baby, are you?"

Her finger covered his lips, and she shook her head. "No, no. Half the guilt I've felt this week was because of how happy I am about it. But I knew people would count the months, and they would know that we conceived out of wedlock. I worried that you didn't want a child right now."

"'Course I do, so long as it's with you." He kissed her soft lips once, twice. "And I wasn't exactly tryin' hard to keep it from happening."

Poppy's eyelids had drifted to half-mast at his kiss, and she leaned in for another. "So, you're not ashamed?"

Beneath the water, he hardened. "Hell no." His lips twisted in a mischievous grin. "Shotgun weddings are a Williams' specialty."

LATER, WHILE THEY lounged naked in bed, Sol was half asleep when Poppy told him about Alwine. His eyes popped back open.

"You're sure it was her at the Smithes?" he asked, wanting to make certain.

"You sound like Deputy Ellis," she chastised, snuggling deeper into his arms. "He said the same thing."

"But doesn't that lady have a wagonload of dolls—wait. You talked to Harold Ellis about it?"

"Don't be jealous."

"I'm not." He was. But mostly, he was upset. Scared, even. Did Alwine's disappearance connect with the other missing girls in the adjacent five counties, or was it merely a coincidence?

"Don't be angry," Poppy began, slipping her hand in his, "but I went to The Dusty Rose to see if Alwine was there—"

"You what!"

"I didn't see or hear her, but that doesn't mean anything. Deputy Ellis said they cleared the house and abandoned it right after that. If Alwine was there, she's long gone now."

When Poppy slid his hand over her stomach, Sol spread his fingers protectively over the place between her hipbones. "I'm sorry, shug."

He kissed the crown of her head. "Promise me you won't go to that place again."

"I promise."

Chapter Twenty-One

Poppy's footsteps sang a happy tune along the boardwalk. It was a beautiful sunny Monday afternoon.

Life was wonderful. Sol was happy with her unexpected pregnancy, not dismayed. After making love all night Friday, they spent the weekend traveling from house to house to relay the information to family and friends about their upcoming nuptials.

Sol was in town today to talk to the reverend, and she was so giddy with joy that she trembled with it.

But first, she had to make a dress delivery to Mrs. Smithe.

Knowing he was at the hotel waiting for her, probably patiently listening to an excited Isa map out wedding plans for the big day, turned Poppy's lips up.

Had things changed so much in one month?

Lucy's mouth had gaped at the news. As promised, Poppy had told Lucy first.

"You were here for one month, and already you've snagged our most confirmed bachelor," Lucy had accused in mock anger. "It took me months to get Ben to marry me. Months!"

A child in a wagon with his family waved at her, and she waved back as she crossed the road.

She would have her own child soon.

Her and Sol's.

They would raise him or her in a cocoon of safety and love. There would be no repeats of her own childhood.

Or Alwine's.

Her happiness dimmed into introspection. Why had Alwine been at the Smithe's house? The assumption that the girl had followed Poppy didn't fit. She thought of all the ways she could ask Mrs. Smithe indirect questions about the event and discover exactly what her young friend had wanted in that foyer.

Wagons and horses passed behind her while she knocked on Mrs. Smithe's door, the covered dress draped carefully over an arm. The housekeeper opened the front door a tiny crack, beadily surveyed her, then opened it wider.

"Yes, may we help you?" she asked, eyes scanning the street.

"Hello, I am here to deliver Mrs. Smithe's dress. Is she in?"

The door widened further. "Oh, she must have forgotten. Come in, come in. Let's not dally on the doorstep."

Poppy was ushered in, and the woman shut the door firmly and locked it behind them. "Can't be too careful," the housekeeper said. "Mrs. Smithe is feeling poorly." She gestured to the foot of the stairs. "She's abed. Let me see what she'd like me to do."

The squat woman in the apron and mobcap ascended the stairs while Poppy twiddled her thumbs in the foyer. Her thoughts bounced between concern for Alwine and ecstatic happiness. To her left was the closed parlor door and across the entrance was another closed door.

Curious if there was another piece of Alwine's doll, she scoured the floor near the door to the right. There was nothing. The hardwood gleamed, the baseboards were free of dust. This close to the second door, voices from within the room were more distinguishable.

Two men were in a discussion, one man perturbed, one pacifying.

Of course. Mr. Smithe was home.

Again, Poppy wondered what he looked like. Perhaps she should ask him if he'd seen Alwine the Monday before or if Mrs. Smithe had relayed more frank information about who had been escorted out the back door. Glancing up the empty staircase, Poppy edged closer to the closed door.

"—believe that little bitch followed me home from the general store," said a man viciously. There was a thud and an answering rattle of glass.

Poppy covered her mouth with a gloved hand.

"And you're sure you've taken care of it?" the man continued, his voice a low threat.

"Yes, she shan't bother you again. I vow it." The other voice was higher in pitch, lightly placating.

Thoughts swimming, Poppy's feet carried her backward toward the front door, and the first man turned the conversation to bank drafts. The office door's brass doorknob turned. Poppy's eyes widened.

"Take the bank drafts to Laredo after this last shipment. I have a man there that knows what to do." The door opened fully, and Poppy pretended to admire the painted vase.

A man with dishwater blond hair and spectacles settled a felt bowler hat on his head, which he tipped when he noticed Poppy. He looked like a banker, professional and pleasant. "Miss," he said with a little bow, and she gave the briefest curtsy. He disappeared around the corner, but not before sending a grave look to the other man.

Poppy's heart began to pound.

The other man exited the office, oddly familiar.

The wave of recognition moved her mouth before her brain caught up.

"Ace?" she blurted, disbelieving.

His head darted up, and she thought vaguely, *I did see him in church*. With the realization came a series of painful memories that tightened the inquisitive expression on her face.

The man from her past, and the father of Alwine's child, was Mrs. Smithe's husband.

Ace was Nelson Smithe.

Ace was of medium height with a middle part smoothed by hair oil, a thin mustache, and an expensive suit with a gold chain peeking from the front pocket. He looked surprisingly young, at least ten years his wife's junior. A frown of sudden concentration deepened rivets in his otherwise smooth skin. He was almost pretty.

"Do I know you?"

It was him.

How could he be here, in this town, in this house, at the exact moment she was visiting?

She had never known Ace's real name when he'd visited the brothel. When her mother had introduced them twelve years before, the Faro-loving Poppy had thought "Ace" such a dashing name for such a sweetly handsome face. Now, over a decade later, a hardness in his eyes opposed the softness of his features. He advanced, footsteps slow as he searched her face, revealing lines that had settled where once there had been none. Mutual recognition evaded the baby blue eyes that had once dazzled her.

Poppy could understand why. Compared to the shy little girl in rags, she was as different as apples were to oranges in her striped muslin day dress, lace gloves, and delicate ivory hat.

Vivid memories flooded her other senses as if they happened now.

All the gifts he'd bestowed, drinking in her happiness. The ribbons, dresses, the kind, flattering words when Mama wasn't around.

The doll.

That's right, she thought in dawning horror. *Ace's family were successful dollmakers. They even had their own factory.*

She would have laughed at the absurd coincidence if it wasn't so horrible. The pieces fell slowly, filling in the empty spaces that made up the connection between Mrs. Smithe and Alwine. A young, pretty girl living in a rough-and-tumble home. Her new, expensive doll. Her pregnancy. Alwine screaming, causing a scene in the foyer, smashing her most prized possession on the floor. Her subsequent disappearance.

It was more than just a coincidence.

Nelson Smithe, the man who fostered an inappropriate affection for little girls, squinted at her and took a step closer.

Poppy took one back.

"Do I know you?" he repeated, using his kind, gentle voice.

Another recollection of that tender voice, whispering to her amongst bedsheets in a dark bedroom.

Don't tell your Mama.

Her skin crawled. "I do not believe so." Her voice had no force or substance. It felt surreal.

"You said a name." His disarming smile was the same. "You must think you know me from somewhere."

"I was mistaken." Her stomach, always so sensitive lately, flowered open, threatening to purge.

To her dismay, he eased nearer. Had he sensed her unsurety? Did he think she was afraid? She wasn't, not quite. Revolted, deeply furious, but shock nailed her feet to the floor. He was so close now. She could see how his large eyes turned sea blue in the light of the foyer window.

"I do know you from somewhere. I remember those freckles. Did I work with your papa?" He spoke to her like a child. Nelson stopped creeping closer and put his hands in his pockets, a relaxed stance. "Why did you call me Ace?"

Chin firming, her expression soured in contempt. When his same vacant smile remained fixed, she felt the impulse to lash out. To wipe it off. "You got Ally with child."

"Ally?" Understanding blanked his face. His hands grew more defined in his trousers. "How do you know Alwine?"

And there it was, better than an admission of guilt. *Al-veen.*

And you're sure you've taken care of it?

What had he done to Alwine?

"Ally is my friend," Poppy said, Mrs. Smithe's wrapped dress clenched in her arms. "You were the one that gave her that doll."

Nelson said nothing, but something crawled across his face like a many-legged bug.

Fear.

"I have no idea what you're speaking—" His face blanked, then transformed into a mad kind of excitement. "I do know you."

"What did you do to her?" Her pulse beat so hard she could hear it, like ears pressed to the seashells sold by peddlers. "Did you hurt her? Would you hurt your own child?"

"That child could belong to any man across the county line." He laughed. He tugged his hands from his pockets, and she backed toward the front door, the space between them shrinking. She held the dress like a shield. "She's just a whore."

"Why give her the doll, then, if she was just a whore?" A tremor made cracked Poppy's words. "You gave me a doll, too, if you'll recollect. And you're still at it."

"I don't know to what end you expect to gain by telling atrocious lies, but I won't hear it. If you know what's good for you, you'll keep your mouth shut, or you'll meet the same end as her."

There was a noise from above; he turned, and Poppy looked up, staring hard at the second-floor landing. There was no one there. Nelson pivoted and closed in on her, but she had already retreated, her hand reaching behind her. He was so close now that she could smell him, pomade and cigars, a hint of his afternoon lunch. Stomach roiling, she fumbled behind her for the doorknob and wrapped her hand around the brass when he grew still, looming over her.

"Poppy Mae?" he breathed.

"You'll be hearing from the sheriff soon." She wrenched the knob. The dress dropped at their feet.

Face hideous with rage, he grabbed for her, but Poppy wedged herself through the crack in the door and fled down the street without a backward glance.

SHE WAS RUNNING, then jogging, but her sides were splitting, so she leaned against the nearest building once she reached Main Street. No one pursued her.

Nelson hadn't touched her, but it was worse. Slimy hands had stroked her from within. Winded, breast heaving, she pushed away from the wall.

She needed to find Sol.

He would know what to do.

Several people halted their stroll on the boardwalk or peered down from their buggies to watch her pass. She ignored a hailing call from a woman from church and didn't stop until she reached the hotel.

Isa was in the dining room waitressing, and Sol teased Minnie in the corridor's kitchen doorway.

Dangerously close to tears, she avoided Mr. Ricci and a pair of women descending the hotel stairs. She did not stop her purposeful walk until she was almost indecently close to Sol's side.

"Sol? May we speak for a minute?"

Squinting down at her, he stood from his relaxed slouch against the doorframe. "You all right, shug?"

Forcing the words out, calm and steady, she replied, "Of course." Then, lip wobbling, "*No.*"

With a quick glance around to ensure no one was looking, he pulled her into the family staircase and closed the door behind them. "What is it? What's wrong?"

Eyes swimming, she looked up at him. "I found Ace. He's Mrs. Smithe's husband. And I think he hurt Ally."

"I'M SORRY, MA'AM, but I can't talk to Mr. Smithe until tomorrow morning."

To his credit, Sheriff Robinson did look regretful, his sad brown eyes drooping low like his salt-and-pepper handlebar mustache. "We've got an important lead on the missing girls case. Go ahead and give your full statement to the deputy in charge until I get back. And try to keep it to yourselves. We find that if word gets out that someone's a suspect of something foul, they tend to hightail it before statements can be made."

Poppy and Sol watched the sheriff and his deputies mount their readied horses and kick them south of town.

The deputy in charge was none other than Deputy Ellis, but nothing in his façade hinted at the flirtatious young man from the month before. He was all cool efficiency, asking pertinent questions with a professional tone.

She told the deputy everything she had told Sol while facing the dusty wall of the office, eyes fixed on a tiny spiderweb in a wormhole in the board. Everything from the doll, the words that had filtered from the office, Nelson Smithe's ugly words that the child could have been anyone's.

"And the disruption at the luncheon last week *was* Ally." She finally looked at the deputy, who scribbled furiously. "She must have seen him when he visited the general store. He said she'd followed him home, and she was who we heard in the foyer. He's the reason she disappeared. And I'm afraid he's going to find another girl, and another, and do it all over again."

Deputy Ellis' pencil was suspended over his notepad, and his eyes seemed far away. "You said he'd given you a doll, too, when you were a child?"

She explained her history with Nelson Smithe and how he was one of her mother's regulars. The deputy didn't blink at that, and she was grateful.

"What kind of doll was it?"

"An expensive kind, with porcelain and real hair. The dress was made of satin and had a matching bonnet. And it was made to look like me, just as Alwine's was."

Deputy Ellis' notepad now had two pages filled, front and back. "Can you give me a physical description of this Nelson Smithe, alias 'Ace'?"

While she gave it, ignoring the creeping, crawling sensation, she didn't see the recognition in Sol's eyes. He shifted his feet and said nothing.

THAT WAS THE bastard that talked to Isa in front of the library.
Sol would swear it on his grandpappy's grave.

When he dropped Poppy off in her attic room, kissing her forehead and giving her one last glance as she stripped off her clothes to scrub and scrub at the washstand, he returned to the sheriff's office to provide a second statement to Deputy Ellis.

The deputy wrote Sol's statement down, every now and then shaking out a hand cramp. Excitement lit his eyes. He mumbled under his breath.

"It's all connecting, isn't it?" Ellis said, rolling a cigarette with some difficulty. "Once Robinson gets back, I'll get his okay and head over to the Smithes."

"Can't you go now?" Sol asked, almost impolitely.

Deputy Ellis grimaced. "The sheriff is funny about us doing things without his say-so. Makes it a real—well, he'll be back in the morning."

"What if Smithe leaves?"

"Then, we'll go get him."

Sol left with balled fists. Instead of turning left to the hotel, he went right toward Carolina Drive, eyes peeled for a big blue house sheltering a rat. Darkness descended, and a pair of teenage boys went from streetlight to streetlight, lighting them. The Smithes lamps were lit, but no shadows crossed the windows. He waited an hour before a side door opened, revealing the silhouette of two men. Sol jogged across the street and leaned against a signpost, waiting for the unfamiliar man with a bowler hat to leave. The two talked in low, tense voices before parting.

After the second man with the bowler hat melted into the street, Sol sprinted to the door, wedging a boot in just before it shut. Shocked blue eyes bulged. Sol gripped Nelson Smithe's lapels with two hard fists.

"What the hell did you do with that little girl?" Sol growled.

Nelson struggled, his toes barely brushing the floor. "I don't know what you're talking about! Release me!"

Sol struck him right in his lying mouth then yanked him back up before he could fall to a heap on the hardwood.

"Like hell you don't." Sol yanked the man up even higher until Nelson's shoulder pads were even with his ears. "And if you so much as look at Poppy again, I'm going to put a bullet in your head. The law won't have to take you in hand. I'll do it for 'em."

He released the coward, who crumpled like a fainting auntie in the doorway.

"Nelson?" called a tremulous voice from the stairs.

Mrs. Smithe rushed to the kitchen.

But Sol was already gone.

Chapter Twenty-Two

S ol slid out of bed the next morning and lit a lantern. The round attic window revealed a black sky. Morning dew fogged the panes.

Words muffled from burrowing her face in the bedclothes, Poppy asked, "Where are you going?"

"I'm gonna see if I can bring Ben and Junior out here to the sheriff's office in case that bastard tries to do somethin' slippery. Can't have too much backup." Sol washed up, scrubbing his face with soap, eyes squeezed shut over the basin. His words spluttered with water. "Before the day is up, Smithe will be in the hoosegow, and everyone will know what a mudsill he is."

Poppy didn't reply. One sleep-swollen blue eye peeped over her arm at his long, bare feet. Isa had moved her things to the room below at Sol's request, and he had held Poppy all night. Once, she'd woken up in a clammy sweat, and he'd soothed her back to sleep with sweeping strokes along her spine.

"What are you thinking about?" Sol asked. He sat on the bed next to Poppy, face falling. Her pillow was damp. "Hey, it's going to be all right, shug."

Whispering against her pillowcase, she declared, "This is going to end badly, I can feel it. Mrs. Smithe will claim I'm lying, and everyone will learn about my past. Franny will be so angry; she told me to keep everything to myself. I'll be run out of town." Her voice broke. "I wish I had been born someone else."

Sol stroked her loose hair with his big, rough hand. "Well, I don't. You can't help what happened to you. And no one will say a bad word about you. Not in front of me. Or the Hobbs. Or the Riccis and

Stones. You'll be a hero, speakin' your truth and maybe saving some other little girls while you're at it. Worrying about it just means you suffer twice."

Before he left, he settled beside her, rubbed her back, and spoke of normal things. What kind of animals they'd raise, how they would make one of the smaller bedrooms her sewing room, how excited he was to marry her.

"I can't wait to walk you around town in one of your fine dresses, show you off to all the old-timers. They'll be wishin' they were twenty years younger."

Calmer, she smoothed his eyebrows with her fingertips, following along his high cheekbone to the stubble he'd yet to shave. "I feel better now."

"It'll pass. All things do." He gave her a soft, soap-scented kiss and squeezed her tightly against him. "Soon, it'll be spit in the wind. We'll be too busy bein' happy with a baby to love on, a home to fancy up, and all the time in the world to grow old together."

"You're right." She rose on an elbow to kiss him again, but he pulled back, brows settled in a straight, serious line.

"Promise you won't go anywhere until I get back? Just to be safe?"

"Well, I need to drop some orders off with Mrs. Hobb before we leave for the sheriff's office. Some women are expecting them this morning."

He thought about saying no but was afraid to. Their relationship was too new. He didn't want her to think that he'd barely gotten her to agree to marry him and now he felt he could walk all over her.

Amusement quirked Poppy's lips.

She batted her eyelashes. "It's just the storage room. All I'll do is cross the alley."

"Hm." He wasn't convinced. "I don't know. What if that fellow is waiting around for you?"

"By two of the busiest buildings in Main Street?" she queried.

Groaning, he buried his face in the fragrant curls spread across her pillow. "Fine, but you'd better hightail it back to the hotel and wait for me. And make sure Isa knows before you go."

"I shall." She gave him one last smacking kiss before he rolled out of bed and finished dressing. He swatted the generous curve of her bottom, brushing against the black taffeta material of the dress she'd laid out the night before on his way out. It was one of her mourning dresses, the only one she hadn't sold. She'd claimed it would be fitting to wear it because the law would only take a woman seriously if she appeared to practice temperance.

He thought it shouldn't matter what a woman looked like. If any of them were threatened or harmed, they deserved help.

Sol locked the family door behind him and took the long way out of town, riding by the blue house on Carolina Drive with his hand against his holster.

All was quiet.

BEN AND JUNIOR flanked Sol, the sun shining weak, gilded light through the pines bordering the eastern side of Dogwood. Each wore gun belts and uninviting stares.

Though Ben and Junior shared different mothers and were often night and day in personality, they both reserved a fierce loyalty for their family and friends. Sol hadn't spent five minutes explaining Poppy's and Alwine's situation before both men turned their backs on him to saddle their horses.

Sol couldn't have asked for more loyal friends.

Ben left a worried Lucy clutching her night wrapper in a fist on the porch. As for Junior, most people thought his pretty face meant he was empty upstairs, but Sol laughed at that. Anyone who could keep up with Isa had to be quick of wit. During the two-hour horse ride back into town, Sol answered each of their questions the best he could, mindful of Poppy's privacy. Ben, who knew the gist of Poppy's past, kept his mouth shut while Junior interrogated Sol.

By the time they hitched their horses in front of Dogwood Hotel, their eyes threw harsh, no-nonsense sparks.

"Go ahead and get some breakfast while I gather Poppy up," Sol suggested.

Junior and Ben nodded and disappeared into the diner while Sol approached Tony's concierge desk.

"Mornin'. Poppy come through here yet?"

"Good morning. Yes, I had the pleasure of speaking to her just before we opened for breakfast."

"Did she go next door?"

"Sure did, had a whole armload of clothes. Isa went with her. I believe they're still there."

"Thanks, Tony."

In the warm, fragrant kitchen, Minnie handed Sol a mug of coffee and a plate of food. He ate while she ordered the other women around, teasing her occasionally. Before he left, he leaned in and pecked her cheek, but she caught the silver dollar he tried to sneak into her apron.

"You think I haven't caught on to you by now?" she chortled, flipping the coin in the air spryly before tucking it back into her pocket. Her brown eyes twinkled, and she shooed Sol out of the kitchen.

Before he left, he leaned back into the crack of the door and asked, "You know if Poppy ate this morning?"

"Sho'nuff. Isa brought her some plain biscuits earlier." Her knowing eyes slid Sol's way, but her lips remained tighter than a drawstring purse while the kitchen teemed with other women.

He maintained an expression of the utmost innocence. "Isa working the diner today?"

"Nope, she's over at the store, says she's gotta help with inventory. They know a good thing when they see it. That girl's got a head for numbers."

Assuming Poppy was also helping at Hobb's General, Sol finished his coffee on the back porch with a couple of hotel patrons, tossed his mug's dregs into the bushes by the porch, tipped his hat, and sidled over to the general store.

Isa was counting under her breath in the storage room, tallying a paper on the clipboard in her arms.

"Mornin', Legs. Poppy upstairs?"

Isa didn't look up. "Morning. No, she's at the hotel."

"No, she isn't over there," Sol denied, pulling his thumbs out of his belt loops.

"Yes, she went back about three hours ago."

Three hours ago?

Sol felt a whisper of worry. "She's not over there, Isa."

"There is no need to yell." Isa's eyebrows were high, and she sounded like Ms. Persimmony when someone spoke above a whisper at the library.

Cursing too low for her to hear, Sol turned on his heel and strode back to the hotel. His footsteps were light when he took the attic stairs two at a time but were stomping on the way down. The attic was empty. He opened every room, saying her name, getting louder and louder at each door. He even checked the water closet at the end of the hall.

Poppy was gone.

Convincing himself to remain calm and not to jump to conclusions was hard when he was already breathing hard, his heart pumping frantically with the fear that something had happened to her. He wanted her to walk around the corner and chastise him for getting upset over nothing. Sol checked the diner where Junior and Ben were leaving money on the table. The only other people there were a pair of older women and a young couple.

"What is it?" Ben's gaze sharpened.

"I can't find Poppy. C'mon, maybe she's upstairs at the Hobbs."

They strode across the alley and entered through the storage room where Isa, once seeing who followed Sol, set her clipboard down. She hadn't spoken to Junior since the morning after the dance, but he pretended not to see her and disappeared through the doorway leading into the store's front. They heard him ask Mrs. Hobb if Poppy was upstairs and Mrs. Hobb's quick steps as she ascended the stairs to find out.

"Isa, Minnie said she came over here with you."

"She did." A note of fear cut through the defensiveness in Isa's tone. She kept her eyes averted from Junior. "But that was hours ago. She told me she wanted to eat her breakfast on the back porch."

Mrs. Hobb chose that moment to look around the doorway. "She's not upstairs. Is something wrong?"

Sol didn't answer. Blood whooshed in his ears. Isa was on his tail while he slung the storage door open, fully intending to ask the patrons on the porch if they had seen a young woman with freckles and beautiful sky-blue eyes.

But something caught his eye, and he froze. Isa smacked into the rigid line of his back. On the ground, half-covered in glistening ants, was an uneaten biscuit.

Isa saw it, too. "That might be Poppy's. We had biscuits for breakfast."

As though madness had taken hold of him, Sol reached for the biscuit, brushing the ants away. He glared at the dirty biscuit, willing answers out of it.

Ben strode to the stable in the backyard, and Junior crouched by the stoop to squint at the dirt. He shook his head. "There're too many tracks. No telling which ones are hers."

"Did she say if she was feelin' poorly?" Sol asked Isa, still cleaning the biscuit of grit.

"No, just—Sol, what is going on!" She'd had enough. Grabbing his arm, she yanked him around so hard that the biscuit went flying.

"Snap out of it! Poppy comes and goes all the time, why is today any different?"

"Maybe because they were going to the jailhouse today to make an official statement against someone well-respected to get him brought in and questioned, genius," Junior supplied, now investigating the ground near the hotel.

"I didn't ask you," Isa snapped at Junior, then paused. "Why would she need to make a statement with the sheriff? Does it have to do with Alwine? Did she find something?"

Sol had almost forgotten Isa was as embroiled in Poppy's life as he was.

"She found out who got that girl from The Dusty Rose in the family way," he said. Isa's eyes widened. "And we told the sheriff before he left yesterday. He should be back today."

"She's not in the stable. Maybe the sheriff came and picked her up while she was out here," Ben reasoned, striding from the backyard.

Relief was swift, rinsing away the grunge of his worry. "I bet that's what happened." Though it wasn't like Poppy not to leave a note.

"Let's go check it out. I'll go unhitch your horse." Junior made his way toward the exit of the alley.

"You stay here in case she comes back," Sol ordered his sister, and it was a testament to how worried he sounded that Isa didn't argue. She nodded, confused and unhappy with the instructions, but she listened.

POPPY WAS NOT at the sheriff's office. According to Deputy Ellis, the sheriff hadn't even been in the office for half an hour. When none of the men acted overly worried about Poppy's missing status, Sol put his foot down.

"No, I told her to stay at the hotel before I came back."

"Well, listen," chuckled the sheriff. "I know you're newly engaged, but women don't tend to listen even when they're *married*, son."

"You don't understand," Sol said, a note of pleading in his voice. "She's scared of this Smithe fellow. We agreed this morning that she would keep low until I got back. And there's somethin' else. She's...expecting."

Junior's lips parted. Ben's eyebrows snapped up.

Deputy Ellis frowned at Sol briefly, measuring him, then tapped the sheriff's desk. "I'll go, sir. I left Mrs. Daniel's statement in the top drawer, and I think you should have a look."

With a sigh, Sheriff Robinson nodded and pulled the drawer open.

The deputy mounted his horse and followed Sol and Junior back to the hotel.

"I'll start lookin' in all the stores," Junior said.

"Good," Deputy Ellis said, scratching his head. "Let's get Mrs. Hobb to visit all Mrs. Daniel's friends. There's a better chance she'd be there than...anywhere else."

Sol nodded. Copper's ears swiveled back. Twice the horse side-stepped nervously, sensing his owner's strange mood.

But Mrs. Hobb was already on the boardwalk in front of the general store. She met them on the road, her moles standing out in relief in the cloudy light. "I talked to Franny. She said she saw Poppy get into a covered buggy with another woman this morning." She pointed directly across from the general store. "Right there."

The deputy leaned over his pommel a little, looking at the tracks. "Does she know with who?"

"The woman was veiled and wearin' a fur-trimmed coat. Poppy's wearin' a black dress and her sewing apron but didn't even have her bonnet on. Franny said they looked in an awful hurry."

"What direction did they go?"

"South."

South was where low town was, west and east were residences, and north of Main Street was the sheriff's office. Where the hell were they going? He had asked Poppy to stay, and the first thing she did was leave. Frustration combined with Sol's worry, boiling just beneath the skin.

"Anything else?" Deputy Ellis asked, eyeing Sol.

"There's more." Mrs. Hobb's eyes flickered up at Sol apologetically from the folds of her skin. "She said she saw two riders—men—come out of the alley and follow after them."

Sol's stomach dropped.

"Did she mention what the men that followed looked like?"

"No, but we can ask her."

But when Mrs. Hobb came back, she shook her head. It had been too dark to see the men beyond the fact that one wore a bowler hat and one had long hair.

A bowler hat?

Poppy had explained that the man that had visited with Smithe the day before had worn a bowler hat. That same man that had left the Smithe's kitchen the night before.

Sol began to panic.

ISA HAD THE terrible sense that she had done something wrong, but Sol was close-lipped and taciturn.

When he, Ben, and Junior had left her to go to the sheriff's office, she had hightailed it to the stable behind the hotel and hitched up her little chestnut pony. Pavo—named during her short-lived interest in constellations—shook his mane at her.

"I already fed you," she said distractedly. Once saddled and resigned to his fate, she walked him down the alley. Her pace quickened when she saw Mrs. Hobb talking animatedly to Sol, Junior, and a deputy in the middle of the road.

Their faces were grave.

"What is it?" she asked, mounting Pavo and wheeling him beside Sol's leggy roan.

A mask hardened Sol's normally pleasant features. "Poppy rode off with a woman in a buggy this morning. You sure you didn't hear anything in the alley?"

Everyone was looking at her. Even the deputy, who was generally friendly, didn't wink or smile at her. Heat climbed up her collar.

"No, I didn't hear anything, but I also wasn't listening."

"Nothing right outside the storage room?"

"I don't know." Isa felt like a child during an exam she hadn't studied for, but the test was evidence, and the weight of a whole school board drilled into her with their eyes instead of a lone teacher. Finally, she cried, "How was I supposed to know, Sol? No one tells me anything!"

"All right, all right, let's just settle down," the deputy interjected. "Where was the last place Mrs. Daniels was seen?"

They retraced Poppy's steps from that morning, with Sol claiming he'd spoken to her in the family hallway on his way out. That was a fib. Isa knew he'd skulked down the attic stairs, but she kept that to herself. Instead, she disclosed that just over three hours before, Poppy had left the storage room to eat on the hotel porch. Directly after that,

Francesca saw Poppy abscond in a small covered buggy with a veiled woman, where they quickly traveled south, followed by two men on horses.

Deputy Ellis divided everyone up.

Mrs. Hobb was to visit all of Poppy's friends and customers. Junior would ask store owners on Main Street if they had seen Poppy, and Ben was to do the same in low town. Sol would visit all the doctors in the area, and Deputy Ellis would get the sheriff to question the Smithes.

"What about me?" Isa called out to the deputy.

"Stay here and wait in case Poppy comes back," Sol snapped, and Deputy Ellis nodded in terse agreement.

Mrs. Hobb patted Isa's boot sympathetically before she went her separate way, everyone darting off in opposite directions while Isa sat motionless in the middle of the street. Less than useless. What didn't make sense to her was why Deputy Ellis hadn't sent someone to the livery to ask if anyone had rented a buggy early that morning.

No, she needed to go inside like Sol said. She'd never seen her brother so upset.

And yet...

"C'mon, Pavo," she whispered between her horse's ears, tapping his sides with her heels.

Hoping no one caught her riding off on her own, she trotted to the livery. It wouldn't hurt to ask. It was barking at a knot, in any case. She'd come straight back as soon as the stable owner waved her off.

It was busy in the livery, and she waited her turn to be seen behind an older gentleman who needed a wagon long enough to fit his sister's pine box. Finally, looking harassed, the middle-aged owner beckoned her over.

"What can I do for you today, miss?"

"I don't need anything, per se, but I would like answers to some questions."

He attempted to look politely expectant, but his eyes flicked to an approaching gentleman. "Let's make it quick."

"I need to know if anyone rented a covered buggy this morning before sunrise."

Scratching his scruff, he thought about it. "Yeah, a little covered gig 'bout five o'clock. Woke the stable boy up needing it. Kent! Get over here. Answer the lady's questions, will ya?" He left Isa with a gangly boy her age that blushed from the roots of his hair to his grungy collar.

"Yes'm?" he asked, lisping through prominent front teeth.

She repeated her question, looking at both of his eyes.

"Um, yeah, some lady dressed up for a funeral needed it 'fore we ran out, she said."

"Dressed for a funeral?" Isa repeated in rising excitement. Poppy's companion had been wearing a veil. "Does she still have it, or did she return it?"

"She brought it back 'bout an hour and a half ago, ma'am."

"What was she wearing?"

The stable boy thought for a moment. "She looked fancy. Wore some furry vest or jacket. And a veil. And she was all in black. No"—he shook his head—"her dress was green. Velvet, the kind my ma always wished she had."

Hope sparking, she asked, "Did she have another woman with her? Black dress and very pretty?"

He chuckled. "No ma'am, I'd remember."

Feeling her hopes fizzle out, Isa sighed. "Can you show me the buggy?"

"Sure. I haven't cleaned it off yet. It's a real mess. She must've driven the heck out of it through mud."

Isa could see what he meant. The little two-seater gig parked behind the livery was splattered with red clay up the back of its canopy. Gaze honing in on the wheels, Isa walked behind it, judging the measurement between them.

"Did the woman give her name?"

"No, ma'am, but don't tell Mr. Bowen if you don't mind. He gets real touchy about stuff like that. The woman paid me extra not to write it down. I'm—I'm not in trouble, am I?" He sounded suddenly worried, checking to see if Mr. Bowen was close enough to overhear. In profile, his chin was weak.

"Of course not," Isa soothed, not knowing if it was true and not really caring. Why would a woman traveling to a funeral race through mud fast enough to get it all over the back? And that early in the morning, to boot?

She left the livery, retraced her steps back to the hotel, then continued south where Poppy had allegedly traveled. There were too many streets, pathways, and alleys for Isa to possibly track, but something kept her going until she was on the road leading to The Dusty Rose. It wasn't as well-traveled, and Isa followed the road for half a mile before she finally found the thing she was looking for.

Two pairs of buggy tracks, the exact length of the one at the livery.

One pair of tracks left town, and the other pair returned. Was it the same buggy?

Knowing full well it could be coincidental, Isa dismounted, led Pavo by his reins, and squatted in the middle of the empty road. She wasn't as good at tracking as Sol and Junior and couldn't be sure which horse prints were fresh and which were old. What had Poppy said The Dusty Rose looked like? White and run down?

After a fervent wish that it wouldn't take much longer, Isa mounted Pavo, followed the buggy tracks another mile, and stopped.

In the distance, a white house stood, empty with blank windows. But what was interesting was the road. The tracks did what Sol called "telling a story". Isa dismounted in a flurry of skirts, tugging Pavo behind her. The hoofprints had deepened and were wider apart, and Isa had to lift her skirts calf-high to avoid the mud puddles that littered the ground. The buggy horse had been run hard through the mud, and there, to the right, was another set of tracks with deep, wide-set hoofprints. Another horse running.

Chasing?

But where were the other horse's tracks?

There! To the left.

"I shouldn't be walking you on the evidence," she told Pavo matter-of-factly as though her heart wasn't climbing her throat. After tying him to a shrub, she returned to the prints in the mud and tried to see the "story."

One horse had ridden parallel to the buggy on the right. The second horse had run in the opposite direction from the other end of the road, and now there were footprints. But strangely, the footprints started in front of the old house as though someone had jumped off the buggy and ran back toward town. Isa was familiar enough with trained cow ponies to recognize that the horse had herded the person on foot. A person with *small* feet. And those feet stopped not even fifty feet away from where they had started. Isa made her stride small like Poppy's and gauged the length of the strides. If it had been Poppy, she would have been running hard, with a horse fast gaining on her.

Isa no longer felt the euphoria of solving a mystery.

If these tracks proved her theory correct—that Poppy had been run down by men on horses—then it meant nothing good. Stalking alongside the road in the grass, Isa followed the tracks past the white house, but they veered left into the woods beyond The Dusty Rose. The buggy, however, made a complete turn and led back the way it had come so the mysterious woman could return it.

But who was she?

And where was Poppy?

Chapter Twenty-Three

Five men and one woman occupied the sheriff's office. Sol stood, muscles tense and squared, and focused on the well-to-do woman in a dark green velvet dress.

Her face was allover bruises, and she wept openly in the chair across the sheriff's desk. Junior leaned casually against the trim surrounding the barred window with a set jaw and crossed arms, choosing to look outside rather than at the female's theatrics. Ben stood similarly beside Sol, stoically watching the back of the woman's head. Sheriff Robinson sat in his own chair across from her, elbows on the table while he asked a constant flow of questions, his forehead a sea of wrinkles and his eyes earnest. Deputy Ellis stood at the sheriff's shoulder, writing on a yellowing notepad, watching the woman like a hawk.

"Mrs. Smithe, it's imperative that you answer all our questions truthfully. Now, you came down here in good faith, but what you've said isn't adding up."

Mrs. Smithe's only response was to blow her nose indelicately into a handkerchief.

"When Deputy Ellis and I visited your house this morning, your maid answered and said neither you nor Mr. Smithe were home."

"The help is advised to say that in every household, sheriff, not just mine," Mrs. Smithe managed. "As you can see, I have been...indisposed." In the light from the window, her purple bruises seemed to deepen in color before their eyes.

"You gonna tell us who got you that way?"
A head shake.
"All right, can you at least tell us where your husband went?"
Another head shake.
"When did he leave?"
"Last night," she said.
After I hit him in the mouth.
Sol tamped down his guilt.
"You know why he left so suddenly?"
She glanced to the side. Sol was convinced she would point the finger and blame him. "No." Instead of feeling relieved or reassured, Sol's spine prickled with distrust.

"Were you aware that Poppy Daniels visited your home yesterday at approximately three in the afternoon?"

"My maid mentioned that our seamstress paid a visit."

"Did your husband remark on anything about Mrs. Daniels?"

"No."

"Were you aware that Mrs. Daniels made a statement against your husband directly after she visited your home?"

"How would I know that?" Mrs. Smithe asked, her shrill defensiveness making every man grind their teeth.

"And you're not aware of your husband doing anything wrong?"

"No—I—"

"What about the young girl that went missing last week? Do you know anything about her?"

"I have no idea—"

"Is it true that your husband is a partner of a company that manufactures and sells dolls?"

"Yes."

"Does he often give dolls away to children?"

"What? I-well-we don't have children or any in our family, but I'm sure he—" Mrs. Smithe broke off, looking panicked and confused by the simple question.

Sheriff Robinson's handlebar mustache was more bristled than usual, but his drooping brown eyes were sharp. "Did the young girl Alwine visit your home at your last lady's luncheon?"

"I—I don't know of anyone by that name—"

Liar.

"Blonde, thirteen or fourteen, she speaks German and, according to several eyewitnesses, owned one of the dolls that your husband's company manufactures."

Silence.

"Were you aware that Alwine claimed to have been with child?"

Mrs. Smithe hid her face in her handkerchief.

"Did the girl and your husband speak when she caused a commotion at your house during the lady's luncheon?"

From behind the handkerchief, Mrs. Smithe mumbled, "He had to help escort her out, but she wasn't speaking English."

"What happened to your face, Mrs. Smithe?" asked Sheriff Robinson.

For a long moment, it looked as though she was fighting a losing battle, but when she raised her head, mouth open to answer, the door flung open.

It was Isa. Her blonde hair was windswept, and her eyes sparked in her flushed face.

"I found something, Deputy Ellis," she gasped, holding a stitch in her side.

Deputy Ellis and Sheriff Robinson looked thunderous.

"Sol, get your sister out of here while we talk to Mrs. Smithe," Ellis snapped.

Isa acted as though she'd been slapped. Her eyes went from the deputy to the sheriff, and her color heightened. Then, they settled on Mrs. Smithe, who had turned in her chair to gape at the sudden entry.

"Isa, get out. We can talk later," Sol gritted. For once, he had no patience for his meddlesome sister. He felt ill with worry and wanted to strike something. Hard.

"But Sol—"

"I got her," Junior said, grabbing Isa's arm above the elbow to steer her outside.

"Do not touch me," she hissed, yanking her arm away. Her eyes were enormous and suspiciously wet. "I'll be right outside, but if you think I'm going any further, then the both of you have lost your wits."

The door didn't quite slam behind her. They could see the back of her head nearly brushing the window just outside the door, the lines of her back stiff and angry.

"I apologize for that, Mrs. Smithe, as you were sayin'?" Sheriff Robinson asked.

"No one did this to me, sheriff," she said after a long silence. Her voice was light. Strained. "I tend to sleepwalk. Sometimes I wake up covered in bruises at the foot of the stairs."

Sol, Ben, and Junior shared an incredulous look behind the woman's back. What did she do this time, sleepwalk right into a saloon brawl?

Neither the sheriff nor the deputy twitched a muscle.

"So you're sayin' you woke up like this?"

She nodded and pressed the handkerchief back up to her nose.

"Did you go anywhere this morning, Mrs. Smithe?"

"What do you mean?" she asked carefully.

"Did you leave your house at all?"

"No."

"Around what time did your husband leave last night?"

"I don't know."

It went back and forth for ten more minutes while Mrs. Smithe became increasingly tightlipped. Finally, the sheriff sighed and pushed his chair back.

"We'll let you go for now, but be prepared for another visit from us. And Mrs. Smithe," he said sternly, "don't leave town. And if your husband shows up, you come straight here and tell us. Do you understand?"

"Yes." Stiffly said. Mrs. Smithe donned a black bonnet that was so deep her face was mere shadows. When she walked out the door, neither Sol, Ben, or Junior opened it for her. They watched her with hard, immovable expressions. Isa's head turned and watched the woman all the way into the road then the little busybody was a whirlwind through the door again.

Sol ignored her and strode to the desk. "I went to the Smithe's house last night around nine o'clock. I threatened Nelson Smithe and hit him in the mouth. And I know damned well that woman knows about it because she was coming down the stairs when I did it. So why did she lie and say he would have no reason to leave last night?"

Sheriff Robinson cursed tiredly. "What you did wasn't smart, but him running now is nothing less than an admission of guilt. Men like him would usually have their lawyers knockin' at my door first thing this morning crying battery."

"That woman *is* lying," Isa seconded, shutting the door behind her and focusing on Sheriff Robinson, who scrubbed his face and leaned back in his chair. He looked like hell.

"What makes you say that?" Deputy Ellis asked, still writing pell-mell on his notepad.

"She said she didn't go anywhere this morning, but I know for a fact that she did."

"How do you know that?"

"Because I went to the livery and asked if someone had rented a buggy early this morning, and they said a woman in green velvet had, that she was dressed up to go to a funeral."

Sol unfolded his arms and stepped forward. "Isa, I told you to stay at the store and wait—"

"I know, and please don't be angry with me, but I thought it would be a good idea to ask! And the woman that rented the buggy fit Franny's description. The stable boy Kent said she wore a green velvet dress and brought the buggy back after only a couple of hours and that it was covered in mud. I looked at it, and it was, and so was that woman's skirt!"

Sol felt hope override his anger at Isa. They had another piece of evidence if this was true. They could be one step closer to Poppy.

Sheriff Robinson, however, merely looked weary and unimpressed. "There are mud puddles all over the road, girl. Every lady's skirts are muddy."

Isa strode to the desk and shook her head. Her hair drooped further. "Not exactly. See, that woman's hem has dark mud on it, but all along the left side of her skirt was *red clay*. That's the exact same mud on the back of that borrowed buggy!"

"I don't know, Miss Williams—"

"There's more, and please don't be angry, Sol, but"—Isa took a breath—"I had a hunch where they might go if it was south. Poppy wouldn't just leave for any old reason. She'd told me about the time she had gone to The Dusty Rose to check on Alwine—"

"When?" Sol burst. Had she gone back after he'd asked her not to? Isa ignored him.

"—so I followed that road and sure enough, the buggy tracks matched. The road turns into red clay, sheriff. Not only that, but a set of tracks followed the buggy."

"There were two," Deputy Ellis interjected, frowning. "Two men followed, according to Francesca Hobb."

"The second rider flanked them." Isa was leaning over the desk. The deputy didn't interrupt again. Her words were coming quickly now, her hands gesturing, and Sol had difficulty following. It was as if his ears were filling with batting. "The buggy horse started to run, its tracks were all over the road, and the man behind it ran his horse, too. Then the second rider came out of the woods beside The Dusty Rose like he was just waiting for her. From there, footprints jumped from the buggy and ran toward town. They were the same size as Poppy's.

She's running, and the second rider starts to herd her, and then...her footsteps disappear. Like he'd picked her up and thrown her on his horse. The hoofprints go into the woods behind that brothel, and the buggy turns back toward town."

It was deathly quiet in the aftermath of her story. Sol and Ben stood erect and shared another look. Junior stared at Isa. If that was true....

But Sheriff Robinson had had enough.

"God's eyes, girl, what are you goin' on about?" he barked, goggling at her as though she were a bewildering puzzle. "We ain't got time for no wild goose chase, Miss Williams."

"But, Sheriff," she started, her mouth flattening.

"No 'buts,'" he grunted, standing from his befuddled slouch. "We've got enough going on with the missing girls' case, and now this—Lord, but I don't know why this always happens all at once."

"But if we leave right away, maybe we can catch their trail and find her—"

"Isa," Sol warned. He approached her from behind and encircled her arm with a staying hand. If she angered the sheriff, the chances of them helping to find Poppy went from low to nil. "Let the man do his job, all right?"

"I appreciate the concern," Sheriff Robinson said, his voice rose higher to drown out another one of Isa's interruptions, "but we must assume that if anything did happen to Mrs. Daniels, then the likelihood is that she is one of two things. One, she is not missing at all and will be back before you know it with an adequate explanation for her absence. Or two"—Here he rounded the desk and clapped Sol's shoulder with a hand—"maybe she's with the other girls. If that is the case, we have a lead, and the more manpower we have behind us, the better."

Despite Sol's readiness to help, he felt a nagging doubt in the back of his mind when he glanced at Isa's hurt eyes from over the sheriff's head. "You know I will always offer whatever support I can. What lead do you have?"

"We've had a tip that this is a group of either Comancheros or Bandidos. Organized crime in these parts is rare. They must be poaching girls further east to get the west Texas law off 'em."

Sol was glad the sheriff couldn't see Isa's grimace of disbelief.

"What do I need to do?"

"Sol, I don't think it's that, it just doesn't fit." Isa's voice rose.

"Isa, I think you need to go back to the store now."

"No, I want you to come and look at these tracks! You'll see then, you'll see that I'm right—"

"Isadora," he shouted, all the pent-up worry and fear spewing out. "I don't need you interfering right now! You go back to the hotel or store, or you go to Ma's, but either way, you need to let the men do their job. You're not bein' a help, you're being a pain in the ass, go!"

He pointed a shaking finger at the door.

Although he hated the expression on her face—he had never shouted at her like that—he wouldn't forgive himself if she entangled herself in something that could hurt her. And she would. She would nose around in things that didn't involve her if he didn't nip it right in the bud.

After sending him a withering, hurt look, Isa stormed out. He watched her get on Pavo and gallop south toward the hotel. He pinched the bridge of his nose, squeezing his eyes tight. Sheriff Robinson's voice was kind, his hand an unwelcome weight on Sol's shoulder.

"That's the best thing you could've done for her, son. We can't have women involved in these things. Just makes 'em worse."

Sol had never felt more like cow shit on the bottom of a boot.

ISA SHOVED THE ten-pound sack of sunflower seeds into the saddle bag. Her movements were cool and collected as she mounted Pavo and nudged him toward the livery, but her mind was a tumultuous, roiling thing. She repeated her plans to herself over and over, but questions popped up between the thoughts.

The goodbye note was written and left on her bed.

How could he not believe me?

Her supplies were packed.

He should know I would never make up stories.

Now, to get Pavo's shoe removed.

How could Sol talk to me like that?

When she led Pavo into the open livery barn, Kent did a double take at her bib overalls and braids. But even with her breasts bound and her figure hidden in one of her brother's old duds, it didn't take much to convince the stable boy to remove one of her horse's shoes.

"It'll lame him if you ride him too much like this," Kent warned, glancing around for Mr. Bowen.

She was aware of this but kept a civil tongue in her mouth. "You have a spare hammer and nails for me to put it back on?"

If he thought her request odd, he kept it to himself and brought the requested tools. Isa placed them and the horseshoe in the bag with the sunflower seeds. She gave him a nod of farewell, and he watched her leave with his hands deep in his pockets.

Pavo's gait had altered imperceptibly, but it was important that the horseshoe remained off until she found Poppy. Because, despite what that sheriff said or what Sol believed, Isa had a gut feeling that it had been Poppy's tracks in the dirt by The Dusty Rose. And that Smithe woman had everything to do with it.

It was high noon when Isa retraced that morning's steps and followed the road leading southwest out of Dogwood. The sun was trying to break through the cloud cover, and for that, she was grateful. She didn't need rain to cover her tracks. Once she reached the abandoned brothel, Isa's sharp eyes searched the ground. The tracks were still there, but other hoofprints muddied the clarity of that morning's prints, and she added spit to the mud with force.

"Where'd they take you, Poppy?" Isa asked aloud.

Dismounting, she opened the flap of one of her saddlebags and reached into the drawstring sack of sunflower seeds. She crammed a handful into each pocket, paying particular attention to the two sets of horse tracks that disappeared into the woods. It was a good thing that the ground was soft from that night's rain; the hoofprints were deep and visible even on the forest floor. With Pavo walking behind her, she sprinkled a sunflower seed or two behind her at every other step, following crescent-shaped tracks deeper into the woods behind The Dusty Rose.

After a couple of miles of this, however, the ground grew dense with underbrush, and Isa had to strain at the dirt, looking for crushed leaves or broken twigs. There was nothing but endless trees and brush. She tied Pavo to a tree and walked in the same southwestern direction, cursing low and fervently when she could see nothing on the ground. The leaf litter was so thick that she couldn't find hoofprints. She wanted to scream.

Then, a glitter of silver on the forest floor caught her eye.

Gasping, she dove beneath the tangled brush and vines, reaching as far as she could until her hand closed around cold metal. It was a thimble.

It had to be Poppy's.

Isa grabbed Pavo and led him southwest, looking for more hints of Poppy.

She was wearing her sewing apron. Things must have fallen out of it.

After half a day of walking, Isa lost the trail again and had to back-track, despairing.

"Why couldn't Junior have come?" she asked Pavo. She had lost all anger for the fool. They could put aside any fights until they found her future sister-in-law. Another half hour of searching proved fruitful.

A length of red silk thread had wrapped around a leaf on a Virginia creeper.

"There you are," she whispered, leaving the thread and dropping a few sunflower seeds next to it. Her luck improved after that. The leaf litter thinned, and the ground softened again. Hoofprints were once again visible. Isa quickened her pace, a tiny flash of red from one of Poppy's silk threads visible along the trail. Isa was so grateful she could choke. Poppy was leaving a trail for them.

A silk trail.

When dusk settled and prevented Isa from seeing the trail, she made camp and vowed to find Poppy tomorrow. Too frightened to light a fire, she was about to drag off Pavo's saddle when Isa saw something that made her gasp.

A campfire flickered in the dark at least a mile away. Could it belong to Poppy's abductors?

She cinched the saddle again, ignoring Pavo's irritated head toss, and pulled him along. The little fire in the distance was nestled in the foothills and easily visible, and Isa imagined Poppy sitting next to it. She must be terrified. Isa's palms sweat as she eased down the hill, keeping her footsteps light. She almost expected to hear the cock of a gun or a low, deep voice in her ear telling her to put her hands up.

When she got close enough to see the silhouette of a man sitting beside the fire, she paused. If she got any closer, their horses would smell Pavo and neigh a welcome. She didn't want to alert them, so she kept Pavo saddled, wrapped herself in a blanket and an oilskin, and tried to get some sleep.

The next morning, her eyes popped open, her heart racing. But no one stood over her like in her dream. Warily, she rolled her blanket and oilskin and strapped it behind her saddle. A quarter of a mile away, the campfire was still warm.

Two horses, three sets of footprints. The smaller ones had to be Poppy's.

Isa was faced with a dilemma, teetering between riding back to convince Sol that there was a trail right beneath his nose and keeping going and letting him find her later.

You're not bein' a help, you're being a pain in the ass, go!

The memory decided her. With a stubborn tilt to her chin, Isa nudged Pavo's sides and melted into the thickening woods, leaving a trail of sunflower seeds behind her.

Chapter Twenty-Four

The morning Poppy went missing, Sol left her full of restless energy. Once she had decided there was no point in waiting around for Sol to come back, she dressed.

Through the attic floorboards wafted the scent of frying bacon and baking buttermilk biscuits. For the first time in days, she breathed in the breakfast aromas and felt no nausea. Grateful for that small blessing, she slid the key to Mrs. Hobb's storage room into the small pocket in one of her skirt's pleats. Her stomach growled beneath the stacks of dresses, trousers, and petticoats piled into her arms.

Just a quick jaunt to the kitchens before I go next door, she thought. She had missed Minnie, anyway.

A sleep-tousled Isa met her on the landing.

"Are you helping in the diner today?" Poppy asked. As far as she knew, Isa had no idea about Nelson and his relationship to Alwine. She wished she could talk to her or Lucy about it, but it would have to wait. It was better to relay everything to the sheriff and a lawyer first.

"No, I'm to go to the general store and inventory all those supplies that came in yesterday," Isa replied through a yawn. She squeezed her amber-green eyes shut and gave Poppy's dress a second look. "Is there a funeral?"

Poppy wished it were that simple. "No, I have a bit of business to take care of and need to look—"

"Serious?" Isa offered, squeezing around Poppy and her bulky clothing to crack the door open. "Ms. Minnie, can I sneak some breakfast before work?"

"'Course you can, honey. Come on in," came Minnie's friendly reply from the area of the stovetop.

"Want anything?" Isa glanced at Poppy.

"Um—a couple of biscuits?"

"That's all?" Isa sounded dubious.

"Yes, I'll eat a large lunch to make up for it." Poppy avoided Isa's penetrating look and chatted with Mr. Ricci at the front desk.

"Here you go." Isa returned with two handfuls of biscuits. One pair had bacon sandwiched between them, a proclivity rubbed off from Lucy.

"My hands are full. Let's drop these orders off at the general store, then we can eat. Well, then, I can eat." Poppy amended. Isa had already polished off half a bacon biscuit.

Poppy led the way on the back porch, crossed the empty alleyway, and unlocked the door. It was still dark enough outside that the morning was mostly mist and shadows. Swirls of fog hung heavily around the tops of the buildings, weighing the air down. A rider passed the front of the alley, facing them. At first, Poppy went stiff, focusing, but his hair was too long to be Nelson. Her shoulders relaxed.

Holding the door open, Isa polished off the last of her second biscuit. She was just like her brother; always eating and quick about it.

Mr. Hobb hadn't come downstairs yet, so Poppy hung the orders on the rack behind the counter, labeling each with a yellow tag and length of twine. Nausea encroached because of her proximity to the shelves of hair pomade and cigars.

"I'm going to eat these on the back porch, Isa." Poppy raised her biscuits in a salute and opened the storage room door, inhaling the outside air before her mouth filled with bile.

Isa's answer was a distracted grunt over her clipboard.

It was only a little lighter outside, the promise of more rain in the air. The fog refused to dissipate, and the air's moisture exacerbated the stench of the alley. Poppy held her breath, closed her eyes, and chewed through a biscuit. She remained very still, afraid that any sudden movement would encourage retching.

Halfway through the first biscuit, her stomach settled.

Opening her eyes, she took a tentative gulp of air. According to her calculations, she was approaching four weeks since her last menses. Would she feel this queasy her whole pregnancy?

Her hand was halfway to her belly when movement caught her eye.

For one bizarre moment, she thought Franny was crouched in the alley with her.

A woman in a dark green dress and a black, outdated pelisse straightened from her hunch and stepped away from the hotel wall where the shadows were deepest. Poppy almost choked on a biscuit crumb before she realized that Francesca was much taller and broader than this veiled woman.

"May I help you?" Poppy asked, fighting a quiver of uncertainty.

Odd people always visited the general store. Even the strange had to eat, and the Hobbs were kind souls known to never turn away someone in need. Sometimes beggars did as Alwine did, knocking on the side door to avoid drawing attention to themselves.

But Poppy didn't recognize the woman until she drew nearer, the large setting on her ring winking in the grayish light.

"Mrs. Smithe? Is that you?" It wasn't a comfort to know that the dark figure was Nelson's wife, and Poppy's eyes swept both ends of the alley. There was no one else.

"I heard you yesterday," Mrs. Smithe said behind her veil. It ruffled with her breath. In, out. In, out. "I stood beside the stairs. I heard everything."

Discomposed, Poppy remained poised at the foot of the storage room stoop, the last biscuit between her fingertips. They stood six feet apart, two blackbirds in a face-off over something rotten. Why had Mrs. Smithe worn mourning clothes when pastels were her color of choice?

"Why are you dressed so?" Poppy asked stupidly. She could not bear to mention Nelson. He'd remained nameless in her mind for so long since her sixteen-year-old awareness had discovered that being intimate with a grown man as a child was wrong.

"Because my marriage is dead," Mrs. Smithe whispered. She strolled closer.

Poppy sidestepped the stoop and faced the street, her back to the hotel's backyard, but paused in her escape when Mrs. Smithe lifted the veil attached to her hat.

The woman's face was a map of bruises.

Deep purple ringed Mrs. Smithe's eye from her brow to her cheekbone. The eye itself was half-closed, the skin dark red. Her lips were split. Maroon had blossomed from her chin to her ear along her jawline. Poppy was familiar with this type of bruising; hard fists attached to angry customers existed at every saloon. Moira had bruised easily but was slippery as an eel and could always escape after the first two blows.

"Did I cause this?" Poppy needed to know.

There was an expression on Mrs. Smithe's face, a curious blend of devastation and wryness. "You did not throw his fists for him, did you?" was her non-answer.

"I am so sorry." She didn't feel comfortable enough with the other woman to reach a hand out to console her. Even now, Mrs. Smithe's body language was aloof, her hands in tight knots in the fur of her pelisse. Voice gentle, Poppy asked, "Would you like to stay in a room at the hotel until it's safe to go home?"

For a long moment, Mrs. Smithe's pale eyes stared at her. "You are very pretty, you know."

Poppy's discomfiture heightened.

"So was—is, that foreign girl." Mrs. Smithe forced out a tight laugh. Her lips looked so painful. "That's why I came here. You said you knew the girl, so yesterday I went looking for her."

"You what?" Poppy felt her forehead wrinkle.

Mrs. Smithe talked faster. Her hand slid inside her coat. "After the girl ruined my luncheon, I asked Mr. Smithe who she was. He denied any knowledge of her. But I confronted him last night after your cowboy visited and bloodied his lip. I'd overheard the two of you, and I wanted answers." Her voice climbed to just above a whisper. "He finally admitted to me what he knew, that she was taken care of."

Poppy shrunk back infinitesimally. Something about the woman's air denied gestures of pity, a low, hostile vibration. She tried to calm herself. To tell herself that it was common for people to respond that way to hardship, to be angry and unapproachable. "Please. What has he done to Ally? Is she hurt?"

Mrs. Smithe's answer was to pull a derringer from her coat and point it directly at Poppy's stomach. Its dull sheen taunted her, the black hole at the end of the muzzle staring menacingly.

"Get in the buggy across the street and I won't shoot you." Mrs. Smithe's words were hard. She yanked her veil into place with her other hand.

"What?" Poppy breathed, disbelieving.

"There are two men in the alley across the street with guns on you as well. If you don't make a fuss, you won't get shot." Mrs. Smithe shoved the muzzle of the gun against Poppy's corseted belly. "Move!"

Dreamlike, Poppy reluctantly allowed Mrs. Smithe to prod her across the street. She attempted to make eye contact with the three people she saw going about their daily business, but it was as though she were invisible. It was still dark enough outside that everything was murky, and no one caught sight of the gun pointed at her back from the recesses of Mrs. Smithe's coat. When they reached a covered black buggy, Poppy glanced across it at the black void of the alley. Two shadows stared back, their horse's heads illuminated in the dingy light. She imagined the barrels of two guns pointed at her.

She climbed in the buggy without complaint, feeling faint and sick.

Behind them, just out of view, a curtain in a second-floor window opened. Mrs. Smithe grabbed the reins and steered the buggy onto the street, two men on horses emerging from the alley to follow.

MRS. SMITHE CONTROLLED the reins one-handed, the other tucked hidden in her coat.

Poppy was unbearably conscious of the gun pointed at her through the old-fashioned pelisse.

It was obvious Mrs. Smithe was unused to driving.

"Where are you taking me?" Poppy's throat was desiccated with fear.

"You will see," Mrs. Smithe murmured through molars clenched in concentration. "When we moved here, Nelson promised me to stop his hedonistic ways. I am beyond dissatisfied with moving, you must understand, Mrs. Daniels. From town to town, we have absconded, and in each one, he would get into hot water, and we'd be off again."

"How would he get into hot water?"

"Don't play the fool, if you please," Mrs. Smithe sneered. Through her black veil, her eyes were narrow slits of dislike. On either side of them, the overcast sky turned the foliage dark, vivid green. There were far fewer people out and about today than Poppy liked.

A frisson of anger inched its way through the fear. "You're saying you knew he was committing adultery."

"He was unfaithful, yes."

"And you were aware that these were not women but children? That he was taking their innocence?"

"Innocence, pah," Mrs. Smithe spat, the veil billowing from her mouth. "There is nothing innocent about any of them. Little temptresses in training. And folk want to make such an ordeal about the ones that went missing, knowing their sinful way of life got them into the mess to begin with. What a farce."

Disgust extinguished any remaining pity Poppy felt for the woman.

"I wouldn't expect one from the lower circles to understand." Mrs. Smithe paused. "But then, you were one of his, weren't you?"

"I was never anything of his," Poppy expelled vehemently. "I was a child, and he was a villain of the most despicable sort, preying on the weak and destitute."

For a quarter mile, Mrs. Smithe said nothing. Her silence turned contemplative. Then, "You must understand, I did try to stop him."

Poppy refused to look at her but couldn't help listening.

"I followed him one night and caught him visiting a saloon. I confronted him, and he cornered me. I just knew he would finally kill me and end it all. But Mr. Williams—your intended—he saved me. Nelson fled. I have tried to stop him. But in the end, I always end up looking the worse for wear."

That was why Mrs. Smithe always watched Sol.

"When I heard of the missing girls in every county Nelson had visited, I was too afraid to speak up. Imagine the scandal." Mrs. Smithe shuddered delicately.

"What are you—" Poppy gasped as more pieces fell to make a larger, more disturbing picture. "Are you implying that Ace is behind the girls' abductions?"

"He had promised he would stop—oh!" The livery horse, feeling the tension in the reins, tossed her head and started running. For a moment, Mrs. Smith pulled her other hand from her jacket, still clutching the gun, and tried to control the mare's movements.

Poppy saw her chance and wrenched the reins from Mrs. Smithe.

The gun clattered to the boards at their feet then fell beneath the buggy. Mrs. Smithe squawked a warning to the men behind them.

"Hyah!" Poppy screamed, flicking the reins hard against the buggy horse's broad back. The mare whinnied and jolted forward, knocking the older woman hard against the back of the canopy. They galloped fast, Poppy's eyes anxiously scanning for a property with a home. In the distance, she could see the dilapidated, ramshackle building of The Dusty Rose with its rotting picket fence.

"Stop it! Stop, you're going to kill us!" Mrs. Smithe screeched. Her veil flew up, revealing her discolored face.

Poppy was beyond hearing. She could feel the thunder of hoofbeats behind them like a drum in her belly, and her teeth clenched so hard that her jaw ached. Both women's eyes streamed with tears, buffeted by the wind whistling past them.

They weren't going to make it to help.

Eyes flaring impossibly wide, Poppy watched as a second rider with long, scraggly hair burst from the woods at their left. He leaned low over his horse, steering his mount to flank their buggy horse and take control of the halter. Realizing she would never outrun them, she sawed back on the reins. The first rider behind them passed the buggy, and Poppy noted he was the bespectacled man with the bowler hat. He wheeled his horse tightly around. When the buggy slowed enough not to break her leg, she jumped, grunting as her black lace-up boots impacted the sandy road.

"Get her!" shouted the first rider from ahead.

The second rider rounded his horse in a tight circle and charged her. She zigzagged in a panic-induced haze, but the man's horse mirrored her every movement as though she were a recalcitrant calf at branding time. Its knees dug rivets in the dirt to her left, and she had one final look at the sad white house with the missing shutters when a cruel, wiry arm hooked around her throat.

She was suddenly airborne, tethered only by the arm that held her in a choke-hold, her feet running in midair. It was shocking to be held by one's neck in such a way, slinging around like a rag doll as the man with the punishing grip trotted back to the other man. Something terrible became clear at once.

She was going to die.

Poppy felt trapped as surely as if the arm was a noose and she was dangling before her executioners. Never would she see Sol. Never would she share candy, hear his jokes, or kiss his soft lips. She clawed the arm of steel beneath her upthrust chin, wishing she could scream at the loss of everything precious.

Mrs. Smithe's features were set and white when they rounded the gig.

And as everything went fuzzy, then black, Poppy saw pure hatred on the other woman's face.

POPPY CAME TO in a rush of the sound of slapping tree limbs, horse-like snorts, and the occasional squelch and crunch of hooves stepping on twigs and mud riddling the forest floor.

Blearily, she forced her eyelids to open a crack. She had a crick in her neck, and she rotated it. More discomfort. A glance at her aching, burning wrists revealed a rope wrapped around her wrists. She was efficiently tied up and helpless on a horse in front of another person.

Her heart thrummed like a hummingbird's. She tried to slow her breathing. To keep her body relaxed.

"I know you are awake," said a man's calm voice behind her.

She didn't answer.

She was riding with the bespectacled man on a dun mustang. The long-haired man who had caught her had ridden a brown and white Appaloosa.

Poppy decided that pretending was pointless, and she asked in a voice husky from abuse, "Where are we going?"

"To the others," the man answered cryptically.

Nostrils flaring, smelling the damp earth around them, she looked and failed to recognize their surroundings. It could be any forest in southeast Texas. "What others?"

"The other girls, of course." His voice was still politely conversational. "You know, even if I hadn't seen you in the foyer, I'd have known you'd be pretty. All the girls he wants taken care of are."

Taken care of? "Do you mean that Ace wanted me killed?"

The shoulders behind her shrugged. "You know something that will get him locked up. That is typical. He finds a girl, woos her, and if they're stupid enough to get too close"—he made a noise like a discharging firearm behind her head—"he sends us to take care of them."

"Is that what happened to Alwine?" she asked, almost afraid to know.

"It was the plan. But, 'tis a shame to snuff out what could make a pretty penny instead."

Something must be wrong with her brain. She wasn't making connections like normal. Did he mean to say that Alwine was alive? Were they to be put to work? Bringing her bound wrists upward, she massaged her forehead.

"Your head aches?" he asked genially. "I told Hoodoo to be gentle; I wanted a good look at you first."

The man had an underlying accent almost too faint to catch, a southern boy trying to sound like a Yankee. And despite the friendly tone, Poppy was under no illusions that he was the gentleman he appeared to be at first glance.

Tell him your name. Make yourself a person to him, not just chattel.

"My name is Poppy Daniels," she said softly, deferentially.

"Poppy, the flower of Morpheus, the god of dreams." His own voice was faint. "The poppy was my mother's favorite flower. For its medicinal uses, however, not its beauty. Are you medicinal?"

The question was so strange, this conversation in the middle of nowhere so surreal that she stammered, "I-I know how to care for people who are sick if that is what you imply."

He chucked against her drooping hair. Her instinct was to move away from the sensation, but she fought it, holding very still.

"Do you? That is delightful to know. Remember, Little Poppy, the more useful you are, the more you will find a place amongst us. But, if you are not, then I have no qualms about meting out the end that our friend Ace so succinctly had planned for you. Do you understand?"

Quelling any tell-tale tremble of fear those words instilled, Poppy nodded. "Yes. I understand perfectly."

"Good," he replied jovially. "As for me, you may address me as Mr. Hall."

They rode in silence for hours. Poppy's stomach growled. She hadn't had anything to drink that day and suffered for it now. For a time, she imagined how Sol was feeling, and her misery increased.

The second man, the one Mr. Hall had addressed as "Hoodoo," eventually rode up beside them and spoke in an indecipherable language. It reminded Poppy of Lou Lou, and she wondered if he was also Cajun French. Hoodoo was middle-aged but was as spry and wiry as a man half his age with a sparse beard and long hair.

While Mr. Hall spoke in what sounded like fluent French, Poppy pondered the many revelations from her conversation with Mrs. Smithe.

Nelson had been behind the abductions of the missing girls. And these men? They were his accomplices. Alwine must be alive, but she wasn't supposed to be, according to her captor. And Poppy and the other girls were to make money. Her first thought was prostitution. And they were traveling southwest. Nelson Smithe had mentioned taking bank notes to Laredo for a last shipment. Were they traveling to the border? If so, they would travel for weeks.

Would that give Sol enough time to find her?

Poppy didn't see how. No one would ever suspect Mrs. Smithe capable of such duplicity. Survival instincts made her thoughts and pulse race. It wasn't the first time she'd been in dire straits. She would survive this, and as she was no longer at the mercy of her mother's poor choices, she would make all the right ones.

Think, Poppy, think.

Mind focusing, she glanced at Hoodoo to her left. He looked straight ahead, listening to Mr. Hall drone on and on in French. Slowly, she reached into her sewing apron and prayed her things hadn't fallen out in the scuffle.

Thankfully, the pockets were deep, and the only thing missing was her scissors. Fingers splayed, fumbling around, she found her silver thimble. Using the giant knot of rope that bound her wrists, she hid her actions and flicked the thimble to the right. She held her breath.

Mr. Hall hadn't noticed.

The next time she reached into her apron, she found her spool of red silk thread. Finding the end of the thread took so long that her lower back prickled with sweat, her face damp and stiff. Finally, she felt the end wrap around a finger. Clenching the spool in a fist, she pulled her hands out of her apron pocket. While the men conversed, she snapped a length of thread off, keeping her movements slow, and flicked several inches of red silk thread onto a vine on the trail.

THEY STOPPED FOR camp a couple of hours before the sun set.

Mr. Hall dismounted and, without waiting for permission, grabbed Poppy beneath her arms and pulled her down. It was a feat of strength to keep her shaking legs from buckling. She had never ridden a horse astride for so long. He steadied her, and she took her first good look at him.

Mr. Hall had a bespectacled, even face. He was in his forties, ashy blond hair cut neatly beneath a bowler hat that paired well with his well-tailored traveling clothes. His dark eyes were beady and shrewd upon her but impersonal.

"Are you in mourning?" he asked with mild interest.

She said the first thing that came to mind. "I'm a widow."

"No chance of a babe?" he asked, eyes narrowing on her trim, corseted waist. "We cannot have our girls in a delicate condition where we are going."

Hiding the flare of panic in her eyes, she shook her head. "No. No babe. My husband has been dead a year."

Satisfied, Mr. Hall grabbed the rope dangling from her wrists. Her fingers were slightly discolored and swollen, and she shifted her hands uncomfortably but kept mum as she followed behind. Hoodoo built a campfire, and she was pushed inexorably to the ground beside it. It didn't take much. The slightest pressure from Mr. Hall had her knees buckling. The earth was pungent with rich soil and the faint undertones of forest floor rot. She watched Hoodoo's hands pile kindling and layer on slightly damp wood. His fingernails were black with grime, his hair in greasy strings around his rough face.

Skin crawling, Poppy remained immobile as a statue. Her mind raced, and fear made her hands tremble. If these men made demands of her body...

Don't think of such things!

What had Sol said? *Worrying only makes a person suffer twice?*

In the end, she worried for naught. Mr. Hall remained polite, if cryptic, and made no inappropriate overtures toward her. He was clearly educated and charming enough to engender friendliness, but there was a coldness to him that prevented formality. He reminded her of a stray she'd befriended as a girl, a cheerful little mutt that played with her and charmed her with his doggy smile. She'd named him Rocky and fed him scraps from her plate for weeks. One day, she'd approached him and reached down to pet his narrow head. She hadn't seen the bone he was chewing between his paws. It had happened in a flash of bared teeth and a vicious growl.

Rocky had bitten Poppy's hand to the bone.

The worst part, she remembered, was sobbing over her bleeding wound several feet away from the dog she'd considered her closest friend. Rocky, having immediately gone back to his bone, ignored her weeping in stoic unconcern. Men like Mr. Hall were the human version of Rocky. Smiling and playful one minute, reactive and biting the next. A common characteristic between the two was the lack of empathy once they bit.

If Sol ever hurt Poppy, remorse would consume him. Despite his teasing and jokes, he was a man who felt deeply, especially about others. Thoughts of Sol made her nose sting, and she struggled to control herself. It was not the time to get maudlin. She must maintain control.

HOODOO RETURNED FROM the woods in a troubled state the following day, his words quick. After a few terse instructions, Mr. Hall reined in his dun horse, dismounted, and tied it to some brush. He pulled a gun from his belt and tipped his hat up to look up at Poppy, still bound and mounted.

"Make a sound, make a move, and I will shoot you, Little Poppy," he whispered up at her.

When he didn't blink, Poppy nodded, unnerved.

He turned his back to her and crouched beside the tree they hid behind.

Hoodoo hitched his horse and circled back on foot.

Excitement and fear warred within her. If they were nervous and circling back, someone was following them. Isa had claimed that Sol and Junior were expert trackers, especially with Hog's help.

Please be Sol, she prayed. Then, she prayed that it wasn't. If Sol were hurt....

They were silent for so long that Poppy began to relax behind the tree. Whoever it was that Hoodoo went back to get must have gotten away.

Then, a scream in the distance made her and the horses jump in unison.

Animal noises grew closer, like a struggling bobcat, and the thunder of horse hooves receded from where they hid. The wild noises, however, drew closer. Frowning, Mr. Hall stood from his crouch and rounded the tree.

Hoodoo dragged someone who seemed to have more than the usual amount of arms and legs flailing all over the place. It wasn't until Poppy caught a glimpse of flying honey-blonde braids and bib overalls that she gasped.

Isa?

What are you doing here, you fool?

Isa's struggles abruptly ceased when Mr. Hall pointed the steady barrel of his pistol at her. Hoodoo, winded and bent over at the waist, huffed something out.

"Hoodoo said you were following us," Mr. Hall said. "Why?"

Isa closed her lips tight, but her enormous eyes ruined the effect.

Mr. Hall cocked the revolver and pointed it close enough to Isa's face that her eyes crossed. "Now, I will only ask one more time, girl.

Who are you, and why are you following us?" Mr. Hall's tone was light, but his eyes were hard behind his spectacles.

Do something!

"That's my cousin," Poppy cried, breaking the tension. They turned to look at her, Isa included. She went limp in Hoodoo's straining arms.

"Poppy," she breathed and closed her eyes.

"Is this true?" Mr. Hall demanded.

"Yes." Isa opened her eyes but only looked at Poppy. "She's my cousin. I followed her."

"That is impossible." Mr. Hall uncocked the pistol but didn't lower it.

Isa swallowed and admitted, "It was difficult. But I have an affinity for tracking."

"Do you?" Mr. Hall smiled. It was not a nice smile. "Stand her up, Hoodoo. Who else is with you?"

"No one," Isa said hastily. She stood so tall that she was eye-to-eye with him. "I didn't trust that Smithe woman and followed her tracks in front of that bordello. I saw signs of a struggle." Her eyes briefly passed over the faint greenish bruising beneath Poppy's jaw. "And then I followed two horses' tracks into the woods. No one was with me."

"Hoodoo?" Mr. Hall asked, ignoring this. "Where is her horse?"

Hoodoo, still breathing hard and standing in widespread readiness behind Isa in case she got any ideas of escape, shook his head. He said something in Cajun French.

Isa tilted her ear, listening.

"Don't just stand there. Tie her up and go find it!" There was a hint of temper in Mr. Hall's voice. Rocky, indeed. The other man tied Isa's hands with a length of rough rope, mounted his horse, and melted into the woods around them.

For a moment, Mr. Hall was silent, ignoring Isa's shifting feet and Hoodoo's hoofbeats in the distance. Finally, he murmured, "*Equo ne credite.*"

As though confused, Isa blurted, "Don't trust the horse?"

It was the first time Poppy had seen the man with the bowler hat show surprise. He raised a brow and tipped his hat mockingly. "The Trojan horse, if you will."

"Oh." Isa looked unsure. "Well, I'm alone. A bunch of armed Trojans won't come exploding out of me."

Mr. Hall's eyes narrowed in calculation. He circled her. "What is your name, child?"

"Isa." When he stared at her, she added, "Short for Isadora."

His mouth barely turned up. "Isadora. Gift of the goddess, Isis."

"The Egyptian goddess? Is that what it means?" Isa's attention occasionally shifted to Poppy while Mr. Hall's brows rose again.

"How is it that you know Latin?"

"I read a lot. There are Latin dictionaries in the library."

Mr. Hall conceded, "That is true. What else do you know?"

His words from the day before echoed in Poppy's mind.

The more useful you are, the more that you will find a place among us.

"She is good with numbers," Poppy said from the horse, tightening her face as though preparing to be shot. Mr. Hall didn't even glance at her.

"In what way are you good with numbers?" For the first time, his question wasn't rhetorical. He was serious, unamused, peering at Isa through his thick lenses.

"Sums come easy to me," Isa shrugged as though it were nothing. Her eyes never left his gun. "I can write solutions to difficult math problems in my sleep. I can solve most equations. Give me multiple numbers in an equation, and I can give you the answer."

"How are you with bookkeeping?" His eyes glittered with sudden fervency.

Nose wrinkling, Isa's answer was almost flippant. "It's child's play."

Poppy glanced at her, a warning in her eyes.

But he smiled. From within his vest lining, he pulled a tiny stitched journal. "Are there any discrepancies in here?"

"You want me to look at the whole thing?"

"No, no. I would like you to review October of last year to April of this year."

"Sure."

Poppy waved away mosquitoes at her neck while Isa made audible tsking sounds. She awkwardly scanned three pages, flipping them with her bound hands.

"Here." Isa stepped forward to show Mr. Hall something midway down the last page. "This number. The total has deviated by one thousand two hundred because of this entry here."

He glanced at the paper, plucked it from Isa's hands, and pocketed it. "Very good. Do you have any other uses?"

"I can tell you how many seconds old you are," Isa said slowly, but her fists clenched at his words. "But that is not useful. I suppose I don't know what you consider useful. Sir."

Be calm, Isa. Remain steady.

"Why, anything that can produce money, of course," he replied.

Later, Hoodoo returned with the unfortunate news that Isa's pony had escaped, and she was reluctantly loaded onto the back of the Appaloosa with him. No fire was lit when they camped that night, and the two men kept Poppy and Isa separated.

On the third day of Poppy's abduction, they entered a clearing. An abandoned barn listed to the left, close to collapsing, and as the small party entered it, a lookout hiding in the loft called out.

Two men exited from the barn, and Poppy saw three wagons within its depths.

For the first time that day, Mr. Hall addressed her.

"Shall we meet the other girls?"

Chapter Twenty-Five

Having dwelled in Mr. Hall's presence for three days, Poppy felt his tension as though he had reached forward and gripped her. Something was wrong.

The two men that exited the barn strode as though racing to get to Mr. Hall first. The first to reach them was a stern-looking man with plain clothes, a beard that came to a point, and a bald head hidden by a hat. He hooked a thumb at the second man. "Cash brought men in last night, Ed."

The second man, Poppy noted, was the same one that had grabbed for her at The Dusty Rose. He opened his mouth to say something, glanced at her, then did a double take. "What's she doin' here?"

"The question, Cash, is why you brought strangers into our camp?" Mr. Hall's tone could have frozen brimstone.

"I got the right to make money with my girls," Cash insisted defiantly, shifting on his feet, spurs jangling. Silver accents glinted at various parts of his body. His cuffs. His gun belt. The tips of his pointed boots. His ruby shirt was ostentatious, his jeans expensive. The engraved Colt on his gun belt had pearl grips.

Ignoring him, Mr. Hall dismounted. "Sid, where are they?"

"Three around the fire, and one's in the loft having a tumble with Mina."

"Hoodoo, chain the girls up with the others and see to the horses."

The three men strode away, fury in every line of Mr. Hall's slight figure. At the side of the barn was a campfire surrounded by men. One, a bald behemoth in suspenders, rose and greeted Mr. Hall effusively. Hoodoo had just pulled Poppy and Isa down when gunfire erupted near the group of men. Mr. Hall had drawn his gun and shot at three men who attempted to scramble away from the fire. Return fire from a survivor clipped the bald man, who roared and fired his own six-gun, ending the skirmish.

Several feminine screams pierced the air from the barn, like a half dozen kettles releasing steam, then went quiet. A man in long johns unbuttoned to his hairy stomach darted out of the leaning building, gun drawn, but Hoodoo's revolver flashed and fired. The man crumpled to the grass in a graceless, faded red heap. Poppy had dropped to her belly, attempting to cover her ears with her tied hands. Isa, however, crouched and looked wild-eyed for cover.

As though it was nothing out of the ordinary, Hoodoo holstered his pistol and tugged at their ropes. Isa helped Poppy up, and they clung to each other as they walked, the whites of their eyes gleamed, scanning for more surprise shoot-outs. They were led like sheep into the barn. Eyes adjusting, Poppy saw three wagons parked tailboard to yoke in a line. They rounded the smallish chuckwagon, and their breath caught.

The first two wagons, whose canvases were rolled and tucked up, were full of girls and women of varying ages. Blank eyes in faces that were brown with dirt turned their direction like a dozen curious owls. Hoodoo ignored the girls in the second wagon, who watched Poppy and Isa with callous eyes as they passed. She recognized two of them from The Dusty Rose.

Most shocking of all were the iron shackles adorning their necks, tethering each manacle with an attached chain.

"They are being transported in coffles," Isa breathed, horrified. "Traders used those types of shackles on slaves before the war."

Poppy swallowed. Her heart ached for them.

Near the front of the second wagon, two more women stood out. Neither wore chains. The heavyset proprietress of the Dusty Rose stood to the side with her arms crossed, her thin mouth curled in a sneer. Big Maude. Her chin was upraised while Poppy was escorted past her to the first wagon. A sinister riding crop was clenched in one fist.

The second woman had dark hair and eyes and had just completed her descent from the ladder leading to the loft. She was the woman Poppy had freed Alwine from.

Big Maude said you broke Mina's nose.

Mina watched Poppy pass with naked loathing and absently touched the bridge of her nose. A large, unflattering bump sat atop it like a knob on a live oak limb.

After dismissing the hatred in the dark eyes, she investigated the first wagon as they flanked it. There were more girls in this wagon than the first—six altogether—chained to each other by their necks. The difference between this group was that their eyes displayed true fear. It rolled off them in waves. Hoodoo, the rope still in hand, rummaged in the side compartment of the wagon. He pulled out a pair of shackles and a length of chain. Rather than fight Isa to don the restraint, he simply pointed his gun at her. Isa closed the hinged manacle around her neck, her burning eyes promising retribution. As Hoodoo closed and locked Poppy's, a horrible sense of claustrophobia overwhelmed her. She breathed hard through pinched nostrils and closed her eyes. Isa's hand touched her shoulder.

"Take slower breaths, Poppy," Isa whispered. Her voice was tight. "Don't faint, please don't faint."

"I won't," Poppy said and opened her eyes. Her weakness shamed her, and she forced a smile. "I'm fine now."

Hoodoo, who had spent that terrible minute connecting the long, weighty length of chain to their cuffs, shushed them. Then, he dropped the tailboard of the first wagon and unceremoniously shoved them in and chained Isa to a youthful brunette. As soon as he left the barn to gather the horses, Isa bent to Poppy.

"Are you sure—"

"Quiet!" screeched a voice behind them.

She had just enough time to duck as Mina yanked the crop from Big Maude and struck Poppy with it. Thankfully, the shackle had caught most of the blow.

"Hey!" Isa exclaimed, half-rising. "She wasn't even talking!"

"Sh!" Poppy hissed, pulling the impetuous girl back down.

Hoodoo, who had just returned with his and Mr. Hall's horses, intervened. He spoke hotly to Mina, grabbed the crop from her unresisting hand, and stalked to an open stall. Mina whirled away in a huff in the direction of the men.

For the rest of the afternoon, everyone sat in silence.

WHEN DUSK SETTLED, Big Maude was relieved by a stout, dirty man that Poppy could smell from the wagon.

All at once, the atmosphere relaxed, and the girls began to speak to each other.

Poppy was desperate to learn more about the girls. After stilted introductions, she managed to get the one Isa was chained to, Gretchen, to open up.

Gretchen was seventeen, the oldest, and intelligent. She was also one of the first to go missing, and had been taken from Brazos County three months before.

"Who took you?" Poppy whispered, mindful of the constant, low murmuring in the second wagon. The stout man, who rested on a rusty overturned bucket, scratched his groin through his trousers. The girls, curious, clustered around Poppy so that they could hear.

"That Hoodoo man took me, Caroline, and Pilar. But the other one, Mr. Hall, brought Vera, Gloria, and Prudence. They were like you."

"What do you mean 'like me'?" Poppy frowned.

"Extras. You were supposed to go to ground." Gretchen was pragmatic and unemotional. Even the youngest girls didn't blink.

"Oh." A chill went through her, and, hoping she was wrong, she asked, "Did they know Nelson Smithe?"

"Who's Nelson Smithe?" Gretchen asked.

"You might know him as Ace."

The youngest of the bunch with the filthiest face raised her hand. "Ooh, I know Mr. Ace. He gave me a dolly." Vacant good humor in her eyes implied she was tetched. "He gave it to me for bein' so good."

"I had one too," the girl chained to Gretchen said, lip wobbling. "But that mean Hoodoo man took it."

One of the older girls, Pilar, nodded to the nearly emaciated girl chained to her. "Gloria used to cry every night about losing her doll."

Poppy donned her gentlest expression and leaned toward the children. "And were these very special dolls? With ribbons and nice clothes?"

All three nodded, and Gloria whispered, "Mine had real hair."

"And that nice man gave them to you?"

More nods.

After more prompting, Poppy discovered that Nelson had taken a liking to the three girls, each from a different town but similar in their youth, their neglect, and their desperate lack of love and attention. Some knew him by other aliases, and each explained that they lived in places where men came and went all the time. Every one of the girls remembered their mothers, fathers, or aunties growing angry with Ace and that not long after that, Mr. Hall stole them away in the night, leaving their dolls, clothes, and families behind.

Gretchen pointed at the next oldest girl, Caroline, who was sixteen. "Caroline is from Grimes. She heard a lot about what's going to happen to us."

Caroline was blonde and pretty, with an air of perpetual sadness. "My father is French, so I understand most of what Hoodoo and Mr. Hall say. They're taking us to Laredo to be sold at the border."

Silence expanded. Pilar crossed her arms, Gloria chewed her hair, and Gretchen pulled the weeping child chained to her into her lap.

"Laredo is a long way from here," Poppy murmured. Her mouth was so dry that her tongue was a clumsy thing in her mouth. "Where did they keep you all hidden for so many weeks?"

"That big mansion," the dirty-faced girl helpfully supplied, smiling wide. Her teeth were in the beginning stages of rot.

"The Dusty Rose is a *casa de putas*, Prudence." said Pilar. "Not a mansion. Not a castle. It's a prison."

Prudence's smile dimmed.

"They kept us holed up in the cellar with Big Maude," Gretchen said, rife with loathing. "I hate it there. That woman is the devil."

Caroline nodded, her golden hair lank and falling from its braid. "She is an evil woman."

"They are all evil," added Pilar, making the sign of the cross. "Those poor girls in the other wagon...."

"What about the girls in the other wagon?" Poppy asked, looking to Gretchen for an answer.

"Hush, Vera," Gretchen murmured to the sniffling girl in her lap. "The second wagon belongs to the other boss-man, Cash. He lets the other men—" She broke off and glanced at the youngest girls, whose ears practically wriggled in their heads. "Well, Mr. Hall does not let anyone touch us but Hoodoo and his brother. Cash, he lets his men do whatever they want with the others. And Big Maude and Mina aren't even prisoners. They work for Cash. They punish the other girls as they see fit."

"Mina thinks Cash will marry her one day," Pilar sneered, her nails digging into the dirty sleeves of her dress. "She'll do whatever he wants, even lick his boots, just for a smile. I hate that one even worse than Big Maude."

"It's a sin to hate," Prudence said, picking at her frayed hem.

"It's also a sin to kill," Pilar rejoined.

At Poppy's mystification, Gretchen leaned closer and lowered her voice. "There was another girl in their wagon that Mina would pick on something fierce. She thought that girl had eyes for Cash, but we could all see plain as day that she was pretty, and Mina was just jealous. Well, one day, we were on our walk to answer nature's call, and we heard screaming. There was Mina, standing over the girl with her chain in hand. Mina had broken her neck, and the girl couldn't move except to scream."

Poppy's hand had gone to her mouth, and she tasted the dirt under her nails. She dropped it back into her lap. None of the girls cried anymore, but the fear was back in their eyes. "What did Mr. Hall do?"

It was clear now that Mr. Hall was the leader of this unsavory operation.

"Nothing," Caroline said softly. "It was not his girl. But we could tell he was angry."

Prudence made a face in which her eyes were big, and her lips pulled thin and tight over her teeth, pretending to be Mr. Hall, and when the young girl broke character and laughed innocently at everyone's disturbed expressions, Pilar shivered.

"Your bread was not baked all the way," Pilar said, making the faintest motion of the cross with one finger.

"No, Mr. Hall couldn't do anything about it. He and Cash have rules." Gretchen held up three fingers. "Cash's group can't touch Mr. Hall's stable, and that also goes for Mr. Hall. He can't do anything about what Cash's men do to his stable." She put one finger down. "No fighting with men from the other group." Another finger. "And no bringing strangers into camp." The last finger went down.

"That's why they killed those men," Isa said lowly to Poppy. "They probably don't want any of those men telling tales about all these girls."

"One of Mr. Hall's men was shot," Poppy said.

"Who?"

"The tall, bald man."

"Oh. That's Gary," Gretchen said.

"I hate guns," Gloria said. "They shot them, and I was scared."

"Me, too. We screamed so loud." Prudence giggled, rocking back and forth in excitement.

"Gary always gets shot." Pilar's eyes narrowed on the repetitive motions of the other girl in disapproval. "He's a legend. He gets shot all the time but never dies. He'll have to ride in the supply wagon with the loco girl."

"Loco girl?" interrupted Poppy.

"Yes, Big Maude's niece. She's as mad as Prudence." Pilar leaned around Gloria and Caroline to flick Prudence's knee. "Stop that. You're rocking the wagon."

Prudence's rocking stopped, and she went back to picking her hem apart.

"Do you mean Ally?" Isa looked excitedly at Poppy. "That means she must be alive!"

Poppy smiled for the first time in days. She'd been afraid to ask the girls. Ignoring the comment about Alwine being mad, Poppy asked, "Why is she in the supply wagon?"

"She was in a family way," Gretchen explained sagely. "Mr. Hall doesn't like that. So he had Big Maude get rid of it."

That cold clamminess came back. "How...horrible."

Caroline wiped her eyes suddenly. "It was horrible. She screamed for hours."

"I wanted her to die," Pilar admitted, looking down at her tightly crossed arms. "No one should suffer torture such as that. At least death would have been peaceful."

It was a feat of strength not to drop her hand protectively over her womb. *Oh, Ally.*

Isa recalled something. "Whatever happened to that other girl, the one that woman—Mina, hurt?"

Strangely, a reluctant silence grew. None of the girls would look at them. Even Prudence grew still.

The one that finally spoke, however, was little Vera from Gretchen's lap. "She's in heaven now. That's what Gretchen said."

A chill passed over them despite the summer humidity that frizzed their hair and invited the whining drone of mosquitoes. They sat in the wagon bed and shivered.

Chapter Twenty-Six

It had been a false lead. Sol, Junior, Ben, and the Dogwood law enforcement rode like an incoming storm through town. Twenty-four hours had passed since Poppy's disappearance.

Easygoing Sol had lost his mind when the Hunstville marshal shook his head sadly and admitted that the lead had gone nowhere fast.

"The group of Bandidos we'd been tipped off on was just a family running a farm. They hadn't even been in town the whole month."

"We had another lead in Dogwood, and you're tellin' us we rode all the way up here for nothing?" Sol had shouted from the back.

All the men in the room had turned to him as one.

Sheriff Robinson, eyes round as eggs, had put a pacifying hand on Sol's shoulder. "Son—"

Sol had shrugged the hand off. "There were tracks near an abandoned whorehouse in Dogwood. My fiancée went missing just like all those girls; she wasn't even the first in our town. There was a younger girl that went missing last week."

Deputy Ellis stepped forward, ruddy with embarrassment, while the crowded room of men murmured. "We checked that brothel. Everyone had cleared out. She wasn't considered missing."

Motioning with flattened hands as though to suppress all the grumblings, the Huntsville marshal yelled over everyone. "All right, all right, just calm down. We heard your piece, Mr. Williams and all of us agreed that your fiancée didn't fit the pattern of the other girls. She is neither young enough nor from a downtrodden residence. It doesn't fit the bill. Her disappearance is an isolated event."

"She was meddling in something, that's why it happened to her!" Sol felt a red haze of helpless rage wash over him, irritating his vision, making the veins throb along his temples. "It's all connected—"

"That's enough, son," Sheriff Robinson had said firmly, steering Sol toward the door. "If you can't keep coolheaded, you can't stay."

Ben, understanding Sol's grim, questioning glance, had remained with his arms crossed and jaw firm, listening to the rest of the meeting while his friend was ushered out. Junior loyally trailed behind.

A day later, they thundered up Main Street on lathered horses, praying for good news. But the sight of Mrs. Hobb pacing the boardwalk in front of the sheriff's office drained all the hot blood from Sol's face. She held a white sheaf of paper and looked beside herself.

"Sheriff! Sol! Thank God you're back, thank God!"

They dismounted, and Sol rushed to Mrs. Hobb. Her face was white and trembling, hearty strength absent. Taking the paper thrust at him, Sol barked, "What's wrong?"

"It's Isa! She's gone!"

"What?" Junior bit out, stomping forward to rip the letter from Sol's hands. They scanned it together, and any fury that worry had melted returned full force. "Goddammit, Izzy, what the hell are you doin'?"

Sol reread the letter as though through a tunnel. Certain sentences jumped out at him.

I left as soon as you rode out.

The tracks indicate that Poppy was abducted on the road in front of The Dusty Rose.

Pavo is missing his left hind shoe.

Follow the sunflower seeds.

If I am right about everything, I will continue to follow their trail. Find me, and you'll find Poppy.

Please do not be angry. All my love, Isa.

Deputy Ellis was an unwanted presence at Sol's back, breathing down their necks.

"I'll come with you to The Dusty Rose." He sounded weary and turned to divulge the letter's contents to the sheriff.

Sol looked up at Mrs. Hobb's wringing hands. "And you haven't seen her since yesterday?"

"Not since she asked for that ten-pound bag of sunflower seeds. We were busy. I didn't even think to ask what in the world she wanted to do with it." Mrs. Hobb's deep voice quivered with worry.

"You couldn't have known," Sol reassured, but the words felt empty. Insubstantial. No one knew the thoughts that lived in Isa's head. Now that she was gone and hadn't returned, he felt her suspicions were not only valid, but obvious.

And I made a real ass of myself yesterday because she was trying to help, he thought nastily, folding the letter, and shoving it deep into his jeans pocket.

"Mrs. Hobb?" His voice was distracted, and he was looking at Junior and Ben. "I'm gonna need you to put together some supplies for us. About a week's worth of travelin' for a few men."

"You're goin' after her?" Mrs. Hobb's voice retained fear and relief in equal measures.

Deputy Ellis led his horse and caught the last of Sol's words.

"If Isa didn't show up today...that means she found them."

RELIEVING ONESELF WHILE attached at the neck to another person was an obscene kind of humiliation, especially for Isa, who wore bib overalls and had to half-undress to answer nature's call. They took turns standing sentinel in front of each other, men watching with mild interest, rifles propped in the crook of their elbows.

Poppy hated them but hid it.

Isa hated them and hid nothing.

They waited for the wagons to be hitched to mules and took turns drinking long draughts of water from Hoodoo's canteen. Big Maude spooned gruel into tin plates for the line of Cash's girls, and Poppy's stomach groaned an empty lament when she heard Mr. Hall approach.

He grabbed her by the iron manacle, retrieved a large, strangely shaped key with a leather tie from his inner vest pocket, and unlocked the hinged iron ring. The chain and shackle were heavy and clinked solidly to the ground, her neck oddly barren and weightless.

She watched the key slide back into his vest.

"Come with me."

Poppy shook her head at Isa, who made as though to dispute this turn of events, and dutifully followed the man in the bowler hat.

Big Maude's skirt was dangerously close to the fire, and Poppy felt no guilt for wishing it would light up like an autumn bonfire. When Mr. Hall led Poppy along, the sweating woman looked across the fire and leered. Maude called something out to Poppy, but it was in German. Mr. Hall's eyebrows rose, and he asked Big Maude a question in the same language. The woman scowled and went back to her spooning. Poppy tried not to look at the state of those hands. Her stomach was hollow and complaining; she couldn't afford to be picky about hygiene when she hadn't eaten anything the night before.

"What did she say?" Poppy asked, feeling the eyes of a group of Cash's men near the second wagon.

"Nothing for your ears, I daresay." He glanced back at her, his bowler hat casting a narrow shadow over his brows. "She has the manners of a pig. Which is why she could never earn a profit or keep regular customers. Why young Cash has her overseeing his girls is a mystery to me."

"Yes, I have met her." Poppy recalled being pelted by obscenities, dirt, and rocks.

"Have you?" He had an interesting way of asking questions to which he did not honestly want an answer. Like a hummingbird, his mind flitted hither and thither. It was as though he had assumed the identity of a perfectly polite gentleman, a banker's skin, but it was all a façade. He wasn't interested in how she knew Big Maude, just as he wasn't interested in the life he had robbed her from. She had only seen him have an honest concern for his brother, Gary, and a disdain for monetary waste.

Mr. Hall led her to the back of the third and smallest wagon.

A muffled voice through the canvas urged, "C'mon, littlun, drink some of it. You're gonna die if you don't get some water in ya."

It was the legendary Gary.

Their footsteps quickened, and Mr. Hall opened the canvas in a gust of mildew, old blood, and unwashed bodies. Poppy averted her face for one weak moment, tucking her nose in the crook of her elbow. Her nausea, absent for so long in the stress of the last few days, returned with a vengeance. Her mouth drooled, and she spat out bile while Mr. Hall was occupied.

"What are you doing? Here, give me your head. Damnation. You are burning with fever." His disgust belied the gentle hand upon the reclining Gary.

Producing a kerchief from her apron, Poppy pressed it to her nose and approached the wagon.

Gary was a mountain of a man. Prostrate, his feet stuck out past the lowered tailboard, and he took up a third of the wagon. Alwine was a dark, tiny lump in the corner. Ignoring his brother, Gary nudged a ladle sloshing with water at her. His head was a stubbled boulder encased in shadows.

Mr. Hall turned to Poppy unhappily. "You said that you knew how to care for the infirm. My brother is in need of your assistance."

An idea sizzled like ozone before a lightning strike. This was her chance to care for Alwine.

"Suppose I stayed in the wagon and tended your brother during the journey. It cannot be helpful to his condition to be here alone. The ill cannot care for themselves in my experience."

While Mr. Hall fell into a thoughtful silence, Poppy imagined her stomach as a cast iron tank, impenetrable and still. Shoving her kerchief back into her apron, she climbed into the back of the wagon, her bound wrists making the endeavor difficult. A large, hot hand cupped her elbow and helped her in.

The hand belonged to Gary.

Hiding her surprise by slipping on the mien she'd adopted during the days of Mrs. Daniels, Poppy sat in the claustrophobic little wagon and tucked her skirts demurely around her legs.

"Hello. I'm Poppy Daniels."

Gary's small eyes were wide and fever-bright on her face. "Gary, ma'am. You one of them angels...them death angels?"

Poppy didn't move but carefully skated her eyes to the side to meet Mr. Hall's nonplussed gaze.

"No, just a woman."

"Oh." Two deep rivets between his brows became cavernous as he thought hard. "I think I'm dyin'."

The wagon creaked as Mr. Hall braced two hands on the tailboard. "You are doing no such thing. Mrs. Daniels will be doctoring you, and you are to do everything she says. And if anything happens to you"— he broke off and met Poppy's gaze, his round spectacles flashing silver—"it'll be on her head."

Poppy nodded, her teeth clamped so hard together that her jaw ached. He returned her nod.

"Good. We have an understanding." He shoved away from the tailboard and dusted his hands off. "I'll send Mina with another bucket of water."

Although she was beyond uneasy in Mr. Hall's presence and her pulse raced faster than any rabbit, Poppy cleared her throat and asked, "May I have some soap, as well?"

For an uncomfortable moment, Mr. Hall stared. "Anything else?" His voice had no inflection or warning that her request had stepped over a line.

"Yes. Clean bandages or rags. The strongest whiskey you have. A basin." She rattled off a few more things she thought would help a gunshot wound and, hopefully, whatever wound ailed Alwine.

Mr. Hall left without another word.

Shoulders relaxing, Poppy closed her eyes and rotated her stiff neck. "Shall we see what this bullet wound looks like?"

Gary's fingers were clumsy and slow on his shirt buttons, so Poppy used his distraction to check on Alwine. The girl was in a deep sleep, her body on fire with a fever that burned even hotter than Gary's. Her legs were akimbo and bared to her knees, skirts wrapped awkwardly beneath her. A foul odor emanated from her body. It smelled of living decay, some poisonous infection that should only ever hover over wounded soldiers on a battlefield.

Such signs of infection should never cling to healthy children.

"How long has she been asleep like this?" Poppy forced herself to turn her back on Alwine.

"Uh, since after we camped here, I reckon," Gary mumbled, closing his eyes and rubbing his rough palm over the bristles of his crown.

"And when was that?"

"'Bout a week ago."

She placed her cool hands over Gary's chest, fingertips bracketing the ragged wound that gaped so wide between his left pectoral muscle and armpit that it never stood a chance at knitting together naturally. It would need to be sewn or cauterized. Older bullet wounds glinted in the light that filtered in from the front and back openings of the wagon. His body was riddled with silvery raised scars. "How many times have you been shot?" She couldn't keep the wonder from her voice.

For the first time, a grin split his wide, thin mouth. "Near about eight. This was my ninth bullet. Ed reckons I'm a cat or somethin'."

"Cats only have nine lives. You must be dearer to your body. You may not survive another bullet wound like this one."

Gary had the same beady brown eyes as Mr. Hall, but his features were coarser, asymmetrical, everything magnified twofold: nose, jaw, teeth. "You should let me die. Ain't no good."

Poppy heard footsteps near the wagon, the slosh of someone using the water barrel that was braced against the side of the wagon bed.

Leaning lower, she said gently, "Why don't you live and change, make it better?"

Gary stared at the roof of the wagon cover and pondered that while Poppy crawled backward, flashing a worried glance at Alwine.

Mina appeared from around the wagon with a bucket, a sack and a petulant expression. She wore her long, dark hair down and over one shoulder. Her movements were excessively sensual when she swung the bucket up on the tailboard, arching her back in a provocative display. Covertly, she slid her eyes to the side to assure that men were looking.

When it appeared as though Mina would stand there all day, the sack of supplies in hand, Poppy cleared her throat. "Thank you for bringing me everything."

The woman reluctantly faced her. She didn't hide the naked dislike twisting her mouth. "I didn't do it to be nice." Her declaration was forceful as though she had waited with bated breath for the right moment to say it. "And from now on, you can get your own shit."

Poppy said nothing even though her heart pounded and her hands felt jittery. She hadn't been spoken to in such a way since she was a girl traveling from town to town with Moira, a constant interloper at saloons and cathouses. Once a pecking order was already established, new girls were a threat. She had always been an easy target, quiet and solemn, but one thing she never relinquished was tears.

They would never get that part of her.

The two women sized each other up, unmoving. Mina had a broad, crooked nose that flared wide, like a bull ready to charge. Her eyes were small and a smidge too close together, and her lips were a tight, angry rosebud. She had the look of a fighter, hardened over time from fending for herself. There was nothing soft in her demeanor, no gentle nature.

"I'll take that," Poppy finally said in the growing silence and tugged the sack from Mina's clinging fingers. She dismissed the seething woman and crawled back into the depths of the wagon.

Poppy could feel Mina fighting the urge to attack. It reminded her of the other girl, the one whose neck had been broken in a fit of rage. Poppy vowed never to turn her back to the woman again.

"LET ME CUT those ropes off ya," Gary repeated.

Poppy sighed. "No, Gary, your brother will be angry."

"Naw, not at me."

From a sheath attached to his gun belt, Gary withdrew a knife with a deer horn handle and a wicked-looking blade. She had hardly blinked before he had snagged her wrists, slid the long edge between the ropes, and began to saw. Her fingers had long been discolored and stiff, and the lack of dexterity had made wrapping his cleaned wound difficult. She held as still as possible, but her arms jerked forward and backward with the violence of his sawing. She imagined him growing angry and stabbing into the soft belly of someone, slashing up in the same rough way, disemboweling them. The wagon rocked a little with his movements, and when the rope finally gave way, she had to turn her face away so the knife didn't impale her in its last upward swing.

"Thank you," she managed, unraveling the rope and holding in a moan of pain and relief. Sucking her lips between her teeth, she massaged the circulation back into her fingers. The ropes had left deep purple marks on the skin of her fiercely throbbing wrists. She flexed her hands repeatedly, eyes closed and sweat popping out on her upper lip from the tingling agony, as the feeling returned.

"I reckon that smarts real bad," Gary murmured, watching her.

The rising sun had appeared behind the thick copse surrounding them on every side. The light illuminated the angry red flesh she had bathed, sterilized with whiskey, and sewn together with her red silk thread. Gary had cursed a blue streak, twitched, and writhed, everything she had calmly asked him not to do.

Mr. Hall had materialized during this unsavory job with a feral expression. The deep, terrifying lines had smoothed into something more congenial once he'd realized she was stitching his brother's wound, not murdering him.

"Putting him back together?" he'd asked, then had turned on his heel and disappeared from view.

It was Poppy's dearest wish that Mr. Hall never looked at her in such a manner again.

Now, Gary was sewn up and bandaged with an old but clean shirt. He lay back on his bedroll with a sigh, sheathing his knife and closing his eyes.

"Have you eaten yet?" Poppy asked, knowing that he hadn't. She still wasn't sure how she felt about this man, but she recognized the danger of not caring for him properly. "You must before you rest."

Yawning hugely, revealing gaps in his molars, Gary's eyes remained closed. "I'm not real hungry. Just tired."

Pursing her lips like she used to when Mrs. Daniels went off eating during her bouts of melancholy, Poppy said, "I insist. What kind of doctor would I be if I didn't care for my patient?"

"Women ain't doctors," he laughed, finally opening his eyes. His expression sobered at how small her mouth had shrunk.

"I shall return shortly. When I get back, you will eat, drink, and sleep in that order. Then I will see to Ally's needs."

"Yes'm." He was properly contrite.

After wiping her hands on a damp rag from the basin, Poppy scooted backward out of the wagon, brushing her skirts off and stretching her aching back. She felt faintly sick from the hollowness of her stomach and approached the fire. Men surrounded it; rolling up bedrolls, eating gruel, leftover beans, and biscuits, or drinking spirits from bottles of amber liquid shimmering in the morning light. Big Maude was nowhere in sight, so Poppy eased between two grungy men to reach the fire.

"What are you doing?" asked a voice behind her.

Poppy flinched and shoved her hands into her apron pockets, turning to look at Mr. Hall's fancy, polished shoes. "I was hoping to get something to eat for Gary and Ally. They need to get their strength up if they are to mend."

"Lester," he barked. "Get her three plates."

The same short, stubby man in filthy brown trousers that had watched the girls the evening before heaved himself off his bedroll and grabbed three abandoned tin plates on the ground. "Yessir."

Stepping closer, Mr. Hall spoke softly enough that no one could hear them. "Why are your hands untied, Little Poppy?"

"Your brother cut them off. I told him you would be angry."

Some of the tension relaxed from Mr. Hall's shoulders. "You did not tell him to do it?"

Poppy's eyes bolted up to meet his, and she shook her head. "No, sir. Although, it would have been nice if he had cut the rope *before* I stitched his wound."

Sighing, he leaned past her to take one of the tin plates from Lester. "It does not surprise me that he did not think to do so. He always was a flower short of a bouquet."

Again, Poppy refrained from comment.

"When you are done caring for them, get in the wagon with the other girls. If you disobey or attempt to escape, I will rethink my decision to leave your hands unbound."

Poppy nodded, accepting the other two plates from a curious Lester, who smelled rancid enough to curl hair.

"Good." Then, he repeated, "Good."

He followed Poppy back to the chuckwagon and pushed the food on a sleepy Gary. Mr. Hall chatted with him for an hour while she attempted to cajole food and water into a nearly unconscious Alwine. The poor thing didn't even recognize her.

She washed Alwine, wiping blood, dirt, and grime from her friend's emaciated form, and broke her own rules against shedding tears by weeping into her kerchief. Then, she threw out the dirty, bloody wastewater along with the tears.

What did that horrible Maude woman do to you?

Hell would be too kind of a place for that woman.

When Alwine was finally clean, Poppy dressed her in a spare shift from the sack that must have belonged to Big Maude. It settled over her thin body like a circus tent. Wedged in a corner of the wagon was a curry comb, and she snagged it. Poppy had washed the matted blonde locks as well as she could, but wads of hair and tangles from dirty braids came out with the comb. *Wrapping the girl's hips in rags and an old oilskin would make waste cleanup much easier,* she thought with a tired sigh. Poppy tucked the girl in with a thin blanket and decided that Alwine's slumber appeared more restful now that she was dry and clean.

Mr. Hall beckoned Poppy all too soon, and they made their way along the little wagon train. The men were mounted on their horses, more than a dozen altogether. Sid, the man with the pointed beard, held Mr. Hall's saddled dun horse.

The two long lines of chained girls stood to the side, waiting to make the careful climb into their wagons. Mr. Hall, who had just locked Poppy in her shackle beside Isa, turned when a dirty, unkempt Cash strode over.

"I want the last two in my wagon," he demanded, throwing a filthy shovel to the side. "Grady, put that up." A man by the second wagon dismounted and followed orders without a sound.

Hoodoo spat out a stream of angry words on his Appaloosa near the front.

"Speak English or shut the hell up!" Cash shouted at Hoodoo, whose hand slid closer to his knife. The younger man didn't notice.

Mr. Hall—Ed—looked at Cash's filthy hands thoughtfully. "I take it by your current state of dishabille that you've taken care of the mess you made?"

"Yeah, I buried 'em," Cash sneered. "But me and my men are gettin' the raw deal here, Ed. You've got twice as many girls as I do. It's time we divvy it up."

"We have twice as many girls because you cannot play nice with your stable."

"That's a damned lie. Half your girls were supposed to be shot. All I gotta do is tell Ace the truth about your little side business—"

"You won't tell him anything," Mr. Hall said mildly. "Because if you do, I'll let out a few little secrets of my own, Cash."

The men around them were tense. None had their backs to anyone and a circle of men formed around the wagons. Fingers twitched near guns, eyes shifted from side to side, and one spat brown tobacco juice on the ground.

Cash, mouth resentfully tight, said nothing. Then, his eyes swept Isa dismissively. "That one ain't even much to look at. Probably won't get you more than twenty dollars."

Poppy felt Isa stiffen and stand taller. She clenched the girl's arm.

Don't speak, don't speak, don't speak.

Isa proved she had brains behind that sharp-tongued mouth and remained silent.

"That one, though"—he nodded at Poppy, his eyes hot upon her—"she and I have unfinished business. Had the law crawling all over the house looking for Maude's brat. She'll get you a pretty penny. Come here, sweetheart. Aren't you tired of bein' cramped up in Ed's wagon?" Cash kissed the air like he was calling a dog, and his men laughed. "Want a taste of a real man? You got that look about you, don't she, boys?" He cupped his genitals in a vulgar show while his men hooted and catcalled.

Knowing his game, Poppy kept her eyes down for several moments before glancing at Mr. Hall. Although Mr. Hall didn't appear overtly pleased, the creases around his mouth smoothed. He cocked his head at the first wagon. "Girls, load up."

Poppy didn't dare look at Cash again.

All the while, she felt Mr. Hall's eyes on her and remembered his words.

His promise.

She would be allowed to live so long as she remained useful.

Chapter Twenty-Seven

"How could you come alone, Isa? How could you let yourself get caught?" All the words had built up inside Poppy until the right moment when the two of them could finally speak in private. The night before, after everyone's introductions, Big Maude had returned with a new crop in hand. There hadn't been another moment to speak.

Now, the little wagon train rattled and bumped along the undeveloped farmland that they were no doubt trespassing on. Not even the driver at the front could overhear them. Nevertheless, Poppy still whispered near Isa's ear so the other girls in the wagon wouldn't eavesdrop. Her shaky breath moved the tendrils of Isa's braid from her ear.

"I didn't do it on purpose, Poppy," Isa defended, rubbing her ear of the ticklish sensation.

They were uncomfortably crowded. Their height differences put them close together, and the six-foot chain between them felt like three. The chain curled like a coiled snake at their sides, the metallic smell of rusted iron pungent.

"I know," Poppy breathed, feeling like she was suffocating between Isa and the wagon bed's wall. The canvas had been lowered and tied, its drawstring pulled tight at the back so only a circle of light was visible. "Of course, you did not get captured on purpose. But this is very, very bad."

"Well, if the sheriff and Deputy Ellis had just listened to me, then Hoodoo would have confronted a group of lawmen out there, not me." Isa's words pulsed with frustration. "I was digging a rock out of Pavo's hoof when he came up behind me out of nowhere. I wasn't even anywhere near the camp."

"He scouted," Poppy said, stretching her neck at the uncomfortable bite of the manacle. How the other girls slept with theirs on, she would never know. She hadn't gotten a wink of sleep last night. "What did you do when Hoodoo caught you?"

"I fought like hell," Isa whispered grimly. Her features were stony and disappointed. "He came up behind me and wrapped an arm around my neck, but Junior does that stunt to me all the time. I tucked my chin and broke out of it as easily as breathing. But he's fast. I hadn't gotten one foot in the stirrup before he was dragging me back down. We wrestled for a good half hour. He almost broke my arm, and I just about ripped his soft bits out."

Poppy was surprised she could find it in her to laugh, and she muffled it into her hand. Was she hysterical? Her mind reeled between despair and the surreality that she and Isa were indeed together in a wagon full of missing girls who they'd read about in the papers.

Unable to hear her disordered thoughts, Isa continued, voice still carefully lowered, "He dragged me at least half a mile. I hadn't realized how close I had camped, and I've been cussing myself ever since. I hope Pavo finds a homestead somewhere."

Her horse had bolted when Isa had been ripped from his saddle.

"I'm sure he will," Poppy consoled, curling her legs up higher. "Do you think that Sol will find us?"

"I left a note and a trail an infant could find," Isa replied, even quieter now. Their chains rattled at their bolts as they sidled closer, knees touching. "Sol and Junior could be on their way as we speak."

"But"—Poppy cleared her throat, hiding the tremor—"that's what I'm afraid of. They'll be shot."

"No, they'll have reinforcements."

"There are more than a dozen men here, and they are all killers. If they were to catch sight of one of our men—" She broke off, and they sat, minds whirling. Finally, Poppy whispered, "Ally is still alive."

Isa made a noise of quiet jubilation.

"Isa, I have to tell you something else. Come closer."

In the privacy of their corner, Poppy told Isa her most precious secret. Then, she disclosed Mr. Hall's ominous question that first day and the current condition of Alwine in the wagon behind them. She could sense Isa's fear spike higher. Isa clenched Poppy's arm, their breathing rapid. Knees drawn up to block her actions from the other girls, Poppy covered her womb with a shaking hand, protecting the tiny piece of Sol that lay within.

BY THE TIME they broke for camp at a shallow creek, the wagon's occupants were flushed, soaked through with pungent sweat, and dry-mouthed with thirst. The road had been dry, and grit filtered through the boards, clouding the air with swirls of fine dust.

At midday, the driver handed a handful of hardtack to Isa, who passed it out to the famished girls. It helped Poppy's queasy stomach until suppertime. Several girls groaned and stretched when the driver parked the wagon and engaged the brake. Hoodoo arrived, tugged the drawstring entrance open, and ordered everyone out for their "nature walk". When they returned, half the men disappeared through the trees, rifles laid across their laps and pistols loaded in their holsters. Guarding the perimeter, no doubt. It would take a few days to familiarize herself with their faces, but for now, every man was a stranger.

Dusk approached, and the girls were positioned to sit in front of the wagons which were parked in a half-circle. One of Mr. Hall's men built a cookfire straddled by a tripod. It took two men to carry an immense cast-iron Dutch oven and lash it to the tripod to hang like a great black pendulum above the fire. The girls watched hungrily as Big Maude poured an aluminum bucket of soaking pinto beans into the pot, unwrapped cheesecloth from a cut of desiccated salt pork, and cut off chunks into the beans. Once again, her skirts were dangerously close to the fire.

"That's one witch I wish would roast," Isa muttered.

On the other side of Poppy, Gretchen stifled a laugh. She stopped abruptly when Hoodoo's shadow covered her. He held a galvanized tub full of filthy clothes, soap, and washboards. In unison, the girls stood up. Looking at each other uneasily, Poppy and Isa followed suit.

"Go," he said, thrusting the tub at them. Poppy grabbed it, as she was the only one with her hands unbound.

The yellow lye soap beckoned her, and she felt her heart beat happily that she would get to wash. They lined up at the creek bank, getting their boots, skirts, and stockings wet and sandy. In an assembly line, the first girls would soap the clothes, the next few would scrub them on the washboards, and Poppy and Isa rinsed, wrung, and draped the clothing over bushes to dry. Behind them, Hoodoo stood sentinel, rifle braced in the crook of his arm.

They were on the last few articles of clothing when Mr. Hall approached Hoodoo.

"Bring the last two to me."

Standing from their crouch, Poppy and Isa held still while Hoodoo unhooked Poppy's chain from Gretchen.

Mr. Hall led them to the cookfire and told Maude, "Make four plates. You two, meet me at the supply wagon." His eyes rested on Isa. "If you run, it will not go well for you, or your cousin. Do you understand, gift of Isis?"

Isa nodded once and averted her gaze. Once he was out of earshot, she stepped closer to Poppy and murmured, "I think he reads minds."

"You may have met your match in him, if only in wits." Poppy inched closer to the campfire, trying to ignore the blatant stares from Cash's girls at their second wagon and the people seated around the fire.

Big Maude sat on an overturned log but heaved herself up when Poppy drew closer. Two men sat around the fire, Lester and a stranger with tufts of chaotic white hair. They were typical "coffee boilers," preferring to sit around the coffee pot rather than help, all the while claiming they were keeping an eye on the girls. Poppy was dismayed when Mina sashayed up, hips swaying.

"It's good to see you off your high horse." Mina smirked, waggling a finger at Poppy's iron shackle. "It suits you."

"You know what suits you?" Isa fired back.

"Isa, no." Poppy tugged on the taller girl's arm.

"I can't tell if you're a boy or a girl," Mina scoffed, giving Isa's overalls and boots a once-over. She folded her arms.

"That's probably because you were busy on your back while everyone else went to school. They teach biological science, not just what-goes-where."

Lester and the other man burst into laughter, wholly entertained.

Dislike darkened the woman's face. "Want to know what happened to the last girl that got fresh with me?"

Poppy pulled harder on Isa's arm, but she didn't budge; she was strong as an ox. "Why don't you show me? I could take you with my hands tied."

The open hostility in Isa's face, paired with the taller girl's slightly crouched fighting stance, made Mina falter. Instead of stepping nearer, Mina spat at her and flounced away. The foamy white spittle had just missed Isa's boot.

"Isa, enough!" Poppy hissed, hooking her arm through her friend's and stumbling them closer to the fire. "You can't make enemies with everyone. We must keep level heads."

"Did you see the way she looked at you? I couldn't let that stand."

"You're going to have to." She lowered her voice even further. "There are bigger fish to fry right now, or don't you remember?"

Isa quietened. During the long, sweltering trip in the enclosed oven of the wagon, they had whispered about possible escape plans. At almost every one of Isa's ideas, Poppy had discarded it. There was a lot the younger girl didn't know about the cruelties of men. What they needed was more information and good timing.

"You want some eatin' irons?" Lester asked, pulling a tarnished fork and spoon from his trouser pocket.

"No, thank you." The first thing Poppy would do would be to stow away a couple of forks. The state of some of the men and girls' mouths were atrocious, their teeth rotting or missing. The thought of sliding something that had been in their mouth into hers made her queasy.

Big Maude leaned over the fire, digging around for the ladle. Her dress from hem to skirt was blackened with soot, her face greasy and hair lank. Poppy imagined she saw something crawling in the woman's graying roots. It made her head itch. While Maude spooned beans and lumps of salt pork on the plates, Lester passed them over to Poppy and Isa.

On the fourth plate, Maude lifted a jaundiced eye to Poppy.

"For you, *Hündin*." Big Maude gave a deep, pig-like snort—and hawked a wad of phlegm onto the fourth plate with the smallest portion. Then, she cackled and plopped the plate on one of the others while Poppy struggled to balance them.

That miserable old hag.

Isa made a noise of disgust that promised an incoming tirade.

"Aw, Maude, that ain't right," Lester chuckled uneasily, scratching his flaking scalp with his fork.

The second man whistled, gawking at Poppy, who passed with her chin high.

Isa muttered about everything she'd like to do to Maude on the way to the chuckwagon, the kindest suggestion that they push her into the fire. At the chuckwagon, Gary sat on the tailboard in discussion with his brother. When he saw Poppy, he sat straighter and beamed at her. Aware of the watchful Mr. Hall, Poppy nodded tentatively back.

In a display of solicitude, Gary took a tin plate from Poppy's hand and passed it along to Alwine, who was still tucked in the darkened wagon interior. But when he made to grab the plate on top of the last, Poppy stopped him.

They played tug of war until she said, "That one is mine."

"What's it matter?" He blinked at her owlishly.

"Big Maude added a secret ingredient just for me. You do not want it." When he continued to look confused, she compressed her lips.

Isa set her plate on the tailboard and cast a dark look at the campfire. "She hawked a loogie in it."

Poppy opened her mouth to ease the sudden tension, but Gary stood brusquely, the irascible anger on his blunt face stymying any placation. The wagon bounced up several inches behind him. Tall and broad as a mountain in a bloodstained shirt, he struck a frightening picture as he stormed toward the fire with the tainted plate of food in his fist.

"Oh, no." Poppy set the last plate of food on the tailboard and circled the wagon, her fingertips brushing her lips. Isa followed close behind.

With a hint of a smile, Mr. Hall moved beyond them for a better view, his hand on his gun. He did nothing to stop Gary.

The two coffee boilers stumbled to their feet at Gary's violent approach, but he overtook them without a look. He stopped in front of Big Maude and showed her the plate.

"Did you spit in this? Huh?" His plodding voice wasn't so slow when he was riled and shouting. It sounded as though he were showing a guilty dog its piddle on the floor. "Well, did ya?"

Big Maude gripped the log she'd reclaimed and glared up at him resentfully. The glower didn't fool anyone. Her posture was tense. Afraid.

"Yeah, I thought so." He shoved the plate against Maude's enormous bosom, and she reflexively grabbed it. "Eat it. Right now."

Mouth pinched into a broad, toad-like line, she shook her head.

"I said," he growled, grabbed her by the back of her squat neck, and forced her to her knees, "eat it!"

Poppy and Isa watched in horror while he smashed the plate of beans into her face. Crying out, Big Maude turned her head to the side, and the lump of cooling beans fell to the ground. Gary merely picked up a handful that was coated with spit, dirt, and leaves and smashed it against her mouth. Cash's men shifted on their feet, but no one stopped Gary as he force-fed every bit of beans to Maude with bruising insistence.

It was either choke or swallow.

Big Maude swallowed.

Disturbed and queasy, Poppy turned her back to the scene. The wind rustled in the trees, and squirrels barked warnings at each other. A horse snorted, and a brave bird sang far above them. Juxtaposed with the noises of nature the sounds of the woman eating on her hands and knees were macabre.

Isa mirrored Poppy, equally unsettled.

Finally, Gary's voice carried over to them. "Now, since you had yourself two helpings of supper, I don't see why you need breakfast tomorrow. Go wash this off and bring it back."

Big Maude obeyed without argument. She came into view, flushed and crying, the lower half of her face covered in filth. Poppy and Isa shared a repelled look while the woman washed the plate in the creek with shaking fingers and brought it back to Gary. Anger had transformed to concentration while he smoothed and flattened the plate, scraped beans onto it, and trotted back to Poppy.

"Here you go, angel. Now you can eat."

Angel?

An idea sparked in Poppy's head. A wisp of one, really. If she thought about it too much, reason would quash it and it would never fully form. But intuition nudged, so she followed it.

With everyone watching closely, Poppy took the plate...and gave Gary a worshipful smile.

AFTER SUPPER, MR. Hall's girls washed the tin dishes, cutlery, and cups.

Poppy remained in the wagon, spoon-feeding Alwine and listening to Gary's exhaustive knowledge of birdcalls. Mr. Hall had unlocked Poppy's shackle and pulled Isa toward a tent behind him. At first, she had panicked and clung to Isa, but Gary had knowingly mollified her.

"He don't do that with the girls, angel. It's bad manners. Don't you worry none."

Mr. Hall had sent Gary a disapproving look before vanishing into the little white canvas tent with Isa. As she could see their silhouettes in the lamplit interior, Poppy calmed herself, glancing over every now and then to ensure their shadows remained suitably apart. Once Alwine had eaten half her beans and had drank a cup of water, Poppy asked Gary to turn his back so she could clean Alwine. He stood and guarded the wagon entrance, and once Alwine was clean, dozing, and cocooned in her blanket, Poppy scooted to the tailboard.

She hadn't had time to discuss her plans with Isa and hoped her friend would understand.

She reached over and touched Gary's sleeve. He turned, uncrossing his arms.

"You need somethin'?" he whispered.

It was dark enough outside that bats flew around in the twilit tree-tops, catching the mosquitoes that constantly plagued them, stirred up by wagon wheels and warm bodies.

"Thank you for championing me this morning." Poppy hoped her smile reached her eyes.

"It weren't nothin'. You just gotta remind them who's boss. Can't have them forgetting who they are."

Poppy ignored her distaste and nodded as though he made sense. "I understand."

"There was a madam in New Mexico that was worse'n Maude. Ed stripped her naked and made her walk behind the wagon for two days." He giggled at the memory.

"What had she done?" *That way, I never do it.*

"She sassed Ed when he was in one of his moods. Don't poke the bear, I always say. You don't ever want Ed mad at'cha."

"So you've had a wagon train of girls in New Mexico, too?" She kept her voice politely curious and hoped he couldn't hear her heart racing.

"Pshaw, all over the place." Gary leaned a thigh against the tailboard. He was very close to her.

She gentled her voice and looked up at him, pretending she was looking up at Sol, asking for a kiss. "Don't you ever get tired of it?"

Gary didn't speak or move.

She leaned closer.

"Don't you wish to settle down one day? Have a family?" She paused. "A wife?"

"I guess." His voice was deeper, but he sounded confused and shoved his hands deeper into his pockets. "I thought about it. But I don't want to leave Ed. He's the only family I got."

"Mr. Hall does not wish to settle down?"

"Hell, no. This is his life. And he's saved my hide more than a dozen times. Busted me out of too many hoosegows to count. I wouldn't be here without him."

"I see," she whispered and lowered her head. Her heart hammered when a thick finger tilted her chin up. If he tried to kiss her, she wasn't sure she could return it. She'd thought she could do this, but her hands wanted to slap him away. Her feet wanted to run. Instead, Poppy made herself smile and look away like a blushing virgin.

There was a smile in Gary's voice. "You're a 'sure enough' lady, ain't you?"

"I suppose."

"I ain't used to those. Reckon I'd have to court you proper."

Poppy made her face look sad. "Would your brother let you? He's only keeping me to sell me at the border."

Gary's laughter was loud, exhilarated. "Ed would let me do anything." He stepped closer, the seam of his trousers brushing against her knees. Her heart stopped. "So, I'm courtin' you. We could seal it with a kiss."

Her smile was too broad to be genuine. More like mad. Hysterical. She lifted her hand. "Gentlemen kiss ladies' hands, Gary."

He grinned, wrapped his fingers around her hand as though it were fine crystal, and pressed a kiss to it. It reminded Poppy of Sol's first kiss on her hand in the hotel corridor, and anguish pierced her.

"Gary!" Mr. Hall ducked out of his tent and squinted through the darkness, Isa right behind. "You're on first watch."

"All right," Gary called back. "'Night, angel." He dropped her hand reluctantly.

He disappeared in the gloom, and she crossed her arms hard to stop the quaking, resisting the urge to wipe her hand. Eyes were everywhere. Mr. Hall crooked his finger at her. She scampered off the tailboard to them, saying nothing while he linked Isa's chain to her shackle. Once Hoodoo reclaimed them and they were attached to the other girls, Isa crept nearer in the wagon bed and whispered, "What are you up to, Poppy?"

Hiding how unsure she felt, she replied, "I have a plan."

Chapter Twenty-Eight

Once Sheriff Robinson had Deputy Ellis' word that there was indeed a trail with the evidence of a suspicious amount of people traveling, Sol finally had begrudging permission to form a posse.

Sol was well-liked, and a posse of over a dozen trusted men arrived within a few hours.

Ben, Junior, and Sol sat on their horses with tight, dark expressions while the men in the posse looked back and forth between them and the sheriff with his deputy on the boardwalk.

"All right, boys, there are rules about these kinds of things. We can't just storm in there without a plan. That's how people get killed. I'm sending a wire out, gonna get us some Texas Rangers so everything will be official and go smoothly."

Sol gripped his saddle horn so hard it felt like the leather gloves encasing his knuckles would split. "You're tellin' me that even if we catch up to them after a couple of days, we'll have to wait out these Texas Rangers?"

"That's exactly what I'm telling you." The sheriff's droopy eyes were steady on Sol's. "And if you disobey orders, you're off the posse."

"They could be doing anything to Poppy and Isa," Sol retorted. Every tendon and muscle in his face, neck, and body stood out. "We've got to get them away from whoever has them as fast as we can."

There were several rumbles of agreement.

Someone from the back of the crowd yelled, "And that bastard Smithe ran off while you were gone, so we can't get more information!"

Sheriff Robinson's face grew florid, and he raised his arms to settle the men. "And we've got men after him! Not a single soul will harbor him once word gets around. We will question him and get answers when we have him in our custody."

And what about my sister and future wife, Sol wanted to scream. They could be killed by the time the Texas Rangers caught up to issue orders.

Poppy could be dead already, lying somewhere in the woods, alone. His sister could walk right into a trap to meet a similar fate.

God, why had he left her that morning?

"Sol." Ben's voice was low beside him, his hand firm on Sol's rigid shoulder. "Try to breathe. Calm down. You won't be any help to them if you're kicked off the posse."

This must be what lockjaw felt like. Incapable of vocalizing, Sol gave a curt nod and blinked fast.

Shooting Sol a wary glance, Sheriff Robinson gave the final orders to the men.

They left at high noon.

On the first day, the trail was easy even without the sunflower seeds and scraps of thread that Sol took, pale-faced, and pocketed.

On the second day, they found Isa's horse. Hog had veered away from the group of men, nose to the ground, and began to bay. Pavo whinnied in response, his eyes rolling. His saddle had gotten hung up in overgrown vines, and he'd been stuck for who knew how long. Luckily, no predators had found him first. Sol slid from his saddle and hacked at the vines with the help of Ben and Junior.

They had her. They had his sister.

It felt like he was having a heart attack. But with a dozen men watching him, grounding him, he maintained a façade of calm.

"Come here, Hog," Sol said, holding a piece of jerky to the coonhound. Once the treat was devoured, Sol brought out one of Isa's dirty stockings then tied a lead rope to Hog's collar while the dog got a good sniff. "Go get her. Find Isa."

Hog was off in a flash, straining against his rope, Sol jogging behind. They had zigzagged for half an hour near the trail when Sol found where Pavo had veered off, his unshod hoof distinguishable from the others. Holding the hound close, Sol crouched, eyes squinted.

"Looks like someone came up behind her. You can see boot prints here where her horse startled." If Isa had fought too hard and proved to be too much hassle, her captor could have decided she wasn't worth the hassle. Sol stood, almost afraid to learn more. "Find her, Hog. Come on."

Hog followed the scent to an old campsite, and Sol breathed easier.

"Whoever caught her brought her to camp," Sol called back to the others.

The tension lessened amongst the men, leather saddles creaking as they sighed in unison.

"I'll find Pavo some water," Junior said hoarsely from the front, leading the mud-caked, trembling pony behind him.

Ben handed the reins of Sol's horse over and said nothing. His eyes stuck to Sol like a cocklebur.

On the third day, torrential rain forced them to stall in an abandoned barn in a nearby field. The barn showed signs of at least three wagons and dozens of footprints. Deputy Ellis called a halt to the posse while the weather was so foul.

"They won't get far, Sol," Ellis said staunchly against several protestations. "Not with three wagons. And I got my orders, too. Now's a good time to wait out the Rangers."

Sol strode into the woods wordlessly, Hog at his side.

It came as a shock when the bored coonhound found a fresh grave within the first hour.

At the sound of baying, the men abandoned the barn and rushed to the wood line. They discovered Sol on his knees, digging through the shallow grave with his hands. One of the men found a rusted shovel by the barn, and every man took turns digging in earnest.

The first body was a man in his long johns, a gunshot wound to the chest. Sol cursed when they found another body directly beneath the first. Soon, they had four bodies of men lined up beside the mass grave.

Isa wasn't in it.

Covered in mud, black with it, Sol clambered out but stayed on his knees to whisper his thanks.

And still, Deputy Ellis refused to let the men continue the search.

Sheets of rain drenched them for days, and the men clustered in a resentful huddle in the abandoned barn.

Once the sun shone its weak light over the horizon on the sixth morning, Sol ignored Deputy Ellis' admonitions and took Hog into the woods across the field. There, they followed the grooves of wagon wheels made mushy by three days of rain. He followed them until the ground hardened and the trees cleared. Several times the wagons had detoured onto a narrow road, and it was at one of the cut roads that Sol halted, teeth gritted. The orders to stop, to wait, tortured him.

"Sol!" Junior's voice was an echo so faint it was almost drowned out by Hog's snuffling.

Sol lifted his shadowed eyes. The sun was at high noon.

It was easy to ignore his grumbling stomach, but when a glance revealed that Hog's ribs were leaner than they had been a week ago, Sol felt a crushing wave of shame. He hadn't even fed his dog that morning.

His knees hit the ground.

"Aw, Hog. I'm sorry, pal." His voice was rough, his face and hands grimy against the dog's glossy coat. Hog shoved his filthy nose against Sol, tail wagging, oblivious to the torment in the man's face.

"Sol!" Junior's voice was closer. "Come back! The Texas Rangers, they're here!"

WHEN SOL ARRIVED back at the abandoned barn, all the men were mounted and ready to ride, three strangers talking to Deputy Ellis at the forefront. The Texas Rangers.

Junior handed over the reins to Sol's gelding, and Ben passed him a handful of hardtack and jerky. Sol immediately fed everything to Hog, and Ben's jaw clenched.

While Sol untied Hog from the lead rope and mounted Copper, Ben rode close so the other men couldn't hear. "You need to eat something."

His own jaw clenching, the knotting pressure of keeping his rampant emotions tamped down huge in his chest, Sol grunted, "I'm fine. I'm not hungry."

"You're no good to them if you starve, damn it."

"What if they're not eating?" Sol finally looked at Ben, his face so stiff it could break. "It's been a week. What if no one has fed them, and they're hungry right now, Ben?"

Ben's mouth worked without saying anything, then, "You don't know that. And you're gonna get weak. That's the last thing we need on this trail. A weak man. We need everyone sharp, and right now, you're as useless as an unloaded gun."

Fury, hot and blistering, compelled Sol to seriously consider releasing some of his emotions and striking his friend. He wasn't weak. He wasn't useless. He and Ben stared at each other, neither blinking, for nearly a minute.

Leaning even closer, Ben gritted through tight lips, "Eat and take care of yourself or I'll have Deputy Ellis drop your sorry hide at the next town. *Comprende?*"

This time, when Ben handed Sol another handful of hardtack and jerky, Sol bit into it. He chewed and chewed, but it sat in his mouth like swill, unable to pass the blockage that had lodged itself in his throat since the morning Poppy had disappeared.

"Williams. Stone." Deputy Ellis motioned to them.

Avoiding each other's eyes, Sol and Ben nudged their horses to the three strangers, Junior trailing behind.

At first glance, the Rangers looked like ordinary men, but Sol noticed something indefinably different in the oldest two compared to the family men in the posse. They had hardened faces, grooves etched deeply, each prematurely weathered. The oldest one leaned forward and offered a hand. Sol shook it, clasp firm.

"I'm Captain Lawson. This is Lieutenant Havelard and Private Pines."

"Sol Williams. This is Ben Stone and his brother John."

Each man nodded to the other. Captain Lawson had a beard that rivaled Ben's during the winter months, but it was steel gray, and his wiry eyebrows brushed the low brim of his hat. Captain Lawson's eyes were as dark and clever as a wily old fox.

"We were on patrol a couple days' ride north. There are fence-cutters up there causin' trouble for the local farmers. Shooting and killing over some barbed wire, if you can believe."

"I appreciate you finding our trail and helping us," Sol said. A tiny firefly's glow of hope lit his insides. "How'd you find us in this rain?"

"Rain doesn't stop a Ranger," piped Private Pines, the youngest of the three.

Lieutenant Havelard cut his eyes at the eager private, and the latter sat back in his saddle as though chastised. Havelard leaned forward against his pommel and offered, "We asked some questions before we left. Sent wires. There's word that some wagons were seen headed southwest."

"We reckon they're headed toward the border," Lawson added. "Had a farmer tell us he spotted wagon tracks on his property, so we found 'em and came straight here. Found your tracks, too."

"We ride day and night," Private Pines couldn't resist adding.

Seeing Sol's eyebrows raise, Havelard hooked a thumb at the young private. "He's fresh. Still finds it all exciting."

Meeting Captain Lawson's eyes, Sol attempted to keep his feelings hidden. "My woman and my sister are in those wagons. And we've lost three days."

"We'll find them, Mr. Williams." Lawson smiled, showing a missing front tooth. "We always do."

IT WAS A camp divided.

After Cash returned from his patrol shift, he and Mr. Hall rowed. Mr. Hall must have won the argument because Cash skulked off to his wagon and dragged Mina out. Stumbling, she followed him to a secluded area behind some trees. Less than a minute later, moans filtered through the brush.

The daily monotony of traveling through rain or shine, completing daily tasks, and being watched by a crop-wielding Maude was only broken up by bursts of arguments between the men and the occasional scrap of a fight. One night, Cash's men lit a fire several feet from the cookfire. Mr. Hall had exploded, shouting and waving his gun, his eyes bright with rage. He and his second-in-command, Sid, had their hands full keeping the two groups in check. Cash, however, did nothing to stopper the flow of dissension between them.

Then, the rains came. For two days, the girls endured the cacophony of heavy rainfall on their canvas roof that drowned out all other sounds. Isa and Poppy used the constant noise to their advantage, speaking plans freely to each other in their damp corner.

"If I cannot convince Gary to get the key to free us, you must use the time when you're not chained to me to steal a horse and flee."

"I'm not leaving you," Isa spat, arms crossed and chin at a stubborn angle. "If we escape, we go together."

"Two of us on a horse will slow it down," Poppy argued. "And I can barely ride. You will have to leave and get help."

"Well, Mr. Hall has shown me a lot of banknotes given to him by Nelson Smithe. You know, I do believe Mr. Hall is laundering the money but Smithe doesn't realize that he is planning to steal it right out from under him."

"What?"

"Sh! Yes, he has had me double and triple checking his accounts, and he's only going to put a fraction of the banknotes in that bank in Laredo. But some of it is going to the banker, some fellow named Mr. Frederickson, and the rest is going with Mr. Hall and Gary to Mexico. And what is even more interesting, he mentioned that Cash thinks he's getting half, but I'm growing suspicious that Mr. Hall is planning something far more sinister."

Poppy pressed her fingers into her eyes, dizzy with all this information. "None of this matters. We need to make a plan so you can get to a town and safety."

"Well, come up with a plan where we escape together."

Poppy had never wanted to pull her hair out more.

Despite storms that had impeded swift travel, Mr. Hall led the wagons on. They took trails and backroads, staying far away from the soft ground of the woods that had otherwise brought them protection from curious eyes. They kept the canvases pulled tight any time they traveled on a public road, armed men posted a few feet away in case a girl got too curious and did something stupid like press her face against the laces.

One evening they had parked the wagons behind a stand of trees on some high ground near the Colorado River. Poppy was familiar with this river. It was close to Austin and the town she'd lived in for the past decade with Gerald. Their proximity to the river made her body tingle with the need to bathe. It felt as though she hadn't been clean in a year.

She was pulling out Gary's stitches, much to his complaining, when she asked, "Do you suppose you could convince your brother to let us bathe in the river?" Afraid he would say no, she ran her fingers across his healing gunshot wound. "This looks much better. There's no longer any swelling or redness."

Gary blinked down at her hand on his bare chest. "I'm just glad those stitches are out. They itched like a sumbitch."

"I can sympathize. Ladies are used to bathing often, and I am long due for a bath. I smell like a pigsty."

He bent over and sniffed. "Smell all right to me."

"Please, Gary?" she asked, flattening her palm against his hairy chest. The heart beneath her hand thumped faster and faster.

"I can try." He grabbed her hand from his person and kissed it. It was a habit that elicited eye-rolls from Isa behind his back and stony expressions from Mr. Hall. He hopped from the chuckwagon's tailboard with a bounce and strode to his brother, who had set up a portable table covered in ledgers and maps.

From behind Poppy, Isa shifted forward. "I don't know how you do it," she muttered. "He is vile."

"They all are," Poppy replied after ensuring no other ears listened. "'You can catch more flies with honey,' my mother always said."

Isa snorted. "That only works for some of them. Being nice to Junior never did a thing."

Poppy's lips quirked. "That's because he gets his enjoyment from pestering you. If you start being nice to him, there's no fun in it."

"I never thought I'd say it, but I miss him," Isa whispered. "And Sol and Pa most of all. I even miss my pigheaded mother."

Poppy laid her head on her young friend's shoulder, aching for her. Her voice was so low it was barely a breath. "I know. Which is why you need to escape as soon as possible. Steal a horse, ride as fast as you can. Find someone that will get word to a sheriff."

Isa was uncharacteristically quiet while they waited for Gary to bring back an answer, and Poppy's hopes were buoyed. If Isa was quiet, it meant she was thinking about it. And even if any warning to law enforcement was too late for Poppy, at least Isa would be free.

THE STIPULATION FOR washing up was to launder the enormous pile of clothes, mildewed from the constant rains, before bathing.

Washing the stinking pile of clothes was worth the fifteen minutes Hoodoo allowed the girls to bathe. Even Cash's girls joined in, and Gary stood with his pistol cocked when the men attempted to traverse the steep river bank to join them. He wouldn't even let them watch, aiming the six-shooter at the closest man.

Poppy could have kissed him.

It was awkward washing in their dingy white chemises and combinations and even more uncomfortable donning their damp dresses before they had completely dried. But being clean for the first time in a week made up for the wet, heavy clothes.

Later, she asked Gary if he would let the girls eat by the fire in the open air instead of the wagon. As though bolstered by the warm reception from the girls, he didn't ask Mr. Hall. He ordered them from his brother's wagon to sit around the wagon to eat as a reward for their good behavior. When Isa gritted her teeth at this clumsy announcement, Poppy dug an elbow into the girl's ribs and smiled broadly at Gary.

Mr. Hall made an appearance, watching the girls with an indecipherable expression. "You are going soft, brother."

"Naw," Gary said blithely, giving Poppy a crooked smile. "I reckon I'm atoning for some past sins. Maybe I won't go to Hell after all."

The fire reflected in Mr. Hall's glasses. It lent him a demonic air, and Poppy glued her eyes to her plate of rice and beans.

After Isa and Poppy ate and brought a tin plate to Alwine, Gary followed with an odd request.

"I've gotta stand guard tonight, but I thought I could brush your hair."

Poppy's hair was drying in riotous tangles and curls. The thought of him yanking a hairbrush through the mats made her want to cringe away. Isa's look of horror behind the hulking man was so comical Poppy fought a hysterical laugh.

"It's an awful mess," Poppy warned, moving aside so Isa could climb into the wagon and hand a curious Alwine the plate of food. "And I am a bit tender-headed."

"I'll be gentle," Gary promised, shifting his bulk on the tailboard with Poppy. The wagon lowered a few inches on its axle. He reached in the wagon bed for the curry brush, finger combing her hair with shaking hands. She tried to ignore his rough breathing. "When we're married, I'll do this for you every night."

"Hmm." She could manage nothing else. Something was happening to her chest and throat. They were blocked and hot.

It felt like when Gerald had died.

It felt like grief.

A mixture of bottled rage and that hot, aching grief stirred within her. She clenched her trembling hands together, willing herself to calm. She didn't know how long she sat still for Gary's clumsy ministrations, for no matter how gentle he attempted to be, her head jerked at every other stroke. She welcomed the pain; it distracted her from wishing she was anywhere else, even holed up in a tree hollow on the run from these men.

Finally, the drag of the curry comb slid smoothly from root to tip. The urge to rip the comb from his hands and fling it grew and grew until her knuckles stood like spikes against her fists. She hadn't known how much longer she could have taken it.

"It would have been easier if this damned shackle wasn't in my way," Gary muttered, dropping the comb to run his hand over and over her hair. He petted her like she was a helpless rabbit.

Which, she supposed she was.

Poppy swallowed. "You could unlock it. I won't run."

"Can't. Only Ed, Cash, and Hoodoo got keys." He sounded disgruntled about it.

The stroking of his hands over her head and hair drove her mad. Poppy focused on other things.

Night had fallen over the camp. One of the men poked the fire, sending light flaring and stretching. The wagon canvases glowed orange, shadows shimmering across their smooth surfaces as men stood and dispersed to their nightly duties. Mr. Hall's tent was small in its usual spot behind the supply wagon. He was a dark, crouching shape within it, his lamp on its highest setting.

"I'll braid it," Isa interrupted from the dark. Her voice wasn't quite steady.

Sighing, Gary pushed the comb into a nook in the wagon bed and stood. The wagon creaked when it bounced up. Poppy hoped Isa couldn't see him adjust the front of his trousers.

Praying she didn't sound as repelled as she felt, she offered, "Your shirt is almost in tatters. I'll mend it tomorrow if you'd like."

"I'd like that right fine, angel." He pulled her hand from her lap. "Your hand is colder than a river rock." Gary chafed it and pressed a kiss to the back.

By the time Gary left for his watch, Poppy was shaking all over.

"How can you stand it?" Isa whispered, sitting crisscrossed and plaiting Poppy's hair with some difficulty because of her bound hands.

"Because we need him," Poppy reminded her in an undertone. "Just like you have to pander to old Ed, I must beguile the brother."

"In the tent," Isa whispered, "Mr. Hall talks to me about Latin, art, cities, and culture. But he expresses so much hatred for the common folk. It's...alarming. Some of the things that have come out of his mouth are things I have thought."

"You are not like him, Isa," Poppy said firmly.

Isa was silent as she tied the end of the braid with a worn leather strip.

A movement from beside them startled them.

Alwine had scooted forward. Her little face was almost skeletal, her hair lank, and her wrists dangerously thin. Some of the fire that had lived in her, the wild fierceness that had plucked at Poppy's heart-strings, had returned in slow increments throughout the week.

Alwine murmured something in her language and pressed her hand against Poppy's breast.

"What is she saying?" Poppy closed her cold hand over Alwine's warm one.

Isa shook her head a little. "I'm not sure."

"Strong heart," Alwine said clearly.

Both Poppy and Isa held their breath when the girl leaned forward and kissed Poppy softly on her cheek, brushing the corner of her mouth. Eyes pricking, Poppy wrapped the girl in a tentative embrace. Alwine squeezed her then pulled away and eased back to her pallet in the wagon. They heard her murmur something else, a chant or song.

"She's praying." Isa looked peculiar, her eyes vacant. There was a softening to her, a sadness, and she averted her face.

"I'm glad she's better." Poppy grabbed a thin blanket and draped it over their young friend, tucking her in the way children should be before bed. "It looked bleak for so long. And, despite our feelings for him, Gary has been a significant help. For that alone, I feel no regret for my actions with him. I only hope that Sol will understand."

If he even comes.

The thought was small and unfair, based on fear, and she dashed it away. Sol would come. He was probably close enough to smell their fire but had to bide his time. There was a reason. There had to be.

"He would understand," Isa said hastily. "He's not like anyone else I know. He would probably give you tips."

For the first time since their bath, Poppy smiled. "That is stretching it."

Isa chuckled, then sighed. "I guess we had better go to the first wagon before Hoodoo comes to fetch us. You're sure we couldn't just sneak off right now?"

"With six armed men ready to shoot at anything in the dark?"

"I thought you'd say that."

They told a dozing Alwine good night and were halfway to the first wagon when a shadow passed over them.

Poppy stiffened, and Isa yelped, fists raised.

Cash laughed darkly at their reactions. Behind him, Mina stood at the second wagon's entrance. She leaned against the dropped tailboard, face pinched.

"And just where are you two going?" he asked, blocking their path.

"None of your business." Isa's bound fists were still clenched.

"Oh, but it is," Cash said, casting a glance of dislike at Isa. His up-and-down look disparaged and dismissed her. A smile slithered across his face when he turned his attention to Poppy. "I do believe this is the first time I've caught you alone, Red."

"She's not alone."

Cash pretended Isa wasn't there. He stepped closer to Poppy and stretched out a hand, grazing his fingertips along the line of her jaw.

In his eyes, Poppy saw only emptiness. There was calculation and hunger, yes. But there was also animal hunger in any starving cat or opossum, lacking all the warmth and empathy needed to be human. Her mother would have fallen head over heels for this man. Moira was renowned for her singularly bad taste in men, and this one ticked all the boxes that guaranteed instant infatuation. Cash looked for easy prey and assumed, because of Poppy's quiet nature, that she would stumble willingly into his web.

She stepped away from his grasp, her bearing cold.

"What is it, Red? You shy?"

"No. I'm not stupid," she contended softly, mindful of Mina listening to every word. "Why would you believe I'd play Gary false?"

Cash dropped his hand and matched her step with one of his own. Lips twisting mirthlessly, he mocked, "Play Gary false? Everyone sees what you're doin' with that fool. You're playing him like a fiddle. And don't think you're the only one to do it, either. But Ed always cleans up the mess afterward. With Gary, there's always a goddamn mess."

If he thought she would come to her senses and heed his warning, he was the fool. Forcing her face to twist defensively, she shot, "Gary isn't like that. He's different. He cares about me."

Instead of being disgusted, Cash's eyes glowed with mirth. "Hot damn, you really believe it, don't you? Well, if it's missing a man that has your brain addled, I've got something that'll get your mind off that halfwit."

Her voice was chilly. "I haven't the slightest idea of what you're speaking of."

Again, his hand reached and caressed her, stroking along her high collar. "It's the itch that needs to be scratched. You're a widow—you know that itch."

"You can go to Mina for whatever ails you."

"What 'ails' me, I like that. Maybe it's not something Mina can help with. Maybe it's something only you've got a cure for."

Behind him, Mina stood from her lazy recline, fists clenched. Poppy kept her eyes on Cash.

"It sounds like whatever you have, even a doctor couldn't cure," Isa broke in, tone rich with revulsion. "Don't let him touch you, Poppy."

Cash turned on her, his spurs jingling as he stalked Isa's way. He was only an inch or two taller than her, even with his expensive heeled boots. "I'm about tired of you butting in where you don't belong, little girl. You keep runnin' that mouth, and I'll put it to good use."

"You put anything near my mouth, and it'll get bitten off," Isa promised. Her eyes reflected the fire, her stance hostile.

"I'd like to see you try and bite this," Cash sneered, lifting his left fist and clenching it hard enough that his knuckles popped in front of Isa's angry face. "I'll add some more gaps to those teeth of yours."

"Cash, what the hell are you doing? Girl, get over here." Mr. Hall's voice fumed, his footsteps so light they didn't hear him when he had materialized from the shadows.

"Nothing at all," Cash replied innocently, using his fist to wipe his nose. His dark eyes shifted back to Poppy. "Have a good night, sweet thing. Think about what I said."

He strode to the campfire and passed Mina without a look. The woman's expression worried Poppy. She wasn't just angry; she was shaking, near tears. There was something off-putting about Mina, and it reminded Poppy of what had happened to the last girl who had received Cash's attention.

Well, Mina can have him.

Anger built while she allowed Mr. Hall to grab her wrist and pull her to the first wagon. She held still while he attached Gretchen's chain to Isa's shackle, and she imagined she could see through his vest pocket to the key that hid inside its lining. She wanted that key so badly that she dreamed of it during her sporadic bursts of slumber.

A bit of that hunger must have shown in her eyes.

Mr. Hall gripped her chin between the curve of his forefinger and thumb.

"I have not seen this look before," he mused, moving her head from side to side. Beside them, Isa watched, worrying her lip with her teeth. "Has a cat been hiding behind the mouse?"

The light from the campfire illuminated half of her face. For half a breath, she let him see how she truly felt. She wanted to tell him how she couldn't wait for someone to catch them. That seeing Ed Hall and his men swinging against the backdrop of a starlit sky was the only thing that would bring her the peace for a full night's sleep.

Instead, she remembered their plans.

"I do not like when that man speaks ill of Gary. And of you."

The curiosity disappeared from his face. "Oh?"

"He is vile."

"What has he said?"

Poppy shook her head and made her lip tremble, just once, for effect. His fingers pinched hard.

"Tell me, Little Poppy, or it will go badly for you."

"He believes you as much of an idiot as your brother. That I had better get on his good side because once he's in charge and you are gone, he'll make me wish for death."

It was a bluff. Isa's eyes were huge. Afraid. If Mr. Hall marched Poppy back to Cash's bedroll, not only would it go terribly for her, but she could be the one stumbling naked at the end of a rope behind the wagon procession.

Or worse.

Mr. Hall released her chin. His spectacles were black from this angle, concealing his eyes. "Girl," he addressed Isa without turning. "This is true?"

With only the slightest hesitation, Isa whispered, "Yes."

While he appeared lost in thought, Poppy didn't dare look at Isa. Instead, she tucked her chin and stared at her worn boots, full of fear and a bubbling, turbulent resentment.

"My brother is of the mind that you are in love with him," Mr. Hall said slowly. The subject change made Poppy blink. She raised her head. "If you hurt him in any way..."

"I would never hurt him," Poppy said vehemently. When she said it, she pictured the way Gary's boots would dangle so much lower than Mr. Hall's while they hanged by their necks. "He has done nothing but protect and help me care for Ally and the other girls. He is a good man."

"'The lady doth protest too much, methinks,'" Mr. Hall murmured, smiling. It was not a pretty smile. "I cannot abide liars."

"Quoting Shakespeare is for the stage or parlor rooms, not for places like this." Poppy waved a hand toward the wagons full of chained girls. "If I were lying, it would cost more than just a scolding or a scandal. It would cost my life. Why would I do such a thing?"

"I have yet to discover that." Mr. Hall jerked his head toward the half-open wagon. "Get in."

He waited until they had crawled into the open spot behind the driver's seat before tightening the drawstring opening and knotting it. As soon as his footsteps faded, they curled together and began to whisper.

"I think I can get the key from him the next time I'm in his tent," Isa announced. "He drapes his vest over a chair every night, and I can unlock my shackle if you start a distraction. Scream or something, say you saw a snake. Then I can set his tent on fire. He has enough important stuff in there to want every man's help."

"If you do that, you must get on a fast horse and ride as far as you can—"

"I won't leave you here," Isa hissed. "If we escape, then we escape together."

Poppy shook her head fervently, tired of this same song and dance. Their chain rattled against the boards beneath them. "No. You are faster, quieter, and know your way around horses. Stick with the plan. Steal a horse, and ride like the wind."

Isa clenched Poppy closer. "I won't leave you with that Cash fellow skulking about. I'll not leave you to that bastard's mercy!"

Wrenching away, fear giving her words a bite, Poppy argued, "You will, and that is final. There is no other—"

She broke off. Footsteps rushed their way, crunching through the brush until they reached the wagon, which rocked from the weight of Hoodoo's body. The moonlight revealed his craggy face hovering above them.

The slap surprised Poppy so much that she didn't move for several seconds after it had whipped her head around. Even Isa took several breaths to register what had just happened.

"Quiet," he spat at them.

Thankfully, he retreated before he saw Isa scrambling up to go after him.

"Stop, Isa," Poppy grunted, pulling a straining Isa back to the wagon's floor.

"I hate it here," Isa growled after giving in and allowing herself to be manipulated back into a supine position. "I hate all of them."

The left side of her face throbbing, Poppy said nothing. When Isa sniffled and turned on her side, Poppy wrapped her body around her, thoughts racing and praying for help to come.

Chapter Twenty-Nine

"What's wrong?" Isa shook Poppy's shoulder, breaking her out of a trance-like state. "Are you feeling poorly again?"

"No." Poppy shook her head and broke her staring contest with the canvas wall. They had traveled for hours, and she felt like a steaming biscuit in a Dutch oven on wheels, the sun hotter than fire in the sky. "Something just feels different."

"It's probably what Gretchen told you this morning." Isa was grim, braiding and re-braided her hair for an hour, bored and fidgeting. When Gretchen looked up from her lap, she asked, "Gretchen, are you positive about what you heard between Gary and Ed this morning?"

Gretchen nodded, dull-eyed. "Yes. He wanted to go to town to get a gold ring, a *real* gold one, he said. And Mr. Hall kept telling him he was making a mistake, that it wasn't smart to marry someone you just met. Gary got mad and stormed off, and that's when Mr. Hall knocked into me, and I spilled the nighttime bucket."

The nighttime bucket was the smelly thing in the corner they had to use between stops to answer nature's call. All of them sat as far away from it as they could.

Gary's persistence in courting her was just one of the many reasons Poppy's guard was up. Their plans to exacerbate the division between the two groups of men had worked, but with it had come consequences. Several fights had broken out between men, and each time they were docked a percentage of pay and made to patrol an extra night.

However, what worried Poppy the most was Isa and Cash's continued animosity toward each other. Every insult Cash volleyed Isa's way would breed two from the girl.

"Don't know what good you are to Ed, looking like a boy the way you do," Cash snickered one morning while Isa stood in line for breakfast. "You got some extra parts under those overalls?"

"You scared I have something bigger than yours?" Isa shot back.

Lester had coughed to cover up a laugh.

Sneering, Cash grabbed his bulge, one of his favorite gestures. "Come on over and find out."

"Whatever you had probably fell off a long time ago," Isa had scoffed, holding out her tin plate for a serving. "That's what happens when you stick it anywhere and everywhere."

Cash had slapped the plate from her hands and pressed himself an inch from Isa's face. "You know, you don't talk much like a lady should. Makes me wonder if you're going to make a good whore after all."

Terrified that Isa would strike him, Poppy wedged between the two. "Please. Please, let's not fight."

Pressed that close to Cash, Poppy saw powder burns on one cheek and dirt in his pores. His scowl had turned into a sickly-sweet smile. "Now here, this is what'll get you the gold." Poppy had allowed him to tap the end of her nose with a finger, using his distraction to push Isa further behind her.

"Boss," one of the men had murmured, a warning. Gary was lumbering their way.

Cash had winked at Poppy, scowled at Isa, and melted amongst his group of men.

Later that night, when the girls lay down to sleep, Poppy tried to convince Isa to keep her head low and stop humiliating Cash.

Isa had whirled on her.

"He insults me first!" She had never sounded more like a child than then.

"I understand that," Poppy had breathed, using the same calm, patient tone she'd employed with the Sunday school children. "But this is different. He's not some churchyard bully. He's a murderer. If you go too far—"

"I don't go too far with these people, Poppy. I tell the truth, even if they don't want to hear it."

"It's dangerous to mistake speaking out with little thought for speaking the truth," Poppy had snapped back, her frustration sharpening her tone. "You will get yourself killed, Isa. Staying alive is worth more than our pride right now, don't you understand?"

Isa's only answer was to turn her back and lay like a stiff, resentful log.

Luckily, Isa had a short fuse that burned out after a bad night's sleep and was now looking down at Poppy with sisterly worry. She laid the back of her hand against Poppy's forehead.

"You don't feel too warm. Clammy, actually."

"I'm well, Isa." She grabbed Isa's hand and squeezed it, but she couldn't prevent the line of worry that made its permanent residence between Isa's brows as of late. "I just worry."

Isa was quiet for a moment, the only noise the creaking and constant rolling of the wooden axles, then, "I'm worried, too. I left a good trail, but there's still no sign—"

She broke off and turned to the driver's seat, wiping her face on the shoulder of her secondhand shirt. Poppy wrapped her arm around her young friend, wishing for the hundredth time that she had run at the first sign of Mrs. Smithe in that alley.

"What if they're still out of town on that false lead?" Isa asked, face still averted. "What if my note fell under the bed?"

"And what if a group of men is following behind, waiting for the right moment?" Poppy rubbed Isa's sharp shoulder blades. Sometimes she forgot Isa was just a girl who needed comfort like any child. But Isa's strength was drawn out in other ways. She didn't love coddling and comforting, though she accepted Poppy's stoically. Having been joined to Isa by the neck, Poppy discovered some things about the curious younger woman. Poppy nudged her a little.

Isa sniffed but didn't turn around.

Poppy shouldered her harder, their chains rattling.

Finally, Isa turned to look, barely hiding the irritation that crept through the cracks of her despair.

"Buck up," Poppy said. "What would Junior say right now if he were with you?"

Instead of looking more upset as Poppy feared, Isa's mouth grimaced. "He'd tell me to quit boohooing like a baby and use my brain. Then he'd do something idiotic, like give me a wet willy."

Poppy stuck her finger in her mouth.

That quick white smile blinded her before Isa clamped it shut and held her hands up to block Poppy's disgustingly wet finger. "You keep that away."

Pretending her heart wasn't five pounds lighter, Poppy sighed and wiped her finger on her dusty black skirt. "All right, then, I'll do the former. Stop boohooing like a baby, Isa. Let's use your big brain to get out of this mess." She lowered her voice, "If anyone can do it and save these girls, it's us."

For several seconds, Isa chewed on her chapped lower lip, drawing her knees up and propping her forearms on them. Then, she glanced at Poppy, fire rekindled. "You're right. Let's get back to planning. Crying never helped anyone."

"You are right, by damn." She nodded, and Isa gifted her with another smile.

They passed the time whispering amongst themselves, their spirits bolstering as they fine-tuned the impossible means to become free from their situation.

By the time Mr. Hall had found a good spot off the path, they fidgeted with high-energy nervousness. Isa had agreed that they needed to try to leave tonight, hopefully before Gary returned with a ring and a proposal.

"What if Gary comes back and asks for your hand before we get a chance to leave?" Isa asked again while they followed Hoodoo in a line to relieve themselves. "Would you ask him to set you free?"

"We'll cross that bridge when we come to it," Poppy murmured, glancing to guarantee no girls were listening. The truth was, she was afraid that Gary would expect something more in return for the ring. Freedom from the shackle meant being chained in other ways. Ways too awful to think of right then. And if he wanted intimacy before marriage, she could continue to demur, but she didn't know how much longer she could keep her distance from him. Gary grew bolder each night, brushing full against her with his body and breathing slack-mouthed down her neck while he brushed her hair. Her skin crawled almost as much as when Cash touched her.

She had an insane wish that Lucy was here so she could ask her opinion on which would be most repellent to have relations with—Gary or Cash?

Lucy would say Gary.

Poppy thought Cash would be worse.

Either would make her want to scrub until her flesh sloughed off, to shed her skin like a snake and start anew. She thought of how difficult it would be to let Sol touch her again if she were forced to endure lying beneath a different man. He deserved someone whole and untainted.

She had felt like damaged goods since she was thirteen, and if she were to lie with anyone other than Sol, would there be a wedding? A future?

And what about the baby?

Her morning sickness had dissipated to mere queasiness in the morning before eating. Gary had supplied hardtack at her request, and she had stockpiled it in her apron like a squirrel, nibbling on it in the mornings before sunrise.

Now that it was suppertime, her stomach growled angrily, demanding food. She hardly noticed anymore. The other girls' stomachs did the same, as they only ate once in the morning and once at night. How long had she been traveling now? A week and a half?

Gary was still absent when they returned to camp, and Poppy shook off her misty-eyed woolgathering. Her brain felt slow and forgetful lately. Days blended into one another, and it grew harder to remember life before living chained to another. For the other girls, it must feel as though they had never lived a life other than this one. Would they be able to return to society after suffering through this?

Since Gary wasn't at camp, Mr. Hall told his girls to return to the wagon with their food. Isa and Poppy got in line last, as was their habit. They were to bring Alwine her evening meal. She was getting stronger. Mr. Hall had mentioned that she would return to the first wagon once she had stopped bleeding and could walk. Poppy didn't even bother complaining about how cramped it would be; he would not care.

They were next in line for their flavorless beans and salt pork when one of Cash's men rode up to Mr. Hall in a hurry, saying something urgent in hushed tones. Isa frowned and strained to hear.

"Hoodoo, watch the girls while I'm gone," Mr. Hall barked, mounting his horse and riding off after the man into the darkening woods.

Isa was still frowning.

"What is it?" Poppy asked, disliking the nervous energy radiating from Isa.

"Why would he come up to Ed with news instead of Cash? And to not even tell Cash what had happened? That's odd."

"Perhaps something happened with one of the men on patrol?" Poppy suggested, but her eyes were everywhere.

It couldn't just be her imagination that most of the men watched her. They were always watching. Leering. Only Sid and Mr. Hall kept their eyes to themselves except for when they were making sure no one scampered free from the camp. Hoodoo had turned to check on the first wagon, standing with his half-eaten plate of food, when one of Cash's men walked behind him. Poppy had gasped a fraction of a second before the butt of the man's rifle connected with the base of Hoodoo's skull.

Hoodoo crumpled to the ground without a sound.

Some of the girls watching in the first wagon cried out.

"Shut the hell up!" growled the man with the rifle.

The girls immediately hushed, the older comforting the younger.

"Poppy, Poppy," Isa was whispering, backing into her and dropping her tin plate. "Get behind me."

Lester stood, his hands up and eyes as wide as dinner plates, the ladle dripping bean gravy. Across the fire, another of Cash's men held a pistol, its black muzzle pointed right at him.

Isa was muttering under her breath. "That's why the man went to Ed. It was a distraction. Most of Mr. Hall's men are on patrol tonight, including Sid. Oh God—"

"There's gonna be a change in leadership from now on, boys," Cash called from the left with a broad grin, two cocked pistols, and glimmering, excited eyes. "Ed's men, drop those guns until we hash it out. I don't think your old boss will be comin' back tonight."

There were muffled thumps of heavy six-shooters and rifles hitting the grass. Cash ordered the four men that remained at camp to line up beside the fire and hit their knees, hands up.

The aggressive man with the rifle strode behind them and lifted its muzzle. "Don't make any sudden movements." His smile was mean, left eye blackened from a tussle a few nights before.

Cash's walk was a strut, and his obnoxious laugh made Poppy's teeth grit. When his eyes settled on her, she knew something dreadful was about to ensue. She felt Isa go rigid where the younger woman stood slightly in front of her, a human blockade. If Isa thought Poppy would cower down and let another person fight her fights for her, she was sadly mistaken. Lifting her chin, Poppy moved sideways away from Isa.

Cash followed with his eyes, then he stalked her way.

"To celebrate," he smirked, holstering both pistols, "I think I'll steal a little kiss."

Poppy turned her face away, but his hand was hard on her face, turning it back toward him with bruising force.

There was a flurry of movement from Poppy's right.

Isa had tried to push Cash away.

"You get your filthy lips away from her," she snarled. The snarl turned into choking.

Another man came up behind her and grabbed her chain, pulling her back by the chain and her two braids. Her floppy hat fell beneath their struggling feet where it lay, squashed and sad to the side. Poppy stumbled forward to keep enough slack between their chain.

"Stop! You're choking her," she pleaded.

"Chain that bitch to the wagon wheel!" Cash shouted, his cheeks florid, nostrils flared. All his celebratory euphoria had curdled into a dark rage.

Didn't Isa know that to make him look weak now, at the most critical point in this organized mutiny, was the worst thing she could have done? It would have been better to have let him have his kiss. As terrible as it might have been, it would now be worse. She saw the promise in his eyes, the promise that pain was imminent. Cash followed her and yanked her back with an arm across her chest, pinning her wrists down where her hands had grasped the chain.

A key slid into the lock, twisting, and he opened the hinge with a wrench. The shackle fell to the ground with the key still inserted.

"Wrap this around a spoke and lock it," Cash ordered the man struggling to hold Isa. He grabbed Poppy's shoulders and whirled her. "All I wanted was a goddamned kiss, but now I think I'll take it all. Unbutton your dress."

Poppy shook her head as that familiar hot stab of shame returned. She wouldn't. She wouldn't do it. He'd have to make her because she wouldn't make it easy for him.

"No!" Isa screamed from behind her. There was a masculine grunt of surprise, and then two long, slim arms wrapped themselves hard around Poppy. "No!"

"Jesus Christ, Butch, how hard is it to hold one little girl?" Cash roared, wrapping a fist around Isa's loose chain and pulling.

Butch limped over, teeth bared with fury and pain, and struck a glancing blow at Isa's head. Poppy could feel the impact as if it was she he had struck, and she screamed.

"Stop!" Close to sobbing, she pulled desperately at Isa's clenched fingers. "Isa, please let go, they'll kill you. Let go, it's all right. It's all right."

It took both men to free the girl's grip from Poppy's waist, and Isa shrieked when she fell backward. She swore, cursed, and fought like a wild thing, ignoring slaps and blows from the men as they dragged her by her hair and chain, strangling her.

Poppy, who had tumbled down into the grass during the struggle, sobbed while they chained Sol's little sister to the wagon wheel. They threaded the chain through the spokes, pulling it tight until Isa's back was against the wheel. Her booted heels dug fruitlessly into the ground.

Breathing hard, Cash stood and pointed a finger at Butch. "You watch her because if she gets loose one more time, you're getting a licking so bad you'll be pissing blood."

"I'm pretty sure I'll already be pissing blood because of that hellcat," Butch groaned, bent over and clutching his stomach.

At once, the mood lightened; several men chuckled.

Some of the deep lines in Cash's forehead smoothed, but his smile wasn't genuine. When he looked down at Isa, Poppy could plainly see hatred burning in his eyes. It scared her more than anything. And when he turned on his boot heel towards her, the hatred turned into something else.

"Well, Red, looks like it's just you and me."

There was another smattering of laughter.

Poppy dried her eyes. Isa was still struggling to get free, but quietly, and she looked Poppy straight in the eye. The misery on her face was more than Poppy could bear, so she looked down and made to stand.

"No, no," Cash tutted, strolling closer to her in a half-circle. His spurs jingled with every step like a gunslinger from a dime novel. "No, I like you right where you are. On the ground." He paused and smiled. This time it was genuine. "On your knees."

The words she had told Isa rang in her head.

Staying alive was worth more than pride.

Had she said that? It must be true. But why did it feel like she would rather die than feel the way she was feeling right now?

Because you can't leave Isa alone with these men. She needs you to be strong.

Poppy stayed on her knees.

"Unbutton your dress."

Chapter Thirty

If a dozen people holding their breath could make a sound, then Poppy heard it at that moment. It was like a pulse. A crowd's heartbeat. For some of them, a heartbreak. Lungs expanding, holding, eyes burning into her. She looked around. All the men watched her. The men who stood with guns. The men who were on their knees like her. The frightened eyes in the dark, shadowy recesses of the wagons. Big Maude, smiling. Isa, grimacing. And, to Poppy's dismay, Alwine had crawled out of the supply wagon, her hair unkempt, her face thin and pale. She watched too, in obvious pain. Whether it was from her healing injuries or from Poppy on display, she didn't know.

Poppy bit her lip and looked up at Cash, shaking her head involuntarily.

"Oh, that's right. You're shy." He sighed dramatically and strode to her, spurs jingling.

Clink. Clink. Clink.

Her throat was unbelievably dry.

"Let me help you." He bent over and started undoing her buttons. Her hands fluttered over his as though to stop him, but he slapped them away. She knew stopping him would only make it worse. Even though touching him would make her ill, it could always be worse. He was halfway down her bodice, her lacy muslin combinations revealed, when footsteps from the second wagon interrupted them.

It was Mina.

"Cash, you promised," she said. She had been crying, and her tears made streaks in the brown layer of dirt coating her face.

He stood from his crouch, and Poppy closed her eyes when his hand raised. She didn't see the slap that knocked Mina to the ground. Hearing it was enough.

"Promises to a whore don't mean anything, Mina," he said coldly. "Get back to the wagon."

When Poppy opened her eyes, she caught Mina sprinting past the wagon. Before the shadows in the surrounding woods swallowed her, she turned and sent Poppy a look of purest loathing. A sensation of spiders crawled up Poppy's back.

"Where are these women coming from?" Cash asked, scraping his sweaty hair from his forehead with both hands. He waited until his men had finished laughing before he reached for his belt buckle. "Lay on your back and lift your skirts. Don't make me ask twice."

Clenching her jaw, ignoring Isa's exclamation of dismay, she did as she was told.

I'm sorry, Sol.

The warm summer air felt cold. Her thighs shook, and her hands were claws in her skirts. When she felt Cash get to his knees and spread her legs, she squeezed her eyes shut. When he pulled the neckline of her undergarments lower to expose her breasts, she forced herself to slow her breathing.

He whistled low but said nothing else, and for that, she was thankful. Control would be impossible if he narrated what he saw.

She heard him popping open the buttons of his jeans, felt him lowering.

Everyone was frozen.

And then...laughter.

High, hysterical laughter.

Poppy's eyes flew open, and she gaped, lips parted, at Isa.

"Ha! What were you planning on doing with that thing," Isa called, "bait a hook?"

Bruises had bloomed into maroon splotches on Isa's face, her teeth gleamed while she screamed with laughter. She looked deranged. Mad. The erection against Poppy's leg flagged; Cash abruptly tucked it away.

"Don't worry, Poppy!" Isa's voice rang out, reaching every ear. "It probably won't be so bad. I reckon you won't even feel it."

There was absolute silence besides Isa's guffaws.

Poppy made the mistake of looking up at Cash, who, still suspended, glanced down at her. Their eyes met. His face flooded with blood, turning crimson then puce. He scrambled to his feet, buttoning his pants. Poppy hastily covered her legs and pulled her neckline up, warily backing away from what looked like dynamite about to explode. It got worse when Lester started to choke.

The man next to him sniggered.

Then, all the men gave in to the bizarre hilarity of it.

Even Cash's men had to hide their amusement behind fists or turn their backs completely, their shaking shoulders giving them away.

But Isa was the loudest of all. Adding insult to injury, she crooked her pinky finger and wiggled it.

Poppy knew it had gone too far and was already on her feet and running.

Cash beat her there.

Roaring at Isa to "Shut up!" he barreled into the girl, stunning her. As soon as she recovered, her whoops of laughter were even louder. When Cash pulled an arm back, fist clenched, Poppy grabbed it and held on for dear life. He ended up striking a wagon spoke. Isa reared her long legs back and kicked him as hard as she could; he fell to his back with an "Oomph."

It was pandemonium.

BOOM!

Everyone jolted. Some men looked around to see who had gotten shot.

"What the hell is going on?"

Mr. Hall had ridden his horse into camp during the fray, Hoodoo swaying behind him, the back of his collar soaked in blood. *He must have woken up and crawled off during the distraction with Isa and the men*, Poppy thought.

"I said," Mr. Hall bellowed, aiming the double-barrel rifle right at Cash's gasping, supine face, "what the hell is going on?"

Cash groaned and scrubbed his eyes.

Poppy clung to Isa.

Everyone else was still as death.

"Call your men off, or your skull will be nothing but crowbait in the next five seconds." Mr. Hall's city twang had shifted to something coarser, his eyes glassy behind his spectacles.

"Put your guns down, boys," Cash ordered hoarsely.

Most complied readily, but the one with the shiner sneered at Mr. Hall.

Hoodoo said something from behind him on the horse. Mr. Hall listened, gun still trained on Cash's face, and nodded.

There was a boom of gunfire. Several girls squealed, and all the men jumped except for Mr. Hall and Hoodoo. At his hip, Hoodoo's gun smoked.

The man with the black eye fell to the ground screaming.

Gutshot.

"Don't just sit there while he screams," Mr. Hall said. "Put the dog out of its misery."

Hoodoo dismounted and, despite his pleas, shot the wounded man between the eyes. The back of Hoodoo's head looked nearly as bad as the dead man's. His long hair was matted with dark, congealing blood.

On the ground, staring into the two black holes of the rifle muzzle, Cash said slowly, "Ace isn't going to like that you just killed one of my men."

"I will lose no sleep over it. That snake almost killed Hoodoo, a far larger part of this operation than you, my yellow-bellied friend. Shall I wire him at the next stop? Confess my sins?"

Cash said nothing.

"No, I don't suppose that would put you in a very good light. Family or not, I expect Ace will be quite put out with you when he finds out you tried to kill the brains of this yearslong campaign. Now, because of your idiocy, three of your men are dead."

Cash's eyes bulged. "Three?"

Juggling to hold his rifle one-handed, Mr. Hall unsheathed a blood-stained bowie knife. "You cannot think I would allow men that tried to kill me to survive, can you?"

"You can't just—"

"I not only can, but I did."

"I didn't kill any of your men!" Cash sounded like a child.

"No, but you tried to kill *me*." Mr. Hall's voice lowered. "The only thing keeping you alive right now is Ace. And once I tell him of your perfidy, your services in this business will no longer be needed. As for you boys," he called to his men, who had stood and sidled away from the bleeding body in the grass, "take care of the bodies. Anything in their possession is yours. I imagine your cut once we reach Mexico will be sizable, with fewer men to divide the profits.

"Lester," he barked. His forced city accent was thick. "Unchain the girl from that wheel, shackle them together, and put them in the wagon."

"Yes, sir." Lester, smelling pungent of unwashed body and fear, took the key and rushed to Isa and Poppy.

They trembled and avoided eye contact while Lester followed instructions, locked them together, and pulled them mercilessly to the wagon.

"Lester, can you make sure that Ally has supper?" Poppy asked. Her voice sounded far away. She glanced at Isa, who crawled into the wagon, the girls parting like the Red Sea to let her through. "And Isa?"

"I'm not hungry," was Isa's muffled reply from the dim interior. "But you should eat."

"I am not hungry, either."

"Poppy—"

Poppy avoided her censure, but Lester, with an indecipherable expression, deserted them before she could make any more requests.

Chain taut between them, Poppy climbed into the wagon, ignoring the staring eyes of the other girls. None offered words of comfort or showed concern for her well-being, and she was thankful. The quicker she could put it behind her, the better.

He did it, not you. It's not your shame. It's his.

She internally chanted this repeatedly to drown out the red flare of her other thoughts, the thoughts that screamed to take over the rationale that kept her calm. Kept her sane.

Now that it was over, a pleasant numbness seeped over her, coating her body and mind with a capacious gauzy cobweb. She didn't wish for Gary to come and avenge her. She didn't wish for Sol to come and save her. And if Cash lived to be a bent-backed old man that never atoned for his sins, she did not care.

She didn't care about anything.

That's what she told herself. It was easier that way.

But when Isa lay on her side and turned to face the corner, Poppy wrapped herself around her and held tight. She would feel it if someone came for Isa. It would wake her up, and she could hold on and never let go.

They both lay still except for the persistent tremor in their bodies. They were quiet except for the growling of their bellies.

Neither slept for hours.

SLEEP FINALLY CAME just before dawn, long after the men had concluded their conversation. The urge to empty her bladder had roused Poppy, and she was appreciative. The dreams of her mother in a ditch had morphed into Sol and Isa.

Ignoring the pulsing headache that had followed the rush of last night's memories, she sat up and tucked her head between her knees. Her dress smelled like dirt, and she yanked her head away from the black skirt. Her bladder was nigh to explode, mouth filled with sticky saliva. Her hunger turned into nausea, flipping like a coin, and she took gradual drags of air.

"Poppy?" Isa croaked. Her voice was a bullfrog's. "You well?"

No. Poppy wasn't well. Not at all.

"Yes. And you? Your poor voice." Poppy reached, her hand a pale blur in the gray morning light, touching the metal collar on Isa's neck. Her hair had come loose from her braids last night and was a tangle on the wagon bed. Poppy picked a twig out, swallowing.

"I'm well as can be expected," Isa whispered, like a convalescent with laryngitis. "I expect I discovered what it feels like when you hang. My throat feels like I tried to swallow a sock filled with rocks." She grew quiet.

The cobwebs of apathy were lifting, drifting away as though a gentle breeze had caught them. "And your head? You were struck quite hard."

"Naw, he hit like a girl."

Poppy covered her mouth to hold in either a hysterical laugh or a sob, she wasn't sure which. When that didn't help, she bit her hand.

"What are you doing? Stop that." Isa smacked Poppy's hand away. "I knew you'd be hungry after not eating last night, but cannibalism isn't the way."

"It's my fault," Poppy gasped, her cheeks flushed with dry, chapped heat. "Everything. I should have stayed in my old town. I should never have come. It's what I deserve. I understand that. But not you, Isa. You shouldn't be here."

Isa sat up. Their chain dragged dully along the boards. "What do you mean 'it's what I deserve'? Don't be foolish."

"It is." Poppy chewed on her nails, tasting dirt. "I was born to this life, didn't anyone tell you? My mother was a scarlet woman, just like your sister Katherine. But my mother, she didn't give me to family. We didn't have any family. All we had was each other. And when it was my turn to help, to work, I shirked my duties. I turned my back on my mother, and she died because of it. This...this is my penance. I'm being punished for killing her."

At this, the three oldest girls stirred. Gretchen, Pilar, and Caroline sat up to listen. *Good. Let them hear.*

Eyes as large and bright as citrine gems, Isa shook her head. "That's crazy talk."

"It's the truth. She needed me, and I ran."

"You're telling me your mother wanted you to whore with her? How old were you?"

"Sixteen. Old enough to work. But I ran and hid at a church like a coward, and that's why they killed her."

"They?"

"The men she stole from."

"Sounds to me like she brought the trouble to her doorstep, Poppy." Isa's voice hardened. "What if it had been me? Because I'll tell you right now, I'm sixteen, and I would run, too. Would you sit there and lecture me that I deserved something bad because I didn't want to follow that particular family tradition? Could you say that to me?"

Poppy said nothing.

Isa nodded slowly. She knew she was right.

Pilar's voice, husky from sleep, startled them. "My sister did it so that I wouldn't have to. After Padre died, she kept the men away while I watched our little sisters."

Gretchen nodded. "My ma tried to keep me away from it. We had a little shanty by the river, and I never stepped foot in the saloon she worked at. She did everything so I can finish my schooling." A ghost of a smile drifted across her face, and she brushed her knuckles against sleeping Vera's forehead. "I want to be a teacher."

Caroline worked at separating a knot in her yellow hair. "I don't have a mother, but *Père* took me with him to gambling dens. It's been an interesting life, but I know he would never expect of me what your mother expected, Poppy." Her voice broke. "I miss him terribly. What must he think has happened to me?"

They sat in contemplative silence until footsteps broke it. Hoodoo's familiar brisk gait. The other girls awakened to the hiss of canvas ties being pulled out of their knot.

They did their routine mechanically; answer nature's call while Hoodoo watched, wash clothes and tin plates in the river, splash their faces before being dragged away, and then return to the camp for breakfast. The numbness threatened, hovering above Poppy, a protective vapor. The only time it cleared was when she managed to catch sight of the purple bruising around Isa's throat and face. Plans circled around and around in her head like buzzards, and she chanted them internally while they stood in line for breakfast.

Despite Isa's curious looks, the girl didn't push, perhaps assuming that Poppy was still overwrought from this morning. This morning had been a moment of weakness. Self-pity came out of nowhere sometimes, but it could easily be brushed away like grits of dirt clinging to a hem. Lester ladled food into two tin plates for Poppy. He had never returned with food and didn't apologize for it now. He did look at her, however. She refused to return his gaze and hoped he could feel the hate she held in her heart for him. For all of them. She hoped it felt like needles stabbing directly into his eyes. On the way to Alwine's wagon, she played out a scene where she tackled Lester, screaming to drown out his own cries, her missing sewing scissors in one hand, its target his wide-open eyes.

The closer they got to Alwine's wagon, the less the scene held any satisfaction.

Mina sat on the tailboard of the second wagon, smiling secretly.

Cash must have gone to her last night, his version of licking his wounds.

Alwine's wagon was quiet and still. Poppy hoped the darling had managed to sleep. The last she had seen of her young friend was her terrified pale face and childishly mussed braids. Strangely, the canvas entrance was only halfway closed. Had Alwine loosened the drawstring herself? That was a good sign. She must be feeling better. Poppy placed the plates of gruel on the board and climbed in, Isa directly behind her. Ducking under the half-open canvas, she saw Alwine's dirty feet poking out of her thin blanket.

When we are rescued, I will buy her shoes.

"Ally," she murmured, crawling nearer. A fly landed on Alwine's toe, and Poppy shooed it away. "Ally? It's time for breakfast. Wake up."

The shape under the haphazardly laid blanket didn't move. The fly landed back on Alwine's toe. It looked stubbed, bruised. The nail had broken, caked with dried black blood. Both feet looked discolored, in fact, especially the heels. Poppy's pulse started to pick up.

Something was wrong. Had Alwine tried to escape last night?

"What on earth happened to your feet?" Poppy reached over and brushed the fly away again, grabbing the girl's foot with the intention of turning it toward her to see the extent of the injuries.

Alwine's foot was cold and stiff.

Jerking her hand away with a high-pitched, whooping gasp, Poppy fell back on her bottom.

"What is it?" Isa's voice had risen too high from her abused windpipe, and the words broke like an adolescent boy's.

With revulsion and fear in equal measures, Poppy rolled to her knees and yanked the blanket from Alwine's body.

"Nooo," she moaned. It grew deeper, guttural, drawing out.

"What!" Isa hoisted herself into the wagon but stopped when she saw what the blanket revealed, her mouth a round, disbelieving 'o.'

Poppy's inhale dragged on and on, her airway thin and compressed, but nothing constricted the long, piercing scream she released like a steam whistle once her lungs had filled. All her grief and horror were released with it.

It made Mina's fixed smile melt.

Made the men around the fire scramble to their feet and draw their guns.

Made Isa cover her ears with her teeth gritted.

The young girl Poppy had nursed back to health lay on her back as though asleep, throat a blackish-purple bruise.

Her hands looked very small.

When rough fingers dragged Poppy out, she didn't fight. She made no noise because she could no longer breathe. Her eyes were squeezed shut, her mouth opened wide in the silent echo of the scream that had raised hairs on every neck.

From somewhere in the distance, Big Maude began to wail.

"Poppy, breathe!" Isa wept from somewhere, shaking and shaking her.

When Poppy's lungs finally functioned, the sound she made was was the croak of a first whooping inhale after the breath was knocked out.

Her body folded, hunching in on itself.

Someone had killed Alwine.

She was dead.

Chapter Thirty-One

Two buzzards circled overhead, and Sol nudged his horse closer. "See that?"

Junior squinted up at the harsh blue sky. "Yep. What do you think it is?"

"Another animal, I reckon."

"Let's go see."

Their faces mirrored each other, both tense and alert. They had grown accustomed to scouting ahead during the day, unwilling to lose the tracks they so fruitlessly followed after several days of waiting out the storm. True to the Texas Ranger's words, the posse had eventually rediscovered the trail but had lost precious time.

They had been following for days, but Captain Lawson insisted they wait until they caught a man on patrol and got more information. So far, there had been no captures. Sol figured the Rangers and Deputy Ellis were too busy arguing about what tactics to take, filibustering instead of getting off their pant seats and saving those girls. The stalling drove him mad. Sol slept less. He ate because Ben glared at him until he did, and he had to admit his friend was right. Sol felt stronger, his mind clearer, when he ate. He was no good to anyone if he withheld food.

But in his own way, he was rebelling.

"We're getting pretty close to them, aren't we?" Junior asked softly, his eyes cut left, right, left, right, his hand poised over his exposed holster. Something had changed in him in the two weeks they'd been on the trail. His edges had sharpened; his eyes could cut glass. He looked progressively more like Ben as their journey continued. He practiced unholstering his gun around the fire for hours in front of the campfire. At first, the townsmen teased him, trying to lighten the mood. But he paid them no mind, and the jokes trailed away awkwardly. It became a ritual for everyone to watch Junior whip his gun out every night, quick as a blink, the metal against leather more fluid than water.

Sol had never been any good with pistols. He would aim and aim and the shot would go wide every time. His aim with a rifle, however, was always true. But his specialty was hand-to-hand combat. The minute he got his arms and legs around a person, it was over for them.

"You see that?" Junior asked. His voice was half an octave higher than usual.

Hog didn't see anything, but he smelled it. He didn't bay, but the wrinkles in his face deepened, his nose frantic along an unseen trail. Whines escaped the hound.

Fifty feet ahead, they saw the two buzzards land, waddle, and flap around something large on the ground. A deer?

With a feeling of foreboding and one eye turned upward at more carrion birds roosting in the sunlit trees around them, Sol pulled his rifle from its saddle holster, his mouth sour. Copper edged closer, Junior at Sol's side with his elbow out and fingers twitching.

The moment Sol saw filthy light-colored hair splayed along the forest floor, littered between the buzzards, Junior had already unholstered his gun and was shooting in the air, once, twice.

Sol knew that gunshots were bad this close to their quarry, but all he could feel was fear.

Isa had hair that color.

The gunshots did their job. The buzzards panicked, falling over each other to fly their big bodies up and up, through the trees and into the sky. Sol and Junior dismounted with the speed of veteran cowboys, their horses unmoving and waiting patiently.

"Oh, Jesus," Junior sobbed, half a step behind Sol's long-legged stride.

Hog began to bay.

"Hush up," Sol barked through a parched throat. He was running, stumbling, then falling, crawling toward the body that the buzzards' absence had revealed. Even though the girl wore an enormous shift, not overalls, that suspended terror didn't leave his chest until he rolled the body over by the shoulder.

"Is that—" Junior broke off and immediately turned, drawing his black kerchief over his mouth and nose, eyes squeezed shut.

"Ally," Sol whispered, letting his hand fall away. The hair that had appeared to be Isa's honey-colored tresses from afar was a light blonde up close. Her hair was just filthy. "Oh, Ally." His voice broke. The back of his hand hovered over Alwine's hair, but he couldn't bring himself to touch her again. He stiffened his resolve and brushed the hair away from her face and throat. "She's been strangled," he heard himself say, the words tight. "Looks like she was dumped pretty recent, too."

Junior's voice was hot and vicious. "Yeah, someone dropped her right off their goddamned horse."

"Looks like it."

"I thought—"

"Yeah. Me too."

They were quiet, Sol still and gazing down at the ravaged girl, Junior restlessly pacing with his hands locked behind the crown of his Stetson.

Finally, "You got an oilskin in your bags, Junior?"

As respectfully as they could, they wrapped the girl in the oilskin, tying the end and middle with spare loops of rope. Since Junior's horse was younger and skittish at the smell of the mysteriously shaped oilskin, Sol gingerly laid Alwine between the pommel of his saddle and his horse's neck. Copper's ears drew back, but he remained still. They had hardly mounted when they heard hoofbeats.

They shared a quick, worried look.

"That's not coming from our camp," Junior said.

They were coming from the west.

A dangerous eagerness lit Sol's eyes, but his words were grim. "Let's flank 'em. Get your rope ready."

Junior's eyes shared Sol's fervent intensity. He nodded, checked that his pistols were free from his jacket, and they split in two directions. Both freed their ropes from their saddle horns. Sol stopped by a large oak and slowly, slowly lowered Alwine against the trunk.

"Stay, Hog. Guard." Hog sat, whining softly.

Sol and Junior got in position behind two different tree clusters, nodded at each other across the several yards between them, and waited.

The man on the horse was cantering warily nearer, muttering under his breath. Sol held still, arm raised and waiting, Junior mirroring him.

As soon as the stranger rode between their two hiding places, they burst into motion.

Sol executed a header, looping his rope over the man's shoulders and yanking him violently off the saddle, twirling the other end of his rope round and round his saddle horn. The horse ran on while its rider fell on his shoulders and neck. When his legs flew up high, Junior executed a heeler, jerking the rope taut once it had secured itself around the man's ankles.

Stunned, his arms trapped against his sides and his legs equally helpless, the stranger lay still, gaping like a banked fish. When his breath finally whooped into his lungs, he groaned. He was an older man, his scalp pink beneath sparse white hair that stood on end like raw mohair.

Dismounting, Sol strode to the pathetic sight.

"What's your name?" Sol squatted so close the fringe of his leather chaps brushed the man's sunburnt cheek.

"I-I—" His watery blue eyes flitted to Junior, who had remained in the saddle, keeping his rope tight. "Danny."

"Got a last name?"

The man's lips tightened in a grimace. "Can you call your man off, son? I can't even think."

"I figured being trussed up tighter than a Sunday chicken would have you thinking faster, old man, not slower. Now, how 'bout you tell me where you came from."

"Up yonder a ways."

"What were you doing there?"

"Just—just out for a ride, son."

"Quit callin' me *son*," Sol gritted, leaning closer. Alwine's sweet face would be permanently branded in his mind. "You're out for a ride, you hear gunshots, and you come toward them. Why?"

"I just thought someone might be in trouble, is all."

"You happen to see three wagons with a helluva lot of men around it come by?"

Danny clamped his lips shut. Junior pulled on the rope, backing his horse up. Danny's body bowed off the ground, stretched taut between the two horses. Sol's horse was trained well; Copper didn't move an inch. The old man started talking fast.

"All right, yeah. Yeah, I came from the wagons!"

"Why did you ride this way?" Sol demanded, grabbing the man's jaw and squeezing.

"I had to check the—" He stopped again.

Blood boiling, Sol leaned down further. "Yeah, I know what you came back to check, you no good sonuvabitch. Danny, I reckon you're gonna come with us. And we're going to see just exactly what the posse of men following y'all have to say. How's that sound? It'll be a jumping good time."

Danny's small blue eyes had flared, and he was still shaking his head when he was wrapped tight as a drum and thrown indelicately in front of Junior's saddle.

Sol recovered Alwine's body, placed it once more in front of his pommel, and mounted. He tried and failed not to think about the contents of the oilskin. He could hear Junior talking to Danny, making threats, ignoring the jouncing grunts from the old man's blood-red face. Before they left the wooded area, Sol roped Danny's horse, whistled for Hog to follow, and led the way back to camp.

CAPTAIN LAWSON FOLLOWED Sol back to the area where Alwine's body had lain.

The older Ranger had questioned Danny profusely, while men had wrapped so tight around the captive that they were a wall of pure menace. Entombed in such a way, furious eyes glittering and fingers twitching over gun holsters, the weak-willed Danny had had no choice but to blurt every single detail of his last six months with a man called Edmund Hall.

Hog was a silent companion trotting beside Sol and Captain Lawson. Junior had wanted to come, but after considering the bristling young man, the captain suggested he help the other rangers guard Danny and retrieve more information from him.

"Show me how she was lying and where," Captain Lawson said once they had found the disturbed earth.

Sol explained the body's position, angle, and condition.

"Didn't even bother to bury her," the captain growled, shaking his head and squatting by a nearby tree. He wrote notes in a pocket-sized journal with a carpenter's pencil. It put Sol in mind of Deputy Ellis. "I'll take the body to the town's doctor before we continue and give the local sheriff my notes. They'll verify the cause of death and wire the marshal over this case."

"What about Danny?"

"I'll leave him with the sheriff. He can rot in the cell until he's tried in court."

A sudden baying in the woods several yards away brought Sol's head up.

"Hog?" Sol called. He sent out a sharp whistle between his teeth.

Hog's baying became snarling. Grabbing Hog's lead and his rifle from the saddle, Sol sprinted into the woods despite Lawson's urging to "Hold up." If the man thought Sol would leave his dog to fend for himself, he was as crazy as a bed bug. Cursing, the Ranger mounted his horse and followed behind. Sol cocked his rifle, slipping his way between barbed vines and tangled underbrush, his footsteps quiet and stealthy from years of hunting on foot.

From his peripheral vision, Sol saw a crouching man raise his rifle to his shoulder and aim. He ducked instinctively, but the muzzle wasn't pointed at him. It was pointed at Captain Lawson.

"Watch out!" he bellowed, crouching to his knee and taking aim.

Sol's bullet hit its target's solar plexus half a second after the man's gun had fired. From behind him came a grunt and a crash of underbrush. Captain Lawson had been shot off his horse. Part of Sol wanted to keep going and find Hog, but he turned back and ran zigzag between trees.

Captain Lawson's horse had shied a few feet away, its owner lying on his side, cradling his hip with a hand. Blood seeped between his fingers, absorbing into the tan material of his trousers.

"I'm all right. Got my hip. How many more are there?" Lawson spoke through gritted teeth and blinked profusely.

"Don't know, at least one more, and he has my dog." Sol listened but heard nothing. Had there been a third shot? He didn't hear Hog any longer. "Damn it," he hissed under his breath. He cocked his rifle again, the sound unbearably loud in the surrounding woods.

"I don't think I can sit a horse," Lawson admitted, "but the men will have heard the shots."

Dog snarls followed by a man's screams rent the air again. The screams became cursing. Then, Hog yelped.

Sol was up and running before the Ranger could stop him.

"You want your dog, you better come out with your hands up," shouted a hoarse voice that was both nervous and titillative. "You don't want me to hurt him, do ya?"

To answer was to give away his hiding spot. Sol crept around an enormous dead oak choked by a tangle of overhanging muscadine vines. Hog's trembling rear stood out from behind a thick pine a dozen yards away, his tail curled between his legs.

Son of a bitch.

On the other side of the pine, a man's squatting back and rear was visible, as though he was holding the dog by the scruff of his neck or his head. It might not kill the fellow, but if Sol shot the man in the ass, there'd be no getting up and running off. Feeling sweat curl the curtain of hair at his brow, Sol shook it back, raised his rifle, and aimed.

"Lower it, or I'll blow the top of you right off."

The voice came from right behind him. Cold lead filled Sol's veins.

In the distance, Hog struggled harder. Sol didn't move. Something cold and hard bumped the back of his head.

"Last time I'm sayin' it. Drop that shotgun, or you'll be a head shorter."

Sol lowered the shotgun, set it against the great oak's tree roots, and straightened with his hands raised.

"Did you get him?" asked the man behind the tree, clearly struggling.

"Put your hands behind your back," ordered the voice. "No sudden movements. My finger's real twitchy."

Sol did as he was told, jaw bulging, the pulse in his temples throbbing.

"Lester, get over here and tie him up."

"You got him?" Lester cried gleefully. Then, "But what do I do about the dog? He just about chewed a hole in me."

"Shoot him, dumbass."

"No!" Sol moved to step forward, but the muzzle of a rifle struck him at the base of his skull.

"Don't move!" The disembodied voice behind him was harsh through ragged breathing. "I swear to God that's your last warning."

"Goddammit," screamed Lester.

"Hog!"

"Shut the hell up!" The barrel slammed into Sol's neck.

There was a *BOOM* and a yelp, and between that and Sol hollering for Hog, he didn't hear the swing of the rifle before it cracked against the back of his head.

SOL WAS SEMICONSCIOUS when the two men dragged him away, but the trees above him were fuzzy and overly bright. Stunned and sluggish, he tried to bring his hands up to cradle the back of his aching head, but they were tied in front of him. He began to struggle.

"Slow down, Cash, he's heavier than he looks, and he's fighting."

"Knock him back out."

"Aw, hellfire."

"What?"

"That his dog followin' us?"

The click of a gun cocking had Sol shaking his head, trying to wake up. Hoarsely, he warned, "Hog, back!"

The sound of the revolver firing was deafening.

"I think you missed," Lester noted.

"Shut the hell up and tie him to my horse."

Slowly, Sol regained his faculties, but he was woozy enough that every attempt to free himself was easily slapped away. It was like a dream where he tried to defend himself from mortal danger only to stumble when he ran, legs like limp rags, fists as insubstantial as feather pillows. He felt the drag of a second rope string between the one that tied his fists together and got to his knees.

"Might as well stay down, Cowboy," sneered the one that had knocked him out. "I'll be goin' fast. Ain't no way you can keep up."

"Hey," Lester said timidly, "you think we should go back for Sid?"

"He's dead. Didn't you see the hole this fellow blew in him?"

"I was pretty well busy at the time," Lester defended, holding up his bleeding hand.

The other man—what was his name, Cash?—finally came into Sol's view. He had a face the ladies would swoon over and a pout that Ben and Sol saw a mile away as a work-shirking tenderfoot. "Did you finish off the lawman like I asked?"

"He was dead."

"Did you check?"

After the smallest hesitation, "Yep. Dead as a doornail."

Cash grunted, but his hand flew to his hogleg when Sol stood up. "You're a tall sonuvabitch, ain't'cha? Ed's not gonna like you, no sirree. You killed one of his best men. They were almost as close as brothers, weren't they, Lester?"

Lester's mouth was clamped shut, looking up and up at a clearly enraged Sol.

"Did you kill my dog?" Sol rasped, trying not to weave on his feet. Had they cracked his skull? His brain felt like mush, his head so sore that it throbbed with his heartbeat.

Lester shook his head, but Cash stepped forward, eyes narrowed on Sol. "I think I got him that last time. You better hope he doesn't come back, Cowboy."

Sol said nothing.

"Cash, we better go before somebody shows up looking for them. You sure we shouldn't just kill him?" Lester avoided Sol's sharpening gaze.

"Hell, no. Can you imagine Ed's face when I show up with the man that killed Sid? And he won't be able to do a damned thing about it, not with that fool 'code' of his." He mounted his horse chuckling, spurs jangling, and dug them in his horse's sensitive flanks.

Leather chaps were an amazing thing, and Sol was never more thankful for them than now. He ran as quickly as he could in the brush, but Cash made his horse wind around trees several times, wrapping Sol's rope around trunks. He was forced to sprint to catch up or have his arms broken against the pressure or scraped raw against the bark. This went on for an hour, but it felt endless. He had a pounding headache but was made from hardy stock, and his legs managed to keep up with the horse.

It irritated Cash. "Hyah!" he cried to his horse, which bounded forward at a hard gallop.

They had made it to a clearing near a river, where the banks couldn't decide if they were made of sand or round rock. Sol fell on his belly and knees, the breath knocked out of him. Sand and grit flew in his eyes from the horse's hooves, and he tucked his head, blinking out what felt like glass. At first, he rolled over and over, bouncing along the ground like a rag doll.

Self-preservation kicked in. Using the muscles in his abused stomach, he stabilized his body's wild rolling to remain on its front. Then, muscles flexing in his shoulders and arms, he pulled up on the rope and held his torso as far away from the careening ground as he could, utilizing his leather chaps to focus most of his weight. His hands went numb and turned dark purple from the weight of his body, but he was more worried about the flashes of metal from the horse's sharp hind hooves. They looked close enough to his face that one kick could send him straight to his maker.

Even though he felt he'd been strung along for hours, that would have killed him; it couldn't have been more than ten minutes. Cash had stopped and simply looked back, waiting. Sol rose shakily to his knees. It was almost impossible to stand, but there was no other alternative. The rest of the day went by in a haze. They saw no one, riding through the woods in circles, backtracking, going through the river thrice until Sol thought he would drown. Finally, as dusk settled low over the sky and the cicadas sang their high-pitched chittering, through the wet fringe at his brow Sol saw a camp with three wagons.

"You think Ed's sure about this pig farmer keepin' us hidden?" Lester asked from above Sol.

Cash snorted. "He better. He already got his pecker wet with half my girls to keep his yap shut."

"Ed's gonna kill him."

"Probably. Pig boy talks so much I wouldn't mind plugging him right in the mouth."

They continued in this vein until they rode directly into camp, Sol stumbling behind, covered in dusty blood and his shirt in tatters. Several men around the campfire stood, guns drawn.

"Where is Sid?" asked a faintly accented voice. The smallish, bespectacled man strode forward. He wore a bowler hat and a fussy suit, but his air was confident. When he looked at the sagging Sol, a tic in his jaw warned of an impending temper. "Who is this?"

Sol recognized him immediately. This was the man that had left Nelson Smithe's house the night before Poppy was taken.

"Well, now, Ed, that's a funny story," Cash began, staying on his horse as though he were in no hurry to dismount or untie Sol.

There was a feminine gasp from near the wagons.

"No!" screamed two women in unison, and everyone turned.

"Isa? Poppy?" Sol slurred.

They ran forward, connected at the neck by a single heavy chain. But they were alive.

His girls were alive!

Overcome, he dropped to his tender knees and held his tied hands out.

"Stop right there," barked Cash. He dismounted, hustling around his horse to plant his feet between the women and Sol. "How do you know this cowboy?"

Poppy's mouth opened and closed, her eyes full and bright, the tip of her nose a vivid red. She'd been crying hard and wore the same dress she'd disappeared in, along with her sewing apron. Isa looked like a wild woman, and he strained to see past Cash. Were those bruises on his sister's face? Her neck was one blue bruise beneath the shackle. He got back to his feet.

A gun pointed in his direction. He saw it from the corner of his eye. The man, Ed, had drawn his Colt, centered right on Sol's chest. Sol stopped moving.

"Tell me what happened to Sid," Ed said quietly.

"Sid shot and killed a Texas Ranger. And this fellow plugged Sid right back. Figured I'd bring him along with us." Cash did a poor job hiding his glee.

Showing no emotion at this information, Ed kept his gun centered on Sol. "Did you find Danny?"

"Nope. I think they got him. We were looking at tracks when this one's dog came for us. Didn't have a choice but to draw them out. They took one of ours, so we took one of theirs."

"Except they killed one of my men. This one must die."

"No!" Isa cried. She looked very young with her hair down around her in a rat's nest, her bib overalls covered in trail grime. "You can't kill him!"

"And why not?" Ed's eyes flicked just the slightest toward Isa, though his pistol never wavered.

"Because he's my brother, that's why." Her nose ran just as fast as her eyes, and she scrubbed at her face with her sleeve. "Please, Mr. Hall. I feel as close to my brother as you do about Gary. Please."

Sol had never heard Isa beg this way before. She'd been switched twice as often and twice as hard because of it growing up. She never apologized, never begged. It made his chest feel queer hearing her do so on his behalf to a strange, violent man when she had never done so for herself.

"Whoo-wee, did you just say that this man over here, *my prisoner*, is your brother?" Cash began laughing. He doubled over with it. When Ed slowly, slowly lowered his gun, Cash's laughter turned to an angry sneer. "It doesn't matter what she says, Ed. He's part of my wagon now. You can't do squat with him without my say-so. Ain't that right?"

Without another glance at Isa, whose look of dumbfounded horror made Sol's wariness rise yet again, Ed holstered his gun. "Those have always been the rules. But I do not see the gain in keeping this man. He is better off dead."

Isa moaned. They ignored her. Sol noticed a mountain of a man walking close behind Poppy. The slack expression on his face had as much vitality as carved rock on the face of a mountain, now that Sol thought about it. However, there was a bit more animation to the giant breathing down Poppy's neck. He looked wholly infatuated. His platter-sized hand cupped her shoulder. She didn't appear to notice.

"I could think of a few things he'd be worth. They need road workers in Mexico just as bad as whores, though I won't get as pretty of a penny. And then there's entertainment." Watching Isa, Cash turned and kicked Sol's legs out from under him. He fell like a log, too exhausted to catch himself. He tried to dodge the next kick.

"Stop, please!" Poppy screamed, the mountain behind her holding Isa and her back by their chains.

"Only cowards kick a man when he's down," Isa shrieked, fighting her tether.

Cash pulled his gun and pointed it at Sol.

Everyone grew still and silent again.

How many times had someone pointed a gun at him? Sol wondered tiredly. He'd never had a gun pulled on him, not even by rustlers. Today, it had happened half a dozen times.

Speaking softly, Cash waved the gun in emphasis. "If I want to put a bullet in his brain right here, right now, there wouldn't be a damned thing you could do about it." Frogs croaked in the woods around them. "If I wanted to cut pieces off him, a little bit at a time, you'd have to sit there and watch. So, I suggest you keep a civil tongue in your mouth."

Isa didn't speak. For once, the fire in her eyes had been doused by fear.

"That's what I thought." Cash smiled, uncocked his gun, and tucked it in his fancy engraved holster. "Get up, Cowboy."

Why? So the little piss ant could kick him down again?

With no little effort, Sol stood, trying not to let the girls see his knees knocking. He rolled his shoulders and tried not to wince at the screaming pain. From every direction, he felt eyes on him. Unable to resist, he smiled broadly at Isa and winked at Poppy. They looked like they wanted to cry harder, but he was floating on air. It didn't matter what they did to him. Just seeing his sister and his woman alive and whole was worth any pain. He had so many questions.

Who had hit Isa? Why did Cash act like he hated her? What had happened to Alwine? Why was the big son of a bitch acting like he owned Poppy? How was their baby?

The questions he wanted to ask made his head swim.

Ed moved closer, ignoring Cash.

"What did your men do with Danny?"

Flexing his fingers, Sol said, "He's probably in jail right about now."

"Did he tell the Rangers anything?"

How should he answer this? What would this stranger do if he admitted that their man Danny had explained the operation in minute detail? He figured these men would get rid of the evidence and scatter to the four winds, the evidence being all the girls and himself.

Maintaining steady eye contact, Sol answered, "He couldn't. I'd knocked him out and he wouldn't wake up."

"How do I know you're not lying?"

Sol knitted his brow in pretend confusion, letting a little of the anger he felt color his words, and shot back, "Why would I lie about stoving in a killer's skull? I found the girl he dumped. The bastard didn't even bother burying her."

Poppy made a noise of grief.

Ed's lips tightened.

"Yep," Sol continued with a bite, struggling with all his might not to glance at Poppy, "all we had to do was follow the buzzards, and our men found her. We shot off a couple of rounds, and he came running back. Guess he got scared someone would find the body and you'd have a mess on your hands. It wasn't anything to overpower one old man. Too bad I was so rough with him. He probably could have made a good witness on the stand. Guess next time I'll be a little easier."

"There won't be a next time," Cash said, walking threateningly closer.

The leader simply looked at Sol, measuring his words, deciding if he believed them. Sol stared right back. Finally, "Cash, grab a neck iron from the supply wagon. We don't need this one getting loose, hm?"

Sol was fitted to a hinged manacle that pinched his neck when it closed, much to Cash's amusement, and was subsequently chained to a skinny sapling behind the supply wagon. It was dinnertime, and an ill-humored, heavyset woman stirred food under Lester's supervision. Another woman from the second wagon slunk over. She embarrassed Sol, climbing all over Cash, posted close by in case the prisoner got any ideas. Every now and then, she made disparaging comments about "The Cowboy."

"What backwoods trash heap did you get this one from, Cash?" The woman giggled, running her hands up and down the man's chest without once taking her eyes from Sol. "He looks just like a bean pole. Why do you have him?"

"Because it gets under Ed's skin, plus free money is free money. Don't you listen, Mina?"

Pouting, Mina let herself be pushed away, but not before she spat at Sol. He pulled his boot back just in time, and she smirked. She had defensive scratches on her hands and neck, and he wondered if Isa had had anything to do with it.

When Poppy and Isa attempted to bring Sol a plate of beans, Cash ran them off.

"He's not part of your wagon, don't let me catch you over here again."

With a look of the utmost loathing, Isa turned away. But Poppy's expression surprised Sol the most; she stared at Cash blankly for an endless amount of time.

"What, Red? You want something? Want me to finish what we started the other night?"

Without a word, she glanced at Sol, unhappiness written all over her face, and allowed Isa to lead her away. The large man, who seemed to always be watching, left the fire to hover around her while she made her way back to the first wagon.

Unable to help himself, Sol gritted, "What did you mean 'finish what you started the other night'?"

Cash blinked, confused, then swigged from a half-empty bottle of whiskey. "That's right. She's your cousin, ain't she?"

He didn't answer, just glared.

Chuckling, Cash shook his head. "Your cousin is a hot piece, Cowboy. Couldn't keep her hands off me, so I gave her what she was askin' for."

Sol lunged.

"Shit," hissed Cash, spilling his bottle in his hurry to back away, crablike. A fierce scowl replaced his shock once Sol's chain had lost all slack. He scrambled to his feet and looked around. Only Poppy and Isa were watching them, faces tense. Swiping his greasy hair back with rough fingers, Cash said, "You do anything like that again and I'll put you six feet under. Got it?"

Not too much later, Cash grabbed a smiling Mina from her wagon and pulled her to a secluded area behind a leaning outbuilding. The noises that the woman made had Sol's ears burning, but a quick look proved that Poppy and Isa weren't perturbed. In fact, neither looked at Sol at all. Poppy was gazing up at the giant drooling at her feet, her blue eyes wide, lips parted, and fingers delicate on his arm. Isa listened raptly. The man nodded, glanced around, grabbed the tin plate that Poppy handed him, and strode with long legs Sol's way.

Pretending he wasn't burning with jealousy, Sol gave the man a wary smile.

"Howdy," he said, hoping being friendly made the girls' lives easier.

Ignoring his greeting, the man squatted down. "Here. Eat this fast before Cash is done."

"He that quick?" Sol quipped, earning a puckish grin from the other man. "Help me out? I can't hold the plate and spoon it in at the same time." The rope was still so tight it cut all circulation from Sol's fingers.

The man nodded and held the plate while Sol shoveled beans into his mouth. He wasn't halfway done before the man grabbed the spoon and took off with his dinner. He returned to the fire, basking in Poppy's praise. Not even a minute passed before Cash swaggered around the corner, buttoning up his fly, Mina primping behind him.

But Sol wasn't watching them. All he saw was Poppy letting another man lift her hand to his lips for a kiss.

And he worried mightily.

Chapter Thirty-Two

B reakfast was more cold leftover beans and hardtack. Poppy ignored the beans and stuffed her apron with hardtack. She'd noticed immediately that Sol had not been given any breakfast, and he sat stiff and alert, watching them. Her strained smile was interrupted by Hoodoo. The women and girls were taken on an expeditious journey to the wood line, but there was no time for their morning washing up. Hoodoo motioned with his hat for them to load into the wagon like he was herding especially stupid ragtag and bobtail. Isa and Poppy craned their necks while Sol was herded similarly into the supply wagon at gunpoint. While Hoodoo loaded the girls and fastened the canvas, Mr. Hall stood out of sight, his words low.

Poppy and Isa looked at each other.

Gary, Big Maude, and Lester were in charge of guarding the wagons while the remaining men confused their trail. *No posse would find them after they were finished*, Mr. Hall vowed. They heard snippets of plans for a spare wagon, bought off a nearby farmer, and murmurs of an ambush.

After the men rode off, Gary stuck his head by the slit of the canvas.

"Angel, I got a surprise for you."

The surprise was a secret trip to the supply wagon.

"Figured you'd like to doctor up your cousin the way you did with me and the little one."

The little one.

The pain still took her breath away.

But now Sol was here, and elation warred with grief.

As soon as Gary had freed her and Isa from the wagon ties, Poppy embraced the giant in a tight hug. She had never hugged him before. He squeezed back so hard that she wheezed.

"You know I'd do anything for you, angel," he vowed into her hair, breathing her deep. "I'd die for you."

Feeling a mixture of pity and gratitude, Poppy stepped back and held his large, prickly face in her hands. "You're growing to be such a good man, Gary."

"Does that mean you'll be my wife? Because Ed said—"

"Sh, it doesn't matter what Ed says," was her non-answer. Gary had arrived at the camp, ring in tow, to find Poppy too distraught to consider any proposals of marriage. "Now, can I get a few supplies and water before you take me to...my cousin?"

By the time Gary opened the supply wagon's canvas, she and Isa held a canteen, a basin of water, and half a bar of yellow lye soap. Isa trembled beside her, and Poppy felt as though she could dance a jig. She would finally talk to Sol! And if Gary decided to make himself scarce, maybe she could hug him.

Touch him.

"Sol?" she called softly.

"Isa? Poppy?" It came from the front of the supply wagon.

Blinking back tears of happiness, she turned and smiled widely at Isa, who was having difficulty holding back her emotion. They pushed the supplies in and climbed over the tailboard.

"I'll be makin' a couple rounds around the campsite. That should give you plenty of time to doctor him up before I get back." He kissed Poppy's hand and strode to his horse.

"We had better hurry, then," Poppy whispered to Isa, snapping the canvas flaps closed behind her. But Isa was already across the wagon bed and in Sol's arms.

Sol was chained to the wagon and sat beside the same ratty blanket that had covered Alwine. Poppy tried to ignore the cloth, tried to suppress the howling anguish. They still didn't know who had strangled Alwine. Mr. Hall had been quietly furious, but all he had threatened was that once he figured out who had done it, their pay would be docked the price of the lost girl. None of the men had come forward, and she could see no guilt on anyone's face except the perpetual smirk that graced Cash's.

"—I don't know whether to be glad you're here or to be angry with you," Isa was telling Sol when Poppy broke out of her daze. She could hear Gary's horse trot out of camp. Lester and Big Maude probably sat unmoving by the fire, keeping a wary eye on the wagons.

"I've been worried sick, Isa. And I'm sorry as hell for not listening to you." With gentle affection, Sol shook Isa's shoulder with his tied hands.

"How long have you been following us?"

"Since the day after the two of you left. Where are you, shug?"

Poppy crawled forward and was immediately enveloped in an embrace that she had thought she'd never experience again.

"Careful," he chuckled hoarsely. "I was tenderized pretty good yesterday."

Pulling back, sniffing, Poppy croaked, "I cannot believe you are here."

"Me either," Isa sniffled. "I thought for certain something had gone all wrong, that you and the sheriff had gone up north on that false trail."

"We did," Sol said grimly.

While Poppy tore another strip from her rapidly deteriorating petticoats to lather it, Sol recounted returning to Dogwood to find Isa gone, forming a posse, and following the trail until they'd been forced to wait the storm out. He mentioned the Texas Rangers, Ben, and Junior, talking around Poppy's ministrations with her homemade rag on his face and scalp. At Junior's name, Isa finally smiled. The basin water had turned a dull, brownish-red by the time he'd told the tale, and Poppy was unhappily picking the tatters of his shirt from the dried blood of his lower torso.

"We need to clean this, too, Sol," she murmured when he hissed and flinched away. "The last thing you need is for your wounds to putrefy."

"Do what you gotta do," he sighed.

"Here. I saved these for you." Poppy handed over a handful of hardtack from her apron which he tore into with a grateful noise.

Unbuttoning his shirt with deft fingers, Poppy listened to the siblings bicker.

"And you"—Sol pointed, mouth full of stale hardtack—"You need to stay out of trouble. Look at your face. Ma would have a fit."

"Would you look at the pot calling the kettle black," Isa jibed, crossing her arms.

In the golden light of the sunlit canvas around them, sweat dotting his lip, he leaned forward and said with undertaker's seriousness, "I mean it, Legs. We are this close"—he held his forefinger and thumb up with only an inch dividing them—"to getting you girls out of this pickle. It's time to play it smart before you end up like—well, just be careful. Lay low, keep your mouth shut. Venting your spleen to these men isn't worth getting your neck broke. Looks like they almost managed it." He nodded to her neck.

Isa absently massaged her grimy neck beneath the iron shackle, her face grave. "When I pictured you here, it wasn't like this. If I have to keep low, then that goes for you, too." Her eyes looked yellow beneath her straight, solemn brows. "No matter what they do."

Poppy had finally gotten Sol's shirt undone. She bit her lip at the abrasions scabbed over his lean stomach. "Oh, Sol. Your poor belly." She ran gentle fingers down the russet-colored scrapes that started from his chest and grew worse toward his belt buckle.

"Well, I think I'll go out here and let you clean him up, Poppy," said Isa, quickly averting her eyes. "I'll be looking out for Gary or the others. I'll tug our chain if he comes back."

Sol and Poppy's gaze held while Isa made herself scarce and pulled the drawstring tight once she had clambered outside the canvas and blocked the open space. Their chain swung heavily between them.

"Sol, can you scoot this way?" Poppy asked softly, backing up to get more slack in the chain.

He followed, eyes dark in his face, their flecks of green hypnotizing her. Without thinking about it, her hands rose to touch his face, where the thickening growth tickled her skin. The backs of her fingers trembled as they grazed over the soft bristles. Poppy swallowed.

"I'd better wash you before we run out of time."

His belly flinching at the touch of the cold scrap of soapy cloth, they watched silently while she gently cleaned his wounds.

"How are you? You haven't said much about what you two have gone through." She had forgotten how deep his voice was, and he lowered it even more so it wouldn't carry to the ears outside. "Are you and Isa all right? How—how is the baby?" It was his turn to gingerly touch her, his warm palm resting over the hard barrier of her corseted bodice.

"I think the baby is well," Poppy whispered, leaning closer to pick at the brush and debris trapped between his belt and his jeans. "It's hard to tell this early. But I'm not feeling so sick in the mornings. And my bladder is constantly full, which is blasted inconvenient."

Two large, hot hands cupped her cheeks and made her look up. "I'm damned sorry I didn't get to you sooner."

"Hush." Poppy dropped the rag in the dirty basin, resting a finger over his lips. He kissed it, the lips satin soft and warm. The small action brought heat to her cheeks.

"Give me a kiss." The twinkle in his eyes was finally back. He brushed her hair behind her ears and brought her head closer.

Giving in to a smile, Poppy ducked her head. "Very well, but first—" She dabbed her finger in the froth on the cracked yellow bar of soap.

"What are you doing?"

"Cleaning my teeth if I'm to kiss you," she retorted, scrubbing her teeth and mouth viciously with the glistening finger. Lye was caustic and burned her gums and the flesh of her cheeks, so she quickly rinsed her mouth with a swallow of her canteen and spat in the basin.

He scoffed. "You think my breath is any better?"

"In that case." She lathered the finger again and stuck it in his mouth before he could dodge it, trying to quiet her laugh at his grimace from her invading finger. It was the most ridiculous thing she had ever done. "Been a while since you've had your mouth washed out with soap?" she teased, pulling her hand away.

Eyes promising retribution, Sol took the canteen, pulled a mouthful of water, gargled it, and spat in the basin. He took another swig from the canteen, glaring over it while she beamed and shook with suppressed laughter. "You think you're funny, don't you?" he asked finally, capping the canteen, and tossing it aside.

"Yes."

"Come here. You don't know how hard it is, looking at you and not being able to touch you. That's the real torture, worse than anything." He was trying to joke, but his eyes were fierce. Intense. "C'mere," he repeated, low and gravelly.

Poppy could do him one better. Her smile had dropped, breath coming faster, and she slid her leg over his thighs and straddled him. When her bottom settled on his lap, he groaned, and she stifled it with her parted lips. He tasted clean but salty from perspiration, his mouth warm, and his tongue moved sensually with hers. Their kiss was slow and languid, but her fingers were fast between them. She brushed aside his tied hands and unbuttoned his belt, swallowing another one of his groans. Behind them, on the other side of the canvas, Isa tapped a bored rhythm against the tailboard with her fingertips.

"We have to be quick," Poppy gasped against his ear after breaking away from the searing kiss.

"You'll be lucky if you get a minute out of me," he grunted under his breath, raising his hips so she could pull his jeans down enough to free him from his fly. His erection sprang up between them, big and hot to the touch.

Throbbing between her legs, more ready than she'd ever been in her life, Poppy wanted to tell him how much she loved this part of him, how much she loved him. She slid her fingers over the flushed, plump head, gripped him firmly, and positioned him to the open slit of her combination drawers. Rising to her knees, flinging her skirts away with one hand, she guided him inside of her wet heat.

"Quiet," she whimpered at the muffled growl he made, sinking lower, lower until they were both gasping, lips clinging to each other. With his hands helpless between them, she was in control, and she tried to be as discreet in her movements as she could. Their breaths came out like forge bellows, their kisses lush and tongues soft while Poppy slid up and down. The pace was slow enough that it didn't rock the wagon, but they both sweat and gritted their teeth. Even with the leisurely pace, Poppy's face and neck reddened, and her eyes glittered with an impending climax. Whispered words poured out of her mouth, barely audible, unable to be stopped. "Sol, I missed you so much. You feel so good, so good—"

It made him jerk against her, reaching a deep, sweet angle that stopped her flow of words.

She broke off and flew apart, mouth wide, eyes squeezed shut. A steady, rhythmic pulsing inside of her explained the sudden rigidity of his legs and body. He became the tether, grounded and solid, while she went airborne, endlessly flying. Sol kissed her throat, her jaw, her parted lips, while her movements became progressively gradual.

"I told you," he managed to pant against her neck.

Opening her eyes, she looked blearily down at him. "What?"

His slow white grin made her heart twist inside the confines of her chest. "That it wouldn't be a minute."

Rotating her hips, she said, "I believe I won this particular race."

Eyebrows raised, he made a face of allowance. "You did lick me on this one, didn't you?"

She nodded and hid trembling lips against his neck. "I love you, Sol."

"What?" His bound hands came up and lifted her chin. "Say that again."

"I said I love you, Sol." She'd never felt so vulnerable, not even when she'd been beneath Cash with her skirts up. "I love you so much I could die."

"Well, don't do that," he tried to tease, but it sounded strangled. "Because I reckon I love you, too. Have for a while now."

"I know. I have, too. I was just—stupid. And afraid."

"No, no. Not stupid." His fingers stroked the delicate, petal-soft skin beneath her jaw.

And then her chain tugged hard enough to wrench her head away.

Their eyes went wide, and they scrambled apart. Poppy had to set him to rights, dragging his jeans up while he tucked himself back in. She had just started buttoning his shirt when they heard Gary's horse snort outside their wagon, its hooves muffled against the grass and underbrush. Isa was explaining how seeing Sol's wounds made her feel poorly when Poppy finished the last button.

They mouthed quick, soundless endearments as she left the canteen, grabbed the basin, and crawled backward to the opening. His eyes were anguished, but he winked and blew a kiss after her as though they were still in Hobb's General and he'd see her for dinner.

But they weren't in Dogwood. Sol was only alive to feed Cash's need for revenge on Ed and Isa. She couldn't forget that. What if Cash tired of him and killed him before the Rangers arrived?

Gary led Poppy and Isa to their wagon, and she fought tears while she climbed in, turning her back to the other girls to face the corner. Scenarios of Sol's possible death chafed at her, but when Isa settled cautious fingertips on her shoulder, Poppy dashed the moisture away and turned to her friend as though all was well.

JUNIOR WATCHED THE lieutenant squint into the gully where the crashed wagon lay.

The posse had been thrown off the scent for two days after finding Captain Lawson lying on the ground, hip shattered from a close-range rifle shot. They'd fashioned a travois, loaded the captain onto it, and hightailed it out of there. Sol's horse hadn't moved, but they couldn't find hide nor hair of Hog. Junior and Ben had located Sol's tracks and discovered what had happened next.

Sol had been dragged behind a horse into a river.

That's where the trail had grown confusing.

"They put us on a merry goose chase," Lieutenant Havelard said while scanning the crevices and pits of the gully below. "Then suddenly they lead us here, not even bothering to wipe the trail."

The eager Private Pines nodded as though he agreed. Havelard ignored him and turned to Junior.

"What do you think, Stone?"

At first, Junior thought Havelard was asking Ben but then he then remembered Ben had followed a different trail. While frowning at the wagon in concentration, Junior pulled out a spyglass, opened it, and gave it another look.

"The canvas is still tight as a drum."

"Yep. You'd think for a wagon rolling out of control to the bottom of a ravine, its canvas and frame would be in worse shape. Wouldn't surprise me if there was someone in there, just waiting for some stupid bastard to go riding down into range."

Hearing it put that way, Junior thought it sounded obvious. He dropped the spyglass and tucked it away. "It's an ambush."

The Texas Ranger spat and grinned, smelling a trap a mile away. "Leave it," he ordered the men surrounding them, wheeling his horse around to backtrack the trail. "The other wagons have the girls. This has 'ambush' written all over it."

Private Pines looked like he wanted to argue and ride down the ravine himself to check, but thought better of it and followed orders instead.

From afar, a man wearing spectacles looked through his own spyglass at the retreating figures, seething.

Chapter Thirty-Three

Cash, Lester, and Gary were left in charge of the women the next night while Hoodoo scouted.

Not even Isa knew what the other men were up to, just that Mr. Hall had returned the night before in quiet anger.

Something must have gone horribly wrong.

They'd heard him pace his tent and throw the occasional hard object. What was worse, he had Cash drag Sol out from the supply wagon for prolonged, intense questioning. Sol, a mulish twist to his mouth, had refused to supply Mr. Hall with much information. Poppy and Isa had shouted indignantly when Cash had proceeded to backhand Sol so hard he'd fallen to the side.

They had to be escorted back to the first wagon by a disapproving Gary.

Now, Poppy and Isa watched miserably while the sun sunk below the horizon, and the men grew drunk from a newly purchased bottle of whiskey. Mina and the men treated Sol worse than a dog, whistling, pretending to call him over to be pet, and throwing scraps from dinner at him. Poppy's fists clenched each time, and her burning eyes promised vindication. Sol, however, stayed relaxed and unbothered. In fact, he looked half-amused by it all.

"If they thought they could make him mad, they've never met a man like Sol before," Isa mused, glaring at Mina as the vile woman poured a little water into a tin plate and offered it to Sol to lap up. She laughed cruelly when he didn't rise to the bait.

"Mina, come here." Cash snapped his fingers.

Throwing Sol a smile and a backward glance, Mina sashayed to the fire where Cash, Lester, Gary, and the pig farmer sat, playing cards and swilling whiskey. As the night wore on, the sky black and starless, the men grew rowdier. Gary had insisted on having Poppy next to him for luck. Ironfisted Maude watched the girls in the wagons with her usual jaundiced eye, crop in hand in case one got fresh with her. Poppy was increasingly aware of Sol's attention on her as Gary became drunker and bolder. He tweaked her ear, ran his palm across her precarious coiffure, and once grabbed her face between his sausage-like fingers.

Chained to the sapling a few yards away, Sol's expression grew less easygoing and more thunderous.

Dangerous.

His eyes never left her.

When the amber liquid in the bottle that was passed around was three-quarters of the way empty, Mina began to dance. Isa didn't hide her shocked disgust as the woman leaned down and gifted every man with a long, wet kiss. When she reached Gary, however, he gave her a not-so-playful shove.

"Watch out," Cash hooted, "You can't kiss a man when his intended is right next to 'im."

Glaring at Gary, Mina stumbled around the fire and sat in Cash's lap to sulk.

But Gary was paying no mind. He had passed out across Poppy's lap, snoring between her knees.

"Gary, wake up and get off of me," Poppy said firmly. Her only answer was another snore, and the other men laughed.

"Dance for us again, Mina," crowed the pig farmer, his eyes shining keenly at her.

The men's attention turned from her to Mina.

At Gary's waist, his deer horn knife beckoned.

An idea formed, and before Poppy lost her nerve, she reached down to the dark leather sheath attached to Gary's gun belt. The men were fully distracted, but Isa caught the movements, eyes flaring. Knife freed, Poppy hid her maneuvering under her skirt, stowing the long blade in her right stocking. It was cold, knobby, and uncomfortable. Adrenaline rushed to a fever pitch.

As though sensing Poppy and Isa's excitement, Cash glanced at them.

Keeping her voice soft and penitent, Poppy asked, "May I bring our cousin some supper?"

Cash scoffed. "I don't think so, Red."

Sol hadn't eaten all day. Cash had ignored her request that morning, too. And for dinner, he and the other men had thrown bones at him and told him to eat up. She decided to try one more time, looking at Cash as though he were a hero. "Please?"

Eyes roving down Poppy's pleading face, to her neck, to her bosom, he said, "Mina. Make a plate for our cowboy friend and bring it to him."

Poppy expected the woman to resent such an order, but the drunken flush in Mina's cheeks grew. "Sure, Cash." She heaped a tin with whatever was left over in the bottom of the pot and weaved toward the sapling to which Sol's chain was attached. Sol's eyes, dark beneath the curtain of his chestnut hair, followed her.

Across the fire, Cash started a bawdy tale of past excursions that he, Mina, and another whore had done. Lester and the pig farmer were a rapt audience.

Poppy paid no mind to this.

She sat with a spine of steel, straining to hear the conversation near the stand of trees.

"Hey, Cowboy, you hungry for supper?" Mina slurred, swaying in place just a foot out of Sol's reach. When he didn't answer, she giggled. "What, cat got your tongue? Maybe you're hungry for something else." She let her half-unbuttoned bodice droop, revealing large, conical breasts with dark nipples.

Sol averted his gaze, lips in a flat line.

Poppy's heartbeat was in her ears, and she stood without realizing it. Isa tugged at Poppy's wrist. Gary rolled to the dirt beside the log.

Mina cackled. "You shy? I like when they're shy. How about a kiss for your supper? You don't wanna starve, do you?"

Through the wool in her ears, Poppy distinctly heard Sol reply, "I think I'd rather starve."

Poppy's incandescent joy was immediately replaced by a red haze when Mina yanked up her bodice and threw the tin plate at Sol's head. He dodged it easily, and a hint of humor creased his cheeks. He could not, however, evade the spray of sand and rocks she kicked at him. Cursing, he scrubbed his eyes with his forearm.

Poppy was running, Isa at her heels.

Lester interrupted from the fire, "Uh, Cash..."

When Mina turned to face the approaching footsteps, Poppy shoved the other woman with all the bottled-up contempt she'd reserved since The Dusty Rose. Mina fell to the ground, skirts flying up to her knees. Before Mina could scramble up, Cash was there, pulling Poppy back with an iron-hard arm.

"Whoa, whoa, what's going on here?" he asked, none too steady on his feet.

Claws extended, Mina went for Poppy, but Isa swiped Mina's feet out from under her, and she landed with a grunt back on the dirt. Still holding Poppy, Cash reached with his free arm and struck Isa's temple with a hard fist.

Isa went limp and fell, unconscious, to the ground at their feet.

Poppy screeched, and Sol bellowed, straining against his chain, red-faced and veins bulging.

Taking a wary step back, Cash shouted, "I'm about sick n' tired of these goddamned crazy women. Maude! Get over here and put this bitch with the others. As for you two"—Cash unlocked Poppy's shackle and pushed her with no little force toward the unsteady Mina—"time for you two to duke it out."

Though no love was lost between them, Poppy and Mina stared at each other circumspectly. Mina was obviously pie-eyed, as wobbly on her feet as a buoy in turbulent waters. Distractedly, Poppy watched Big Maude huff over and grab a stirring Isa by her bound wrists, dragging her behind the wagons adjacent to them.

"Isa, you all right?" Sol called hoarsely, but there was no answer. He stood and towered over them, not close enough to touch, chained as he was to the base of the tree. "When I get my hands on you, you'll regret every time you ever touched my sister."

"Oh?" Cash asked, a drunken grin spreading over his face. "What about all the times I touched your cousin? I have an intimate knowledge of her, you could say. Don't I, Red? She's pretty as a peach under all those skirts."

Sol grew very still.

"Not that you should know, but wait." Cash pretended to think. "What was it you told me, Mina? You saw these two kissin' in the chuck wagon yesterday morning? At first, I thought she was lying; she tends to do that. But now—hell, I'm not sure. Now I'm startin' to think you two are kissin' cousins after all! Just wait until I tell old Gary." His laugh was high and irritating, a hint of violence about him. "Now, if you girls want to fight, let's up the ante. Make it interesting."

Excitement rising, he called to Lester and the farmer at the fire. "What do you think, boys? Care to make a bet?"

The two called out bets, digging for coins in their pockets. Gary still snored in the dirt across the fire. Poppy looked helplessly at Sol, feeling sick. He shook his head slowly, casting a meaningful glance at her waist.

No, don't fight. Think of the baby.

But what other option did she have? If she announced her pregnancy, she would end up like Alwine, neglected and dying from a botched surgery in the back of the wagon.

"And I'll tell you what, Red," Cash was saying to her, running his palm across her lower back above her bustle. "If you win, I'll let your cousin live. But, if Mina wins"— he grinned across the space between Poppy and the scowling woman—"he'll be pushing up daisies before the sun rises."

Mina flung her hair out of her face, spreading her arms. "He's a dead man," she jeered at Poppy. "And you'll be wishing *you* were dead by the time I'm through with you."

Cash's presence at Poppy's back disappeared, and Mina attacked. She rained slaps over Poppy, grabbing her auburn hair and scattering the few pins left in the messy pile. But Poppy was fast; she squirmed out of the other woman's clench, losing several strands in the process.

"Hit her with your elbow," Sol's voice said to her right over the other men's whoops and catcalls.

She listened. Poppy's elbow crunched into the side of Mina's head, who screamed and held her left ear. Bloodthirsty now, Cash yelled his own advice, feeding the other woman's fury.

With a scream, Mina tackled Poppy.

Sol tried to help.

"Swipe her feet!"

"Move, watch her right hook!"

It helped that she was small and quick, but Mina's greater size and strength eventually resulted in Poppy on her back. Poppy's skirts had come up, garters showing, and Cash made lewd comments at their left while at their right, Sol strained to get closer. To help.

"Don't you hurt her!" he bellowed at Mina, his voice deep and carrying.

The men at the fire had come closer, laughing, nudging Cash drunkenly.

Above Poppy, Mina stank like sweat and unwashed bodies. Her hair trailed down into Poppy's eyes, their hands gripping each other's arms, fighting furiously to get the upper hand.

Leaning closer, breath caustic with whiskey fumes, Mina whispered, "I'm going to enjoy seeing your cowboy die. Almost as much as I enjoyed seeing your precious foreign brat die."

"*What?*" Poppy grunted.

"You heard me." Mina giggled a little. She sounded far away. "And it was worth it just to see the look on your face right now. Comin' into camp, nose in the air, always thinkin' you're better than us. Just like that one girl Cash brought. Well, she learned that you fall even harder off that high horse than when you're in the dirt with the rest of us."

Sol said her name, but Poppy wasn't listening. She felt a comforting blankness, a surety of what her next actions would be that laid a calm balm over her raw face, her sore scalp. She reached, reached until her fingers encircled the hilt of the knife in her stocking. The three men to the two women's left were howling, yipping coyotes, but Sol had gone quiet, hearing everything.

Seeing everything.

He saw Poppy free the knife from her stocking, saw her strong legs wrap tight around Mina's hips. Poppy, body coiled and jaw tense, plunged the blade of the knife once, twice, thrice, into the shocked woman's side.

Once for the nameless girl.

Once for Alwine.

And once for Sol.

Each time, Mina grunted and tried to squirm away, but Poppy's legs were vises around her. It wasn't until the third plunge to the hilt that Poppy extracted the knife, rolled Mina off her, and crawled to Sol. Mina bled in the dirt, speechless, touching her crimson side. Poppy sawed frantically at Sol's bonds, shielding her actions from the other men with her body.

"What are you doin', girl?" Cash chortled, stumbling close and nudging Mina with the toe of his boot. "Fight isn't over 'til it's over." He leaned over and touched the scarlet blood that was spreading into Mina's dirty blouse. "What the hell—"

"Cash, the supply wagon!" Lester cried, hands in his sparse hair. "It's on fire!"

Everything happened at once.

An ugly look wrinkled Cash's face with hatred. Eyes mean slits, his bloody hands reached for Poppy. "You—" He didn't finish the thought. As soon as he came within grabbing distance, Sol had him. His long arms snatched Cash's shirt front and yanked him to the ground. While Sol and Cash struggled over the knife, Lester rushed to help, but something large, skinny, and furry bounded into him with a terrifying, snarling growl.

It was Hog.

Lester screamed as the hound tore into him.

While Cash and Sol wrestled, Poppy grabbed Cash's gun. She turned and pointed it at the pig farmer, who stood drunk and open-mouthed. Hands trembling uncontrollably, Poppy cocked the weapon. The farmer saw it, turned, and ran as fast as his squat legs allowed. She squeezed the trigger, but the bullet didn't hit. The gun's rapport was loud. Gary jerked awake beside the fire. The girls screamed in their wagons, and whether it was from the gunshot or the enormous fire spreading their way, Poppy didn't know. She looked up at the sound of footsteps, expecting Maude.

It was Isa.

She lowered the gun.

"Poppy, give me the gun," Sol said. He had unshackled his restraints with the key. Cash lay dead at his feet, Gary's deer horn knife stuck out at an angle beneath his breastbone. "I've got the key. Let's get the girls freed. Isa, where's that big woman that carried you off?"

Isa stopped in front of them, panting. The pupil in her left eye was dilated. "I knocked her out when she was trying to take me to the wagon. She thought I was unconscious. Then, I lit the wagon on fire and set the horses free." She looked down in disgust at Cash. "Bastard. I wish he was alive so I could kill him again."

"That's enough of that," Sol chastised, then hollered as though just noticing, "Hog! Here!"

The hound released a terrified but alive Lester. Sol strode over and unarmed him.

"Please, please. Don't kill me," Lester begged.

"Get over there by the tree," Sol ordered unsympathetically, leveling Cash's pistol with a steady hand. Put that shackle on yourself."

Lester complied, and Sol locked the iron manacle.

Soft weeping grabbed Poppy's attention. Mina had crawled on top of Cash. Their blood intermingled.

A large, warm hand slipped into Poppy's.

"Come on, sugar. Let's get those girls."

From the corner of her eye, she saw Gary blundering around near the campfire. She felt a strange concern that he would fall in. Then, she was guided away by someone pulling her hand. With Sol leading, the three of them ran behind the combusting wagon. Maude was on her back in the grass, and Poppy was relieved to see that all the girls in the second wagon had already poured out.

Sol grabbed Poppy's face, kissed her hard on the mouth, and handed her Cash's key. "You get started on these girls, and I'll get the others out of the first wagon."

She nodded and turned to the first pair of frightened girls.

"Let's get these chains off you," she told them, voice breaking. Her hands shook so badly that it was hard fitting the key in the hole, but one by one, she freed each girl.

But when the last manacle dropped into the dirt at their feet, Poppy heard something behind her.

Chapter Thirty-Four

Behind her, a masculine shout demanded, "What the hell are you doing?"

To her left, Poppy heard a drowsy, "Angel? What's goin' on?"

She whirled away from unchaining the last girl, but the swaying Gary wasn't what made her face blanch. Mr. Hall leveled a gun at her from atop his horse, expression ferocious, cocking back the hammer.

As if in some slow-moving dream, Isa dropped the rope she was had been knotting at Big Maude's wrists and ran toward Mr. Hall.

"No!"

Gary blinked only once before registering his brother's intentions. He didn't say anything; he dove in front of Poppy.

The Colt fired, throwing the briefest spark. Gary didn't make a sound when the bullet went through him and into the wagon just behind Poppy, wood splintering, the girls crying out and running for cover.

"Poppy!" Sol roared, leaping off the tailboard of the first wagon and racing to them, Colt drawn.

Mr. Hall, who had jumped to the ground to cradle a confused Gary, leaped back to his feet. Seeing Isa, Mr. Hall grabbed Isa by her hair and raised his pistol. Sol halted midstep.

"Stop right there," Mr. Hall said, his lips white against his bared yellow teeth, just like Prudence's uncanny pantomime of him from that first night in the wagon. His eyes were wild, constantly flicking from Sol's pistol to his brother groaning on the ground.

Gary was gutshot. It was the tenth bullet. No more lives were left. There would be no recovery from a wound of that caliber.

Eyes enormous, Isa acted as Mr. Hall's shield as he backed up to his horse.

"Get up," he growled to Isa. To Sol, "Do not get ideas. I *will* shoot her. Gary. Grab that horse."

"Wha—" Gary moaned, glancing at the freed horse that had gotten its lead rope tangled in scrub brush.

In the distance, gunfire popped and echoed.

The posse!

"Get on the horse, Gary!" Mr. Hall screamed, trying to mount his horse behind Isa while still holding the loaded gun to her person.

"Easy," Sol murmured, letting his stolen pistol dangle from his finger, hands widespread. His face had blanched whiter than Mr. Hall's, great shadows darkening his eyes. "Easy."

"Shut up! Gary, get on the horse and follow me."

Even as he rushed the mortally wounded man, who staggered hunchbacked to his horse, he could hear the thunder of hoofbeats.

The posse was finally here.

Gary had managed to climb on the horse bareback when men broke through the surrounding trees. Mr. Hall kicked his horse, and he, Isa, and Gary disappeared into the night.

A horse with a big blond on it rode up seconds after the two horses had disappeared.

"Sol! Poppy! Thank God, I thought—where's Isa?"

Sol was tucking the pistol in his jeans, rushing to Junior. "They just took her. Hurry, we've gotta get her! Poppy—"

"I'll be fine!" Poppy cried, urging him toward Junior. "Go get her, hurry!"

For a moment, he looked at her, anguished. Then, he hopped on the back of Junior's horse and pointed where the two riders had left with Isa. The darkness swallowed them up while Poppy rushed to the group of girls that still needed to be unchained.

Please, please let them find Isa and come back unharmed.

Behind her, the fiery skeleton of the chuckwagon blazed higher.

THEY HADN'T RIDDEN twenty yards when Junior and Sol caught them.

Gary had fallen off his horse and lay groaning in the dirt. His shirt was soaked through with blood, and in the weak orange light from the flaming beacon of the wagon in the distance, it looked like an ink spill. He groaned on the ground, curled into himself, clutching the spreading black spot which glistened wetly.

The leader, Isa's hair still in his fist, leaned over Gary and spoke with a voice-carrying urgency.

"I'll walk up to him," Sol said lowly, tucking the stolen pistol in his waistband at his back and sliding off Junior's horse. "You flank them."

For a minute, it looked as though Junior would argue, but he finally nodded, dismounted, and walked into the shadows of the surrounding trees. Sol drew his pistol and stalked closer.

As though sensing him, Ed stopped talking and straightened, putting the muzzle of his Colt beneath Isa's jaw.

"I know you are out there. Show yourself!"

"I'm right here. Calm that trigger finger down," Sol suggested, eyeing the man's white-knuckled grip on the pistol.

"Ed, I ain't feeling so good," Gary groaned in the dirt. His stubbled head looked like a misshapen white boulder in the firelight. "I think Angel was right. I already used up my ninth life."

Ed's eyes flicked down.

"Why don't you let my sister go, and you and your brother can go y'alls separate ways?" Sol kept his voice calm and persuasive.

"Gary is gutshot," Ed spat. Sweat beaded his brow and lip. "He doesn't have much longer. Let's strike another bargain, hm? A sister for a brother."

"Your men are being tracked down. The girls you took are free and safe. Just let her go, and you'll get a fair trial."

Isa tried to stop him with her eyes.

Ed yanked her hair and held her head farther back, shoving the gun deeper into the skin under her jaw. "Don't even look at him, you conniving little bitch."

"Kept you on your toes, did she?" Sol joked, stalling. Terrified.

Instead of being appeased, Ed's quiet rage intensified. "Ever since the first day, this one has caused problems. I should have killed her from the start. At first, I loved her. Now, I hate her. Strange how that works." He clenched his fist harder in her hair, and the skin around Isa's eyes tautened. He hissed into her ear, "*Fiducia necat.*" Then, to Sol, "You want to know what your sister has been up to all these weeks? Playing whore for all the men."

Eyes manic in the flare of the burning wagon, Ed told story after story of Sol's sister in sordid detail, his body coiled as though ready for the taller man to make a mistake. Even though Sol hoped—no, *knew*—that the bastard was only spewing lies, he couldn't stop a hint of emotion from playing out on his face.

Isa's head turned slightly to the right when a shadow moved.

It was Junior, pistol trained on Ed.

Slowly, slowly, she held her fingers up.

Her mouth moved soundlessly.

One.

Two.

Three.

Isa shoved Ed's gun up and ducked.

Two guns went off.

Ed's shot grazed Isa's jaw, leaving her ears ringing and her skin peppered with powder burns. Junior's shot exploded through the side of Ed's skull; Ed collapsed to the ground in the exact position Gary lay in.

Sol rushed forward and grabbed Isa, squeezing her tightly to him. Junior ran over but stopped to stare at Ed.

"He was lying," Isa gasped, holding her ear and wincing. "None of that was true."

"I knew he was," Sol soothed, tucking her under his chin and closing his eyes. "And look at him. Dead as a doornail, and I've got you right here. Now we can go home."

Isa began to cry at that.

"This one's dead, too. Liver bled out," Junior said. His voice sounded odd, so Sol turned, confirming he hadn't been hiding an injury. Junior's face was pale as parchment, the pink scar above his kerchief gleaming in the dimming light. His eyes were glued to the giant hole in Ed's head.

"Hey," Sol said. Junior blinked and looked up. "Thank you. You saved her life."

Some of the blankness left Junior's expression, and he nodded. He holstered his pistol, hand not quite steady. "I'd do it again if I could."

"Junior?" Isa stood up from Sol's embrace and beelined it to Junior.

She barreled into him and wrapped her arms around his torso.

Sol turned his face away; seeing a man cry was never a comfortable thing.

POPPY COULDN'T RECALL much of that night or the day after.

The girls were doctored, and each made statements at the Gonzales County marshal's office. Lester, Butch, the pig farmer, and Maude were held in the jail cells out of sight somewhere in the building. It was surreal how iron bars and a few walls took all the power from them. Hoodoo had been shot and killed by Lieutenant Havelard.

Isa's dilated pupil returned to normal, the gunshot graze was minor, but the extent of her bruising had raised each of Sol's, Junior's, and Ben's hackles. They circled around her while the doctor swabbed and salved Isa, ignoring her protests that she was fine.

The hotels were filled to bursting with girls and posse members.

After submitting their statements, they found a tidy little boarding house run by respectable spinster sisters. Junior and Isa got their own rooms, Hog bedded down in the barn, and Poppy and Sol snagged the last room under the ruse that they were married.

The boarding house was a cozy two-story with lace and frills at every window, chair, and table. Doilies graced every surface, the books packed into shelves made Isa's eyes light up, and the sizzle of meat frying cleared Junior's cloudy stare.

Sol and Poppy ate supper, ravenous, then asked if there was access to a tub.

"Oh, it's in your room behind the divider, dears," said the youngest sister. "All we ask is that you empty it yourselves. We're not as young as we used to be."

An hour later, Poppy reclined against Sol's chest while steam rose from their arms and knees in an enormous galvanized metal tub. It smelled of rose bath oil and erased the dirt, sweat, and blood from their aching bodies. They were both spotted with bruises, some greenish and faded, some purple and dark. Their necks and collarbones were red and chafed from the iron shackles. The sisters had loaned Poppy and Isa clothing, and Ben had dropped off Sol's saddlebags before tipping his hat and returning home.

During the bath, they told each other everything. Each experience was recounted, good or bad. It was a purge that healed, these confessions in steaming water. Like a baptism. A rebirth. Sol sat quietly and washed her back, shoulders, and neck with a washrag. He asked about Gary. She asked about the Rangers. He asked what Cash had meant about knowing her intimately. She relayed the events and withheld nothing. The washrag squished in his fist, but the arms encircling her were warm and safe. After Poppy had scrubbed his hair, he climbed out and washed hers.

"I had never killed anyone before all of this," Poppy admitted during her second rinse.

"Me either."

"I don't know how I can live with myself."

"We have to, sugar. We have to."

Poppy stood, skin glowing pink from her scrubbing, eyes huge and blue in her face. Sol looked at the gentle swell of her stomach. She was so beautiful to him that it hurt.

"It's still hard to believe you're right in front of me. That it's all over." He smiled sheepishly, unused to sounding so maudlin.

Something changed in her face, brightening. Poppy grabbed his hand. "Feel. Press your hand here," she whispered.

She pushed the area below her navel, pressing his fingers deeper, and he worried about hurting her. When Sol felt a hard roundness, his eyebrows rose.

"Is that the baby?"

"Mm-hm. She's growing."

"She?" He wondered if women had an intimate knowledge of these things. If they knew the sex intuitively.

She gave an abashed shrug, and the ends of her lips curled up. "I wouldn't mind having a little girl to cherish."

A vivid image of a little girl with long hair and a flowery dress running in a field of wildflowers, him chasing her, catching her, and throwing her high in the air, stole his breath. His eyes prickled and felt wet. He closed them and dropped to his knees. Pressing his lips to Poppy's belly, he offered thanks that she was alive and well, that her womb still held the child she had so desperately wanted, and that his sister was coming home with him.

Her voice was tentative above him. "The townspeople will think the worst."

It went unsaid in the room, hovering above them. Poppy, taken by a slew of men to be sold into prostitution, returned weeks later with her belly swollen with child. It wouldn't matter if the two of them knew the truth. Rumors would still haunt them as the population speculated.

"We'll be too busy being happy to worry about other folks," he promised, rising to his feet. He kissed her damp head like she was the most precious thing in the world.

"But if they think I am dirty or ill-used, my business could fail."

"Poppy, if any person holds what happened against you, then you don't need their business anyway." His voice was firm, and he chucked her under her chin.

It amused her. Sol watched her smile spread.

"I suppose you are right."

"I'm always right." He sounded surprised that she hadn't known that before.

Her smile faded as she brushed her hands along his ribs. "You've lost weight. We need to fatten you up."

"You've changed, too." His hands lowered from cradling her face to drift along her heavy breasts.

Poppy's breath hitched and she admitted, "They're sensitive, too."

"Are they?" To test that theory, he grabbed the towel and dried her hair, back, and legs, leaving her stomach and breasts for last. Sol let the soft cotton drift over the seam between her ribs, moving the towel so that it barely brushed over the underside of each breast. The nipples puckered. They looked redder. Darker. His mouth watered. If she looked down, she would see how much she had affected him.

"*That* hasn't changed." Apparently, she looked.

His grin was easy and wide. "Not when you're in front of me, shug." He bent low and kissed her, plucking at her lips, teasing. The towel dropped, and he brushed his knuckles over the satiny skin beneath her collarbones, skimming down the sides of her breasts, avoiding her nipples. She made a complaining sound in her throat, and his grin returned.

"Quit teasing me, or turnabout will be fair play."

As far as threats went, it was probably Sol's favorite. She must have seen it on his face because her smile returned and didn't drift away. Hand slipping into his, Poppy walked him backward toward the bed. She pulled him down for a kiss, and it was like falling into sin. The way this woman kissed was unlike anything. Their mouths made love; she seduced him with her tongue, made promises with the lush way she wrapped her lips around his. It made him harder, made his mind focus on only one thing, and that was settling as deeply inside of her as she could take.

But he wanted to go slow. He needed to relearn her body. They had a lot of time to make up for, after all.

"Grab these," he said, his throat thick, and guided her hands up to the wrought iron headboard. "Don't let go."

Poppy's breasts and ribs rose with her rapid breathing, and he loved how her eyes glazed over. Squirming, she spread her legs, planting her feet wide on the bedspread, toes curling.

Throat flexing, he rasped, "Now, that's not fair, sugar."

"Who said I play fair?" Her soft voice was even huskier, her smile gone. The intensity in her features always set him off, made his blood pump ferociously.

It brought him back to the first time they'd made love in his little room in the barn.

He dragged his palms from her silky knees, up her shapely thighs, but avoided the apex of her legs. She groaned in frustration, and his lips twitched. Tugging the curls between her legs once, he ordered, "Enough of that. Patience."

"I cannot recall the meaning of the word."

Gripping her knees again, he spread them wider until each nearly touched the coverlet. He dragged his lips down one thigh, kissing the crease near the spot that was shiny and wet for him. Unable to resist, he reached over and bit the soft mons that sat atop her vulva. She sucked in a breath and held it.

"Let me take care of you, darlin'," he murmured into her, kissing lower and lower until his tongue disappeared into the hot crease that hid her clitoris. She didn't hold her breath anymore. She panted. By the time he was finished making love to her with his mouth, she was writhing and sobbing, trying to be quiet. But she never let go of the iron, though her hands had gripped hard enough to make the metal protest and creak. He rose to his knees and hooked his fingers beneath her knees, drawing her legs up toward her chest, his too-long hair hanging in his eyes. "Let go, sweetheart. Guide me in."

Poppy complied immediately, reaching down to grab him by the flushed hilt. The head of him was deep red as she notched him against her and lifted her hips. He flexed and broke through the tight ring of her entrance. They groaned as one.

As usual, he couldn't contain his words, his praise. He spoke low, though, so the rest of the household wasn't privy to their activities. Sinking into Poppy was better than soaking in a hot bath at the end of a hard week, better than sinking into heaven, better than anything. The way they fit had him perspiring, straining, and grunting like an animal. Her eyes were closed, but her face was rapturous, her growing breasts bouncing with their movements. Sol brought her heels up and against his stomach, changing the angle of his thrusts, and picked her hips up.

Her bliss turned savage.

They stopped caring about their noises, and the headboard bumped the wall repeatedly until that fire raced down Sol's spine, tightening his sac. Poppy's face was pink, and her hand worked furiously between them, her lips in that familiar round shape that warned Sol that she was close.

Thank God.

He stopped holding his release back and let go, feeling her contractions tighten around him, exploding in dizzying surges, drawing it out. After, he fell dramatically to his back and rolled her with him still engaged. His arms and legs were jelly, and he could have slept for a hundred years.

"That felt even better than I remembered," he panted, blinking unseeingly at the ceiling.

She made a noise of agreement, kissing his chest over his thundering heart.

"Marry me tomorrow."

She didn't even hesitate.

"Yes." Then, she chuckled. "Lucy will be furious."

Feeling his lips spread wide with pure happiness, he laid a smacking kiss on her mouth. "Lucy will understand."

SOL AND POPPY married at a courthouse in the next established town that sold wedding rings.

As Ben had left the day before by train to get home to Lucy and the ranch, there were only Isa and Junior to stand witness. Both did it with somber formality.

Later, when the two stood in line behind the newly married couple at the next train station, it was Junior who made the first move to talk.

"Izzy," he began. Stopped. His beard was fast growing in, giving his pretty features a ruggedness that pleased her.

Raising her eyebrows, determined not to let it grow more awkward between them, she said as though to a simpleton, "*Yes?*"

His quick scowl was comforting. "Never mind."

She rolled her eyes and shoved him. "I was teasing. Spit it out."

But he waited until he had paid for his ticket before he steered her to the side. Poppy and Sol were a few feet away, arm in arm, lost in their own world. "I wanted to apologize."

Now her confusion was real. "You don't have anything to be sorry for."

"Yeah. I do. I wanted to tell you sorry for how I treated you at the dance."

Isa was speechless. She looked up at him—one of the few men she could do so with—and said nothing. That was a million years ago. They were different people then.

He continued, "I think it's been hard for me, seeing you grow up."

Her throat was a trap door, slamming shut.

"You're like a sister to me. And, if I'm honest, in my head, I've thought of you more like a brother. So, when you came to the dance in that dress, all grown up with those worthless bucks panting after you, I got angry. But it wasn't my place. I ruined your first dance. What's worse, I ruined your first kiss. And... I'm sorry." Junior stood, just as somber and serious as he had in the courthouse. His vivid blue eyes didn't shift; they remained steadfastly on Isa's bruised countenance. All the while he looked more handsome than he had a right to.

It wasn't fair. Just because someone was beautiful, it shouldn't make a person's body twist and coil the way hers did.

Yet, another sensation was coming to life, too. Something she had felt but had never put a name to. She became increasingly certain that it was love. Not the kind of childish adoration she'd mistaken for love, no.

True love.

She no longer needed him to care for her in return. She truly loved him from the deepest realms of her soul. It didn't matter if he married someone else or had multiple children, and she had to witness him living happily without her for the rest of her life. This emotion was deeper than all the jealousy and childish misunderstanding that had plagued her nights and days, pining for him.

Isa wanted him to be happy, and not just happy with the exception that he loved her.

She wanted him to be happy, without exception.

It was as though her whole being had undergone some irrevocable shift, a tectonic plate of knowledge grinding away some layer that had prevented her from seeing the truth.

This was love, she thought, wonderingly. *This is how you are supposed to care for someone.*

As though sensing the great shift within her, Junior scrutinized her face, confused.

With this unbearable weight lifted, this heaviness she hadn't known she'd carried, Isa's smile was soft. Unable to speak while he looked at her, she stepped into him, hugging him close, cherishing him.

I love you.

"I forgive you. And I hope you'll forgive me for the horrible things I said to you after the dance. I didn't mean them, and I'll never forgive myself if I hurt you."

He patted her back heartily, but she disengaged before the hug became an awkward embrace. His color was high, and he fiddled with his hat, taking it off and on, settling it this way and that.

Amused, she crossed her arms. "Not used to apologies, are you?"

"Not used to getting them, that's for sure."

She whacked him with the back of her hand, and the watchful lines on his face eased until he became the Junior she remembered.

And wonder of wonders, she was even wearing a dress!

They fell back into their pattern of ribbing and horseplay the entire journey back to Dogwood. Still, even though she maintained that airy, lighthearted sensation of enlightenment, there was another secret part of her that she didn't bother to inspect.

It was an emotion that was newer, deeper, and more primitive. And it had materialized the moment Junior had killed for her.

They were halfway home when Junior turned to her on the train bench. "I forgot to ask." He hesitated nervously as though the question might not be fully appropriate. "What did that Ed fellow whisper in your ear?"

Isa's momentary confusion cleared.

Feducia necat, Edmund Hall had hissed.

Her lips spread in a slow, hard smile and she looked out the train window. "He said, 'Trust kills.'"

Epilogue

1 Year Later

Across the lane from the Folk Victorian house she shared with her family, Poppy showed the blonde baby in her arms the Hereford cattle grazing near the fence line.

Days like these made the events of the year before feel surreal. Dreamlike.

They had arrived in Dogwood, bruised but healing, with Alwine's body. Mrs. Hobb bought a plot and a marble angel, and she wept when they lowered Alwine into the ground. Francesca was absent, but the body had been shrouded in a hand-sewn quilt with patterns of frolicking baby animals. Mrs. Hobb had sobbed to Poppy that Francesca had wanted to give it to Alwine; it had been hers when she was a baby.

Poppy forgave Franny and let herself grieve.

It took the law four months to find Nelson Smithe.

He was hiding in one of his many properties when the Texas Rangers, Junior being one of them, apprehended him.

The trials had been long and taxing. Kitty Power's husband had gallantly offered to defend Poppy and had indeed defended her with the tenacity of a terrier with a bone. Nelson Smithe's lawyer had been crooked and mean-spirited, dredging up Poppy's past and her mother's history of stealing and whoring to the courtroom. The loss of a few acquaintances hadn't bothered her inordinately; she was also supported by the most unlikely of people.

The iron-haired Mrs. Levitz from Mrs. Smithe's luncheons championed Poppy to the Women's Circle and threatened to form her own group if anyone thought to ostracize a lady for the evil doings of others. A terrified Francesca had even testified in court, velvet green dress patterns in hand, more proof that Mrs. Smithe had taken Poppy that warm July morning. Even shy, fearful Bertha testified on the stand, translating the words that Alwine had screamed on that fateful day she had burst into the Smithe's house.

"Right away, I understood what the girl was screaming, and though I did not see her, I heard her words clearly." Bertha had been flushed and squirmed, but her words carried. "She was shouting, 'I am having your child. You promised you would not leave me, you promised.'" Bertha's testimony had caused a ruckus, and Mrs. Smithe had immediately screeched, "Liar!" and was briskly escorted from the courtroom.

But what had caused the most pandemonium was Isa's testimony.

Isa took the stand and, never taking her eyes from Nelson Smithe's pale, furious face, explained in exhaustive detail all the ways Edmund Hall had stolen laundered money from him in the past five years. When she told the courtroom that Mr. Hall's plans were to finally wash his hands of Mr. Smithe, murder Cash, and steal all the banknotes for Gary and himself, Nelson stood from his seat. He was white as a sheet, sweating as though he would cast his accounts all over the lemon-scented polish of the courtroom floor.

The judge had immediately called for a recess.

And it was during this recess that Nelson Smithe got his hands on a deputy's six-shooter and blasted his brains all over the courtroom antechamber.

It was better than a testimony of guilt.

Mrs. Smithe was sent to a women's prison across the state, and Poppy's lawyer, Mr. Powers, managed to acquire enormous restitution for Poppy, Isa, and the other missing girls.

Thoughts of the missing girls reminded Poppy to mail her letters to Pilar, who was married, and Gretchen, who was halfway through normal school so that she could teach. They had corresponded regularly for the past six months, and her heart swelled with joy that they could use their restitution money to create wonderful lives for themselves.

Hoofbeats in the distance pulled her from her reverie, and she glanced up to see two riders approaching.

Poppy gasped dramatically to get the blue-eyed baby's attention and pointed to the riders. "Look, Ally, it's Uncle Junior and Aunt Izzy!"

The eight month old reached a starfish-fingered hand and cooed, revealing two white bottom teeth. Ally had Poppy's blue eyes, but everything else was Sol, from her wide grin to her long legs. When she saw Isa and Junior's familiar horses, she began to kick frantically.

"Sol, Isa's here to say goodbye!" Poppy called, jogging to the yard. Ally giggled, her fine blonde curls bouncing.

Hog stood from his laze in the grass near a year-old boy, the coonhound's belly huge from the steady diet of scraps from the family table. Timothy stood with the dog and was as long and gangly as all the Williams offspring, the shock of dark hair and eyes were all that set him apart. Poppy was grateful Katherine hadn't made a fuss about them adopting her child. They had been overjoyed to take him in once Sol's mother had expressed fear of raising another of Katherine's babes, and Timothy had nursed alongside Ally after she was born.

Spying Poppy running and smiling, Timothy wobbled toward her. Sol, abandoning the task of hanging a rope swing in the shade of the tree beside him, scooped him up and slung him over his shoulders. He dropped a smacking kiss on Poppy's mouth, making Ally laugh, and they strode together to the narrow dirt road.

Isa rode Pavo in the travel dress that Poppy had helped her sew. After their rescue, she hadn't donned bib overalls again, and her natural confidence had spread to her clothing. Isa no longer bound her breasts, her outfits were predominantly split skirts and light bodices with low collars that didn't choke.

"High collars feel like I'm chained up all over again," she had groused to Poppy one day.

The two of them were closer than sisters. After their trials, being feet away from each other for two weeks, witnessing each other's strengths and weaknesses, they could have whole conversations with a single look. Even now, Poppy's eyes grew misty. Isa looked more like an adult at seventeen than ever, with her upswept hair, newly cut fringe, and elegant hat.

She even sat side-saddle.

Sol had claimed that Hell must have frozen over the first time he saw it.

"You look grown up, Isa," Poppy said when Isa and Junior dismounted.

"Tricks and lies," Junior quipped, dodging the hand that had reached over to flip his hat from his head.

"You're a sure enough college lady," Sol boasted, chest puffed out. "I hope Austin is ready for you. Bet they've never seen the likes of you before."

"Try not to get expelled on the first day. Try to wait a week or two," Junior added, chortling and ducking an airborne twig.

Brushing dirt from her hands, Isa shot Junior a quelling look and reached for Ally. "Give me my niece. I won't see her for a while yet. Miss Pickney said the train leaves at three, so we had better make this quick."

Poppy sighed and leaned into Sol. He rubbed her arm with the hand that wasn't holding Timothy. "What an adventure this will be. You must write me every day. At least for the first month. I want to hear everything."

Isa blew a raspberry on Ally's cheek. "I will. The first thing I will do is get a spot in Ms. Jessie Andrew's class. She teaches French and German. Can you believe she's the first woman to have a teaching position at the university? What a pioneer."

"You gonna be a teacher?" Sol asked, not for the first time.

Shrugging, Isa handed Ally back and reached for Timothy, dragging him over Sol's lengthening chestnut hair. "Timmie, come here, you little darling."

"Oh, he'll get your jacket mussed," Poppy fretted.

Scoffing, Isa kissed all over Timothy's black curls. "As though I would ever care. A little dirt doesn't hurt, does it, Timmie?" She looked at Sol and returned to his question, "And I'm not sure what I shall do. Teaching is the obvious choice because I'm female, but I'm partial to numbers. Could you see me owning a bank one day?"

Sol immediately said, "Yes."

Isa's eyes gentled, and she embraced her brother, sandwiching Timmie between them. "I do love you dearly. And I will miss you both so much."

They talked a little more about her living situation with the librarian, Miss Pickney, with whom Isa was to stay. Miss Pickney had a new position as a librarian at the university, and housing came with the position. Isa would board with her during her studies.

As they mounted their horses and reached the lane, they heard Isa say, "One, two, three, race!"

It didn't escape Poppy's notice that Junior had been unusually quiet while they had chatted with Isa. She had also noted that he had drank in the sight of Isa laughing, eyes riveted on her profile. Sol mentioned later that Junior must be having difficulty accepting that his little tag-along had grown up and was leaving.

But Poppy knew it was something more.

Later, Lucy and Ben came over for supper with their three rambunctious boys. Lucy and Poppy sipped lemonade on the front porch and watched the sun go down, discussing Lucy's next cookbook and Poppy's profit from selling sensual nightwear to Trudy. Ben pushed the squealing boys on the rope swing, chatting animatedly with Sol about Junior's future with the Texas Rangers.

When the Stones waved farewell and promised to see them in Dogwood that Sunday, Poppy sighed and laid her head on Sol's shoulder.

"I love you." She said it every day now.

"I love you, too, sugar." Sol held two sleeping babes in his arms and kissed her when they walked inside, joking and laughing softly.

That night, after putting the babies down in their crib for the night, Poppy and Sol made love and talked about their dreams for their family. They drifted off to sleep, wrapped around each other as tightly as a muscadine vine, smiling.

The End

Dear Reader

Thank you for reading *Poppies and Silk*! Writing Poppy's book was a wholly different experience from writing the first book. Her character didn't shout at me like Lucy's had. She had a story to tell but was reluctant to talk about it. Her story was about resilience and an old, deep injury—the kind that makes you doubt yourself your whole life until you find a way to heal it. I knew that even though Poppy appeared put together with her pretty dresses and secrets, beneath it, she was not. And Sol, who is a fixer if I ever wrote one, was immediately drawn to her. But then, the hero can't always save you. Sometimes you have to save yourself.

I hope you enjoyed reading Poppy and Sol's story, and if you'd like to leave an honest review, it would mean so much to me! You can also email me at **authortanyafischer@gmail.com** as I love to hear from readers and get their opinions.

Want news of my next book release? Sign up now

Don't miss *Trail of Sunflowers*: Book Three in *A Texas Bloom Series* where the series continues with Isa and Junior: Coming Soon!

Also By Tanya Fischer

Acknowledgments

I want to thank my beta readers, Dancey and Darla, for their support during the long and emotional process of writing this book.

Thank you to my cover artist, Eduorna, who is so wonderful and always willing to touch things up just how I like it. And I'm grateful for my editor, Britney, who did an amazing job polishing up the book that had too many dangling modifiers and misplaced commas to count. I hope she still has her sanity.

To my husband, who is always my biggest support, and with whom I can talk myself out of a tangle in the plot.

And to the readers that have emailed me and used word of mouth to get the existence of my first book out there, you've made this journey easier, and definitely more exciting to sit at the computer every day.

About the Author

Tanya Fischer lives on a little Texas homestead with her husband, two children, and their pets (of which there are chickens). When she's not reading, she is writing. She has a passion for romance of every genre, though her heart lies in Historical Romance. She left her job in education and has pursued her dream of writing full-time.

She can be found on:

Facebook: facebook.com/authortanyafischer
Twitter: twitter.com/Tanyat_fischer/
Instagram: instagram.com/authortanyafischer/
Website: authortanyafischer.com